Detroit Stories
Rhoda Stamell

Detroit Stories
Rhoda Stamell

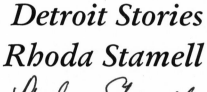

Mayapple Press 2006

Published by   MAYAPPLE PRESS
                     408 N. Lincoln St.
                     Bay City, MI 48708
                     www.mayapplepress.com

ISBN 0-932412-38-6

Cover design by Judith Kerman. Book designed and typeset by Judith Kerman; text and story titles in Giovanni Book, cover copy and titles in Garamond, Garamond Demibold Italic, Gill Sans,

Acknowledgments
"Nelson with the Blood of Kings" was read at the 26th Annual Old Dominion Literary Festival, Norfolk, VA, October, 2003. "Love for a Fat Man," was Runner-up in the Sixth Annual Short Story Contest, *The Boston Review*, published in March, 1999. "Love for a Fat Man," was published in *What Are You Looking At: The First Fat Fiction Anthology*, ed. Donna Jarrell and Ira Sukrungruang, NY: Harcourt Books, 2003. "Also Known as Alonzo Jones" was first published in *The Kenyon Review: Culture and Place*, Summer/Fall 2003.

The author owes a great debt to the Ragdale Foundation and to Alice Hayes, sponsor of the Frances Shaw Older Woman Writing Award of a month in the country for a writer come-lately. Special thanks are extended as well to Writers' Colony at Dairy Hollow for three wonderful summers; the MacDowell Colony for three winter months; the Wurlitzer Foundation for a residency in Taos from high summer and until the first snow fell; to Blue Mountain for a late summer odyssey. Endless gratitude belongs to my students, fifty years of them, whose courage and innocence have impelled me to write about them.

And to Charles Baxter, I owe a lifetime of thanks for the privilege of being his student.

Contents

Nelson with the Blood of Kings

I don't come on to white women because I want to. Me personally, I like my women brown and comfortable. No complications. Have some fun and do some laughing. After that, there's moving on. No hard feelings. So I can't explain Mary because, you know, life is hard enough.

I live with a nice brown woman who doesn't ask me where I'm going or where I've been. A while ago she hung up my clothes in her closet. I thought about putting them back in my suitcase, but I was feeling mellow, and she is a good person. Vanessa.

Thirty-four years old and one suitcase holds it all. I call that freedom. It's easy to leave when it isn't working out, and it isn't hard to settle somewhere else. But the first time I took that one suitcase and started walking, the whole world lying there like a tiger trap, I was scared. One suitcase isn't much protection, but protection only goes so far. So one suitcase is fine.

I tell women that I'm twenty-seven, so they don't expect too much. I say I am a hairdresser. Which is true and it isn't. I don't have a license, but I did work in a shop once where I washed hair and answered the phone.

Vanessa doesn't say much about me not working and all. She leaves a few dollars every day, so I stick around when she's home or stay with her kids when she has the afternoon shift. She's an LPN and works extra shifts just to keep ahead.

Once after a double shift, and she was tired, she said: "Baby, how long you planning on living like this?"

"I'm getting it together, baby. I'm going to get me an associate's degree."

That's how I ended up going to school. You can believe that I didn't want to go by the way I dragged my feet. I was too late to register on time. When I woke up, the bus ride seemed too long. Every thing was too far away and too complicated.

A long time ago when the world was full of promise, my teachers were always going on about how smart I was. Math, science, all the hard stuff came easy to me, but what I loved was to read. When I was reading, I was in the safest, most interesting place I had ever been. I never wanted to come back.

Even though I am dark, I have good features. That's what my mother said: "Nelson, you got such good features like an Ethiopian. Maybe we have the blood of kings. Maybe we are really somebody."

If I had to, I was going to pay the tuition with Vanessa's credit card.

"I got me some credit," she once bragged, "but it's only for emergencies."

I was looking for some weed when I found the Master Card wrapped in tinfoil at the back of the freezer. I didn't need it. During all the long, tedious afternoons I had negotiated financial aid.

Still I had missed the first week of classes.

"Ain't your college started yet?" Vanessa asked on her way out to work.

The tinny voices of cartoon characters came from the living room. Let me sleep, I wanted to shout at the kids sitting in front of the television, but I got up and got dressed.

"Where you going, man, dressed like that?" LaMar, Vanessa's eleven-year-old son, asked. "Why you wearing your winter hat?"

"I'm going to school."

"You look like a crackhead."

"Shut up, LaMar."

"Besides, you already missed the bus. Ain't one coming for almost an hour."

"Damn. LaMar, did your mother give you grocery money? I need to get a cab."

"Can't give you no money, Nelson. Mama say I gotta buy the groceries. She didn't say nothing about giving you money for a cab. In fact, she say not to give you anything."

"I'll pay it back. Just give it to me, LaMar."

"How you going to pay it back? You ain't got no job."

So the first time I saw Mary Porter, I was an hour and a half late for her summer English class, and I was wearing a blue wool hat even though it was eighty degrees. When I smiled at her, I remembered my teeth. Nelson Chapman, with the blood of kings in his veins, was missing four very important teeth.

But it didn't matter. I knew what I knew, and I could feel her knowing, too, as if the two of us had already moved into our brief future. It's always like that. Some people call it love at first sight, but that is just simple minded. It is a knife blade cutting through the present, revealing the moments to come, and then the broken surface is sealed. The clock resumes its movement, but you know what you know.

That's how it happened with my teeth. On a day I knew that violence was coming and the sun was flat and burning. People in nice houses closed the windows and turned on the air conditioning, or they sat on their porches and fanned themselves.

I was living in Highland Park on Woodward in a room where the window only went up three inches, just enough to let in the shouts of the night, the sound of buses, the cars without mufflers, and the occasional crack-crack of a .22 revolver.

Highland Park is the place where you go when you're down on your luck. Detroit surrounds the once-pretty neighborhood, spilling city filth and city troubles into its streets. The trees died, and people started selling. All those hard working people left their two-storey flats and their bungalows, and they took their businesses with them, too. All that is left on those wide streets meant for trucks carrying goods and traffic carrying people to their business, are the broken windows and the boarded-up store fronts.

I had been staying with a white girl named Lisa, but she had disappeared with some dude who had some coke. I don't blame her. I would have gone, too.

We had our little dramas: crying, screwing, smoking pot, fighting, ordering Chinese food, which we ate right in the bed. When Lisa took off, the room got smaller and hotter.

I walked to Palmer Park, named after the family who had owned the land. Their two homes were kept like shrines in the park. The Palmers were ambitious white people, taking a chance with their log cabin among the thick trees. Then when things got good, they built the big house in the middle of fields. Palmer land, Palmer forest, Palmer fields.

Those Palmers would pitch a fit if they knew what was going on in their forest. The fields got turned into a golf course, but the forest belonged to the crackheads and the dopers.

That's where I was headed, not for anything but to get cool in the watery green under Mr. Palmer's trees. Instead I met Bobby, and the moment I saw him, the destroyed, pretty boy, I knew that he was the menace promised to me in the morning heat.

He reminded me of Lisa, who would have been a pretty woman if she had stayed where she belonged. But the city, the one they created for themselves, battered their small bones and roughened their pale skin. They wouldn't recognize themselves in the mirror, hair dark and greasy, the bruised eyes, the frail bones begging to be broken.

Bobby wasn't wearing a shirt like he was in his own backyard. He didn't wear socks either, just dirty docksiders.

"You're a pretty black man," he said.

"And you're a pretty white boy. But I just came here to cool off."

"Fine. That's good. A man of leisure. Wanting to get cool. That's good. I can cool you off. How would you like Bobby to cool you off?"

"No, man. I don't want to get into it."

"That's good. I can handle that. The day is young. I can wait."

"Ain't nothing to wait for. It's too hot."

Bobby stood over me, rocking on his heels. "I know a place where it's cool. Air conditioned. I got friends who have air conditioning and some very nice substances."

"I don't have any money."

"We can trade. We can barter. These are new times, and cash is obsolete."

I didn't say no to the freaked out, skinny child, who should have been drinking beer on the lawn of a fraternity house.

We walked down Woodward, Bobby's arms flailing, his chest thin and reddened, shoes flapping on his bony feet. I was embarrassed, but I followed him to the abandoned motel. I pried off the board nailed across room 27 and pushed open the door.

"This place ain't air conditioned, man. This place is a dump."

"It's not so bad. See, we can sit down. A little later we can get some beer, maybe some weed...."

"I said I didn't have any money."

"I told you. We can trade."

"Trade what?"

"Whatever. Whatever they want. The guys when they come."

"You know, Bobby, I gotta get out of here."

"No, man, no, you don't. It'll be good. Here, sit down on the bed. Let me do you. Anything you want. I'll be your woman, your man, anything. Just stay. Here, let me do you."

And I didn't stop him. I just let him move over my body with his eager mouth. I just lay back and let it happen because it didn't matter, Bobby or Lisa or any mouth in the world.

I lay on the bed, no sheets, just the dirty mattress, and I was holding Bobby in my arms, his child's head on my chest. The light was cool and golden in this room. There was trash everywhere: beer bottles, McDonald wrappers, pizza boxes.

If I had slipped into dreaming at this moment, then it was a dream of a bright kitchen where my mama was cooking, and I was reading. "Oh, Nelson," my mother would croon in my dream, "Beautiful Nelson."

The brightness exploded. They were in the room, bats in their hands, swinging. Bobby was screaming, "No, no, I can explain," and then he was limp on the floor, and I knew he was dead. I don't know if they meant to kill me. There were just the bats and then so much blood, me stumbling out on the light- flooded street, a woman crying out, "Lord, Lord, who done this to you, baby?" Large against the flat, white sun, a brown angel.

It's been a long time, so I don't think about my teeth, not even when I eat. You can get used to anything. Even when I had some money, getting new teeth wasn't a priority. Not that I didn't try to get some. I just took off before the dentist finished them.

He must have been pretty mad to waste that nice bridge. No one will ever know, he said, but something came up, and I had to leave.

One thing I did learn from losing those teeth is to pay attention to the signs of the day. I'm not superstitious, but I always watch for omens. If something doesn't feel right, I listen to that feeling. There are a lot of things I don't do because of that day with Bobby.

It was the first time it had occurred to me that the most casual act can unfold into the complications of the next hour, the next day, the next year.

Mary Porter gasped, a polite, little intake of breath that she couldn't control. I cursed the moment I ignored the warnings that nagged at me that hot, crazy day. I cursed crazy, freaked-out Bobby, who never heard any warning, but I got over the cursing. You don't need to look good to get what you want. You just need to go and get it.

"This the Shakespeare class?"

"Of course. Who are you?"

"Nelson. Who are you?"

"I'm Mary. I teach this class."

"My pleasure," I said, and I smiled, not caring about the teeth. Pleasure is what I felt, pleasure and the whole, rich future spread out before me with all its joy and its terror.

She handed me a script and pointed me toward my partner. "You're Friar Laurence, and she's Romeo. You can practice your roles."

There was only other dude in the class, wearing a white man's shirt with a little horse on it. If she were looking for someone to play a priest, he was the one. But she gave him Lord Capulet, who was only nice when no one got in his way.

Friar Laurence only wanted to make things better, and he didn't have himself in mind. He was the kind of guy who would stay on a sinking ship and try bailing out the water with a little can. All of his hope would be in the power of his little bailing can against the whole ocean of water. He'd be going at it until his last breath of air. When he stood there before the prince, everything in a mess, he offered to die to make amends. The poor guy. He didn't have a chance the first day he got involved with all those people, rich and spoiled, out for themselves.

Friar Laurence said, "He stumbles who runs fast." He's telling Romeo to be cool, to look around and take stock of the situation, but Romeo keeps running until everybody is dead or full of grief. No one is sadder than the friar because he tried to do right.

I'm not saying that I have been a man to do right, but I recognize the aloneness that good people feel. The women who helped me out, the brown women and the black women, they didn't ask for anything, except maybe a little joy in the night. And when I was walking away, leaving nothing behind, they stood there, not crying, not begging, just heavy with regret.

My classmates weren't the kind of people to study Shakespeare. They lived in too-small apartments or rented houses, looking in the registration book and saying: I want to do this. Just once in my life.

Worried people was what they all were, but for a little while they wanted bigger words in their mouths.

My acting partner, Esther, stayed with me the whole semester. She loved being Portia and Gertrude and Juliet, but she did ok as Laertes and Bassanio and Romeo, too. I didn't want to be any of those guys, out for themselves. People I took from would laugh at that. But I only took what was there.

If someone woke me up in the night and asked me what I wanted, I couldn't answer. Before I can gather words around me like armor, there is nothing in my head or in my heart but an empty landscape; endless, rolling fields with long grasses that do not move in the still air.

So a guy like Antonio, who can have everything and who is sad because he doesn't want anything except to be with Bassanio, a greedy, white boy out for himself, a guy like Antonio I can understand. He can march right up and bare his chest to Shylock, the worst guy he can imagine to be his executioner.

My Antonio would urge Shylock on. "Cut out my heart, Shylock. But what you will hold in your hand will be only the facsimile of a heart, and no blood will drip from your fingers."

I wrote that in my essay to get Mary's attention. And again when I was Friar Laurence, my head bowed, accepting the prince's sentence of doom and the world's curse. "How sad," she murmured, and Esther hissed, "That lady likes you," with the disapproval of a black woman when a white woman is interested in a black man.

I am not a black man. That is a political statement, and I am not interested in the politics of blackness. I am only interested in my own brownness and how it has brought me to despair. It has also brought me many women—and men. Perhaps the despair came after all the hands and mouths, but I think it began with my beginning.

Mary. She should have been a nun or a saint, but she liked the things of the world: pretty dresses, books, baseball games, good food.

Mary. Passionate in spite of herself; pale and thin because she is devoured by her longings.

"My pale twin," I wrote to her, "press your hand in mine, and let the world dissolve." She crumpled up that slip of paper, but at the end of class she gave it back with her phone number on it.

I didn't call that number until I had touched Mary. I had to feel the body's words.

"You should let me cut your hair," I said to one of the white girls.

"Don't be crazy, Nelson."

"No. I used to be a beautician."

"Not really."

"Yeah. I always gave a good haircut. Like Mary's. Mary has a great cut. Who did it?"

"No one special. Someone at a small shop."

I placed my hands on her temple and ran my fingers through her hair, let it fall away. "Beautiful," I said as her hair fell against her face.

Let the world dissolve. That's what I was saying to her with my hands. And she heard.

Esther was furious and forgot her school speech. "Nelson, what you trying to do? Can't you see Mary an innocent woman. She don't need your trash. And she don't need to play games in front of the whole class."

"Mary's a big girl, Esther."

"That's half right. She's a girl. The other half is that you an evil, black man. What you doing? Get revenge for your white parts."

"What are you talking about?"

"About your white blood."

"I don't have white blood."

"Well, I don't see too many black folks looking like you, not unless they got white blood in them."

"There's nothing in me that's white or black."

"Then you a nothing man, not belonging nowhere. Is that what you saying?"

I called Mary on a night when Vanessa had a midnight shift and her kids were in bed. Mary's voice was distant as if she lived a million miles away.

"It's Nelson."

"I know."

"Are you sleeping?"

"No. I was waiting."

"For me?"

"For you. For the impossible. They are probably the same thing."

"Like us. Like twins.

"That was lovely, what you wrote."

"I could write our story. I know all the lines."

"But, Nelson, I'm a character in our story, too. I have words of my own."

"I know all the words, Mary."

"It's late. I have to sleep."

"Tomorrow then. I'll call you tomorrow."

"Where are you?"

"Downriver. In Ecorse. Where are you?"

"At the opposite end of the world. In Waterford."

"Near Pontiac?"

"Yes. Why?"

"I was just imagining a bus line that would travel from me to you. I'd be sitting alone on my bus. I'd travel through the night until I get to you. Where you are is the only stop for this bus of mine."

"You shouldn't say things like this, Nelson."

"Why not, Mary? What's the harm in anything we say."

"I'm your teacher."

"I'll drop the class."

"I wouldn't want that."

"I can come to you. Now."

"That bus doesn't run, Nelson. It's the middle of the night, and no buses are running."

"I want to come to you. Hold you gently. Whisper to you in the dark room.

"I'm going to hang up now."

"Tomorrow."

"I don't know about tomorrow."

I didn't know about tomorrow either: what Vanessa's schedule would be, what she would say when she saw the message units and the phone number on her bill. What she would say about the woman I talked to from our poor, hot rooms, a woman who slept in a cool, airy room, the clean, white house brushed by the branches of trees.

I had to get money but more than I could wheedle or hustle, fifty or a hundred dollars, but I needed more than money itself. I didn't have a license, so I couldn't rent a car. I needed to get my teeth fixed, but I didn't have the weeks of time. I needed new clothes, but I had no way to explain why I wanted them.

When the obstacles are so great, you can give up, or you can burst through the barriers, just the way you are. Usually I walk away. Not this time. This time I would see it to the end.

Esther said that Mary was forty. She called her a dried-up woman, no juices flowing. "Those eyes so pale and skin so thin you can the blood running behind it. And pale clothes to match. Why you want such a colorless woman?" I didn't care what Esther said. I just wanted her to talk about Mary.

"And, like I said, Nelson, I don't think she been with no men."

"You're crazy. She's lovely."

"She too skinny to be lovely like you say. 'Lovely' is such a white way to talk. But whatever. If she ever been around, she would know that you are just a lot of trouble."

"She's in another world."

"And you better not go there. Maybe she's playing a game you don't know about."

"I know all the games."

"Might be one you missed, Nelson. Just might be one."

The game I missed was loving someone, but that's not what Esther meant.

I loved Mary. In class when we were acting or talking, I loved the excitement she felt.

"You're so funny and so cute," I said to her one night.

"Don't lead me on. Don't embarrass me."

I loved that woman, too, her melancholy, self-deprecating voice that I had to hear every night, but Mary's body wasn't what I was thinking of.

Once I said to her, "I'm thinking of your bones."

"Please," she said. "I can't talk about things like that."

"It's not what you think. It's knowing how you are made, the bottom line of you. That's what I want to know."

Women always want to be desirable. But the more I told her how I wanted to be with her, the less I meant it. I wanted the talk, the sound of her voice, the sound of mine. I wanted the current between us caught on a word or buried in the lines she spoke or I spoke.

She was reading Portia's part from *The Merchant of Venice*. No one else in the class wanted that part. You can't like Portia if you are black or poor. She was spoiled and rude to her suitors, especially the dark-skinned prince. But she said some great things.

Portia says to Bassanio that she is who she is, and that's okay with her. At least until she meets him. She says, "Yet for you I would be trebled twenty times myself—a thousand times more fair, ten thousand times more rich—."

Bassanio wasn't anyone, just a good looking guy out to marry some money so he can have the easy life. I can understand that. But Portia didn't need him.

That's how it works with women. Even when they have it all, they think there's something they haven't got. I wasn't anything but a Bassanio knocking at Mary's door, not good enough for her in any way.

"There are ways I want to be with you, Mary."

"Please, Nelson. It's not possible."

"What I want is possible."

"It's just talk in the night."

"But I'm close to you. I've never been closer to a woman."

"It isn't enough. It can't be enough."

"Then let me have more. Let me come there."

"No. Not here. If something happens...."

"Nothing will happen that you don't want."

"I don't know what I want."

"It doesn't have to be complicated. Let me meet you. Anywhere. Name the place. I'll be there."

"Let me think about it."

"But you'll do it. You want to do it. To meet. We are talking about meeting."

"Sometimes I don't know what we are talking about."

"Meet me, Mary."

"All right. Saturday. At Cranbrook. The Greek amphitheater. Do you know where it is?"

"I'll find it."

"Four o'clock."

"I'll be there."

The day you know you are shabby is the day when it is important not to be. I had stopped noticing my clothes, except when they got too raggedy to take with me, a shirt too frayed, socks worn too thin. If someone saw in me the remnant of good looks, that was something left over, someone I wasn't any more.

But now there was Saturday at Cranbrook, a far suburban place, and I had to go there as someone else. Not as the Nelson I have become.

Using Vanessa's Master Card bothered me. When I take stuff that isn't mine, I see it as an exchange for what I give. But I gave that woman nothing, not even enough loving because there wasn't much time to love in her scrambling life. Buying those jeans, a shirt, a windbreaker, and some shoes, I was taking more than I could have given even if I had kissed her into melting every night.

Tell you this: It doesn't matter to me if it's a man or a woman who loves me. The gift of their love is all I want. Even when I had to leave, I have always been nice when someone gives me their love. I hold that treasure in my hands, and I would never be cruel.

I washed the jeans and the shirt three times at a laundromat so that they didn't look new. I didn't want to appear too bright with expectation. Then I hid them in Vanessa's winter closet: shirt, jeans, jacket on a single hanger and the shoes hanging in a plastic bag.

Cranbrook Institute is near Pontiac, the first city after the Detroit suburbs ended. So I would have to hitch after I got out of the city because buses don't run that far. I'd be standing on the side of a road, thumb sticking out, expecting someone to stop. I couldn't imagine reaching any destination in that way, and I was afraid that I was no longer capable of movement or of destination.

There is a resolve that is greater than paralysis and fear. That early Saturday morning I dressed quickly before it grew light in the room where Vanessa had been asleep for just an hour. I left the house with the dollars she had put in a bowl on her dresser and with the Master Card in my pocket. I set out on a journey of twenty miles. If I did not take it, I could not imagine another journey in my life.

The morning was cool. No one on the street like they are when it has been a hot night, and people come out early, restless and angry, looking for relief. I told myself that this was a good morning for a journey.

The bus took me to Eight Mile Road and Woodward before nine o' clock, and I had seven hours to kill. That's too much time when you don't have anything but a few dollars and a few miles to travel.

All up and down those big streets, Woodward and Eight Mile Road, people were getting to where they had to be in ten, twenty minutes. I couldn't remember the last time I knew how I was going to get somewhere or how long it would take me. I stood there on a corner while the cars went by, and I was the poorest man in the world without the ingenuity to change the direction of my impoverished life.

So I walked like all the poor brown and black men walked on morning streets to places they had to go. I walked, the sweat forming under my arms, the burning of my feet on the hard sidewalk.

When the sidewalks ended, that's when I had to hitch. I didn't believe anyone would stop, but I had to go forward because I couldn't go back.

"Where're you headed?"

I bent over and looked at the man in the Infiniti. "Cranbrook. You know, near Pontiac."

"No problem. Get in."

You see these kinds of guys in ads, late thirties and sandy colored: light hair, tan skin, pale colors. Even his eyes were pale. A regular white man except that he stopped for me.

"You know that the grounds at Cranbrook don't open to the public until 1:00."

"No," I said. "Actually I didn't"

"They aren't going to let you hang around. It's a fancy neighborhood."

"Maybe I can stop nearby."

"Nothing much around there, not for all the hours until 1:00."

"I'll make out."

"My name is Barry. I'm not in a hurry. We could stop for some breakfast. To kill time."

"Yeah, I guess I need to kill time, but if I could afford breakfast, I wouldn't be hitching."

"Breakfast is no problem at all."

"But there's a problem, right?"

"Only if you make one."

"I'm meeting someone, Barry. This isn't the time."

"It's worth something to me, really, and worth something to you...ah...I don't know your name."

"Nelson."

"Nelson. You are quite the sight, Nelson, and I would like to see a little more of you."

"It's not the right time."

"For fifty dollars."

"To do what?"

"Nothing you haven't done before. Right, Nelson? There isn't much you haven't done. I saw you standing out there, and I said to myself, 'There's a man who has been places. There's a man down on his luck.'"

"Someone you could take advantage of?"

"That's what I thought."

"Look, Barry, tell me something. What is the sign I wear that has you talking to me this way?"

"It's just corruption, Nelson. Beautiful corruption but on the downside."

"That's why it's only fifty dollars."

"That's right."

"And breakfast."

"Part of the deal."

Barry let me stay in the room after he left. The motel was a few miles from Cranbrook, and I could walk there. Rest here, Nelson, he said, because there aren't many resting places in the world. I would have liked him if we had met some other way. We did things that were too intimate for strangers, so I guess if I ever saw him again, we would have to look away. I know Barry's raw cries in a dark room and the hollows of his hips, but I don't know his laugh or the way he would shake hands.

He left me a hundred dollars. I didn't complain. I could take a cab to Cranbrook or pay back Vanessa. I could buy Mary a nice dinner, and we could talk about Shakespeare and drink red wine. That was Barry's idea. "Take the woman to dinner, Nelson. Dinner is the best place to talk to a woman."

That was in my head while I walked down Lone Pine Road among all those fancy Bloomfield Hills houses: asking Mary to dinner, ordering wine, clinking our glasses together. It was beautiful on that road with all the trees, stone walls, lawns that rolled up to houses that were settled and peaceful.

Cranbrook wasn't like Palmer Park. It was public but with guards and museums; private schools for rich kids tucked out of sight; high, brick buildings with ivy blazing as it climbed walls and wrapped around windows. Visitors were strolling around like there was nothing better to do than to look at late summer flowers or lean over a stone railing and watch the swans coasting on the surface of the small lake.

I walked through the little woods to the Greek amphitheater. When Mary came, we would sit together on the stone seats under those tall, elegant pines, and we would talk. I would hold her hands; I would brush her lips with mine and kiss her lowered head. When the afternoon was over, we would go to dinner and hold glasses of red wine in our hands.

The amphitheater was beautiful, the kind of place that Mary would pick "to play out our drama." That's what she said. I sank back against the stone steps and watched Mary come out on the grassy area that lay before the stage.

"This is where the chorus would dance and recite in a Greek tragedy. And this is where we can play out our drama."

"I don't know anything about Greek tragedy," I said. "Maybe I could take the class from you."

"I can't be your teacher any more. We've broken the rules."

"We haven't done anything, Mary. We haven't touched or kissed or even had a cup of coffee together."

"All the nights, all the talk, all the wanting...."

"That doesn't have to mean anything. We can start over. We can go to a restaurant or maybe a nice bar for a drink.. We can be friends, Mary, if that's what you like."

"I want to make love, Nelson. Right here on this grass in the bright daylight."

"Someone might come. This is a public place."

"Don't tell me it would bother you."

"I can't do this, Mary. Why don't we go somewhere, to a room...."

"It'll be too late. Right now. Right now I can do it. Here in the light."

"Are you afraid of me? Is that what it is?"

"I don't know."

"Are you afraid to make love to a black man?"

"You don't want to know about what I am afraid of."

"I don't understand."

"Yes, you do. You just don't want to do it. After all the talk, every night telling me how you wanted to, you don't."

"I love you, Mary."

"I don't want your love, Nelson. I want to make love."

"Why me?"

"Don't ask me that, Nelson. Neither one of us would like the answer."

"Because I don't count."

She knelt in front of me, pressing her mouth in the palms of my hands, first one and then the other. Please, please, please, she said. I tried to draw her to her feet. I can't be your man, I said. I'm not good enough for you. Please, please, please, she said. Help me, Nelson. Someone has to help me.

I can't help you, Mary.

I held her, and through the rough linen of the dress she was wearing, I could feel her heat. I held her because I wanted to run as all my life I have run from neediness and from being needed. I held her because I wanted to be the kind of man I could respect.

"Dearest Mary. If it were right, if I were right, then we would be lovers to light the world."

"Stop your damn words, Nelson. Stop your damn empty words."

Then she was gone. And it was so dark and so cold in that place. So far away from everything. I walked across the the grass and went up the stairs to the stage. If I had known some famous poems, I would have had the right words to say. If I had memorized some of Antonio's lines about the emptiness in him, I would have said them out loud in the empty amphitheater. But I only had my own words.

"This was just a play," I said to the stone seats. "The actors were saying their lines as if they were real people. But it doesn't mean anything. No, I didn't say that right. It don't mean nothing! Nothing at all."

Also Known as Alonzo Jones

After a while school didn't mean nothing to me but a place to hang out. My mama got worried, but she wasn't asking any questions. Except the easiest one. "Shakir, honey, how come you don't got no homework?" I wasn't telling her how it was with me until I worked it out. I didn't want her coming up to school and 'fronting' the journalism teacher about calling me a fop.

I got mad because I thought she was calling me a fag, and I wasn't taking that from anyone, I don't care if she is my teacher. She could see right away what I was thinking. She kinda laughed. "Fop," she said, "A show-off person, a person who uses clothes to show off."

I called her a bitch. Under my breath or to my cousins, Tray and Maseo. Only thing, they weren't my cousins. We all lived on Gallagher since grade school, so we called ourselves cousins.

I am a good imitator of white people, and a lot of times I did her for Tray and Maseo. "'These boys aren't your cousins? People can't go around creating cousins whenever they feel like it.'" They laughed and said that I looked like her when I did her voice. "'Distinctions. It is about making distinctions.'"

Now how am I going to look like an old white lady?

Like I said, we lived on Gallagher since we were small. Gallagher was better than where we came from, which, according to my mama and my daddy, was the ghetto. If the ghetto was falling down poor, then that's about right. But Gallagher was fine. Single houses. No people upstairs banging and throwing and waking you up at night. Nobody letting lawns go so bad until they were all tamped down like cement. That was ghetto lawn, but on Gallagher, there were pale, spring flowers and red autumn shrubs and tall pines—three on our property—and trees with swooping down branches. And it was pretty quiet, too, except when we were little and played kind of loud in the street.

We would run out of our houses like a bell was ringing, all at the same time. We would ride our bikes from Eight Mile Road to Nevada, from Conant to Mound, whooping and hollering, but that was before we got ashamed about riding bikes and not having a car to drive.

We had a hideout, Mr. Smiley's garage, which was full of cardboard boxes, all sizes. We would go in there through the side window so he couldn't see us, and huddle together in a big carton, smoking and talking. We never did burn up anything and never got caught either. You don't want to be caught doing anything by Mr. Smiley. Sometime Tray would try to get a girl to come there, but it never did work out. It was just our place until one day we got too old to crawl into cardboard boxes.

The only time I didn't like living on Gallagher was in the cold winter when it got dark early, and it was too icy to ride my bike. That's when the dogs were out. They would walk real slow, swaying from side to side, a few feet behind some lonely fool out on the street. It was usually me. These dogs, they acted like they really weren't interested, but every time I hurried up my step, then they stopped swaying so casual and hurried up themselves. Of course, I ended up running and them chasing me, maybe two or three dogs. Like it was some game, only I was scared, and they weren't playing.

While I was running, I would be unfastening my belt, knowing they had to catch up with me. Then I would whip it around, sometimes hitting one of them, but mostly just whipping it through the air. All the while I was shouting at those dogs. They would bark and show their teeth, but they would run off. I called them the winter dogs, but I only talked about them to Tray and Maseo.

Black people are afraid of dogs, but if I were white, I would still be afraid of them. They can't want anything but to run you down and to tear you apart, or why would they chase you? It's the wolf in them that makes them sniff you out when you are alone in the night.

On our fence there is a sign: Beware of the dog. My daddy put it there, so no one would bother our backyard. But we never had any dog. No one on Gallagher had a dog. That's why I was so scared of those winter dogs.

The day I met her, it was January and real cold. Didn't matter because I was sharp: silk shirt, baggy pants, gray and black knit cardigan with a shawl collar, $85 shoes, a diamond stud in my ear. It wasn't semester change or anything, but my history teacher told my counselor that I should write on the newspaper. I thought I was getting out of history class, and that was fine with me.

She looked at me, so cool and sarcastic.

"Is that real?" she said, meaning my diamond stud.

I thought about lying, but there are some lies not worth telling.

"I wouldn't wear no diamond stud in this place," I said.

"Any diamond. So it's a zircon, right?"

"Whatever," I said.

"Acrylic sweater, polyester shirt, fake lizard shoes. You can never be warm in synthetics."

"My shirt isn't polyester," I said. "It's real silk."

"Good for you," she said. "Let me have your program change."

I was born Alonzo Jones, but my mama and my daddy were going through some changes, so they took them Muslim names. I got to be Shakir Khalid. Now, when being Muslim isn't anything to us, we still can't go back to the old names. Anyway, I'm staying Shakir Khalid because that's how I think of myself. After I told her about my two names, she had things to say about that, too.

Sometimes she would say my other name, Alonzo Jones.

"You definitely aren't an Alonzo."

Who did she think she was?

In the beginning I hated her. In the middle time I liked her better than anyone. When we did newspaper stories together, going out into the halls and on the street, talking to people, there wasn't anything better in the world.

That first year I couldn't get anywhere with her. I'd hand in an editorial—I didn't like to do reporting—and she would look at it like her eyes were too good for seeing it. "You can't write an English sentence worth printing," and she would give it to Larry.

Larry, write this. Larry, can you help me? This is great, Larry. Larry everything. He was her big favorite. Her editor-in-chief. She talked to him like he was her friend, not her student.

So I asked him once, "Hey, man, are you doing the mash-mash with her?"

I didn't believe that for a hot minute, but I asked him to see what he would say.

"No, man, but she'll do anything for me. Don't even know why."

Because that was the way she was, and all I wanted was to be the special one. More than anything

She would write all over my articles, "I can't stand this careless garbage," and throw them back at me corrected. I would throw back at her: "I'm going to be editor-in-chief of this paper. I'm going to win the big scholarship." She never did say no. She never did say "over my dead body" like I thought she would.

Larry did win the big scholarship that first year. Out of nowhere. There was never anything at our school but the Marching Doughboys with none of them reading off the same sheet of music, and then Larry wins a $24, 000 scholarship. He gets flown to the University of Missouri in a private jet, courtesy of Ford Motor Company. And his mama went, too.

After that, Larry stopped being respectful to her, in little ways but still hurtful, you could see. I guess he thought that he did it all by himself, not that she had done it for him. I promised myself that I would be grateful when it got to be my time.

Whenever the newspaper came out, there would be an article by me, looking so good, everything spelled right, the sentences on the page like birds sitting on a wire, each one important all by itself. She always fixed it up so it would come out right, my voice behind the words. I could almost hear them better than I could see them.

"Is this the lead article?" Like I knew, but I wanted to hear her say it.

"You can see for yourself right on the page."

I was always the lead article even when Larry was still around because he did mostly layout.

Once a month we would go down to the *Free Press*, the newspaper that printed the papers for the schools in the city that couldn't pay for those shiny ten-twelve page papers with all kinds of photos about white people privileges. They were always sending them to us like we cared about their sweet, little lives.

We would be driving down the freeway, four of us packed into her Honda. Then we would be walking in the big lobby past the guard who waved us through to the elevators like we were important. We would be getting off at the third floor like we belonged there, belonged in the city room.

The copy editor in charge of us would get us logged on to the computers. We were supposed to edit the stories and write the headlines, but she never let us change one word of the copy.

"You'll just mess it up," she said and did the editing herself.

In the end she changed all the headlines but the ones I did. Every time she didn't change one of mine, I could see that I was getting closer to having my turn.

I liked the city room. It was big and full of computers and telephones, but still it was very peaceful. We would sit at our computers, never talking to each other much, but just looking at our screens, sort of connected to the keys.

I always got done real fast compared to the other kids, so it was my job to check the headlines or get the other kids out of trouble with their computers. Sometimes some white guys would come by and smile at us like it was some kind of miracle that we could type and get the computers to work for us. One of them, the managing editor, was a big guy who looked those editors you see in those old movies on Cable TV. His tie was always loose and his sleeves rolled up. Only he didn't have pens and pencils in his pocket because everybody used computers. Whenever he saw me, he would say, "How're you doing, son?" I was honored and scared. Not that I can't talk to white people, but I just don't like to. I never know what they want to hear.

The red-haired editor didn't like us. He would sit down at his computer late in the morning before the reporters came in. We were supposed to be gone. He would be doing stuff, and if we laughed or swiveled in our chairs too much, he would give us dirty looks. I could handle that. He didn't want to hear anything at all.

After Larry had left on his scholarship, all tall and light-skinned and slick like he was, I was the editor, sort of in an unofficial way. I would sit in the front seat of her car. Maybe I asked dumb things, but I had to know.

"What do you think all those white people are thinking? About a white lady in a car with black kids?"

"That I'm your mother."

"No. What do they think?"

"That you're my slaves."

"Come on."

"That I kidnapped you. Honestly. They think I'm your teacher."

What I never asked her was if she were ashamed. I mean like we would be walking down the street, say, so we could get to Greektown to eat our lunch. Or we would be on the People Mover. And we'd be shouting and acting like fools. Because people didn't take us to places like that every day to eat and to sightsee. But if I was one of those people on the street, I wouldn't smile at us, yelling and pushing. I would hate us. I would hate the woman who brought black people where they didn't belong.

I know what they thought. We would be sitting in the little People Mover train that carried us above the downtown streets, and I would have to look right into the face of a white person. That white person would look at me, and I could hear the voice of his thinking.

They said terrible things with their eyes.

For the big edition, the last one of the year, all nineteen high schools competing like in basketball, we got assigned to fashion. She wouldn't settle for plain old fashion and what you should wear to look sharp.

"If you ask me, fashion is stupid to begin with."

No, she wasn't settling. She insisted on writing about the social significance of what people wore.

"Don't be asking me to go around the halls asking these dudes about their Nikes and their Tommy Hilfiger shirts," I said.

"We'll go the malls."

"Same people be there."

She called up a bunch of schools, private schools, but all those headmasters and priests and nuns had excuses for not letting us into their fancy, paid-extra-for schools.Then somebody gave her the name of a headmaster who had once been a teacher at our school, only he escaped. He probably let us come over to his fancy private school because he was so glad that he got to leave.

It was a boy's school and run by Catholics. It wasn't too far from Gallagher, but I never dreamed the world could be so different in just a few miles. Like I saw that school before, but I never thought about it being close. The streets were wider, the houses were square and solid and spread out, and trees bent over the streets in gentle, brushing ways. And that school looked just like a palace with creamy walls and a roof of golden tiles. If I had seen it every day of my life, I would never believe it was a school.

"I'm not going in," I said.

"What are you talking about?" She was taking her Nikon and her Fujica from the trunk of the car.

"I don't feel like talking to all those sissy little white boys," I said.

"We have an appointment, and we have one hour to interview as many people as we can. And you aren't going in? No way. You take your notebook and get out of this car and do what you are supposed to, or you can take a bus back to school."

"You don't have to go through all that."

"You can just get out of the car."

Lots of times when I remember the rough way she talked to me, I wonder why I took it. It made me mad, but she could care less. But I didn't stay mad. She was doing the best she could, and we—I was always disappointing her. She would drive us right up to the door, and we wouldn't get out. She must have been disappointed all the time.

Inside it was like any school building but real clean and quiet. We waited in a room until the school day was over. She talked so cool to the headmaster, but he looked pretty nervous to me like he had never seen any black people before. But when the bell rang, and all those guys came out of their classes, a lot of them were black but not like us.

They were black-white guys, talking soft and grammatical and dressed like white boys with sport shirts and ties and sissy blazers and the kind of shoes that rich people wear on yachts. They were definitely not sharp, but they didn't need to be sharp.

It wasn't so bad. Not even with the white boys. The six of us— including our teacher who always piled too many people in her little Jap car—went out on what they called the commons. We just strolled around, talking to different guys about their clothes and school and taking notes. We sat on stone benches under trees with leaves fluttering down in the breeze.

She was taking pictures with both of her cameras. I kept the one she took of the white boy I was interviewing. The Nikon got all the best details: how light his hair was, turning up at his collar; the curl of every leaf in the background; even the look of everything being all right with him. You can catch things like that with a good camera even when you aren't looking for them.

That's how we saw Dalton. We followed the movement of her camera as it turned toward the building. Dalton was walking down the steps to the place where the stairs divided in two directions. He was very dark and wore a loose white jacket and baggy white pants like women wear in a harem. His shirt was black, and a huge cross hung on a rope from his neck. Like he thought he was Jesus, a black fag Jesus dressed in fag clothes, standing at the railing, looking down on all the goody-goodies talking to black kids from a public school in a poor neighborhood. Talking about clothes.

Right then I hated her for real. She didn't have to bring us here and push our faces into it: them and him.

"Who is that dude?" I asked Tim, the white-boy name of my white boy.

"That's Dalton. He's different."

"How come he doesn't follow the dress code?"

"He protested. Said it violated his personal rights. So they leave him alone. He makes the stuff he wears."

I never saw him up close, but I saw the pictures, the processed hair, the long hands resting on the edge of the balcony where he stood. The rings. The folds in the jacket.

"All my materials are cotton jersey with some spandex to keep the shape of the garment," he said in the interview, which I didn't do even though she asked me to. I wasn't going to talk to him. Who brought so much shame to himself and to me. Who didn't have the sense to hide his black, faggot self from the world.

I didn't talk all the way home. I didn't even try to sit in the front seat. I sat in the back next to the the window and watched how the streets changed from clean and quiet to trashy and noisy where we lived. She kept looking at me with worried eyes in the rear view mirror, but I pretended not to notice.

I got over Dalton and all that. And about not liking Gallagher any more. When it was summer, I got a job at Payless Shoes on Eight Mile Road, which was ok because it didn't get dark until late. I could walk home after work, and people would still be out on their porches or talking on the sidewalks. Not just winos and freaks. Then me and Tray and Maseo would hang out and maybe get together with some girls. Mostly we just hung out.

If I were doing an interview like she taught me, at this point I would ask: What were your plans? Did you and your friends have plans for the future? We thought so. They sounded like plans at the time: Maseo playing basketball for some Big Ten—only we didn't know what "Big Ten" stood for; Tray going down south to college and being a football star, and me winning the big scholarship and studying journalism at the University of Missouri like Larry was doing. But plans and dreams are only the same at the beginning. We just didn't know how to make them stay the same.

Like always when school started, I came back looking sharp. Yellow silk shirt, yellow silk pants, black patent leather shoes. Jheri curls all fresh but short on top this time and long in the back. You know she had to say something about how I looked, or she wouldn't feel normal. I was ready for her. She could say that I looked like a pimp or a drug dealer. I was ready for that. Instead she told me that there were people to impress who wouldn't be comfortable with Jheri curls and loud clothes. She said that I had to play by different rules if I wanted to get some privileges.

"You have to decide, Shakir. No matter what, you can be the editor. But you have to decide how far you are going to take it."

I said what I wanted both of us to believe. That I could do it. That I could be Larry all over again. But I wasn't Larry, tall and light-skinned with close-cut hair, preppy like the guys at the Catholic school. I was small and dark-dark, looking ghetto with my silk shirt and greasy curls. So how could I believe it? How could either of us believe it?

We tried. A lot of times we were friends. A lot of times I made her mad, and she made me mad. Like she wouldn't let me do the layout. She would sit at the long table with the dummy sheets, the pica ruler and pencils and grease markers all over the place, just thinking and blocking out articles. Then she'd crumple up the dummy sheet she was working on and start all over again.

"Dammit, I hate this," she would say.

So I would try to tell her what I thought would work—I could even see it in my head—but she got even madder.

"How do you know? You never did this. You don't even know how to do this."

I did know how to do it, but if she didn't think so, how could it be right. Other times she wasn't so cold about it and used my ideas. But she always forgot that I could do it.

Then something bad happened. Or maybe I just understood what was going on all the time. I was reading my published article about choosing the right gifts for Christmas. Don't even know why I looked, but I found the original in my notebook, all wrinkled and pencil smeared. They weren't the same. The article in the newspaper was so funny and so slick, just like I imagined things in my head. But the stuff on those ragged sheets of looseleaf paper that I had grabbed one late night before my copy was due, it was bad. Nothing was spelled right, and the sentences just ran on and on, making no sense. But those were my words, my real words. The words in the paper were her words, only I forgot that every time I saw my byline above an article. I forgot that I wasn't the one who wrote what came under my name: by Shakir Khalid.

It was just a lie.

I could see her doing it. Taking the copy home to type—nobody in the class would type the copy even if they knew how—and changing it without knowing how different it turned out. She probably thought in the end that she was typing what we had written. But all the time it was getting changed, getting polished; words turned here and there until they fit what she wanted. And what she wanted most of all was to believe that we were good. That we could make it.

Larry out there in Missouri, the place sounded so cold, so far away, what did he think when he sat down to write? Where did he think the words went to? Or didn't he care? He got what he wanted. He got out. Maybe he didn't care if he got out on her words. Maybe he thought he could find some words of his own when it mattered.

I stopped going to class after that. She would stop me in the hall and ask me if I would come to journalism, and I always said yes, but I never showed. The day I dropped the class, she came to my house. She stood on the porch and yelled at me. She called me an asshole and a fool. She said that she had done everything for me, and she didn't deserve such betrayal. Then she went away without asking why I had done it—as if I could tell her.

That year the final city edition of the newspaper was real nice, about neighborhoods in the city. Any fool could tell that kids didn't write those articles. I guess she had to do it, write them herself, what with the whole world reading them, at least the whole Detroit world. Her name was on it, too, along with the kids', and she didn't want to look bad. I wanted to tell her that she had done a real good job, that she should be proud of her work, but we don't talk any more.

Love for a Fat Man

She was not beautiful; she was out of place. For one, the soles of her shoes were too thin. Any piece of broken glass could cut through thin soles like that. She knew that. She picked her way delicately among the broken bottles in the parking lot, the pot holes puddled with muddy water, the cans, and the newspapers. She held her skirt as if it might sweep across the filthy pavement. In the beginning anyway because she changed so much that I think I am remembering someone else. In the beginning she seemed fragile and breakable, but not broken. Broken was what she thought she was, but I wouldn't have started up with her if that had been true. Broken women are too dangerous. They don't care enough to be cautious.

The women who worked in the clinic—City Health and Social Services—talked about her in Spanish. The nurses speculated about the cost of the buttery leather satchel that she carried. The clerks envied the paisley folds of her skirts, the ruffled silk of her blouses. Even the pediatrician, who was from Pakistan, remarked on the gold ring that she wore: "True gold, twenty-two carat, and the diamonds are not of glass, I tell you."

I preside over this world of women. Aside from them there is only Xavier, who drives the van, and the medical residents who are assigned here for rotations in pediatrics and obstetrics. The residents cause me the most trouble because there aren't any barriers here between their medicine and the malnourished children; no way to separate themselves from the junkies in Prenatal, from the women who come up pregnant every ten months; from the tea-colored babies brought in by pasty-faced girls. These residents have a lot of flat tires and incidences of the flu, and I report them to their chiefs. "Medicine is about people," I tell the chiefs. It is an effective argument.

I drive here from my home at the farthest edge of Detroit. The people in my neighborhood consider themselves cosmopolitan:

Blacks with solid incomes, Mexicans like me who are professionals, Jews with liberal tendencies. It took me a long time to get there, to the boxed-in area bounded by Seven and Eight Mile Roads, Livernois and Woodward, to the two storeyed houses with three bedrooms, shuttered, and lawns that spread out like aprons. My wife drives a Volvo so that no harm will come to our sons, Rafael, Miguel, and Luis, in the event of a collision.

When I was growing up down here, growing up on 23rd Street, one of those poor streets numbered in haste, too unimportant to be named, there wasn't any clinic. My grandmother wrapped my chest in flannel, gave me tea brewed from ancient memory, and prayed in the Spanish of Indians.

And I survived, unlike my mother, who was murdered by her boyfriend—probably my father—in the Jalisco Bar just a half a block from here on the corner of Fort and Junction; unlike my brother, who slammed a stolen car into an abutment on the Lodge Freeway; unlike my uncles, who died of pneumonia, undiagnosed cancer, mistaken identity, and jealous women.

"Roberto," my grandmother would say to me, "Eat, Roberto. Eat what I make for you. Eat to live. Live, my baby."

And I ate. The beans, slow-baked in the fat of pork; the soups, red with tomatoes, thick with meaty bones, dense with onions, corn, and rice. Tamales, greasy in corn husks. And I ate. Coney Islands from Duly's, hamburgers from Top Hat, chop suey from Ho Ho Gardens, baloney and white bread bought at A&P, wolfed down in Clark Park after school.

It is all the same here as it was when I grew up on a numbered street, but I do not approach it with any particular bitterness because I don't live here any more. I can stand at the window of my office and sever the connection between me and the litter of the street.

So what did she see when she came to my office that first time, up those steps that winded me to walk? What did she see that she thought she could love? A fat man whose eyes were lost in cheeks like bags of candy. A man who grew up in the streets he looked down on from a streaked window of a squat building, cold in winter, hot in summer.

I am trained to be suspicious. There was law school, but I didn't stay long enough to benefit from not trusting what I heard and saw. There was the M.S.W. program. And always there were the numbered streets whose lessons added up.

The cross above our bed taught me suspicion, too, believing as I do that my wife lay beneath me during nights of love to please her Lord and his insatiable appetite for children. Once in an argument, I called her a whore for Jesus, and the way she looked at me, not angry, but as if she understood something about herself, hurt me. For the tidy box of a house, real brick; the sturdy, blue Volvo; three pale boys spared the dark, Mexican sun, she would suffocate under the rolls and weight of flesh and close her eyes against the sight of my body, sloping down in cascades of fat.

So I had my reasons to be suspicious of a woman whose hands were quick, little birds that flew about her words. The delicate colors of her eyelids were taken from a subtle palette. Her earrings were little pearls, irregular and starch-white. Such a woman would wear little pearls.

She talked of the program she had been assigned to administer. Yes, she was new at this kind of thing, used to subject matter, but didn't doubt that she could work it out, goals being realistic, always open to re-evaluation. When her hands came to rest on the fine, woolen weave of her skirt, she said, "I am in terrible pain."

Because she had eyes that didn't see me, I could do what I did. I came around my desk and took her small hands. I tasted the grief in her kiss, felt loneliness in the coolness of her skin. I thought—I remember thinking—this is like the movies. But not really. There was too much pain in that embrace. And I was afraid.

I didn't think that she would ever come back up those stairs. She wasn't like the social workers or the board members of the clinic or the R.N's. They were people like me, from the tall houses and the narrow driveways. Thin, ravening dogs had chased them home from the bus stop after a day of work, a night at school. Women like that I could kiss in my office and not be afraid that I had dared to hold them, to touch them, a short, fat man with small features lost in pouches and caches of fat.

I can talk about the fat now, but then, I wouldn't think about it. What I did think was that she would wipe her mouth with a quick movement of her hand as she went down the worn, waxy steps. She would shake away with little shudders the memory of my small hand, my ludicrously small hand that lifted the hem of her skirt.

Then I thought she was crazy in the way that some people are off balance all of their lives, responding to something in themselves and not to what is happening outside of them. I thought she was one of those people who came at things from an angle intensely her own.

She would hang on the door frame, wearing, for instance, a black corduroy dress with a high neck closed with jet buttons, a dress fitted to the hips and falling in rounded pleats. I loved that dress and paid compliments when she wore it, but I always thought that polyester and rayon were the materials of this place, that she offered us too rich a diet for our starved appetites. At that time she was thin, very thin, and I could imagine her pushing away a plate after a few forkfuls because she was not present enough to eat.

But we never ate together.

So I took her to bed, and I turned her away. I hurt her, but I had to do it.

The room was dirty, I am sure. It had the sense of too many people lying on the thin, bluish sheets; too many naked feet padding across the rough carpet, damp like moss; too many feet on the cold, sticky tiles of the bathroom. It cost twenty-eight dollars for the rag of a wash cloth and the cardboard towel, the bed where no one would go for sleeping, a lamp that crooked its neck like a malignant goose. It cost twenty-eight dollars, and she gave me twenty of it. I took it as if I expected her to pay, to make the choice hers and not mine.

She sat in a chair, wearing her slip. The only light came from the bathroom, but that was too much light for me. If it had been dark, I could have pretended that we were there because we wanted each other. But as long as she could see me, I couldn't believe that she was there for me.

"We don't have to do this," I said, because she looked at me for the first time in that twenty-eight dollar room. My enormous undershirt, sleeveless with a rounded neck, stretched and shapeless. Shorts—they can only be bought at Big and Tall—and my thin legs and the thin bones of my feet.

Then she wasn't crazy or jittery in her high-strung way. She was solemn. Her hands lay quiet where she sat in the brown chair, the white slip shining like moonlight. She said: We came here for a reason, and we don't have much time.

How you feel when you are a fat man, struggling for air on a flight of stairs, whose sacks of thighs push out your feet in a splayed, duck-like walk, and how you feel when you have disappointed a woman are very much the same. You can't think about it. You say things like, "No one messes with a big man." Like "I am going to fuck you to death." But you can't do either: protect yourself from the quick and the strong, or get close enough to a woman to fill her as she desires.

I was tender with her. I kissed the soles of her feet, and she paid me back in pleasures. But I knew.

Still on Monday she appeared in my office, as always pausing in the doorway so that I could see the picture she was presenting to me, a picture she had prepared for me. She wore a gray silk blouse that was almost blue with a tunic collar that she favored at the time, and gray slacks with a lizard belt. There were little heels on boots, and the leather satchel hung from her shoulder. Her earrings were silver discs intersected with black lightning.

I thought she looked elegant. I loved her for how she looked. I would have gone back to that mossy, humid room with her at that very moment and would have found the right way to love her. But for what she did.

She kissed me like a mother kisses her child in a moment when love compels her to press her lips on that child's head. Standing above me where I sat at my desk, she kissed me in this way. It was a kiss too intimate, too tender, and too kind. It was a kiss I could not accept because it had to be a lie.

"You know I am married."

"Yes, but still...."

"There will be too much talk, and my wife comes here."

"Then it was just to get me for that once."

"I didn't mean to do it at all. It was a mistake."

She did not come upstairs after that. She ran her classes on the first floor at the back of the clinic, and we only spoke about the security guard's duties or when the men in her groups bothered the patients. I saw her all the time even when she didn't know it. I saw how she changed. There were the thick-soled boots, orange-tan, and jeans; soft, open shirts, and the parka whose collar lay against her cheek, rosy with winter. I heard her laugh, touch kindly someone's hand, open a door for an old lady. And I wanted to be with her.

But I could not go to her. I could not lumber down the narrow stairs, catch my breath before I reached her door. I could not believe that she would want such a man as I was. I could not go.

Then I fell—into myself, into the maelstrom at whose center was my failing heart. I rose and fell and sank. When I knew where I was, when I knew what had happened, then I thought of nothing but the beat of my heart and its echoing pulse, the circuitous journey of my blood. I thought of nothing but of rising to the moment of waking and sinking to the instant of sleep. In the night I imagined the intra-

venous bead poised like a bird about to drop in a downward plunge.
I could hear it fall in the dark.

Then in the time of full awakening, when the bed was cranked
up and day filled the single hospital window like a painting—false
sky, cardboard buildings, trees bent like wire hangers—and my wife
was seated in the beige armchair as if she had been there forever, they
brought me food. A small piece of chicken, a scoop of rice, some
beans, green and soggy from the steam cart. Food for the heart pa-
tient, but I refused it. I refused the oatmeal and the unbuttered toast.
The tuna and the bowl of greens. The nurse told the doctor. My wife
folded her hands this way and that, imploring me in a low voice so
that no one would hear.

"Roberto, how can you live if you do this? Roberto, if you die,
you bring us down. Roberto, I have children. Roberto, don't do
this."

I didn't want to die. I saw that food was my death, my way of
dying. A different kind of death from my pretty-girl mother's and her
violent brothers, but really no different when it came to willing death
upon ourselves, the deaths that the nameless streets intended for us.

The social worker came, and she had a name that was Greek. Her
hair was black and smooth, and her eyes were innocent and kind. I
could hear the accents of another language in her words. The folders
she gave me described the diet of heart patients, the benign food that
nourished, that would not bring you crashing down in the middle
of an ordinary day when your desk was filled with messages, and the
intercom called your name. But you could not answer.

For her kind eyes and the foreign language at the core of her
words, I ate: small forkfuls, tentative spoons lifted to my lips. But I
was always afraid, not the simple fear of dying but the fear of a person so purely instrumental in his own death, so deliberate in the ar-
rangement of his own end. I had never understood this before falling
into the wide pool of pain. I had never understood the devouring
monster that lived in me, intent on my destruction. Now that I knew
that he—it—was there, I could not please it with my easy dying.

From the woman I received a card, humorous, impartial, no
words that would alarm my wife as she arranged the plants and cards
on the window ledge. "We heard you were ill," cartoon figures, and
her signature.

When I left the hospital and the trays of food, the small portions
that never satisfied the hunger, only the need to survive, I was afraid
again. Afraid of the breads, the margarine, the eggs in their top-heavy
ovals. The chicken bleeding on the counter-top: the stew filling the

kitchen with the rich smell of bay leaf, beef, carrots and onions. The wedge of cheese covered with plastic wrap. The cookies for the boys; the boxes of mix in the pantry; the unopened cans stacked one upon the other, red for soups, green for vegetables, yellow for fruit thick in syrup. They were menacing, tempting, everywhere in my home.

I would walk because I was supposed to and because I had to escape the murderous food. At first, it was just two blocks and home again, past the square lawns beginning to green, the doors brown and cream, shutters thrown open to light and the voices of the neighbors. The sidewalks were dark with rain that had fallen in the night. I had never looked at these streets before, but now I saw them foot by foot, yard by yard, roof by roof, gray and luminous, dark and light.

One afternoon, I toasted a tortilla on the burner, flipped it over and back again, filled it with beans that had been cooked in the oven with pork fat and cheese. I wrapped the tortilla around the beans, thinking, "I am cured of this madness." But with the thought came the fear, coupled and fused: yearning and aversion. I threw the tortilla in the sink and ran from the house.

The Greek social worker arranged that I join the program sponsored by the hospital for people suffering from extreme obesity. There was apology in the way she said the words, 'extreme obesity,' but I did not need her apologies or her delicacy. I was terrified.

The way it works is that you don't eat any more. The food for your life comes in sealed packages, choice of five flavors: chocolate, vanilla, pineapple-banana, orange-lemon, and strawberry. Five times a day the packets are mixed in a plastic container with the measure of water. There are vitamins and herbal teas. That's all. After a lifetime of eating everything, whether it tasted good or not, whether it was raw or cooked, whether you wanted it or not, the only choices were five flavors. Beyond that, there was hunger.

The walks became miles of streets and extended into another season. Other journeys were made on the stationary bicycle, the degrees of difficulty determined by a single lever. While my family ate their meals, I would pedal at number two and try not to hear the fork sing against the plate, the spoon vibrate across the bowl.

When I went back to the clinic, she was preparing to leave. Xavier was carrying boxes of materials to her car. The posters were rolled into cylinders to be spread out, flattened, and pinned up with bright, new stick pins in another place. She had been offered another site and a permanent position. She was wearing slacks of soft cotton and a white shirt with the collar open.

"Why, you look wonderful," she said. "We were so concerned."
She would not say 'I.' That was her revenge on me, a way to take away
the room, the white slip, and the hurried, clumsy moment she could
not have wanted to happen to her.

"I had hoped we might talk," I said.

"There isn't time any more."

A man can wait as women wait. A man can walk the pleasant
streets of the life he has made. He can go each week to his support
group and tell other men and women how he felt when he ate twelve
doughnuts in the alley before going in the house for dinner under
a dim light in the kitchen, his grandmother filling his plate. He can
decided what flavors he will mix with water at 8:00, 11:00, 1:00. He
can buy two pairs of trousers until the next forty pounds are lost. He
can see a thinner man emerge but never lose the outlines of the man
and boy he was. He can grow thinner and thinner and still be afraid.

He can be afraid even when he is as thin as he is ever going to
be; when he dresses in the morning in trousers with a thirty-six inch
waist and a shirt with a collar sized fifteen; when he eats the oatmeal
measured and sealed in a package, a safe, preordained portion. He
can still be afraid.

And he is afraid when he calls her after so many months, more
than a year: that she will not come, that she will never know what he
willed for himself against the devouring other self that lived in him.

She came, herself another person. She was not the woman who
stood in doorways, afraid to enter. She was a woman who hung up
her coat—"thinsulate," the label on the lining read—and who took
a seat at the side of the desk. She wore her glasses and smiled when
she was amused.

"I can't believe this. I would never recognize you. If we met on
the street...."

"Most of the time I don't believe it either. I have to think about
it all the time. It's like being an alcoholic. That's how it's treated."

"Meeting and confessions?"

"Doctors and diets."

"Has it changed you?"

"In a lot of ways. But not about you."

She stood up, and even in her sensible clothes, a dark dress,
washable, and flat shoes, a watch with a broad band, a beige purse of
sturdy leather, she was still the out-of-place woman who had picked
her way across the glass-littered parking lot. Ten pounds heavier, two

years older, she was still delicate. She looked out at the filthy streets, the dirt-covered windows of the low buildings housing pawn shops, junk shops, resale shops, diners.

"Before we were like people in a play, wearing masks, saying our lines to go with the parts we were playing. No sense and no consequences. We were just outside of our lives like on a stage. And I was outrageous. I don't know who I thought I was."

"So it didn't count?"

"No, it didn't. Now, you are just a man who wants to sleep with a woman who isn't his wife, maybe once or twice a month. That's all. Just a regular man with a modest salary and a family to support. And I don't want that."

"You wanted that fat man, the man I was. Is that right?"

"I liked the play acting, the inappropriateness, the thrill of it."

"You can have it again. We can."

"It would just be sordid. Before it was dramatic. I could make you up, bigger than ordinary life. I could find reasons to love you that no one else could think of. It was romantic, even creative. Now it would just be adultery. I don't have time for adultery."

I should have known that, too. About what there is time for and when that time is over. I should have known from the brief lives of the people on this street that stretches east and west in misery. For every wretched girl who comes here with a child in her arms and one opening up like a flower within, there had been a moment when she was lovely; when she and her man were poised on the exquisite brink, a place where only falling was possible. We should have gone to the room as long as it was the place for us, but there were too many things to be afraid of. And they stood in my way.

I can imagine what we would be like now: two ordinary people in a bed, making love, saying too many things, and then the anger that springs from such meetings. I should be content with the memory of her quiet posture and her folded hands. I shouldn't know any more about her.

Outside Verona Walls

There is no life without Verona walls,
But purgatory, torture, hell itself.
            (The Tragedy of Romeo and Juliet, III, iii)

I.

Isabelle walks down Woodward each noon hour. She floats past the flat surfaces of buildings that rise straight up toward the Detroit sky. When it is cold, she wraps herself in a woolen shawl. Her skirt moves like a curtain around her ankles and skims the top of her black shoes.

Her kerchief covers her hair, the thick, wavy hair that she won't cut short because it would look like a trimmed hedge.

When Isabelle walks down Woodward, she imagines herself as immense as a dinosaur, her huge haunches lifting and falling. If she let her arms move freely, they would knock people from the sidewalk, and they would tumble into the street.

She is not displeased with the sense of her own enormity. When she sees her reflection, it is of a tall, full-bodied woman with a thin face.

At night her hair spreads out on the pillow. She is two people, the sleeper and the spy, watching herself between the white sheets and under the white comforter. Her face is calm and pale, her eyes closed, a downward sweep of lashes, pale curve of her mouth. She wants to fan her hair out on the pillow. But she is practicing stillness.

The beloved's eyes are watching her on the narrow bed. Everything is white: blankets, plain curtains tied back with a ribbon during the day, the rag rug on the floor. Her red-brown hair is fire against the whiteness. When she opens her eyes, she is always surprised

that the beloved is not standing there, subdued by the whiteness or
enflamed by the fire of her hair.

II.

Isabelle works as receptionist and executive secretary at the medical school, but she believes only in the healing power of the body. It
is the force that governs her life.

Where she works is pleasant. Her desk is situated so that she
can pivot her chair from her computer to the telephone. Her voice is
slow and melodious. She enjoys the roundness of the words as they
form in her mouth. "Good Afternoon. Wayne State University Medical School. How may I direct your call?" The words curl themselves
into tendrils small enough to snake through the wires to the listener
at the other end where they will unfold like flowers, delicate and
easeful. "One moment, please. I will connect you."

She loves the formulas that make up her day. The dictations become documents under her fingers; papers settle in orderly patterns
when she places them in the multi-colored folders of their origins or
their destinations. The finality as the stamp machine descends upon
an envelope.

On Sunday Isabelle visits with her mother, Irene Zelesky, to help
her with the mid-day dinner. They remember when Isabelle's life was
turned in an unexpected direction, but they do not talk about that
time any longer.

III.

Her father has brought home a suitor, 'a proper man,' and it does
not occur to Isabelle to go against her father's will. She is nineteen.

The man, Tadeusz, wants to be called Ted, but he speaks to Isabelle and her parents in Polish to show his suitability. Isabelle will
not speak Polish. She lets it rain around her, protected from it as if
she were carrying an umbrella.

After the clear chicken broth with wide noodles, the beef and potatoes in a sour cream gravy, fruit compote, and the steaming tea with
sugar cookies, Isabelle and Tadeusz take a stroll in the neighborhood
where the houses present themselves in a harmony of green shutters

and white vinyl siding, tidy lawns and borders of flowers. Neighbors nod at them as they pass by in the summer evening.

Tadeusz wants to go for a drive. He asks Isabelle's parents if they would like hot fudge sundaes from Sander's.

Ladislaw Zelesky is pleased that the walk has been successful. "You and Isabelle go and bring back some ice cream." He reaches into his pocket for money, but Tadeusz waves it away.

In the parking lot of Sander's, Tadeusz kisses Isabelle on the mouth. He kisses her again and then places his hand on her breast, his fingers spread over the cloth of her blouse.

"No," she says in English. "Don't do this."

Tadeusz speaks in Polish. She is his fiancée. He has done nothing wrong. She has returned his kiss. What did she expect?"

"Take your hand away."

They return to the house without the ice cream sundaes. Tadeusz lets her off in front of the house and drives away without saying good night to Irene and Ladislaw.

"Where is Tadeusz?" her father says to Isabelle. He speaks to her in Polish.

"He left." She answers in English.

"You have not been agreeable," he shouts. "What did you say? What did you do?"

Isabelle cannot tell her father that his hand on her breast had sent flames running down her legs, burning her in a place she had no name for. She has no words in English or Polish for what she has felt.

"Nothing," she says.

After that her father does not speak to her in a normal voice. He shouts and then one day he hits her. "If you live in my house, you do as I say."

She goes to her sister's and sleeps on the couch. She gets a job as a file clerk in a downtown law firm. When she has enough money, she rents a small apartment on Second and Willis. With each paycheck she adds to her furnishings with the careful calculations she has seen practiced by her mother.

Ladislaw Zelesky dies of a heart attack at a family barbecue in Lola Valley Park in the late spring.

"I need something black," she tells the saleswoman in the boutique, Once Removed, on Six Mile Road near Hamilton.

"Black dresses are the first to go," the woman says, estimating Isabelle's size and leafing through the rack. "Especially the simple ones. All I have is this." She holds up the long, black skirt, an A-line that would emphasize Isabelle's ample hips.

"You could wear an overblouse," suggests the woman, "or a long jacket. This skirt came with a long jacket, but someone bought it. It was sharp."

The shawl is scrambled among the neck scarves and headscarves.

"I like this," Isabelle says.

"Honey, you're too young for a shawl."

"No, I'm not young at all."

For her father's funeral she has become someone else, someone she welcomes as if it is a return rather than a birth.

IV.

With her next paycheck Isabelle buys a used sewing machine, the old-fashioned, black model. At Haberman's Fabrics, she finds the pattern for a skirt with a narrow waistband and generous folds to the ankle. With extra material she can make a ruffle for the hem. She considers a pattern for a blouse, but she recalls her mother's complaints about the difficulty of setting a sleeve.

She leaves Haberman's with four swaths of material for her skirts: a light, narrow-whaled corduroy of a medium blue; an almost translucent black wool that will require a lining; a beige cotton with a black and purple paisley design; a white cotton remnant with a splash of flowers.

Isabelle discovers that she dislikes meat and is repelled by the scaly pieces of fish laid out on ice in the market; that she prefers green beans, broccoli, cauliflower, red and yellow peppers; cucumbers, radishes, and carrots with the stalks. At Thanksgiving, the first one after Ladislaw Zelesky has died, she refuses the holiday food.

"What's wrong?" her sister asks. "Are you sick?"

"I would rather not eat turkey."

"I bought it fresh, Isabelle. It isn't a Butterball like last year."

"The taste of meat...."

"I knew it," says her brother-in-law. "She is some kind of hippie. I could have told you that would happen when she started wearing those skirts hanging down to the ground."

"I don't know any hippies," says Isabelle.

She does not talk about boyfriends or clothes or babies or television programs with the young women she works with. She refuses their invitations to go to lunch or for a drink at one of the few bars that remain open in downtown Detroit. After the work day is over, Isabelle walks from the law firm on Congress to her apartment on Second and Willis. It is a long walk but she looks forward to it.

"Can I give you a lift?" her supervisor says when they are riding down in the elevator. "It's brutally cold out there."

"Walking in the cold clears my head," says Isabelle.

She discovers rituals that please her. Cooking from the recipes in her second-hand cookbooks. The click of needles as she crochets or knits the shawls she wears and the scarves she gives for gifts at Christmas. She buys a book at the second-hand bookstore, *A Weaver with Needles*, and her scarves have small flowers knitted into the weave or the shadowy outlines of leaves.

She does not own a radio or a television, but she has no guests who would comment. Her sister will not drive to "such a bad neighborhood, full of drunks and students," and Isabelle does not invite strangers into her apartment. When the maintenance man comes to fix the toilet or unstop a drain, she burns aromatic candles when he leaves, exorcising the disturbing aura of the breath expelled from the lung, the faint, pungent odor of the skin.

She prefers, however, clothing that has belonged to other people. A ruffled blouse whispers to her of a woman dressing herself on a Sunday morning in hopes of seeing the man she loves; a long-sleeved sweater, whose snags she has pulled through with a crochet hook, belonged to a girl who wore it to walk through autumn woods. The silk T-shirt, deep bronze, still vibrates with the pride of a young woman with her body, and Isabelle must subdue it with a tight wrapping of her shawl.

Two evenings a week Isabelle takes a class at Wayne State University. She browses among classes as she would browse through the offerings of garage sales, estate sales, and second-hand stores.

She has struggled with the translation of Flaubert from the French and is not sure that she understands Emma Bovary; she has dreamed her way through Music Lit, forgetting to take notes because she lingers too long in the sunlit parlors and courtyards of Mozart and Vivaldi.

She has left the law firm and taken a better-paying job at the medical school. The hours are better, too: 8:30 to 4:30 and no requests to stay "until the work is done for the night." Now she can enroll in a weaving class at the Center for Creative Arts.

She weaves in the colors that have to come to her in dreams: corals and burnt orange, brown with the red tinge of bark, blues that are silver in a certain slant of light. Her dreams are vivid and eloquent.

The medical school is too far for walking, so Isabelle asks her brother-in-law to teach her how to drive. He swears under his breath when she makes a mistake, but he sees her through left turns and backing up.

"You're on your own for parking," he says. "Just stick to parking lots for a while."

Her mother gives her Ladislaw Zelesky's 1988 Mercury Marquis, whitewalls still bright from his weekly scrubbing, the blue-black car gleaming from the waxing and the buffing. Isabelle steers the huge boat of a car carefully down Woodward to Jefferson and back. She feels like a sailor in a sea of small fish darting back and forth on the rivers of these city streets.

V.

On this winter day. On this winter day, she is carrying so many groceries that she uses the elevator instead of the stairs. This day that has not been ordinary from the outset: Anemone, her cat, is not asleep at her feet when she wakes up; a cactus on the windowsill has burst into flower; a storm window shatters and falls like shards of ice to the street.

The boy in the elevator asks her, "Want me to hold the doors open?"

"Please."

Instead the doors slam closed and open again; the boy, not a boy, flushes.

"I pushed the wrong button." He seems angry at Isabelle for this embarrassment.

They are silent as the elevator shudders its way to Isabelle's floor.

"Want me to help you carry your bags?" he asks so reluctantly that Isabelle has to laugh.

"You have a great laugh," the sullen boy who-isn't-a-boy, says. "It sounds like music."

There is nothing Isabelle can think to answer. The doors close.

VI.

Isabelle sees the sullen boy walking down Jefferson, coming from the direction of the medical school. It is raining, but she passes him by, afraid to ask, "Do you want a ride?" Two streets later she stops and waits for him.

He peers into the car, sees who it is, and opens the door.

"I'm soaked. I'll probably get pneumonia. This would never have happened if that son-of-a-bitch, Dr. Aaron, hadn't asked to see me after class. I could've gotten a ride with one of the guys. But no, he wants to talk about how my last quiz score in anatomy wasn't 'up to par' like it's some stupid golf game. And it's raining. So what's the point of talking about a test score that I can't do anything about. I miss my ride. I'm starving. I'm wet. My goddamn books are probably ruined. Look at my shoes. These shoes are my best shoes. They look like cardboard."

"They'll dry out. Just don't put them too near the radiator." These are the first words that Isabelle says to the sullen boy in her car.

"The radiators. Those damn things keep me up all night. Clank, clank, clank. Sometimes I want to pull them out of the floor. They drive me nuts. Look, could you drop me off at the McDonald's on Warren? I have to eat something."

"You can eat dinner with me."

"I don't even know your name."

"Isabelle."

"Brian."

Isabelle warms black bean soup. She peels two sweet potatoes and simmers small pieces in maple syrup, cinnamon, and water. She adds a cup of couscous and some raisins. She slices two large pieces from the loaf of bread she has baked and takes out the butter.

Brian looks around her apartment: the white throw rug, the white upholstered chairs, and the lamps with white shades. Georgia O'Keefe lilies are the only prints on the wall.

"This looks like a nun's house. Are you a nun? I shouldn't haven't been swearing like that in the car. I'm not Catholic, but still I didn't need to swear like that."

"I'm not a nun."

"You look like a nun."

"I like white."

"It's nice. It's peaceful."

The table is set in color. Isabelle serves the soup in splashy flowered bowls and serves the warmed bread.

"I only have tea," she says when she sets the bowl of sweet potatoes and couscous on the table.

"I need caffeine," Brian says. "A coke would be ok, but I bet you don't have any coke, right? You're one of those people into health."

"You're 'into health,' too. You're a med student."

"Yeah, you're right. My mother's big dream. Both of her sons doctors. I said to her, 'Ma, I'd rather be a lawyer,' and she went nuts. How much she sacrificed. Took the bus, didn't have a car of her own because she knew that every extra penny should go for her boys. In winter she was cold because she didn't have a fur coat, not even when she could get it half off. Because her sons' futures were on the line.

"I have to tell you, Isabelle. I think I'm going to be a terrible doctor. I don't get along with people that well."

Isabelle cannot find her voice. She wants to tell Brian that he could take a residency in radiology or pathology or even anesthesiology.

"What is this, sweet potatoes and some kind of rice? I guess you're a vegetarian. It figures, but that's ok. I've been eating crap. McDonald's, Burger King, pizza until I could go crazy. This is a nice change.

"So you work at the school. I thought you looked familiar when I saw you in the elevator. I felt that I hadn't seen you in life but in a dream. You know what I mean? The way you move—like flowing water, calm and silver. A dream river."

Isabelle begins to cry. "Oh, oh," she says, but she does not dare to say more because there are sounds in her heart that she is not capable of uttering.

"What's wrong?" Brian gets up from his chair and comes to her. He puts his arms around her shoulders, and she rests her head against his chest. She hears the quick beatings of his heart. "What did I say? I'm sorry. I like your dinner. I like you. I didn't mean to insult you. Don't cry. I really like you. Don't cry."

Isabelle cannot stop crying. Brian lifts her from her chair and guides her into the bedroom. They lie down together on the white bed. He strokes her hair and cradles her in his arms.

"I like everything about you. You don't have to cry." He holds her around the waist and kisses her eyes, her cheeks, her mouth. Isabelle opens her eyes and looks at the man she will love.

VII.

After work Isabelle parks her car two blocks from the medical school and waits for Brian. When she is asked to move on, she tells the police officer that she is waiting for a sick friend. She is terrified that she will not be where she has promised to meet Brian; that she will miss him while she is circling the block. She will never see him again if she is not in the exact place at the right time.

"Why can't we meet in the school parking lot?" she asks him.

"Do you want people knowing our business, Isabelle?" He is annoyed, and Isabelle thinks he might be ashamed of her, her long skirts, the shawls instead of a proper coat, and the earrings her mother says make her look like a Gypsy.

At the market Isabelle picks out the chickens with the same critical thoroughness she has seen in her mother. She pinches and eyes the bird as if she could detect bad feed or a disease of chickens.

She buys a cookbook, *365 Ways to Prepare Chicken*, and prepares a different dish each day. She numbers each successful recipe: Chicken Marengo, number one; chicken and fettucini with sun-dried tomatoes and carrot sticks, number eight; baked chicken dredged in seasoned breadcrumbs, number fifteen; apricot grilled chicken, number twenty-two; chicken in peanut sauce, number forty-one. Each number is a victory on the calendar of her lover's presence at her table and in her bed.

She doesn't eat the chicken. She cuts it and re-arranges it on the plate. Brian eats quickly; he doesn't notice that she doesn't eat the chicken.

Brian goes to his own apartment after dinner to study. He is gone until midnight or one o'clock in the morning. Isabelle cleans the kitchen, washes clothes, irons Brian's shirts, wipes the sink, bathtub, and toilet with a mixture of vinegar and water. She makes tuna salad or egg salad sandwiches on pumpernickel bread for Brian's lunches. She bakes carob brownies or oatmeal cookies and cuts oranges into quarters. She fills his thermos with hot water and lets it stand all night so that his coffee will be hot throughout the day.

Then she takes a bath. While the tub is filling, she washes her hair in the sink with a mint shampoo. She wraps her thick, curling hair in a towel and soaks in a bathtub in which she pours half a bath oil called Sea Breezes. She thinks of Brian's fingers circling her nipples, filling his hands with her.

Even if her hair is damp, she goes to bed at eleven o'clock, her hair spread across the pillow, her hands folded beneath her breasts. She is waiting for the turn of the key, the door scraping over the carpet, the sinking of the bed as he takes off his shoes and his pants. She is waiting for him to turn to her, to move on top of her. She wraps her legs around him and rocks him into her. Forever. She could rock him forever.

VIII.

Isabelle asks Brian to come with her for Sunday dinner to meet her family.

"It's not like I'm going to marry you, Isabelle," he says, looking at her with annoyance.

Isabelle wonders what will happen: when the school year is over; when she has prepared all three hundred sixty-five chicken recipes. She dreams that Brian is moving away from her, and when she tries to stop his gradual fading from the dream landscape, her hand comes up against a glass wall.

When Isabelle is at work or in her weaving class, she does not believe in the existence of Brian or in the words breathed between kisses. *You are quick silver that carries me away until I cannot return.* Whose words are these? She can't distinguish. *Where you lay your hands, my skin is flame. Take them away, and I will become ash.*

IX.

"I thought I'd go nuts, you know, when Jim told me, 'I think we should start seeing other people,'" Isabelle hears from the cubicle that adjoins her office space. "That means he's already screwing someone else."

"So, what did you do?"

"I said, 'That's a good idea.' And he said, 'I'm glad you see it my way.' Then I lost it. I started screaming, 'Your way, you son-of-a-bitch. Do you think that everything is going to be your way? That I'm just going to fold up like a handkerchief that you can stick in your pocket and pull out any time you want me.' I got out of the car and walked away."

"Did he come after you?"

"No. He got what he wanted. I made it so easy for him."

"You can never stop them from going. When that's what they want."

"Yeah. You think there is a way. Like you could become a blonde or go on a diet or buy a sexy outfit. But nothing works. I tried making Jim jealous by showing up at Brady's with a real gorgeous guy. Like it was my cousin Al, but Jim didn't know that. And he comes up to me and says, 'I'm glad you got it together.'"

"The creep."

"I can't get him out of my mind. I hear he's engaged, and I try to pretend it's ok, but it isn't. I can't figure out why I'm not the one. After all I did...."

Isabelle goes to the ladies' room and looks at herself in the mirror. How can I be the one? I have to be the one.

X.

"What's wrong?" Isabelle says to Brian when he gets in the car.

"They're going to throw me out."

"Who?"

"The dean, the anatomy instructor, all those bastards. And I didn't do anything."

"Then why?"

"They always had it in for me. 'Mr. Raskin, you have a bad attitude.' 'Mr. Raskin, you aren't holding up your end.' Right from the
beginning, they've been giving me a hard time."

"That isn't enough to expel you. There has to be a hearing."

"Oh, there will be all right. I thought you knew."

"About what? What did I know about?"

"The notes."

"Notes?"

"The ones I took into the exam."

"Oh."

"I made them to jog my memory. That's all. Just some notes."

"Where were they?"

"In the sleeve of my shirt. So I could slide them into the palm of
my hand."

"Who saw them?"

"Aaron, the son-of-a-bitch."

"Dr. Aaron is pretty strict about cheating."

"I wasn't cheating, God damn it, Isabelle, I wasn't cheating. They
were memory devices. Little diagrams."

She is silent.

"You'll help me, won't you?"

"How can I help you, Brian?"

"You could go to Dr. Aaron. You could tell him I was under a
lot of stress. Or that you forgot to take the notes out of my pocket
when you hung up my shirt. You could tell him it was an oversight.
So when I found them, I slipped them in my sleeve. Because I didn't
want it to look like I was cheating."

"He won't believe that."

"You never want to do anything for me, Isabelle. You just want
me around, so you won't feel like an old maid. That's why you want
everyone to know about us. Well, now's your chance. Everyone will
know that we are living together, and you forgot to take those notes
out of my shirt pocket."

"I want to help you, Brian."

"My mother will never forgive me. I won't be able to go home.
I'll just kill myself. If I'm not a doctor. If I have to tell my mother."

"I'll think of something," she says. "I'll talk to Dr. Aaron."

XI.

Isabelle's throat is filled with a thickness that is dread. If she cannot convince Dr. Aaron to be lenient, Brian will disappear from her life. She cannot think beyond Brian: Brian at the dinner table; Brian seeking her out in the dark and white room, his hands trailing comets across her stomach; the relief she feels as she watches his quick, angry walk toward the car, as if somehow it were her idea to be secretive. Brian curled around her until morning, and the slow, delicious awakening as he pushes himself into her, hardening to her softness.

She does not care about anything but this. "There is no world without Verona walls, only purgatory, torture, hell itself." Romeo said it about exile, life without Juliet. She remembers these words from a Shakespeare class.

Isabelle wears a long, straight skirt and a white blouse. She tames her hair with a brush and does not wear a scarf. She has bought No Nonsense pantyhose at the supermarket, and she has already caused a run by pulling them on too hastily.

She makes an appointment with Dr. Aaron for 4:30. Of course, she could enter his office with only a knock during work hours, but she wants to emphasize the importance what she has to say.

"Ms. Zelesky, what can I help you with?"

"Dr. Aaron, the young man, the one you believe to have cheated...."

"Raskin. You aren't here to plead for Raskin."

"Yes, I am. You see, he is so much younger than the others. I'll bet you didn't know that. He is only twenty. He is able to do the work, but he gets frightened. He wants to keep up."

"What idiots let a twenty-year-old into medical school?"

"People who thought he was gifted. Don't you think that might be the case? And he is gifted. So quick to learn, serious about his studies."

"But those notes."

"He was frightened. Maybe he just wanted to know they were there, so he could visualize them. He has an incredible memory. He can remember the exact page numbers. Ask him anything, Dr. Aaron. Call him into the office. Ask him the same questions that were on the exam. He can answer them. He didn't have to cheat."

"I can't give him special privileges."

"I know you have standards, Dr. Aaron. I hope that I am not insulting you by asking...."

"What are you asking?"

"For some other punishment. But not expulsion."

"He cheated. He's not fit to be a physician."

"Let him have another chance. He is just a boy. He needs some time to be a man."

"Well, then."

They sit there in silence. She feels that a day and a night have passed before he speaks again.

"He must withdraw immediately and repeat the year. And I won't have him in my anatomy class. He can take his anatomy somewhere else."

"Thank you. You are so kind."

"Mr. Raskin is fortunate to have so passionate an advocate for his cause."

Isabelle lowers her eyes.

"I am sorry. I don't mean to be inappropriate," Dr. Aaron says. "But it amazes me: The human heart is so small and has important functions. But I didn't realize how much the heart is capable of."

Isabelle thinks of a heart, bloody and pulsating. It's not the heart, she thinks. It is the crease of her elbow where he presses his mouth. It is the hollow of her back where his fingers play. It is the rise of her breasts where he places his hands on top of hers. Love lives in all the valleys and the rises of the body.

"The heart is too small," she says.

XII.

Isabelle finds the white dress in Birmingham at a resale shop, Repeat Performance. She has never shopped so far from Detroit before, but the best almost-antique furniture shops are located in the suburbs. She is looking for a wooden bedstead to fit the new double mattress.

Repeat Performance is crowded with coats, suits, dresses, pant suits, shoes, purses, all of which have gone out of style. There are only lamps and occasional tables, no other furniture. She is about to leave the shop when she sees the white dress.

She takes it from the rack and holds it up. There are frills at the neck and it is fitted to the waist, a eyelet skirt over the cotton slip.

"It's such a lovely dress," says the woman who is running the shop.

"It's very nice," says Isabelle.

"You could wear it to a lawn party, maybe a luncheon, but it's a dress more for a costume party. I could give it to you for twenty-five dollars."

Isabelle buys the dress. She imagines herself with a garland of flowers and a bouquet in her hand. The dress will float like mist as she approaches the judge to become a wife. She wishes she could be married in a grove in golden green light. Or on a cliff with the sea curling on the rocks and her hair lifted in the wind.

"Do you like it?" she asks Brian.

"It's pretty. What's it for?"

"It's a wedding dress."

"I thought we were going to keep it simple. Just you, me, and the judge. One, two, three, out the door."

"We aren't going for a driver's license. We're going to get married."

"You do it in the same place. You get a license to drive, get married, start a business. You don't wear a white dress to the City-County Building."

Isabelle hangs the dress in the closet. Something will come up, and she will be able to wear this dress and tuck roses with velvet petals at her waist.

"We should invite our families."

"No way."

"Don't you want your mother at your wedding?"

"She'll find out about it soon enough. I mean, I'll have to tell her. She'll try calling my apartment and get no answer. Then she'll call out the army."

"It isn't right, not telling our families."

"It'll be like a funeral. Me getting thrown out of medical school and then getting married. My mother, she'll go nuts. What am I supposed to say? 'Hi, Ma. I'm getting married. Yeah, and I also got kicked out of medical school. No, Ma. She isn't Jewish.'"

Isabelle wants to say: Don't marry me. But she can't.

She should not love this beautiful boy, but she cannot bear the hours in a day when she is parted from him. Time is frozen from the moment she leaves him until the moment she sees him again. Each day is impossibly wonderful and impossibly horrible.

He doesn't love her, and he is ashamed of her. She has seen him look away when they are in the supermarket or in K-Mart if he sees someone he knows. She has seen him look at girls, eighteen, nineteen. She already sees him leaving.

She thinks: Night is everything to me. He stands in the door of the bedroom where I lie and wait for him. I must always be there first so that I am what he comes to, not the bed, not the place of sleep, but the place where I wait to receive him. I am the gate, and he must enter. He must pass through me.

She thinks: I should let him go.

XIII.

They marry on a Saturday morning at the Thirteenth Circuit Court in Detroit. It is a day that is crowded with marriages. The anteroom rustles with tulle and silk. Bouquets wrapped in lace are set on benches. A mother and father in church clothes sit next to a girl who is pregnant. There is an argument and a young woman in jeans rushes from the room, followed by a man saying, "I didn't mean that. I meant that..." before the door swings closed.

In the judge's chambers, there is a witness. In five minutes they are married.

On this Saturday Isabelle's mother morning is wiping down the kitchen or digging up the flower beds for early planting. She might pause, disturbed by the notion that an important moment has passed. Then she will shake it off. Isabelle's sister will be at her aerobics class. She won't sense anything because the instructor will be shouting above the music, and her sister will be intent on first bending right and then left or marching in place. It won't be quiet enough to hear Isabelle straining toward her with the news and the apology.

When they finally know, they will remember what they were doing as if somehow other tasks had prevented them from attending the wedding. They will blame themselves because they will not want to blame Brian. They will want Isabelle to be happy.

Isabelle and Brian go to New Hellas in Greek town and have flaming cheese, Greek salads, and a glass of Retsina.

"Nothing is different," she says to Brian.

XIV.

An envelope comes from Brian's mother. There are two plane tickets to Philadelphia with open dates and the warning to use these coupons before June 4. It is May 13.

"So when do you want to go?" he asks.

"I don't know. Perhaps you should go alone. I could come a little later."

"I want to get it over with."

"What do you want to get over?"

"Her being mad at me."

"You said that she was understanding about school."

"In view of everything, yes."

"'In view of'?"

"She's not exactly thrilled."

"About me."

"Think about it, Isabelle. My mother never dreamed I would marry someone who isn't Jewish. It didn't even come up because she didn't think she had to say it. So there's that. And she'll be a little upset when she sees, when she finds out that you're older than me. Eight years. She might think, well, I don't know, that it isn't the best thing."

"Do you think it isn't the best thing?"

"What do you want, Isabelle? I can't help what she is going to feel. I can't help what she is going to say. And she's my mother. She's done everything for me."

"So you'll have to listen."

"Sure, I have to listen, but it doesn't mean anything. She'll be a little mad, and then it will be fine."

XV.

Isabelle can hear the argument between Brian and his mother even though she is lying down in the guest bedroom, and they are in the living room. She has closed the door, but the mother is shouting. Brian's voice is a murmur, and she is glad that she doesn't hear what he says.

"This is your solution to a problem? Bringing home a shiksa, a big horse of a Polack old enough to be your mother? You have a mother. You don't need two."

Brian's voice rises.

"There are other ways to show gratitude. Getting married to a Polish woman—and a Catholic—is not the only way to be grateful. You could have lived with her. So what? When you were done with her, you leave. But now you made a mess, and now you have to get out of the mess."

Isabelle can hear the sharp tones of Brian's anger.

"Don't tell me about love, young man. A Jewish boy doesn't fall in love with a Polack. He falls in bed with her. We're talking about sex here. Fine. Sex is good. You can get it anywhere. But her?"

He is shouting. "Ma. Stop it. What am I supposed to do?"

"Send her home. Then we'll work it out. We'll get a lawyer. If I had known from the beginning, I could have taken care of everything. You don't have to make a bad bargain, not with this woman in her Gypsy dresses and her slow-witted eyes. What were you thinking? That she was pretty? That you could spend a lifetime with her?"

Isabelle puts her hands over her ears. If there were a radio in the bedroom, she would turn it on full blast. She wants to shout over the mother's voice: Stop it. Stop it. Stop it.

Brian comes into the room. Isabelle pretends to be sleeping.

"Honey? Wake up. I need to talk to you."

She opens her eyes. She wishes to be blind, to be deaf, to be paralyzed, to vanish.

Brian wants her to go home. He will settle it with his mother. His mother will come around. When he explains how much Isabelle means to him, her goodness, her generosity, everything.

"It's just the Catholic thing, Isabelle. She knew about it, sure, but seeing it is different. I can make her understand. It would just be better if you weren't here, so she can get used to the idea. When I explain everything to her."

XVI.

Brian and Isabelle stand in front of apartment building. Isabelle's flight back to Detroit is at 7:30. It is 6:10, and there is no sign of a cab.

"I'm going in," Brian says. "I'm calling a cab."

Isabelle picks up her overnight case and walks to the intersection where cars stream out of the day into the growing dusk. She raises her hand, and a cab swerves from the far side of the street and pulls in front of her.

"Airport, lady?"

She nods. She is glad that she doesn't have to speak. She has nothing more to say.

XVII.

After a month, Isabelle's sister and brother-in-law rent a U-Haul trailer and move the furniture and Isabelle's clothes from the apartment to Mrs. Zelesky's basement. Brian's clothes are sent to Philadelphia.

Letters from a lawyer have arrived, and Mrs. Zelesky, who has power of attorney for Isabelle, signs the papers and sends them back.

The family physician wants Isabelle in a place "where her medication can be regulated," but Isabelle's mother refuses to put her daughter "in an insane asylum." She is a dutiful nurse to her daughter. When she goes to the market or to get her hair washed and set, she asks a neighbor to sit with Isabelle.

"She won't be any trouble. I just want someone in the house while I'm gone. In case."

In case Isabelle begins to speak. In case she gets up from the rumpled bed and walks to the kitchen because she is hungry. In case this is the day that Isabelle is herself again.

"It's not so unusual," Mrs. Zelesky says to the neighbor who has agreed to look at her programs in the Zelesky house twice a week.

"Once my heart was broken, too. I was a young girl, younger than Isabelle, but still my heart was broken. If I spoke, tears flowed down my cheeks. For a boy, for a nobody, I don't even remember his name. But it was real. Heartbreak is real like pneumonia or the flu. At least you get over heartbreak. It's not like, Heaven forbid, cancer. It isn't permanent, but it can make you sick.

"Isabelle is sick with heartbreak. That's all. I can see by her face that she is beginning to feel better. Any day now I expect to go into her room, and she'll be sitting up and brushing her hair and asking where her black skirt is. She wants to go for a walk or sit on the porch. I know this. I can wait."

Just as her mother predicts, Isabelle opens the curtains of her room one morning. She sees on the small, neat lawns the yellow, bobbing heads of dandelions. She cannot imagine a more joyous sight. She wraps herself in the crocheted blanket that her mother has left folded on a chair and goes out on the porch and sits on the old-fashioned glider that has been repaired and oiled and still rocks without the sound of rust.

Her mother is standing on the sidewalk talking to the mailman. When she hears the screen door slam, she turns and sees Isabelle coming out on the porch. She waves, and she smiles as if she is greeting Isabelle after she has returned from a long journey.

These Mourning Duties

'Tis sweet and commendable in your nature, Hamlet,
To give these mourning duties to your father....
                                        ...But to persevere
In obstinate condolement is a course
Of impious stubbornness. 'Tis unmanly grief.
It shows a will most incorrect to heaven.

                                        (Hamlet, I, ii)

You can always tell when there is going to be a weapon sweep. The building sits so quiet on the street. Inside it's a different story. The gang squad in red windbreakers, officers in uniforms, plain-clothes men. These are not friendly people, like the two officers assigned to the school, men who know everyone. These are outsiders, stony-faced and doing the routine.

Hand over your backpacks and purses. Your beepers and your cell phones. They are illegal even though they aren't weapons.

Is that marijuana you are stupid enough to bring to school? You're going to the precinct.

Resisting an officer? Pepper spray in your face. Later your mother will scream at the principal: My child ain't no criminal.

Is this a box cutter. You are suspended—indefinitely. No explanations. Don't even bother.

Guilty of nothing? Sit in the auditorium. Your teachers can't help you. This is police country, and your teachers are so short and powerless with their tired faces, in their ordinary clothes.

Absent from this ceremony are Ronny Pawlychuk, who died in the school parking lot, and Antonio Spencer, who shot him in the back.

Antonio's hand was on the gun, big against his ribs because he was a thin boy, still child-like. The students leaning on the sides of their cars, smoking in the parking lot, saw it. They knew who he was, a boy who got to be a murderer that afternoon.

"Murderer" is a cold-blooded word for a boy—as if Antonio hadn't ever been hungry or lonely and scared in the days and nights behind him and of the days and nights that he couldn't know about. When he reached for the gun that he had forgotten about, the bulk of it was like the extension of his hand, which he raised, pointing the gun at the back of the boy who was turning away, but not running away. He fired because there was nothing else to do. And kept firing, blam, blam, blam, blam in the bright, blue afternoon.

That's what a murderer would do.

After that everything must have been liquid like a dream. The horrible act is behind him. There is no rewind; there is just the way it is going to be for the rest of his life. He doesn't know who thought of running away. Everyone is talking, yelling, but the only words that matter are the words he can never be boy enough to say: I didn't mean to do it.

"Remember," we will say, "when that boy got killed in the parking lot?"

"Because he was white."

"Because of the gang he was in."

"With a nine millimeter."

"Wasn't it a twenty-two?"

But we won't know. We won't keep those memories because there are the television cameras for that. Our lives have been altered forever, but we won't remember.

I don't remember what I read about myself when I wanted to find my birth mother.

"Malnourished."

"Rashes. Bruises."

"In the care of grandparents with a history of child abuse."

"Neighbors alerted Social Service 8/13/72. Child removed to foster care 8/24/72." "Permanently placed and adopted 4/26/73."

I don't remember any of this, even in dreams. My memories are shadows, moving behind walls.

Ronny is a name on my seating chart, a name in my record book, a clumsy cursive when he scrawled it on the board or with a dull pencil on his homework assignment. This boy did not know he was walking his last steps, turning his back and laughing his nervous, defiant laugh for the last time. He did not know he was being immortalized in exactly this way. Or in whatever way the witnesses constructed their memories of this death.

There were so many stories of the way it was. Three shots, five shots, six. It all depended on the way you thought death occurred in the city or the kind of sound you thought a gun made in the cold, early spring afternoon. However you imagined a sixteen-year-old boy arming himself.

It was his mother's gun, kept under the bed so that she could reach it when there were strange sounds in the house. Or it was a gun he had stolen, searching through drawers in a friend's house, coming upon it, slipping it underneath his jacket, in the waistband of his too-loose jeans. It depended on what you imagined as being possible.

When I think of the death of this boy, he gets to be someone else, someone more important and more vivid. I say his name, Ronny, and I feel bereft. But he was just a boy in my seventh period Basic Algebra class.

He was a gang leader, but the gangs aren't much more than the loosest of connections among the idle children, who have no place to go or very much to talk about. I remember his bravado, and the bad boy toughness is sexy.

He lived in a group home because his parents couldn't control him or didn't want to. He turns in the narrow bed, listening to the breathing of the boy who shares the room with him, someone he didn't know two months earlier when his white world turned black. He wants to ask: Are you awake? Can we talk? But it isn't his brother in the other bed. He will never sleep again in the same room as his brother or hear his breathing again.

My classroom is on the far side of the building away from the student parking lot where the shooting occurred. Not the death. He died in the back seat of his brother's car on the way to the hospital, a jacket stuffed up against the wound of the bullet, his brother saying, "Hold on, Ronny. It'll be ok. Hold on."

By the time I got to the hospital, he was dead. The bloody jacket was on the floor of the emergency room. I only meant to pick it up, but I started to cry, clutching the jacket close to me, facing the television cameras, the emergency room in the background like a scene from the soaps.

I said things I did not know I thought and should not have said for the way they turned out.

"These kids are searching for a world. A gang is just the world to replace the one that has been lost."

"I help these kids. I stand between them and the horror of their daily life. It is my mission. I am on a mission to save the children."

"Ronny was a genius, a beautiful boy. I loved him. Now he is dead, and I am going to keep his short time alive for as long as I can."

The parents, father and stepmother, mother and stepfather, are summoned to the hospital in those quick and brutal ways announcing catastrophe. The telephone rings; a superior calls you to his office; someone breathless comes to your house and cannot look at you while the news is blurted out. In a short time people are gathered where they could not have imagined being. Brothers who have not spoken to one another for months lean against one another, trying to gauge what it is they feel about the lost life.

This family shares with each other what I share with no one I know: hair color, the wide, blue eyes, short, blunt fingers. Whose eyes do I have? Who walks the way I do? Whose blood and breath and body were also mine in the beginning?

I embrace Ronny's mother. "I loved him," I whisper to her. She recoils. "I was his teacher," I say. She softens and sinks against me. I am so peaceful at this moment. She could be my birth mother or my aunt through blood and bone and the millions of frames of shared experience.

The television cameras are pointed at us, and in a short time no one will be able to separate my tears from the family's or my voice from their own words of disbelief and shock.

The detectives arrive, and I leave. In the city the police are the enemy even when they are the only ones you can call when the day erupts in blood and shouts and hollow gunshots. They arrive with their harshness, their business-as-usual, passive faces. The police are not like cameramen; they are not after images. They make the moment disappear. They clear the stage with haste to make room for the sounds of other twenty-two's or thirty-eight's or nine millimeters, for blood-stained jackets, for other weeping mothers. There is just so much room, and space must be cleared.

I intend to go to my mother's house, to Myrna. She is my adoptive mother. She would have seen the news by now.

Then it is dark, and I am sitting in my car in front of the house I was taken from, a starved child with bruises and rashes. My birth grandparents live there, but Myrna says they have moved. I have chosen not to believe her. If I wait out here long enough, she will come out, a short woman, still girlish because she didn't know how to grow up and be a mother. She will have brown hair streaking to a blonde colorlessness and a sharp nose. When we stand next to each other, we will be the same height. We will not have to say anything at all.

When I get home, there are six messages from my mother, from Myrna. I delete them and go to bed. I do not sleep until after it is six a.m. and time to call in sick. For I feel sick in ways I cannot describe.

"Julie," the voice comes to me in a sleep that is half wakefulness. "Julie, answer this phone." It is my classroom partner, Delphine.

"It's crazy here. The kids are quiet, not knowing what to do, and the gang squad is everywhere, running into classrooms, dragging boys out, interrogating them in the conference room, in the halls. Handcuffing some. Taking them to the precinct, downtown."

"I don't believe it."

"Believe it. Anyway, everyone has seen you on television."

"What are they saying?"

"It depends."

"On what?"

"On whether they're white or black."

"I don't understand."

"You know how it is here. Some people say that you wouldn't have gone to the hospital, wouldn't have said anything if the boy had been black."

"That isn't true."

"It's true now. You should stay out of school for a while. Give folks a chance to think of something else."

"I don't care what anyone thinks. Someone had to speak for him."

"No one is saying anything."

"What do you mean?"

"Just that. No one is saying anything. I don't think they will. This isn't the first time. Remember when that boy got shot seven times outside the band room? That's pretty hard to ignore, but nothing.... I went to the principal and asked, 'Isn't there going to be an assembly? A staff meeting?' He said, 'What should I say?' I said, 'These children are afraid.' 'There is nothing to say,' he said. So what do you think he'll say now?"

"I will say it."

"It belongs to the family now. Leave it alone."

"I'm not living with the silence."

"Leave it to someone else."

"It has to be me."

Then I could sleep. I would be a torch burning the shadows falling on this death, burying it with silence. I slept.

I am dreaming about the girl who was my mother. In my dreams she is nineteen years old. She cries because she wants love her baby, but she can't even give me a name. She can't hold me in her arms or give me something to eat. My bed is a cardboard box with an old sheet folded over and over to serve as a mattress.

In the dream we meet. I don't even know her name. She is just "mother" to me.

I will take her to a restaurant, a nice one. That is what I am thinking in the dream. I will treat her to a good meal. We will have wine, but if she is like me, drinking won't be good for her. She might get upset. And a nice restaurant might make her nervous. If she is dressed wrong, if the menu intimidates her, she might try to leave.

We go to McDonald's and sit in a booth. No one gets upset in McDonald's because everything is as it should be. So it is with us, this nineteen-year-old girl and me, her twenty-seven-year old daughter. We are who we are.

"'Mother,'" I say. "I just wanted to say your name. 'Mother.'"

When I woke up, Myrna, my mother, was there.

"Mom. When did you get here?"

"After calling you a hundred times. After worrying myself sick. Someone was murdered where you work after all."

"It wasn't me."

"I know that. I saw you. My own daughter shows up on the five o'clock news. And the ten o'clock. For the whole world to see. Defending her students. Black ones. Little white thugs. That's what my daughter chooses to do with her education. Stand up for the trash in the world."

"You drove over here to tell me this?"

"I didn't know where you were."

"This isn't your business."

"Not my business! If my daughter isn't my business, then I don't have any."

"You don't."

"Don't have a daughter? Is that what you mean to say to me? That I don't have a daughter? Just a stranger I can never understand because—what did you say—because we don't share the same DNA?

Your father and I—can I call him your father or would you prefer
that I call him Jim? What would you like to call your father and me?
Aunt Myrna? Uncle Jim? Or your parents because everyone in the
world has got to have some kind of parents somewhere, and this is
the best you could do."

"Mom, leave me alone."

"There's coffee in the kitchen and some sweet rolls. The kind you
like with pecans."

"Ok."

"When you decide to get up, you can call me."

"I'm going to school."

"At 2:00 in the afternoon?"

"I need to see if everything is alright."

"That's a laugh. Nothing is alright in that place. Not from day
one. But you had to teach there. You had to...."

"Please."

"I'm going."

"I love you, Mom."

"Oh, Julie, I only want to be your mother."

There are things I can't let go of because I am alive in someone
else's memory. My mother, the one who carried me, has to know that
the drum of her heart played across my bones, thrummed against my
skin, and got caught up in my blood. What I know of her is the beating of her heart.

The building was empty by the time I got there except the custo-
dians who moved like ghosts in the drab and brown hallways with
their brooms whish-whishing across the floors.

The light in my room was soaked up by the porous green walls.
I'll paint this room, I thought. Yellow or bright red or orange. A
color that won't swallow light. A color we can live with.

I sat down in Ronny's seat. Ronny's math group would be short
a partner until someone new came into the class, an administrative
transfer, a child who was on the wrong end of the fighting or whose
mother hoped the school would be safe. Someone would take Ronny's place, but I couldn't let him disappear so easily. I took a black
marker from my desk drawer and printed in block letters: Ronald
Pawlychuk: His Desk. I wrote on the board with the chartreuse chalk
I use for bell work: R.I.P. Ronald Pawlychuk.

I was so sure that the next day would be set aside for mourning. Classes would be canceled because death interrupts the daily acts of a community, and the community must gather together in a ritual of comfort. Nothing else made sense to me.

Instead there was the weapon sweep. The red jackets of the gang squad, the black blazers of downtown security, the crisp blue uniforms of police officers.

I went to my classroom and started emptying the contents of my desk drawers into the cartons I kept everywhere for projects, markers, crayons, and pencils that I kept after testing programs. I should label these boxes, I thought, but I just shifted things from one box to another.

Delphine came in with a coffee cup. "Girl, what are you doing?"

"I don't know."

"Looks to me like you are crying. Can't you take the casual violence of a weapon sweep? Don't you enjoy seeing children terrorized?"

"I guess not."

"Good thing you aren't wearing make-up because you are a mess as it is."

"Thanks. Were you in the auditorium?"

"Long enough to wish I had stayed at home."

"I can't stand it."

"You're not supposed to stand stuff like this. You supposed to be scared of the kind of people who send in the troops after a bloodletting. Not the doctors or the nurses. Just more violence, more shoving, more shouting. After the..."

"...the murder of my student. Who was just sixteen. Who didn't have a clue."

"I hope we aren't calling this self-control."

"Compared to yesterday it is."

"Well, work on it. Look, Julie, don't talk to your kids about the murder or the weapon search. There isn't any point. Just give them some fun problems. Keep it quiet."

"Keep the uneasy peace?"

"The kids have had enough. Now they need comfort, a safe place, a peaceful room."

"It isn't safe. Or peaceful."

"Then pretend it is."

"They'll want to know what to do."

"Julie, what makes you think there is something to do?"

"I want people to act like they care. I want them to do something to make Ronny's death...."

"Make sense? That isn't going to happen."

"Then let them pretend, too. Why can't they pretend?"

"You wouldn't want to know."

Someone died on a Monday, and there was no announcement on the p.a. "We regret to announce the tragic death of Ronald Pawly-chuk."

Or if regret wasn't the right word, the official voice could say, "Let us bow our heads in remembrance of Ronald Pawlychuk."

Or a letter, perhaps, telling parents that their children would be kept safe. A statement to the newspapers. Some pretense to make it seem as if the world were sane.

It was on my desk, the announcement on thin, white xerox paper:

Marziuk & Son Funeral Home
18621 Ryan Road, Warren
Visitations: Wednesday 5-9, Thursday 1-9
Funeral: Friday 11:00

I drew a map on the board: Ryan curving out of the city and into Madison Heights, the street getting wider, houses giving way to small stores and strip malls, none of them boarded up. I showed Ryan crossing Interstate-696, throbbing with traffic.

"X equals the funeral parlor. Right here between 12 and 13 Mile Roads. Ask your mothers, your brothers to take you there. Here, look, I've written the times on the board. Let's show Ronny we cared about him."

"They gonna be shooting there."

"But the police be coming, too. His mamma and his stepdaddy is cops."

"People in Warren don't like black folks."

"Ain't no bus on Ryan."

"Anyone who wants to meet me at Ryan and Eight Mile at 4:30, come up to the desk and get a permission slip. Fill it in like I've written on the board. Have your mother sign it."

Delphine was waiting for me in the classroom when I came back from lunch for my fourth period class.

"Staying for a basic algebra class?"

"Don't be cute, Julie. You know why I'm here."

"Delphine, I'm doing it. Whatever you think I'm doing, that's what I'm going to do."

"And what do you think I am thinking you are about to do?"

"I'll tell you. I'm taking kids to the funeral home—to show sorrow and regret and friendship and respect."

"And defiance."

"Since when is going to a funeral home defiant?"

"Right now. In this place and under these circumstances. Look, if these kids want to pay their respects, let them make that decision. Because that's what they want to do, not what you want them to do. Then they'll go, getting there in the ways they always get places, begging relatives, taking a bus that runs on the wrong street and walking over, calling a cab and piling in to share the cost. But I'll tell you this, no black kid is going to go to Warren just because you want them to."

"Who told you about that?"

"Oh, honey, it is all over the halls."

"This is nothing but news, isn't it? For coffee breaks and lunchtime. How did it get to be news?"

"Most things turn into news. And you already are, holding on to that bloody jacket, talking at the cameras like you were Joan of Arc or something. Come off it! You want to feel bad? There are plenty of things to feel bad about. Let this go."

"I'm meeting those kids this afternoon."

"Fine, you meet them. They just won't meet you. They aren't going to go driving up Ryan with their white teacher and into a neighborhood where the signs are written in an alphabet they can't read. Where the people stare at them, hating them for crossing a line that's been drawn so that everyone but you can see it. They don't live in your world. We don't live in your world."

"It's always going to be about race."

"Always. I'm sorry."

"No. Thank you, Delphine. For being so honest."

"I'm trying to protect you."

"I wish you could. I really do."

Myrna came with me to the funeral parlor. I begged her.

"It's not my place. I don't know these people."

"Mom, I can't go alone."

"I don't have a good feeling about this."

"Please."

The parking lot of Marziuk Funeral Parlor was filled, cars blocking each other, spilling out into the street. The side streets were lined with cars. We had to walk three blocks, Myrna complaining that she wasn't used to walking in shoes with heels, and holding on to my arm.

The family members sat in chairs around the casket.

"We should leave, " I said.

"What are you talking about? We came all the way here."

"I can't go up there. I can't look in that casket."

Myrna walked away from me. She doesn't look anything like me, I thought, this woman doing her mother's duties, shaking the hands of Ronny's mother, his stepfather, his father, nodding to the brothers and the half-brothers. Dabbing her eyes with a handkerchief, the one she must have been holding in her hand because I didn't see her take it out of her purse.

"What did you tell them?"

"That you were too overcome by grief."

"What did they say?"

"What they always say when there is nothing to say."

"I'm sorry, Mom."

"You want to do your duty, Julie. I don't mind helping you with it. Now let this be the end of it. Go back to normal."

"I don't know what normal is any more."

"The things you have to do, that's what normal is."

"I'm trying."

My mother and I stand on a dark street in March near a funeral parlor, talking to each other quietly. Two women, who would never have known each other but for the accidents of other people's lives, call each other mother and daughter, but we are strangers in our blood.

Woodbridge Cemetery is in another world, an older Detroit world where people paid attention to death. You could tell from

the ornate headstones and the little chapels that read: "Blankenship, Caroline, Beloved Wife of Henry Blankenship." "Blankenship,
Henry. Revered Father and Cherished Husband." There were a lot of
Blankenships, all laid to rest in the same corner. No matter what had
happened, no matter who had moved away, quarreled or retreated for
five years, ten years, fifteen, they came to Woodbridge to rest in the
same plot of ground. Blood claiming blood; bone mixing with bone
in the earth.

Unless I have children, I will never rest in the same place with my
own kind. Unless I have children, I will be buried with Myrna and
Jim.

Ronny would not be resting with strangers. He had his family
spot with his grandparents, not the Pawlychuks, but with his mother's family. "Rest in Peace, Sally Stubblefield." "Live in God's Arms,
Aaron Stubblefield." "Beloved Son, James Stubblefield." "Eternal
Life, Wilma Lester." Next to these four patches of ground, grown over
with grass, still muddy from the melted snow, was the raw trench for
Ronny, his last place on earth.

They would say that his death was tragic. "What a tragedy that a
boy should be killed." "How tragic that he died for nothing." Then
there would be no blame, no responsibility, no reason to remember
that it had something to do with someone's carelessness. Tragedy
will explain it all.

Tragedy. That's a word to hide behind. No thinking about the
boy looking toward the car where the brother sat, waiting, believing
that his very presence would protect his younger brother, the one he
hadn't seen for seven months.

"He told me," the brother said to the camera, "that these guys,
you know, gang members, said some stuff to him. Threatened him.
Jeez, he was just a kid. So I told him I'd be there for him. I mean
he's my brother. If I had thought the guy was going to shoot him, if I
had been been prepared.... But I wasn't. And now we got this tragedy."

Or potential. That's what the counselor of the group home said,
"Ronald had potential. He was quick, and he knew how to play the
game. He got along in spite of—well, you know, being white and
nobody else...being the only one. He was smart, and he knew to wait
it out. All that potential, just wiped out. It's a pity."

Pity. It catches me in my throat. A sound, not a word, starting
where the pain flared out from the bullet; only a sound to be his last
word. Looking toward his brother, the one he knew to call when

he couldn't face them down alone, his hand fluttering toward him, meaning: Help me. Meaning: Not this. Meaning: Fuck.

Would it be that, an obscenity? Gathered to God with an obscenity. Oh, let Him forgive the child who had no better words. Forgive her, if his last word was: Mother. His mother who never saw her son in the group home. That's what she told the television reporters.

"Oh, I called Ronny a few times—after he was taken away— but they said he didn't have phone privileges. If you knew him, you would understand. He wouldn't cave in if you chained him to a radiator for a month. Well, we never did that. Of course not, but you know what I mean. Then I let the time get away from me."

Mother, the beat of your heart has echoed in the pulsing of my blood. Haven't you heard it? Heart to heart, Mother, yours and mine.

There weren't many people at the cemetery, maybe twenty, mostly family, the mother's and the father's both but divided and standing apart the way divorce makes things turn out. There was no tent over the trench. There was just sky and wind.

Ronny's mother walked toward the casket. She touched it once, shook her head, and moved back to where her other sons and her husband stood. How familiar she looked to me, this short woman with colorless blond hair falling loose under the black hat, the dotted veil, the kind you see in movies. How old could she be? Forty-five, fifty? Around the right age, looking as I imagined she might, but not as pretty as I wanted her to be.

"Mrs. Schemanski? I'm Ronny's teacher. We met at the hospital. I want to offer my condolences."

"I remember you. You were on television about Ronny."

"I wanted to make things clear—about the kind of boy he was. I didn't want the rumors to be the truth about him. When they weren't true."

"But they were. What they say about Ronny is true."

"It isn't. I knew him, too."

"Look, Miss. You should try to understand the kind of kid that Ronny was. You couldn't live with him. Bad blood. Nobody's fault, and I'm not trying to blame his father. It just happens that way. A kid is born bad, right from the very beginning. Not his brothers. They were good kids in spite of everything. But Ronny, he didn't have the patience for being good. And that's why he's dead.

"I've seen a lot of dead kids. That's my job. Juvenile. It's because they were asking for it. All down the line, getting in the way of trouble, wanting to be there. I'm not even surprised. It's Ronny in that box, and he's dead, and I'm not surprised.

"So you shouldn't waste your time. There are a lot of other kids who would be glad to have you care about them. Ronny wouldn't be one of them. He would wait until your back was turned or your guard was down, and then he'd do the worst possible thing he could think of. And you'd say to yourself, 'Damn that boy,' and you would mean it."

"You're his mother. He's dead. And you say, 'Damn that boy!' Like he was no more important than an insect. And not even his mother cares."

"Are you a mother? Answer me that. Did any kid make your life a living hell? I don't think so. I don't think you have the slightest idea about how it can be."

"I have a mother."

"And I bet you gave her some hell-to-pay."

"No, not my mother. Not as far as I know."

"Ask her one day. Ask if it has been all peaches and cream. Then tell me about caring."

After the funeral, I painted the room. I went in during Easter break, and I painted and painted until all the new color seeped into pores of the walls, until all the dead green disappeared under the coats of bright yellow. It was a yellow that jumped back at you, not a yellow like the sun coming through a window. But at least it wasn't the same room anymore. We could go on as if something had happened, but we had acknowledged it. And we painted over it. It was an act in the absence of an act. That was something. I like to think it was something.

Devil's Night

People say I'm too young to have a grown daughter, but that doesn't mean I look good. When I lost heart the way I did, everything that made me pretty went out of me. My skin is ashy. My eyelids are puffy, and you would think I just left off crying. I haven't cried in years. Tears don't mean anything. They run right down your cheeks and disappear.

So my eyes are dry, my hair, too. I can't fix it like I used to.

I don't have those good looks any more.

Being pretty is dangerous. You are like one of those toy ballerinas, going round and round in the snow, and you can't stop long enough to figure things out.

My mother was a pretty girl. When she was thirteen, she looked like a woman. When she was fourteen, she had me. When she was sixteen, she left me. She must have loved me some to stay that long.

My mother came out of her room, all dressed up. She looked good, Grandma said, saying goodbye, promising later. She wasn't taking me.

"Not a tear in your eyes," my grandma said. "Like you knew she had to leave."

She did have to leave. But she could have called to hear my voice. Then hang up. I would have known who it was.

My grandma said that she was probably dead, but I would know. I would have felt her absence in the world.

My grandma was a maid for white people. The night would be half gone before she got home.

She begged the neighbors to take me "just for today," in exchange for doing their ironing or cleaning around the yard. People are kinder than you think. But she ran out of places by the time I was four.

Time can stop, the light stuck in a fixed place in the sky. Only the kitchen feels safe. I am sitting at the table with my coloring book and my crayons, comforted by the murmuring of the refrigerator, the hulk of the old, black stove, the friendly labels of the cans on the shelf.

I was humming. The radio wasn't working, so I had only my voice.

My grandma found me under the table, "Not exactly screaming," she told the doctor in the emergency room, "and not crying. Just a heartbroken sound."

She begged a neighbor for a ride to the hospital where they wouldn't keep me because there was no insurance; where I had my first sedative, and gray oblivion covered me like a shawl.

She had to send me away. School was a year away, and there wasn't any way around it.

I say that my grandma sent me to relatives in the country. I say that each morning before breakfast, I would hurry to the chicken house and collect the new eggs. My great-aunt would make me biscuits and sausage gravy. Then I would dig in my little garden where I grew tiny, red tomatoes and bright green beans and perfectly shaped carrots.

I say that I had a cat and a dog to play with. At night my granduncle would take me on his lap and read to me from Golden Books even though he was tired from his work in the fields. Then my great-aunt would give me a bubble bath in a large white tub. She would scrub my back with a bristly brush and towel me dry and carry me to my sweet-smelling, soft bed where my cat and dog were already asleep on top of the covers.

I was put in foster care.

When you are in foster care, no house is the same except that you have to leave. It's almost as hard to leave a bad house as a good one because you never know where you will go next. The social workers were surprised that they were called so many times to take me out of a house. Then they got used to it.

"Ebony doesn't do as well as most children. That's because of her emotional problems."

I tried not to curl up on the floor and let the sounds take me over. They didn't like it, not even the nice foster mothers.

If the man in the house got that look, the one you learn to dread even when you're only ten years old, it's hard to go to sleep at night.

You're waiting and hoping that it's just your imagination: the door cracking open, the footsteps as loud as heartbeats. "Don't make no noise, honey."

The next day at school, circles under your eyes, you know the teacher's going to report you to Social Services. Then there aren't night visits. You just stop existing. No one says your name or asks if you are hungry. If you are slow coming home from school, the woman will start yelling, "They don't give me enough money to be going crazy about where you have gone to."

That's the first time you know you are worth money.

The first night in every home there might be a nice dinner and even a welcome present, but it never lasts because you aren't blood. I could never puzzle it out: the importance of being connected by blood. My mama left me. And how much more kin could we be?

People think there is nothing more cruel than leaving a child, but there is silence, and there are shouts. There is coldness and the hot place on your face where the hand fell. Aside from what you have come to fear, both blows and caresses, no one ever touches you in ordinary ways.

"She'll last about a month," the social worker says to the psychologist. "Then without fail, I mean as predictable as rain, I'll get that call, somebody screaming, 'Get that kid out of my house! She's wailing like a ghost. Can't even stop her.'"

"Ebony, dear." The psychologist always calls you 'dear.' "Why do you start your...."

"Humming. She says it starts with a little song she hears in her head."

"Let the child talk."

"She isn't going to tell you. I've been through this before."

"Ebony, why do you hum?"

I'm lonely. No one talks to me. Doors close on me, locking me in, locking me out. Everywhere there is no one.

"Ebony, why do you hum?"

"Don't know."

"I told you. I've been through this before."

Seven homes. That's what the social worker said.

In the girls' home, there are rules, and you can sleep at night. There are voices in the halls and in the shower room, and the voice in your head goes quiet.

Casa Eve was the best home I had. It wasn't a pretend family. Everything was simple: getting up, cleaning your room, taking a shower, eating breakfast, getting the van to school, taking it back, doing homework, eating dinner, watching TV, turning out the lights.

Every night you made a bag lunch: peanut butter and jelly, an apple, a cookie, and a juice box, all the brown bags neatly folded over at the top, names printed on the last fold. Kashawna, LaToria, Crystal, Toni, Amber, Tasha, Angela, Kesha.

It was more than some kids got, the ones who lived with mothers or grandmothers, or who maybe just lived on their own.

I lived at Casa Eve for three years, and I never had the clothes I wanted. When we outgrew our clothes, they would go into the community closet. If there was something you liked, a dress or a sweater, you could request it. If someone else wanted it, then you drew straws for it. Wanting was better than getting. The dress was thin and greasy from too many owners; the sweater was shapeless and snagged. The prize was just some old garment that hadn't been new for a long time.

You don't need clothes to be pretty. If that were true, Pluto would not have noticed me, standing outside of school, waiting for the Casa Eve van.

"Come with me," he said, leaning over the passenger seat of his black Jaguar. "Pretty little thing, come with me."

"Leave me alone."

"Let me be your dogg, pretty girl. Let Pluto be your main man."

What makes you pretty is an accident. None of it is in your power, especially when you live in a place like Casa Eve where you get your first lipstick at sixteen and never any eye shadow or mascara. But I was fourteen when I left with Pluto, so I never got that lipstick, Maybelline or Cover Girl. It was a big event, and I missed it.

I still think of that lipstick. When I was sixteen, I remembered that I had missed that lipstick.

Pluto Noyer. "So fine and with money to throw in the street," Amber said.

"Girl, Pluto is a bad person," LaToria said.

"That's one black man," Tasha said, "black in his heart, and that ain't all."

Every day I watched for that black Jaguar coming by the school. Maybe he would ask again. He would say, "Hop in," like in the movies, and I would.

I would borrow someone's blouse or vest to wear with my jeans. I wanted to look good for the next time he came by.

It was November, and I had my hands in my sleeves to keep them warm. The Jaguar pulled up to the curb, and a girl got out. She wore high heeled shoes, tight jeans, and a leather jacket that nothing could fit under. She was pretty, and she knew it.

"Who's that?" I asked Tasha.

"Pluto's woman, Felicia."

"What's she doing at school?"

"He ain't got any use for her today. You better believe there's a long line waiting to take her place. Younger than her, and she's only fifteen."

"She looks grown up."

"That's as grown up as he likes them."

"Who told you?"

"It's all on the street. You sure interested."

"Just asking."

"You're a Casa Eve girl. The police be after you ten minutes after you come up missing."

Someone would say: "Where's Ebony?" There would be the opening and closing of doors, low voices, the calling of the police, people wanting to get me back.

I would dream about Pluto. How I would lay my hand against his velvet-black cheek, and he would press his lips in my palm. When I shivered with cold, he would wrap me in his black leather jacket. I would ride with him in his black Jaguar for as long he wanted me to.

That's not how it happened. But one day I did get into Pluto's car, and I asked him to take me for a ride.

"Anything you want, little girl," he said, and we drove away.

Like in my dream of what it would be like to be with Pluto, we drove; past all the party stores and "liquor sold here" signs; past the bank and the Secretary of State which were the only buildings that never got boarded up; on to the freeway where the speeding cars would draw back to make way for Pluto Noyer.

He said to me, "I told you I'd be your dogg one day, Ebony."

"Who told you my name?"

"When Pluto sees a girl he wants, he finds out all that he needs to know. Ebony Regis is the name of Pluto's queen."

"I should go back to school."

"You can go back to school if you want. First, we're going to get something to eat. You can be back in time for your van. That's Pluto's promise to you. You can ride that van just like you been every day if that's what you want. But right now, I'm pulling into Big Boy's and buying you a hamburger and some fries and a pop."

I had never been to a restaurant except for McDonald's. Now I had a book of food to choose from. I knew to put the napkin on my lap. I learned that at Casa Eve and to eat with a fork.

Pluto ordered a hamburger with everything, fries, and a large coke. Then it was too late to get the van.

His house wasn't anything. It was somewhere to leave. Nothing much in it but a bed, a stereo and a big screen television. A chair in the living room and a telephone.

A child's world is the world of day, illuminated by the sun. In the night world light flickers on the wall like lanterns tossed in a storm, and only what you can touch guides you through the dark: the rough carpet beneath your foot, the pebbly surface of a wall against your hand, the smoothness of the stainless steel wash bowl. Pluto had taken me to the world of night.

"Am I your woman now, Pluto?"

"You just a child. When I see that you a grown woman, then I'll be your man."

"I can be your woman now. You'll see."

"There's time. Tomorrow, next week, plenty of time for you and Pluto. We gonna get you some nice clothes, get your hair fixed. First things first."

Most nights we went out, late, maybe eleven o'clock, midnight. To places you couldn't find during the day. You would have to know the right alley, the exact street, the dark building that was the entrance to an underground world. Down some steps, footsteps echoing, and then bursting into light; a waiter in a tuxedo, all black with a red cummerbund, white gloves, waiting to seat you, to call you by name: Mr. Noyer, Miss Regis, good evening. Only it wasn't evening. Sometimes it was near to morning.

There were women in tight dresses and stiletto heels; diamonds bright as icicles melting from their ears. Men just like Pluto, dressed in black, diamond studs, heads shaved close. Leather rich as cream; fur as soft as feathers, gold bracelets as solid as chains.

They danced alone, mostly women and the men who came along as bodyguards or hangers-on. Red strobe lights, wavering like flames, swept across the dance floor, and the dancers moved as if they were flung by a powerful force. The music was loud, wailing all the time, but it didn't matter because people didn't talk. They ate and they drank, they danced and they laughed; they went into rooms through red doors, and they came out clear-eyed and flowing like water. Anything you wanted, you could get. There was no need for words. There wasn't anything to ask for.

The women were beautiful: some so dark that you couldn't imagine skin being more lovely; some like me, with good hair and thin with bodies meant for clothes; some full and soft so that you would want to sink into them. The white women were blondes or red-heads with skin as chalky as a ghost's.

I didn't think I could hold a light to all that beauty. But I could see that I did—in the eyes of the other men, like Pluto, the kings of night.

The waiters brought food. They always knew what you wanted, or you wanted what you got. Pluto's food sat in front of him. I never saw him eat.

Living with Pluto was like living with a shadow. When he touched me, it was a breath of a touch. Making love was like that, too; like a spirit passing over me, and like a flare-up of a match, there was a spark and then darkness. Whenever I woke up, he was gone.

Every night I got dressed up, waiting to see if we were going to the clubs, not asking for anything. It was just like the foster homes: I could stay as long as I wasn't any trouble.

He would be gone for days, and I would order pizza. I would switch through all the channels until there was a program I liked. I slept most of the day and watched movies at night when he wasn't there.

I never used the phone except to call for pizza. There was no one to call and nothing to say. I had disappeared from the world.

Perhaps someone was thinking of me, like Grandma or the girl who was my mother. Or Tasha and Amber. But their thoughts never reached me.

When men came to the house with Pluto, he would tell me to go into the bedroom. They never stayed long; their voices were low and serious. No one ever laughed or went to the refrigerator for a pop or a beer. It was business, Pluto's business.

Perhaps he still drove the girl, Felicia, to school. She would be dressed in her leather jacket and jeans, waiting in the doorway for the black Jaguar. "Mom," she would call, 'my ride is here," and she would run to the car. The whole of her life would be focused on that little time: getting into the Jaguar and going to school, walking up the littered sidewalk to the building. Felicia of the black Jaguar.

Or there was a woman, someone close to Pluto like a sister. She would put her arms around him and ask in a teasing way, "Tired of your schoolgirls, honey?"

I lived in four houses with Pluto, and they were all the same. No table to eat on or a chest of drawers for clothes. It was a carry-out, go-out life, a life of the clubs, of pizza boxes and styrofoam containers; bottles of pop gone flat in the refrigerator; clothes still in their original boxes or on the floor of the closet; sheets slept on too long and used plastic cups on the counters.

I could be lonely forever. That's why I didn't leave when Pluto didn't come to the house at night.

It caught me by surprise.

"Are you pregnant?"

"I don't know. How would I know?"

"You a woman, ain't you? And you got caught."

"What do you mean, Pluto? How did I get caught?"

"Fucking someone else."

"I didn't."

"You must of, girl. And I don't keep no whores. You gotta go."

I put on my shoes and pulled a sweatshirt over my T-shirt and walked out in a pair of jeans that I couldn't zipper all the way because I was pregnant. It was May.

I meant to go to the park near Outer Drive. There were benches there. But I was all turned around in the night, and I ended up walking the wrong way toward Six Mile Road, past the prison, the burnt-out houses and the closed-down businesses, walking quick under the ovals of light from the street lamps. I wanted someone to say, "Hey, girl, what you doing out there? Come on in." All the houses I passed, though, were guarded with iron gates that pretended to be decorations; they were closed up tight, and only etchings of light framed the dark window shades pulled down against intruders.

Nothing was open on Six Mile Road; not McDonald's or the gas station or the Lantern Restaurant even though the sign said, "Open 24 Hours."

I went to a dark house, where there were flowers planted and the lawn was cut. I walked up on the porch and sat on the wicker lounge.

Even in May, nights are cold. You don't think about it when you are sitting in the house, looking at television. You think how nice it is to feel the soft night on your face or how good the breeze feels coming through an open window. It isn't until you sit through one May night until morning comes that you know how cold it can be.

The doors of the houses on Yonka Street opened early. The old people rose up from their light sleeps and came out to water their shrubs and wash down their steps. They didn't say anything. I wasn't on their porches, so I wasn't their business.

Rose Montgomery came out of her house, carrying a broom. "Look, miss, I don't mean no insult, but this is my porch, and you ain't anyone I know. So if I can help you, I will. If there ain't no help, you best go on your way."

"I'd like some help."

"Then come on in and use the bathroom while I make you some coffee."

On Yonka Street they took care of me. I could sleep at Rose's and eat someone's hamburger dinner or tuna casserole surprise. Closets were turned out, and I had pants with elastic waists and large shirts to wear. No one on Yonka Street asked me where I came from or why I didn't have anything.

During the day when I sat on Rose's porch, I didn't believe in Pluto. At night it was different. In the darkness, I could hear the engines of the Jaguars and the Mercedes as they started up with their expensive power; I could hear the pounding music as if it were rising from the underground world where every night was the same, and nothing grew in the sunless soil.

On Yonka Street every day brought new greens and yellows, red and pinks, out of the earth. The ground was black and moist with turning and watering; the edges of the lawns cut smooth with shears; sturdy flowers planted around the trees.

On Yonka Street when it was pleasant in the evening, the women in their flowered house dresses and the men in their white shirts and dark trousers sat on their porches. Garage doors were lifted by hand

and cranked up over oiled rollers; cars were moved out onto side drives and washed and polished.

The baby was growing and no one asked questions. A summer and part of the fall went by before Rose sat herself beside me on the lounge.

"You should elevate them feet. They sure look swollen."

"I can't get them into my shoes."

"It's like that, carrying a baby. This baby due in about three months, don't you say?"

"I guess."

"Well, you got to think about it, Ebony. You got to make arrangements for yourself. At least for your baby."

"I can leave whenever you say, Rose."

"No, no, honey, I'm not putting you out. I don't mean that at all. But you gotta make plans for the baby. That's your responsibility. If it was just you, why you could sit on my porch forever. I'd have room for you, rain or shine. But this baby got to be provided for. Now we been talking about it, and Mr. Harris, he agree to carry you in his car to Social Services down Six Mile and talk to the social worker."

"I want to keep my baby."

"That's up to you, honey. But you got to do something."

"I can't go to Social Services, Rose. I ran away from them once. And if I went, I don't have any way to prove who I am. I don't have any papers or birth certificate."

"That don't make no difference. You can say that your papers got burned up in a fire. You can give a common name. Say your name is Sue Jones or Mary Williams."

"My baby needs my name."

"Names don't mean nothing, Ebony. Names don't tell who you are. They just words like the ones I'm speaking now. The daddy of this baby, he made plenty of promises once, but he ain't around. He got a name, but it don't matter."

I gave myself a name for the day: Clara Bright. Rose said it wasn't common enough.

"That's the name I want,"

"Well, if it don't work with one social worker, we find us another."

My daughter was named LaFleur Bright.

The pain didn't mean anything to me because it was LaFleur breaking her way into the world. Not slipping into the world, not sneaking into it, but entering with pain that was almost beautiful.

I promised not to leave her. If I ever left her, I said, I would never rest easy in life.

We lived a converted attic, my baby and me. The kitchen behind a folding screen, the stove, sink, and a little refrigerator all in a line. There was a green couch and a lamp on a wooden table, a television on a stand, and a chair near the window. Blue and green fish swam on the curtains.

In the other room the beds were crowded together: her crib and a double bed for me, a chest of drawers, and a lamp on the table by the bed.

Some strangers had made a home for me. They had put milk and bread and eggs in the refrigerator. They had put macaroni and cheese and cereal and raisins and tea in the cupboard; had folded towels and hung them on the rack in the bathroom. They had put toilet paper and extra soap under the sink; had stacked boxes of disposable diapers in the corner of the bedroom.

I would lie in the bed, watching my baby sleep, waiting for her to wake up. Some days I never got dressed. Never opened those curtains either. I just watched those fish swim around in white light that changed and darkened. That's how I knew the times of day: by the light the blue and green fish were swimming in.

Once a week the visiting nurse came with diapers and food from WIC—welfare for women, infants and children. Formula for LaFleur even though I was nursing. ("You can never tell when that milk will dry up, Clara.") Food for me: cheese, milk, a sack of apples, some oranges, peanut butter, canned chicken. Little jars of baby food: applesauce and mashed bananas. Boxes of baby cereal with fat, white babies smiling off the box.

I told the nurse that LaFleur didn't need to eat food from jars. My body made all the food she needed. But visiting nurse frowned and her face got tight.

She pulled back the curtains and the light of noon flooded the front room. "Light and air," she said. "That's how a baby flourishes." Her face got tight again, and later in that week my social worker brought a stroller, folded up like an umbrella, so I could take LaFleur out into the air.

LaFleur deserved the light. So I pulled on jeans and a big shirt and went out every morning.

The visiting nurse still had a tight face. "Do you have any friends? Do you talk to anyone?"

"I talk to LaFleur."

"Do you talk to adults? Clara, do you talk to anyone?"

The landlady invited me to her flat for coffee and cookies. I didn't think to dress myself up or to fix my hair. When I looked in the mirror, I saw someone I had made up, fit to be a mother.

The landlady, Glenda, said, "Girl, you got to fix your hair. Why don't you come down tonight and let me give you a wash and roll your hair? We put the baby in a little basket and have us a fine time fixing you up."

"I don't have any money to pay you."

"Don't need no money for a little hairdressing."

"My social worker talked to you."

"We talk. About a pretty girl living up there alone and on her own. No crime in that. Have these cookies with your coffee. And we can have a nice visit."

"I don't want to be any trouble, Miss Glenda."

"No trouble, honey. I'm glad for the company. Now that is one pretty baby, but she don't favor you. No, not at all. She must look like her daddy. Or one of your kin."

"She looks like her father, but he isn't interested in LaFleur."

"A young, wild man. He just settle once and go on his way."

"Something like that."

"Don't pay it any mind, honey. You doing fine. Always home with the baby, but if you got a yearning to go out and visit with a friend, then leave your little girl with me. You so young, you must have a little fun in you."

"Thank you , Miss Glenda. Don't take it wrong. I just want to stay with my baby."

"I understand, honey. But you just knock if you need some help."

LaFleur. I would touch her small fingers. I would feel the pulse of her life. At night I would make a cradle of my arms; breathe with her into sleep and rise out of it at the moment that she wakened and nuzzled at me for her feeding. In the bathtub I would place her between my knees and wash her scalp with the baby shampoo and soap her body and rinse it off with fresh water in a cup. I would wrap us both in a towel and rock her until we were both dry.

"Clara, don't you ever use the baby's bathtub? I found a dead spider in it."

"I take her in the bath with me, Miss Adams."

"A baby ought to have her own bath water, Clara. Would you like to take a bath in somebody else's water? I know I wouldn't. And I don't imagine LaFleur likes it."

"I'm her mother."

"That doesn't give you the right to do anything you want. Motherhood has its responsibilities. Which you are ignoring. For instance, there were six eggs in the refrigerator last time I was here. There are six eggs in the refrigerator now. I take that to mean that you have not been giving LaFleur her necessary protein in the morning."

"I'm nursing, Miss Adams. The books say that breast milk...."

"Those books are written by radicals, women who nurse their babies until they are six or seven years old. You have to practice moderation when you are a mother, Clara. You have to use your common sense. Do you have all the protein you need? From the looks of the refrigerator, you aren't eating properly either. And those bananas rotting on the counter! The potassium you need. What do you eat, Clara? The cheese is moldy, the apples are rotten."

"I eat peanut butter. I ate some of those bananas."

"Your bed, Clara. It's like a nest. Do you stay in bed all day? There are no toys, the stroller is rolled up in a corner...."

"I take her out, Miss Adams. Every day."

"I will be frank with you, Clara. I am going to speak to your case worker. I am going to insist on some changes."

"There's nothing wrong with LaFleur. She's healthy. She's big."

"Oh, yes. Absolutely. A fine child, flourishing remarkably, thanks to a miracle that I certainly cannot account for. How long do you think this can go on? A child thriving on her own. The baby is what? Three months old? What words has she heard? The little books are still on the table. They haven't been opened, have they?"

" I sing to her."

"I would hate to see a beautiful child like LaFleur fail to thrive. That's what we fear the most: failure to thrive. The most heartbreaking aspect of this job. I can't let it happen, Clara. I am truly sorry, but I can't let it happen."

"Are you taking my baby from me?"

"I'll leave that to your worker. But I know what I see, and I have to report it."

I was enrolled in Second Chance. Every morning I got up at six o'clock and bathed La Fleur in the plastic tub. I boiled an egg every morning and ate what she wouldn't.

I pushed the stroller the six blocks to Second Chance.

All the time I was afraid of Pluto in his black Jaguar, easing down Linwood, his eyes sweeping the street with its ruined buildings, the fallen marquee of the movie house, the boarded-up stores, all brown and gray. He would see me and wouldn't see me, but then he would look, almost without interest, at the baby in her yellow snowsuit, and he would take her because he would know that she was his.

Second Chance wasn't about me; it was about LaFleur and trying to keep her safe. But only love would keep her safe.

"You did very well on your tests, Clara. Where did you go to school?"

"Down south."

"We'll have to send for your records. Do you remember the name of the school?

"I don't guess I remember the last one I went to."

"Well. At any rate, we are impressed with your achievements. Excellent spelling. Good error recognition. Perfect for the word processing program."

"I would like to train to be a teacher."

"You must take advantage of the opportunity being offered to you. Divinely inspired people, visionaries, I would call them, joined together when they heard the young men and women in the city crying out in need. And they answered the cries. With this school. Second Chance was built for you. All you need is to believe in it."

"I don't know what I am supposed to believe in."

"None of us have seen God. Yet we believe in Him."

Some of us have seen the devil. We watch his black car cruising by, his face dark in the shadows. We know him better than we know God, who never shows us His face; who never drives down our streets.

"I guess you're right," I said.

Second Chance was about rules. Two tardies, probation. Three tardies, expulsion. Fifteen minutes between classes. Mothers had an hour during lunch to go the Child Care Center. In the afternoon there were specialized classes: computer technology, engineering drafting, mechanical sciences, automotive technology, medical technology, word processing. That's what Second Chance was all about: technology. The world that was going to happen.

It was a world of machines and the tasks would make you equal to the machines. Learn the formulas. Solve the equation. Label the parts of the sentence. Complete the puzzle. There is nothing to question. There is only to do.

Four forty-five and the buildings fall into stillness, the machines shut down, and electricity is brought to rest. Mothers rush to the Child Care Center, the babies already in their jackets and hats; the toddlers lined up and ready for the bus or the offered ride or the walk home. Five o'clock and in the winter Second Chance is lost in darkness, and I don't have to believe in it until the next morning.

When it snowed, I had to take the bus. If the 7:38 bus was late, then I had to wait. The cold didn't bother me; it was being in the same place every day on the street; the black Jaguar, sleek in the winter morning, a lone car on a street that no longer led to anywhere a person wanted to be. It would travel like night coming, inevitable and dark.

I met James at the lunch break. He was a senior student in the automotive technology program. Everything about James was right, and I wondered why he wasn't out in the world where people managed their lives in regular ways.

"Oh, James," said Teresa, who had the computer next to me. "He had a bad growing-up life. After his momma died, he lived on the streets. Or wherever he could go."

"I'm staying at Second Chance all my life," he told me. "Out in the world every day is like a room with a trap door in it. If you aren't careful, the trap springs, and you fall. You land some place you don't want to be. So I'm not going out there."

"You can't stay here forever."

"I can. After I finish the post-graduate course, I can be an associate teacher in the automotive lab. Jerry, the director, he set it up for me, and Father Morgan agreed. He said they couldn't find people like me every day. Father Morgan said that about me!"

"You're lucky."

"I don't believe in luck. I believe in keeping out of the way of danger. There is no amount of money that will ever make me go back to the dark and evil city. This place is a fortress. Nothing can break down the walls. A solid fortress.

"There won't be much money, but I know how to be careful. I rent in a nice house, and when I am teacher here, I will buy one easy to keep up and cheap to heat. I will have a yard with a high fence, stained a nice oak color with vines and bushes all around...."

"To keep out evil?"

"You could say so."

"I hope you get what you want, James."

"I mean to."

After I got to know James, it wasn't lonely. Every morning he waited for me and LaFleur in his 1982 Chevrolet. He would walk with LaFleur from the porch when I came out and put her in the car seat he bought at a flea market.

"It's the law," he said. "If you keep on the right side of the law every minute, then you'll be ok. But give in to temptation, then you are on a long slide into the pit, and there's no getting back."

I didn't guard myself.

If James had asked, I would have told him about Pluto.

I was never afraid with Pluto, in the watery world where every morning the record was raked clean by fingers of waves; where every night began as if there had been no night before. The same day, the same night.

With James I was frightened. We would go to church every Saturday night, and I would sit beside him, LaFleur in my lap, so pretty in the dress James bought her for church. I would hold the prayer book in front of her, so far away that I couldn't see the words of the hymns, but I wouldn't sing them anyway. If there was a God, equal in power to the God of the dark world, then He would be angry if His holy words came from my mouth. But James, he bowed his head, and his silent prayers rocked his body. He sang loud so that God couldn't help but hear him. Laughter shook itself loose in me.

"Why did you laugh in church, Clara?"

"I was so happy, James. I couldn't help it."

After church we would go to a diner, LaFleur sitting next to James on a little booster seat and him feeding her little bites of his hamburger or his chicken. He loved LaFleur, "like she's my own."

When LaFleur was two and a half, I graduated Second Chance. We wore our robes to the reception with little sandwiches and punch in a big bowl. Glenda was there and James, proud in the audience, holding LaFleur on his lap. Glenda took a picture of the three of us,

James smiling and handsome, me with a light in my face that I swear must have been a trick of the camera, and my beautiful child, her skin glowing dark and velvet, her eyes so deep that you'd be afraid to look in them too long, her soft curls held up in a red ribbon.

"The perfect family," said Glenda as she snapped another photograph.

"Save some film for the wedding," James said.

We were married the next week in the church. All the time I was afraid that a great laughter would rock the church and that I would laugh, too. That when we got outside a black Jaguar would be waiting for us.

"I love you, James," I said. "I promise to be with you and for you for all of our life."

"I will keep you safe, Clara. With all my power I will love you and keep you safe."

And I did love James. I loved his determined innocence. I loved the way he picked LaFleur up in the night when she awoke in her own bed, alone and afraid, and carried her around her room, introducing her to the teddy bear who sat on the end of her bed, the flowers and the birds on the curtains, the little table "where you can draw and write, little girl, all the feelings of your heart."

I loved him, and I became the woman he wanted me to be. I put on that woman like a dress. Some days I believed in her, that young woman who got up and fried eggs and made coffee. The young woman who awakened her husband with a kiss and dressed her child for day care in a clean dress and put her favorite snack in her knapsack. Who was always on time for work. Who helped clean up after church meetings. The young woman who knew only one prayer: Keep Pluto away from us.

I saw the darkness of Pluto in LaFleur, like a shadow falling over her. And then she would run to join the other children on the swings. She would come into the room, and when I turned around, she would be gone. She was everything to me, and I was afraid of her.

"LaFleur's not like you , Clara," James said. "I'm not asking you who she's like. It's just that she is, well, not so straight-forward."

"I'm not straight-forward, James."

"When you come into a room, I feel who you are. I say to myself: My Clara's here, my sweet, sad, innocent Clara."

"James."

"No. There was nothing before us."

So I didn't tell him, and the years fell away. And James and I didn't have any children together. At night he would hold me in his arms, and he would cry.

"It's my fault, Clara. You have God's blessing in your womb, but there is darkness in me. God won't let my seed take root."

"James, no. Don't say it's your fault. I know it isn't. If anything, it's mine."

"We need to pray."

"We could go to a doctor."

"No. This is in God's hands."

I was the darkness, the darkness that had filled me when I was with Pluto, and LaFleur was darkness, too.

She grew tall and by the time she was ten, she was strong. She was motion and power; then she was stillness.

"Oh, honey. I didn't see you."

"I've been here, Mamma, I've been watching you."

"Don't scare me like that."

She was full-grown when she was eleven. Her short skirts floated against the back of her legs. The spill of her curls was shining black.

James loved her. It was LaFleur he asked for when he came home.

He wouldn't let her stay overnight at another girl's house or walk to school with the neighborhood children.

"We are a family. Everything we do, we do with each other."

"She isn't having a normal childhood."

"We never had anything like this. Loving parents, a good home, church and all the good people. If this isn't normal, tell me what is. But I don't think you can, Clara."

"You can know things that you haven't had, James. It is possible to imagine what is good."

"Exactly. What we are giving LaFleur, a good life."

A poison spread in me. It tainted simple words like "Come to dinner" or "Answer the phone." I promised myself not to speak to her that way again, but I didn't have another way to speak, not to her, not to James.

"How you throw your body about, Miss LaFleur Simmons!"

"I work all day, and you just sit around with a book until dinner time."

"Your daddy doesn't have to get up early on a Saturday just to take you to gymnastics."

One day they would leave—together, taking what they wanted most. The precious things: the photographs of the church picnics with the three of us standing against the trees; the three china bowls we ate our ice cream from; the throw pillows splashed with blues and purples that Glenda gave us for a housewarming gift; the cast iron skillet we made our pancakes in. They would take these things, moving quietly in the dark. The engine would purr to a start. They would leave me with the television set and the dishes stacked neatly in the cupboards, the towels folded in the linen closet, the rooms emptied of them.

"That LaFleur. She's getting worse by the day, James."

"What is she doing?"

"The insolence. You can see it in her eyes. Mocking me.... But I can't talk to you about it. You're always on her side."

"I'm trying to be a good father, Clara."

"But you're not her father, are you, James?"

"I try to be, but it doesn't seem to please you."

"You spoil her! How can I be pleased when I see my child spoiled and turned against me!"

"What are you talking about?"

"Nothing. I'm upset. Nothing."

The silence fell on our house when the three of us were together. When LaFleur and I were alone, there were shouts and the slamming of doors.

One day she was gone. Every day before that day, I would hold my breath when I came into the house; she would be doing her homework or talking on the phone, laughing until I came into the room.

"Who are you talking to, Miss? Who makes you laugh like that?"

Questions never answered.

She went to Glenda. I cried when Glenda called me to tell me. LaFleur could stay with her until the trouble between us was over. "Mother and daughter bound to have some differences."

I set the table for dinner. Two plates, two cups, two settings of flatware, two napkins folded neatly under them.

"She's gone," James said when he saw the table.

"To Glenda's."

"I'll make myself something later."

"There was a call from the church on the message machine. A meeting."

"I forgot. I'll grab a bite later."

That's how we lived. Two empty place settings.

"Did you call her today?"

"I talked to Glenda."

"How is she?"

"Fine."

"Going to school?"

"Glenda says so."

"Where was she when you called?"

"I called during the day. From work."

In the night we held on to each other. Once I said: Why don't you leave? He said: I can't.

Devil's Night, October 30. The mayor says that he hopes Detroiters will show their pride in their city. He hopes that we will wake up in the morning and there will be no smoke in the streets. "We don't need the police to tell us what to do. Let's show the world that Detroit is coming back. Let's take Devil's Night out of October 30."

James was part of the Neighborhood Watch, cruising from six to midnight with a partner and a cellphone. He was wearing a cap that said, "Keeping Detroit Safe."

"What are you laughing at, Clara?"

"I'm laughing at your hat."

"I can't talk to you any more."

On Devil's Night we are always waiting for something to happen. The local television channels interrupt programs to show pictures of a warehouse burning; of men and women patrolling the streets in their cars; of the flash of sneakers moving away from a building. "Vigilant neighborhood volunteers have just prevented a housefire," says the excited newscaster on the street, jacket zipped up against the cold night. "Police official bulletins say that 85 teens have been picked up and are waiting to be released to their parents."

The telephone. Devil's Night, October 30, and my daughter is thirteen years old.

"Clara, this is Glenda. You should know. LaFleur left here. I tried to stop her. 'Don't go, child,' I said. 'That man too old.' But she went anyway. All dressed up. She didn't look like no little girl. That was a woman walking out of here."

"There was a car."

"A black Jaguar. When she got in, it moved away like a cat, gliding along. I called out. 'LaFleur.' But my voice wasn't no louder than a squeak."

"You couldn't have stopped it, Glenda."

"You could have stopped it. You the momma."

"Yes. I am the mother."

There is a time in the endless tangle of memory when we have to find the half-forgotten street, the hidden building, and the underground entrance.

LaFleur was sitting on a leather banquette, Pluto's arm around her: father and daughter but looking like brother and sister. LaFleur's curls spilled over a black band. She wore a tight black dress. They looked at me with one face.

"Hello, Ebony."

"I've come for my daughter, Pluto."

"She is mine, too."

"You didn't want her."

"Neither do you."

"I lost my way. I want her back."

"What you got to give me that is more precious than a daughter?"

"What do you want?"

"Something important. Something as important as this child's innocence."

"You are her father! You can see that. For God's sake, a father can't...."

"Paternity got its privileges, Ebony."

"LaFleur, come with me. Let's go home. You can't stay here."

"Pluto, can I dance? I want to dance."

"Sure, baby. I want to see you dance. Your mother and I will watch you."

The dancers turned in their solitary dances among the columns of light that touched them and left them in shadows.

"Let her go, Pluto."

"What's in it for me?"

"My gratitude."

"Woman, that don't mean nothing to me. You wouldn't even miss it. I want something that counts."

"What do I have that you want?"

"Your name."

"My name?"

"That's right. You give me Clara Bright, and I give you LaFleur Simmons. Even trade."

"I would be Ebony."

"That's right. And what would that mean?"

"I would be no one."

"Say again?"

"I ain't nothin', Pluto. Nothin' at all."

"That's more like it. You can get your daughter. I don't want her."

For her child a woman can travel through flame and through darkness. She is smoke among the dancers. She takes her child in her arms. She is shelter and home.

When La Fleur and I walked out into the ordinary night, she said, "There aren't any fires."

"Dad's out on the patrol. When he comes home, he'll be glad to see you back."

"Mom."

"I love you, LaFleur. I love Dad, too."

We sat, the three of us, until it was morning, and all I know about truth I told. But I couldn't look at James.

"I was born Ebony Regis. Clara Bright is the name I made up."

"Not Clara? All the love I spoke to a woman called Clara, and that's not her name."

"I wanted to tell you, James, but you didn't want to know."

"Because I thought I knew. But this….."

"I didn't have the words."

"I couldn't call you Ebony."

"You don't have to."

"Ebony Regis is someone I don't know."

"It's who I have to be, James. But I don't expect you to be with me. Just watch over LaFleur and help her grow up right. Be her father, the one you are."

"I'm sorry…Clara."

In the morning there were streamers of smoke over parts of the city, but it wasn't as bad as most years. James had gone to work, and LaFleur was sleeping. I went into her room. The dress she had worn lay on the floor, and I crumpled it up.

"Don't remember this, my dearest, your night among the lost souls. When you wake up, you will be a girl who belongs to the daylight. Remember that I came for you."

Devil's Night is one night I won't go out of the house. It is the night when everything is on fire, and the streets are full of smoke and shouts rise and spread out over the roofs so that you don't know if they are on your street or on the next street or in your head.

I don't live too far from James and LaFleur, but I don't see them very often. Maybe a few times a year, and always at this time. James will wait in the car while LaFleur visits. That's how short the visits are. I don't even ask her to take off her coat.

"I could tell Dad to go on without me. I could walk back home."

"No, honey, that's ok. You have things to do. And I'm busy. How's your father doing?"

"He's fine. He's thinking about getting married. She's nice. She works at Second Chance. She remembers you."

"That was a long time ago to be remembering. I like to look ahead."

"Are you all right, Mom? You look so thin."

"Let me worry about you. How you are doing in college and all. Tell me about the young men knocking at your door."

"Oh, Mom, I'm not pretty. I'm plain. Men are not knocking at the door. Besides, I have to study."

"You and your father still going to church?"

"Every night. It seems we can't sleep if we don't go to services. We come out so rested, so peaceful."

"That's good."

"I should go."

"Yes."

I had taken the three bowls, the china ones we ate ice cream from, the cold vanilla, the swirling chocolate, the red bits of strawberries. That's all I took from the house. I remember how we held them in our hands, fingers getting icy because the china was so fine and delicate that light could pass through it, and the cold. The spoons would clink against the bowls.

The sirens howl, and it's darker than dark even at 6:00. Devil's Night, October 30 in Detroit. And it's always the same, bad, even when it isn't bad; even when there aren't many fires and nobody is taking your car or puncturing the tires or soaping the windows. No matter what else happens, quiet times, good things, then it's Devil's Night again. You have to think about what could happen and what did happen.

Biographical Note

Rhoda Stamell began writing fiction at the age of fifty. When she was sixty-one, she won the Francis Shaw Older Woman Writing Award and spent a month at Ragdale Foundation in Lake Forest, Illinois. She retired from high school teaching the next year and has been writing fiction ever since.

Stamell lives in the suburbs of Detroit and is an adjunct professor of composition at Lawrence Technological University and Wayne State University.

For a complete catalog of Mayapple Press publications, please visit our website at *www.mayapplepress.com*

Mayapple Press books can be ordered from your local bookseller, by mail or online with PayPal.

RAVENOUS

Necrotic Apocalypse Book One

D. PETRIE

MOUNTAINDALE
PRESS

ACKNOWLEDGMENTS

2020 was a hell of a year.

Life hits hard and I am grateful to all the people that kept me going.

My heartfelt thanks goes out to everyone that has helped a book like Ravenous rise from all the chaos. To Dakota and Danielle Krout, few publishers are as supportive and kind as MDP. I wouldn't be as motivated to write without you both. Most of all, thank you to everyone that has picked up this book. Cause, like, I wouldn't be able to do this without you.

PROLOGUE

Pain screamed through Digby's body as he clutched a hand over a wound on his neck. Blood ran through his fingers, while a sharp spike of agony accompanied every heartbeat. He wasn't sure how many times he'd been bitten. Everything was a blur. It had only been an hour since he entered that godforsaken place, but already his world had been torn inside out.

Witchcraft was real.

Monsters were real.

Curses, were, real!

One impossible thought after another streaked through his frantic mind as water sloshed around the small boat he lay in. The ocean rocked the craft from side to side, taking it out to sea. At least he was away from the ghoulish nightmares that had tried to devour him only moments ago.

Zombies.

It was all so insane. He could still hear the hungry wails of those creatures in his mind as the motion of the waves began to lull him to sleep and unconsciousness threatened to claim him.

"No!" Digby sat back up and coughed out salt water, whipping a lock of wet, black hair from his face. He couldn't die. Not now. Not like this. Not after leading the life he had.

He'd never been one to show up at his village's church for service. If he died now, well, it was no secret where he would be going. He reached into his pocket, grabbing a handful of coins only to throw the useless things in frustration. The money was barely worth stealing, let alone losing his life for.

Digby shook off his regrets and clawed his way up one side of the boat, fighting for every inch against a block of stone that had fallen into the boat to pin his leg to the floor of the craft. He fell back down as a blinding jolt of pain erupted inside him. His heart slammed against his rib cage at an uneven rhythm, sending a surge of pain through his chest with each heavy thump.

Everything blurred except for a word floating in the corner of his vision.

CURSED

Water splashed around him as he spasmed on the bottom of the small craft. In desperation, he reached for his magic, the mana that he'd discovered within him only an hour before.

MP: 0/107

There was nothing left. Even with the power he'd gained, there was nothing he could do. In a dying haze, he reached for the side of the boat again and yanked himself up to gaze back at the coast of England that he'd drifted away from.

A castle burned in the distance.

"Serves you right!"

Digby's words sounded like gravel in his throat as he screamed hateful things back in the direction he'd come from.

"Shouldn't have meddled in witchcraft to begin with!"

Agony burned his chest, consuming what little strength he had. Digby let the anger overtake him, retreating into the comfort of his spite. It warmed his soaked body as darkness began to close in on him. He didn't just curse his enemies. No, he cursed his allies as well.

"You hear me, Henwick! I never should have followed you."

The face of the charismatic hunter that had led him to his death flashed through his memory as his body slumped against the side of the boat. Drained of strength, Digby slipped back down into the seawater that sloshed across the boat's bottom. All warmth left his body. He had nothing left.

Digby closed his eyes, losing the fight as his heart slowed, each beat trailing off into a whimper. The sound of waves faded to silence as he reached one hand out toward the sky and let out one final breath.

"Damn... you... all..."

YOU DIED
All attributes are reduced to 0.
Maximum MP reduced to 0.
CURSE ACTIVATED
RACE UPDATED: ZOMBIE

CHAPTER ONE

Digby stared up at a light. It emitted a subtle continuous buzzing noise as his body lay on a hard surface, unable to move.

He couldn't budge a finger.

Not even an eyelid.

Granted, his eyes were already open. In fact, they had been for quite some time. He couldn't have closed them even if he'd wanted to. They had been frozen that way after all.

Not that he cared.

Digby was a zombie.

He didn't even know Digby was his name, let alone have anything to care about.

Actually, there was one thing he cared about.

Food.

Yes, Digby was pretty hungry. Better make that starving. Though, there wasn't much he could do about it with his body unable to move due to the ice permeating every necrotic cell in his body.

That being said, he was starting to feel a bit... warmer.

A long string of squiggly lines stretched across the bottom of his vision in a seemingly infinite line. It moved from one side to the other. More nonsense appeared on one edge as it fell off the opposite side, like there wasn't enough space to show it all.

Digby the zombie didn't know what the squiggles were, but the same pattern seemed to repeat itself.

You have survived for 1 year. 10 experience awarded.
You have survived for 1 year. 10 experience awarded.
You have survived for 1 year. 10 experience awarded.

The pattern went on like that for what seemed like forever. Though, on occasion, the pattern changed to show a few new lines.

You have reached level 3.
498 experience to next level.
You have one additional attribute point to set.
WARNING: Unable to increase attributes due to a lack of void resources. All attributes will increase by 1 retroactively when minimum resource requirements have been consumed.

Hurry up and eat something already, you imbecile!

That last line of squiggles somehow seemed unpleasant. After that, the lines went back to displaying the same message as before in a seemingly infinite loop.

You have survived for 1 year. 10 experience awarded.

Digby ignored the messages as a voice came from nearby. He couldn't understand anything that was said. All his necrotic gray matter could take in was a bunch of tones and sounds. On occasion, they seemed to form patterns, but after having his intelligence attribute reset to zero when he'd died, Digby lacked the clarity and focus to make anything more of them.

The voice continued regardless.

"You realize this is pretty much how every horror movie starts, right?" The speaker sounded light and airy.

"Or…" a second, deeper voice joined in, "this guy here is a historic discovery."

"Maybe." The first voice paused. "You said he was found by a friend of yours?"

"Yeah, they were doing a climate study up in the Arctic, measuring the icecaps and what not. Said there were some strange lines and markings on this guy's skin, so they kept him on ice and shipped him down to us at the institute."

"That's creepy. How old do you think he is?"

"The boat he was found in dates back to the twelfth century England. It's upstairs at the loading dock waiting to get checked out now. It will make a really cool exhibit in the climate studies wing."

"How did he get all the way up to the Arctic?" The voice sounded incredulous.

"No clue. The poor guy's leg was pinned by a block of stone that must have fallen over on him. He probably died of dehydration at sea and drifted up north. The whole boat was completely frozen. He never would have been found if the ice caps hadn't started to melt."

"Global warming to the rescue." The lighter voice let out a laugh.

"Welcome to the twenty-first century." The first voice laughed.

"Hey guys." A third voice entered the room. "They only had decaf at the commissary, so I got you both a tea."

"Thanks Mike, anything's better than decaf." The shadow pushed away, gliding across the floor on some sort of furniture only to swivel to one side. It snatched something from the newest shape that had entered the room.

"Oh gross," the most recent arrival blurted, sounding like they'd had a mouthful of liquid. "What is that?"

"A corpse his friend found in the Arctic." The lighter voice didn't seem interested.

"Isn't that how every horror movie starts?"

"That's what I said." The slender shape spun back and slapped a limb down on a nearby table.

"You both are just being squeamish." The first voice groaned. "How 'bout you quit worrying and help me get this guy's clothes off so we can—"

"That's what she—"

"Don't even say it, Mike." The lightest voice cut off the last.

"…Sorry."

Suddenly, a large shadow blocked out the light shining in Digby's eyes. Followed by the second more slender shape, and finally, the newest, shorter shadow entered his view.

Something inside Digby stirred, a void deep within him crying out to be filled. It was like a question hanging in the air, to which the three shapes smelled like an answer. A feeling similar to frustration echoed through Digby's gray matter, but try as he might, he still couldn't move.

In the end, all he could do was emit a low gurgle.

"What the hell was that?" The two smaller shadows shrank away.

"Relax, he's starting to thaw. Nothing to be worried about." The largest of the three remained close to jab Digby in the chest. Instinct lit up his ancient synapses; the urge to bite the prey-shaped shadow ricocheted around his frozen skull. That was when a message streamed across his vision. Of course, Digby couldn't read it with his non-existent intelligence, but somehow, he felt stronger.

> **Racial Trait, Ravenous, active. While active, all physical limitations will be ignored.**
> **WARNING: A ravenous zombie will be unable to perform any action other than the direct pursuit of food until satiated. This may result in self-destructive behavior.**
> **WARNING: Ignoring physical limitations for prolonged periods of time may result in catastrophic damage.**

Digby's frozen muscles split and cracked as a false strength surged through his frozen body. He lunged forward at the shadow.

That a boy, get up!

The damage the act caused his body didn't matter. Nothing did. The next few moments were a blur.

"Fu—" The large shadow cried out as Digby's jaws ripped into its neck. A line of squiggles streaked through his vision.

1 common human defeated, 80 experience awarded.

"Shit!" the shorter one shouted, reminding him where it was.

Digby released the first shape and snapped a gnarled hand out at the next flailing limb he found. His jaws bit down, claiming a scrap of food.

The slender shadow made a loud noise as Digby yanked himself forward, throwing his current meal aside to get closer to the next. Driven by ravenous hunger, he rebelled against his non-existent attribute values and sprang off the table. His frozen joints ground together while his body popped and cracked all over with each movement.

The slender shadow turned, moving faster, but Digby was too reckless to be stopped. He landed on its back, slamming it down to the ground. There was a loud snap.

The noise stopped after that.

1 common human defeated, 80 experience awarded.

The shortest of his prey leaped over him, its lower limbs squeaking on the slick floor as it scurried out of Digby's view. One of its limbs left a trail of crimson fluid in its wake. Digby didn't give chase.

He had enough to eat for now.

CHAPTER TWO

Nutritional resource requirements met for level progression.
All attributes increased by 8.
Maximum MP increased to 61.
You have 8 additional attribute points to allocate.

Took you long enough.

A fog began to clear in Digby's mind. Not completely, but enough for him to read the lines of text scrolling across his vision. It took him a bit of time to sound out the letters in his head enough to comprehend them, but still, somehow, he had become smarter.

"Me level?"

Alright, maybe not that smart.

Digby swiped at the words in the air with his hand, then returned to eating whatever he was currently holding. He didn't fully understand what the words meant anyway. Despite that, the last line reappeared a second later as if telling him to do something.

You have 8 additional attribute points to allocate.

Current attribute values:
Constitution: 8
Defense: 8
Strength: 8
Dexterity: 8
Intelligence: 8
Perception: 8
Agility: 8
Will: 13

"Free points… goooooooood." He read over the lines several times, unsure if the values were respectable or not. For some reason, his will was higher than the rest, though he didn't understand why. He blinked twice. None of that was important now. No, what was important was picking which attributes to put his eight available points in.

Intelligence is strongly suggested.

"Hello." Digby waved at the message, unsure who or what was talking to him through the strange text. Then he took another bite of food. He tried his best to focus on the words to make a decision on what attribute to increase. The process felt familiar but also completely foreign to him, like it was something he'd done before, but only once. He took another bite of whatever he was eating as he thought back, hitting a wall of fog in his memory. Some things, like how to steal produce from a marketplace, floated to the surface, but anything related to the strange messages he was seeing was somehow out of reach.

Digby shook his head.

Trying to remember anything only confused him more. Instead, he decided to sit and have a good think to figure out what each of his options might have an effect on.

There were so many choices.

Maybe Defense?

DEFENSE: Attribute related to physical durability. Allocating points improves skin and bone density. Greatly reduces the damage you take. Defense can be supplemented by wearing protective clothing or armor.

That sounded nice. Though, wasn't there something else that was more important?

Pick intelligence, you halfwit.

He ignored the unpleasant message, chewed and thought some more. There was definitely something he needed.

Pick intelligence.

Perception?

PERCEPTION: Attribute related to the awareness of the world around you. Allocating points improves the collection and processing of sensory information and moderately affects mana efficiency.

No, that wasn't it. He looked over the rest, letting whatever was communicating with him weigh in on each.

CONSTITUTION: Attribute related to maintaining a healthy body. Allocating points improves the body's ability to fight off disease and lowers the chance of infection and food borne illness. Greatly affects endurance.

Pointless... the dead don't get tired or sick.

AGILITY: Attribute related to mobility. Allocating points

will improve overall control of body movements. Greatly affects speed and balance.

Definitely something you need, but not a priority.

STRENGTH: Attribute related to physical prowess. Allocating points increases muscle density to yield more power. Greatly affects the damage of melee attacks.

Also not a priority.

DEXTERITY: Attribute related to skill in performing tasks, especially with hands. Allocating points will increase control of precise movement. Greatly affects control of melee attacks and ranged weaponry.

Nope, not this one either.

WILL: Attribute related to controlling your mind and body. Allocating points will increase your dominance over your own existence. Greatly affects resistance to spells that directly affect your physical or mental self.

Useful, but also wrong at this particular moment.

INTELLIGENCE: Attribute related to comprehending information and understanding. Improves processing speed and memory. Greatly affects mana efficiency.

Good god, just pick this one, you simpleton.

Oh, that's it. Thank you.

Digby focused on the word, intelligence, watching the number tick up from eight to nine. A sudden rush of clarity flowed through his mind to clear a little of the fog that was slowing his thoughts down.

Maximum MP increased to 65.

Want more. He focused on the word again to bring the value to ten.

Maximum MP increased to 69.

Yes, that's niiiice. He added another point, followed by another, beginning to feel more like himself with each selection. His mana continued to rise by four with each point.

Almost there. I'm almost as smart as I was before…

Digby dumped the rest of his points into intelligence, bringing it up to sixteen.

…before I died.

"Wait, what?" His words came out raspy as musty air passed through his vocal cords. The sensation was strange, like he had to make a conscious effort to inhale and move his lungs.

That was when he realized he was eating a human hand.

"Gah! What in the hell am I doing?" He threw the hand across the room, immediately having the urge to go over and pick it back up to continue eating.

Digby dropped back into a chair that he'd apparently been sitting in up until now and hugged himself whilst shaking. He was in a large, unfamiliar room with some kind of metal table. It was one of the largest spaces he'd ever been in. He could hardly believe the size. It was like something out of a castle.

There were no windows in the space, but light filled the room from rectangles embedded in the ceiling that held glowing tubes. The walls were smoother than any stone he'd seen, and the floor shined with an impossible gloss. That was when Digby noticed the blood.

"Oh god."

A skeletal foot peeked out from behind the metal table, like someone had gnawed it down to the bone. Even some of its toes were missing. Digby immediately wished he hadn't put all those points into intelligence. Ignorance had been bliss. Glancing around, he tried to convince himself that someone else must have been the culprit. The taste of blood in his mouth told him otherwise, sending a single thought through his mind.

I killed them.

No, worse, he had eaten them.

Digby shook his head and tried again to remember. The last thing he could recall was lying in a small boat, injured, while a castle burned in the distance. He had yelled something back then. Something about magic.

Witchcraft!

"That must be it. This isn't my fault. It was witchcraft. I've been cursed. I didn't mean to hurt these people. How could I?" Digby groaned to himself. "Like anyone will believe that. Hell, I don't even believe it. Likely I'd be burned at the stake if I tried that sort of defense." He furrowed his brow, wondering why he'd had that thought.

He tried to remember what had transpired before he'd found himself in that boat, but his memory wasn't good enough to sift through the information. All he could recall were bits and pieces. He knew his name and that he'd lived in a small village near the coast of England. The castle he'd seen had belonged to a nearby lord by the name of Axton, but beyond that, he had no idea why he'd been there or how it ended up on fire.

More importantly, he had no idea why he was seeing words and numbers in the air or what sort of curse had been placed on him. Despite that, the words and the magic behind them felt real, as if he'd already learned how to use them but just didn't remember when.

Focusing on the fragments of his past, Digby searched for where and when he might have obtained the mana that he could feel flowing through his body. It was cold, like the wind at night. Try as he might though, there was nothing to be found beyond memories of the average life of someone unimportant. He focused on the image of the burning castle, hoping to recall why it mattered but found his memory of the place blank. Something told him the answers he needed were inside.

Digby's mind continued to run in circles, only to come to a screeching halt when he noticed a set of bloody footprints that traveled across the floor. He followed the trail with his eyes to a door. It hung open, a bloody smear leading out into a hallway of some kind. His whole body froze as a horrifying realization struck him.

There was a witness to what I've done.

A vague image of a third person running from the room flashed through Digby's mind just before a new thought demanded his attention.

I have to hide the evidence.

There would be time to investigate what happened back in the castle later. Right now, he had a murder to cover up. Without hesitation, Digby rushed to the door. At least, he tried to rush to the door. It was more like he shambled his way there. His coordination was off, and his body felt heavy.

Digby shut the door, nearly falling in the process. It was only a matter of time before whoever he'd let get away returned with the village guard. Pushing off, he stumbled back around the metal table to the two skeletal corpses. He skidded to a stop, slipping in the pool of blood.

"Gah! I'll never be able to clean this up in time." He scanned the room for another way out. It seemed fleeing the scene was his best option. There were no windows, but there was a second door on the same wall, plus a rear exit on the far side.

"Perfect, I'll slip out the back."

Digby sprinted for the door as his instinct to flee made him forget about his strange lack of coordination. He tripped and fell almost immediately. He didn't feel right, like his body had been ripped apart and sewn back together. It didn't hurt, but it wasn't pleasant either. Just uncomfortable.

A foggy memory of being frozen bubbled to the surface. The sound of his limbs cracking as they moved echoed through his mind. That Ravenous trait, whatever that was, had somehow overridden every limit that his battered body had, probably causing more harm than good in the process.

Digby pushed himself up off the floor. There was no time to worry, he still needed to flee. That was when an obvious question struck him.

"How long have I been in this room?"

He furrowed his brow and glanced back at the skeletal remains on the floor. The question put a hold on his panic for a moment. If he'd already eaten two people, then it stood to reason that more time had passed than he realized. Following that line of thought, a second question came to mind. Where was the witness that he'd let escape now?

Surely, they'd had time to bring back the village guard. Unless they never made it that far? Whoever it was might have gotten lost or had been unable to find help. What if it was night time, and they were waiting until morning?

A wave of relief pulled a weight from Digby's shoulders. Maybe no one was coming. Maybe he could afford to take a few minutes to get his bearings. He stared at his hands, finding his left covered in a tattered leather glove. The other bore various tears and fissures in the gray skin that was stretched tight across his bony fingers.

"What is wrong with me?"

The instant the question left his mouth, a strange circle appeared at the edge of his vision to answer it. The shape glowed a soft green as it spun out from one corner to float, front and center, where it expanded to show a list of words within it.

STATUS
Name: Digby Graves
Race: Zombie
Mutation Path: None
Heretic Class: Mage
Mana: 61/93
Mana Composition: Pure
Current Level: 10 (628 Experience to next level.)

ATTRIBUTES
Constitution: 8
Defense: 8
Strength: 8
Dexterity: 8
Agility: 8
Intelligence: 16
Perception: 8
Will: 13

AILMENTS
Deceased

Digby's heart sank as the last line told him what he already knew. The truth that he had been hiding from for the last few minutes.

He was dead.

Not only that, but he wasn't even human anymore. Nay, he was a monster. A zombie. The word shook a memory loose from his necrotic gray matter. A memory of shambling forms reaching for him. His mind pulled on the thread, struggling to recall every detail of what had happened.

Suddenly, stone walls surrounded him as he fell to the cold floor of the castle from his memory. Teeth clamped down on his arm.

———

"Get off me!"

Digby squealed and kicked at a ghoulish man as it toppled over on top of him.

The creature's skin was sickly pale in the light of a torch that Digby had dropped nearby. Reflected flames flickered in the cloudy white of his assailant's eyes. It bit down harder, shaking its head the way an animal would, tearing at its prey. Pain, like nothing Digby had ever felt, screamed up his arm.

Shadows stretched up a spiral stairway behind him seconds before more of the castle's deceased occupants poured into the hall. In desperation, he reached for his torch, catching the handle with his fingertips. With tears of pain in his eyes, he gave his attacker a hard crack to the head, filling the air with embers as the zombie tore a meaty chunk from his arm.

"Gah!" Digby scrambled away as the monstrosity proceeded to eat what it'd claimed.

———

Just as fast as it had come, the memory faded away, leaving Digby in the room he'd awoken in. Wrapped up in the events that had transpired in his past, he'd fallen again, and was now kicking at one of the corpses in the room as if it was attacking him. His eyes flicked around, coming to grips with what he'd seen.

"That's how it happened! The bite spread whatever curse those wretched souls had to me." His gray, damaged skin made sense now. He was grateful that there were no mirrors in the room. Digby could only imagine what he looked like.

He was a zombie.

Trying to remember more, he tore at the tattered sleeve of what was left of his shirt, only to find the bite wound he'd received, gone.

"Huh?"

There wasn't even a scar.

"But I saw it."

He was sure he'd lost a sizable chunk of his arm.

"Wait a second." A new thought struck him. "How am I thinking?"

In the brief memory of the zombies he'd encountered, Digby hadn't considered the creatures to have all that much going on upstairs. So why, then, did he?

"Is it because," he glanced at the numbers at the lower corner of his vision that displayed his mana, "I have magic?"

The circle that had displayed his status before reappeared to show him his status information again, as if to say, 'Yes, you idiot, that's exactly why.'

"What the hell does all that mean?" Digby argued with the shape as he reread everything, hoping the strange messages might give him another bit of snarky information like before. He swept his hand through the floating status ring when it didn't respond, causing it to shrink back to its home at the edge of his vision.

"Wait, don't run away."

The shape returned as soon as he complained, like it was responding to his words or thoughts.

"What sort of witchcraft is this, and how did I learn magic?"

A line of text appeared to answer his question as if something was listening.

Heretic Seed synchronization stable.
Class assignment, Mage.

Congratulations, you got magic. Lot of good it did you.
You died in less than an hour.

Digby scowled at that last line, irritated at the thought that there was something watching him and listening to his every word. Especially if it was something witchcraft related. Not to mention he didn't like the sound of the word heretic in there. With his luck, some sort of demon was talking to him. At least it had the decency to tell him something useful. If the message was to be believed, then he had only learned magic less than an hour before he'd died in that boat as it drifted out to sea.

"What the hell is a Heretic Seed?"

HERETIC SEED
An unrestricted pillar of power. Once connected, this
system grants access to, and manages the use of, the

mana that exists within the human body and the world around them.

Try to act a little more grateful. It is the reason you're still thinking.

"Yes, yes, whatever." Digby rolled his eyes at the comment, not wanting to give the thing an ounce of gratitude. "So is that what I'm talking to? This Heretic Seed?"

This time, there was no answer.

"Hmm, maybe it can't answer direct questions." Digby scratched his chin, realizing that the Seed had only made comments alongside other more basic messages. It was almost as if it couldn't contact him freely, but instead could only add to the information meant to train new heretics about its functions. Even then, it mostly offered rude comments. Digby decided to play along. "Alright then, what is a mage?"

MAGE: Starting class for heretics whose highest attribute is intelligence. Excels at magic... *and often lacks physical strength.*

"Did it just call me weak?" Digby narrowed his eyes at the message before adding, "What does a mage do?" His status ring flipped to show its reverse side, where a different list appeared.

AVAILABLE SPELLS:
FIREBALL
Description: Will a ball of fire to gather in your hand to form a throwable sphere that ruptures on contact.
Rank: D
Cost: 15MP
Sphere size: 3in
Range: Because this spell only creates a throwable mass, its range is dependent on both strength and dexterity.

REGENERATION

Description: Heal wounds for yourself or others. If rendered unconscious, this spell will cast automatically until all damage is repaired or until MP runs out.
Rank: D
Cost: 10MP
Duration: 10 seconds
Range: 10ft
Limitations: May require multiple castings to repair all damage.

Continue using spells to increase their rank and efficiency. New spells can be discovered through experimentation, using related skills, increasing your heretic level, completing rituals, and unlocking new classes. Creativity and taking risks are often rewarded.

PASSIVE HERETIC ABILITIES:
ANALYZE

Reveal hidden information about an object or target, such as rarity and hostility toward you.

MANA ABSORPTION

Ambient mana will be absorbed whenever MANA POINTS are below maximum MP values. Rate of absorption may vary depending on ambient mana concentration and essence composition. Absorption may be increased through meditation and rest.
WARNING: Mana absorption will be delayed whenever spells are cast.

SKILL LINK

Discover new spells by demonstrating repeated and proficient use of non-heretic skills or talents.

TIMELESS

Due to the higher than normal concentration of mana within a heretic's body, the natural aging process has been halted, allowing for more time to reach the full potential of your class. It is still possible to expire from external damage.

A little late for you there.

"Indeed. Lot of good that does me." Digby scoffed at that last ability. "I've already expired. Being Timeless doesn't help if I'm dead."

"Actually…" A detail of one of his spells jumped out at him. "How did I die if my Regeneration spell will cast on its own whenever I'm unconscious?" The answer became obvious by looking at his mana value that sat at the lower corner of his vision.

MP: 61/93

He had absorbed more since increasing his maximum values. Apparently putting points into intelligence had an impact on how much he could hold. Though, he still needed more. If he had been empty when he died, then his Regeneration spell wouldn't have been able to help.

"No matter, I have enough mana now, so regenerate." He spoke the word to activate the spell. Then he waited for the cuts on his hands and his damaged joints to heal. Several seconds of nothing went by.

"Why am I not healing?"

Regeneration cancelled due to incompatible mana composition. Minimum 10% life essence required.

"What!?" He tried again.

Regeneration cancelled due to incompatible mana

composition. Minimum 10% life essence required.

He stared at his status ring at the edge of his vision to call it back to the center and scanned the information it held for an answer. Before he found it, however, his mind latched onto something else.

"How did I gain eight levels?"

Digby couldn't remember the hour leading up to his death floating out to sea, but he was sure his level had been much lower. Wasn't it only two? Focusing on his heretic level, his status ring flipped again to display a wall of text.

You have survived for 1 year, 10 experience awarded.

The same message repeated itself for what seemed like forever.

"I've survived for how long now?" Digby's mouth fell open as he counted the lines, only to lose track after a few dozen. As if sensing what he wanted to know, the Heretic Seed gave him the information he needed.

Total experience gained from survival: 8,230.

Congratulations, you're older than the dirt you should have been buried in.

Digby nearly fell over.

CHAPTER THREE

YOU DIED

Digby read over the messages he'd received long ago before the wall of text. If the strange words were to be believed, he'd defeated a handful of other zombies prior to his death. By the time of his demise, he had somehow reached level two, making him level ten after gaining experience simply for existing. Whatever that meant. He shook his head. None of it made sense.

Digby returned to staring at the one line that was hardest to accept.

Total experience gained from survival: 8,230.

He divided the number by the ten experience he'd been getting per year. Shouting when he reached the answer.

"I'm over eight-hundred-years-old?"

He fell silent a second later, letting out nothing but a slow wheeze as his lungs released a breath of musty air. His status ring returned back to its home at the edge of his vision.

Everyone I've ever known is gone.

Digby lowered his head to his hands, feeling his cold flesh against his forehead. The faces of a few acquaintances emerged from the fog of his memory. A shop owner here, a bartender there. Absent was the presence of anyone close to him. No family or friends. The only face he could even connect a name to was one of the hunters that had lived in his village, a man named Henwick. Anger flared as he remembered the name. Digby let the feeling go along with a lone sob.

Perhaps I had not been well liked back home.

Digby remained still with his head lowered for a quiet minute. Then, he laughed.

Actually, it was more like a cackle.

"Popular or not, I've outlasted the lot of you." He attempted to snap his dead fingers, with little success. From his reaction, it was obvious that his personality was too abrasive to be adept at making friends. Fortunately, that seemed to make everything easier. There was no need to mourn the dead if he didn't care about anyone. Digby nodded to himself and stood back up.

Sweeping his gaze across the room, he noted how many objects he failed to recognize. He had been so preoccupied with the two dead bodies to notice anything earlier.

Rectangles of glowing glass, each held by metal pedestals, sat on desks on one side of the room. Some of the rectangles were blank while others held detailed paintings. The images were so realistic, almost impossibly so. It was as if the artist had recreated exactly what they saw with perfect detail.

Digby approached one of these glowing windows containing a picture of a man and a woman. The man had his arm outstretched toward the viewer at an awkward angle in front of a background of crystal blue water. The beauty of the image was like nothing Digby could remember from the dreary life he'd led back in his village.

He stared at the strange glowing rectangle, letting curiosity carry him away. The information ring at the edge of his vision snapped out to encircle the device. An uncomfortable moment passed, as if the glowing shape was thinking, before text appeared around the edge of the circle.

Computer: common, information storage and processing.

"That must be my Analyze ability." The corner of Digby's mouth tugged upward, realizing that he hadn't even needed to say anything to activate the function. It had simply reacted in response to his thoughts. Beyond that, he ignored the text; it didn't make much sense, anyway. Instead, a few numbers near the corner of the computer's image window drew his eye. It was a date.

"I'm in the twenty-first century."

That was when the reality of the situation sunk in. He settled back down into a chair to give his deceased body a rest as he wrapped his head around his new existence.

"I'm lost."

With no home or anywhere to go, he was truly and completely lost. All he had left were the clothes on his back, and really, they were soiled to a point that they barely even counted as garments anymore.

"What do I even have left?"

Digby pulled the tattered glove from his left hand, finding a ring of black runes tracing a line around the gray skin of his middle finger. Veins of dark green spread out from the markings to climb up his wrist. They looked awful. He attempted to cast Regeneration again, hoping for just a bit of his humanity to return.

Regeneration cancelled due to incompatible mana composition. Minimum 10% life essence required.

A valiant effort. Stupid, but valiant all the same.

"Oh yes, apparently my magic doesn't work." He checked his mana, finding plenty at seventy-five out of ninety-three.

D. PETRIE

He'd gained a few points since last he'd checked, so there was definitely enough to cast something. "And why does this Heretic Seed thing feel the need to keep mocking me?" He read over that last line of text that told him trying to cast Regeneration was pointless.

A valiant effort. Stupid, but valiant all the same.

Eventually, he shrugged at the snarky comment and attempted to cast Fireball instead.

Fireball cancelled due to incompatible mana composition. Minimum 10% heat essence required.

"Alright, if I understand this, my mana composition has no heat or life essence. So what do I have?"

The Heretic Seed showed him his status list again. This time, it expanded the line that showed his mana to answer the question.

HEAT 0%
FLUID 0%
SOIL 0%
VAPOR 0%
LIFE 0%
DEATH 100%
WARNING: Your mana system is unable to absorb any essence other than death due to deceased ailment.
CONGRATULATIONS: You have achieved mana purity. Some spells requiring death essence will yield better results.

"All I have access to is death, huh?" Digby attempted to cast Regeneration several more times in rapid succession, hoping he could force it to activate with his current mana balance.

WARNING: Continued attempts to cast improperly balanced spells may yield unpredictable results.

Go ahead, keep trying. Maybe your head will explode.

"I don't recall asking you." Digby ignored the unhelpful comment and kept trying, encouraged that the warning message had implied that it was still possible to cast something with his mana. He wasn't about to let whatever the Heretic Seed was tell him what to do.

Then, his mana shifted. It felt like mud being pushed through every fiber of his being. Digby collapsed to the cold floor, his body convulsing as a new spell wormed its way into his mind. A moment later, something snapped into place inside him. After that, he was fine.

Better than fine, actually.

The splits in his skin began to repair themselves and his muscles began to feel more solid. He was a long way off from healthy, but it was a start.

NEW SPELL DISCOVERED
Regeneration has evolved into Necrotic Regeneration.

NECROTIC REGENERATION
Description: Repair damage to necrotic flesh and bone to restore function and structural integrity.
Rank: D
Cost: 10MP
Duration: 10 seconds
Range: 10ft (+50% due to mana purity, total 15ft.)
Limitations: Requires compatible resources to be consumed by target. May require multiple castings to repair all damage.

Look at that, you didn't explode.

"No I didn't, and this is more like it." Digby sat up and cast the spell repeatedly until he got another message.

No damage to repair.
WARNING: Overuse of Necrotic Regeneration may deplete consumed resources. A lack of resources may activate racial trait, Ravenous.

"Damn, that might be bad." Digby did a squat to test his body. He had some trouble getting back up again. "Apparently this is as good as I get for now. Must be because of my low numbers." He looked over the rest of his attributes. "Come to think of it, why are my numbers so low?" He sifted back through his past messages, finding an answer near the beginning of the wall of text.

YOU DIED
All attributes reduced to 0.

"That would do it, I guess. If it wasn't for the levels I gained from surviving all those centuries, my attributes would all still be stuck at zero." He thought about his decision to drop all his optional points into intelligence.

That had been close.

"I could have just as easily put everything into strength. That would have left me stuck in a fog, unable to understand anything beyond hunger. I may be weak now, but at least I know what I'm doing."

With a little luck, he might be able to bring the rest of his numbers up to where they were before he'd died. Out of morbid curiosity, he asked a number of questions trying to get the Heretic Seed to show him his status from eight hundred years ago.

PREVIOUS ATTRIBUTES
Constitution: 17

Defense: 14
Strength: 14
Dexterity: 15
Agility: 15
Intelligence: 18
Perception: 8
Will: 12

You have a long way to go.

Digby couldn't help but agree with the Heretic Seed's assessment. Regaining the values he'd had while alive would be no small feat. He just hoped he would live long enough. Well, maybe live wasn't the right word. *Survive?* Although, with enough time, who knew what was possible. He might be able to become even stronger. On top of that, if magic was real, then there might even be a way to bring himself back from the dead. Thinking about it, he had a lot to do.

"Alright, first things first, I need to get out of here and find somewhere to hide and figure out what happened to me."

Safety was a priority, but so was learning how he ended up connected to something like the Heretic Seed, not to mention finding out what it was. Its description had called it a pillar of power, but did that mean a literal pillar that existed somewhere, or something else? Was it really the thing sending him messages? There was no way to know.

Digby shook his head. There was too much to think about, and he couldn't keep waiting for someone to stumble across him standing over the two corpses he'd eaten.

"Come to think of it…" Digby trailed off, realizing that finding safety and understanding the Seed weren't the only things he needed. No, if he was going to accomplish any of that in his weakened state, he was going to need a way to defend himself.

Unless he already had a way to defend himself?
Maybe…

Digby began casting Fireball repeatedly, just as he had done with his Regeneration spell. He focused on his hand, willing fire to gather in his palm just as the spell's information described. The same warnings about using an improper mana balance flashed across his vision for the first few tries. Then, success.

Digby winced and struggled to stay standing as a new spell slithered through his mind. A moment later, emerald flames coalesced in the air, flowing toward his hand.

Digby grinned.

Then, he screamed.

The fire hadn't been forming in his hand at all. No, it *was* his hand! His dead flesh spat and crackled as his fingers burst into flames.

"Bah!" Digby flailed his arm, the fire streaking through the air as it climbed up his wrist.

NEW SPELL DISCOVERED
Fireball has evolved into Cremation.

CREMATION
Description: Ignite a target's necrotic tissue. Resulting fire will spread to other flammable substances.
Rank: D
Cost: 15MP
Range: 20ft (+50% due to mana purity, total 30ft.)
Area of effect: 10in
Limitations: Ineffective against living targets.

"Argh, the hell? Why would I want to do that? I don't want to set myself on fire." Digby searched the room for a bucket of water or even a chamber pot, finding nothing to douse the flames. He tried to pat it out with his other hand, but that just spread the fire to his other arm.

Stumbling around the room, he set a number of papers on fire before finding two cups filled with what looked like tea. The containers were white and made of a paper-like material. There wasn't time to think about it. Digby grabbed them both and splashed the tea across his flaming hands to extinguish the blaze.

With the problem solved, he stood there panting—on reflex more than anything else, considering he didn't seem to need to breathe anymore. Digby forced a few deep breaths through his lungs before stopping all together. It felt strange that he didn't feel the urgency to inhale that he normally would have if he'd been alive. Instead, the act of breathing simply didn't matter. That was when he realized he couldn't smell the smoke wafting from his hands.

"Oh!" Digby forced air back inside to carry the scent, realizing that there would be no way to smell things without doing so. Not to mention he needed air in his lungs to talk. Apparently breathing still had a use after all.

As he stood there, attempting to relearn how to breathe without actively thinking about the act, smoke continued to waft through the air. Silence fell over the room again. A moment went by, then a new noise blared into his ears, its volume loud and constant.

It began to rain.

"What?"

Digby looked up at a silver device embedded in the ceiling as it showered him with water.

"What!"

The strange alarm continued to sound, sending Digby into a panic. He checked his mana, finding eighteen MP left after his experimental casting. Another Necrotic Regeneration healed his hands, bringing his total down to eight.

It was only a matter of time before a guard or something came to check on the noise. He spun toward the back door and made a break for it. His uncoordinated legs fought him every step of the way before, finally, he reached the knob and dragged the door open.

"What?" Digby stared into an empty closet.

Shoving the door shut in frustration, he turned back toward

the two doors at the other side of the room. There wasn't a choice; he was going to have to sneak out the front.

He traversed the room again, splashing through the water that pooled on the floor. It washed away the blood of the two mostly-eaten corpses. At least there would be less evidence of what he'd done.

Without hesitation, Digby pulled open the front door and shuffled his way out into a hallway. He kept moving. The alarm faded behind him as he passed by several closed doors. There were so many lining the walls. The hallway was so wide that even a castle looked like a hovel in comparison. His memory was spotty at best, but still, buildings this large simply didn't exist back in the time he'd come from.

How do I get out of here?

Digby turned down another corridor, hoping to find a window or stairway that might point him in the right direction. Instead, he found trouble. A man in strange clothes stood in the hall facing away. He wore a lightweight, white coat like some kind of clergyman.

Digby stopped, dead in his tracks, before slowly backing away.

Then the man let out a familiar moan.

Digby winced, his mind flashing back to the single detail that he could recall from the time that had led up to his death over eight hundred years ago. The man turned toward him at a snail's pace. His mouth hung slack as he let out a groan. Crimson stains covered his front.

"Oh God," Digby gasped.

It was a zombie.

He couldn't believe what he was seeing. How could there be another zombie there besides him? Maybe he was mistaken. His Analyze ability reinforced the truth in response to his doubt.

Zombie: common, friendly.

Digby staggered backward just as a second zombie

wandered out from an open side door. A third zombie followed. They staggered toward him and brushed against his shoulder, paying him no mind.

"Just how long was I sitting in that room? And how could these monsters have gotten here?" Sure, he had been back there long enough to eat two corpses, but that would only account for an hour, maybe two. Then again, it could have been even longer. He could have been sitting there in that room for several hours for all he knew, considering his intelligence attribute had been too low to know the difference.

That was when he remembered the third person that had been there when he'd attacked the others. The one that had escaped. They hadn't gotten lost at all. No, he had bitten them.

"Dear God."

Digby clasped a hand over his mouth. "I must have fatally wounded him, only to have him turn just as I had and spread the curse from there."

The only question was, how far had the curse spread while he was casually eating back in that room? All Digby knew was that covering up the murder he committed down the hall had just become a lot less important.

The people of the future had bigger problems to worry about than him.

CHAPTER FOUR

Rebecca Alvarez yawned as she sat in front of the curved one-hundred-eighty-degree display of her work station.

"Why isn't anyone answering?"

She tapped a finger on her keyboard and stared at the message window sitting at the center of the enormous monitor. With an impatient huff, she typed the words 'Awaiting orders' into the input field for the third time and hit send. Afterwards, she sat back and chewed on a fingernail to wait, unable to shake the feeling that something was wrong. Central Ops had never failed to respond before.

After five minutes, she stood up and paced around the living room of her company-provided apartment. Eventually, she gave up and headed to the kitchen.

Grabbing a container of chicken parmesan from the fridge, Becca tore off the plastic lid. It was a strange meal to pick for breakfast, considering she had just woken up. Then again, it was also eleven o'clock at night and no one was around to tell her to eat something more appropriate.

It wasn't like she got to pick her meals anyway. The least she could do was to choose when she ate them. She had her employer to thank for that. The prepackaged container was part of one of those premium food plans that delivered complete meals every few days. The menu was planned out by a specially trained chef to provide nutritionally balanced meals with minimal cook time. Her health and convenience were important after all, and Skyline knew how to care for its employees.

It was a good thing too, because Becca didn't know the first thing about cooking. Remote military operations, sure. She could pilot a drone through a war zone to support Skyline's ground units, but if she was asked to cook a roast, then she wouldn't know where to start. Fortunately, that wasn't her responsibility. In fact, the struggles of basic day to day life hadn't been her problem since she was thirteen.

Becca tossed the plastic container of chicken and pasta in the microwave and punched in the recommended cook time listed on the label. She watched her meal rotate for a few seconds before tearing her attention away. From there, she padded across the high-end kitchen to the fridge and claimed a bottle of mineral water.

The apartment was a nice place to live. Lonely, but nice all the same.

The only people to talk to were the guards down in the lobby, disguised as doormen. Of course, there was a six-inch blast door and forty floors between herself and them, so it wasn't like she could take a stroll down there.

Becca would need the blast door's unlock code to do that.

If she wanted to talk to the guards, she could always use the intercom, but that would be an exercise in futility. The guards never had much to say. She hadn't been reprimanded for disturbing them before, but Skyline always reassigned their guard staff whenever anyone got too friendly.

Obviously, Becca was aware that her secluded lifestyle wasn't normal. It was just necessary. Skyline was the world's leading private military contractor, and as such, its practices were sometimes unorthodox. They had to treat their staff like the carefully cultivated assets they were. Besides, it wasn't like she was a prisoner. She had chosen to be there, in a roundabout way.

Heading to the living room, she plopped herself down on the couch and played a little sudoku on her company provided tablet. It was one of the few approved apps that came prein-stalled since there was no chat function that could allow for outside communication. She wasn't able to download anything more. A beep from the microwave called her back to the kitchen where her meal was ready. Becca punched the open button and grabbed the plastic tub.

"Ah! Hot." She dropped it flat on the counter, causing red sauce to spatter the front of the simple tank top she wore.

"God damn it." Becca waved her hand to one side to cool her fingertips.

Letting her meal sit, she grabbed a light hoodie that she'd left on the back of the couch and zipped it up to cover the stain on her stomach.

"There we go." She ignored the specks of sauce that had landed on her pajama pants. It wasn't like anyone cared what she looked like. Actually, she hadn't put on real clothes in weeks, possibly even months.

Returning her attention to her breakfast-slash-dinner, she blew on a forkful of chicken and shoved it in her mouth before taking a seat at her work station. She reached forward and placed the identification cuff on her wrist to the console's unlock panel since it had timed out due to inactivity while she'd cooked her food. Afterward, she tapped the keyboard, bringing her enormous curved monitor to life. Her rotation should have started fifteen minutes ago.

"Maybe they'll send me somewhere new today," she mused to herself through a mouthful of chicken.

Skyline assigned a drone operator to most of the squads they had in the field. For each unit in the fight, it was a godsend. The fact that they could get eyes in the sky, or send in an expendable scout, saved countless lives. She could even place small explosive and stun charges to initiate a breach.

Most of the missions she'd worked had been overseas as part of joint operations with the U.S. military. Skyline also aided with domestic law enforcement back home, but Becca had never been assigned there. She'd assumed it had something to do with the fact that she was stationed in Seattle and Skyline wanted to maintain a layer of detachment with her assignments. This left her stuck on the night shift to match the time zones overseas.

She glanced to the clock at the side of her monitor. It was late enough for local businesses to be closed. Becca polished off her dinner, then typed another message into her system.

Still awaiting orders.

She checked the time again.

"Hmm." Becca leaned on her elbow and waited another minute.

Impatience getting the better of her, she typed a few more words into the chat window.

Requesting a connection address.

Still, no one answered.

"I hope I'm not in trouble." Becca sank back in her chair.

That was when she noticed a blue light flashing against the wall of the apartment behind her. Pushing off with her toes, she wheeled her chair away from her drone station to peek into the living room.

"That's odd."

The light was reflecting off the windows of the building across the street. Becca pushed herself up from her chair and crept toward the floor to ceiling windows that lined the outer edge of her apartment. The view had a tendency to make her dizzy, being so high up.

It was hard to make out anything while looking down at such an extreme angle, but it looked like there were several police cars on the street below. A staccato of white-orange flashes joined in between the vehicles. Becca backed away from the window.

She recognized gunfire when she saw it.

Judging from the muzzle flash, it was a semi-automatic pistol. As to why anyone would be firing that fast, she had no idea. At that rate, it would be impossible to hold a target. The only time she'd ever seen anyone fire like that had been when a new recruit panicked.

"But this isn't a war zone." She took another step back. "This is Seattle."

Becca spun on her heel and ran back to her console to open a direct line to Central Ops. It wasn't protocol, but she was starting to freak out.

"This is Crow's Nest, requesting information on a situation in progress. Location, Seattle, United States." Her eye twitched. "Also known as outside my window."

No one responded.

"Crow's Nest to Central Ops, requesting info," she repeated the plea.

Still nothing. Becca let out a growl and jumped up from her chair. A moment later, she was standing at the steel blast door of her apartment. She slapped a hand against the talk button of the lobby intercom.

"Hey, anyone, what's going on down there?"

Again, no answer came.

"What the hell is going on?"

Becca ran back to her station and opened every social media site she had access to. She couldn't use any of them to send a message since those features were blocked, but at least she could get some information. She froze as soon as she saw the first news article posted.

BIOLOGICAL ATTACK IN SEATTLE

"What?" The plastic covering of her computer mouse creaked as her fingers tightened around it.

She scrolled down, finding post after post of people begging for information about friends and loved ones in the city. Though none of the posts seemed to be getting any response from anyone inside the city limits. It was as if there was an information blackout.

"Damn it." She clicked back over to voice-comms. "Somebody better——"

"Hang tight, Crow's Nest," a voice cut her off.

"What's happening?"

"You're on standby for now."

"Yes, but what's——"

"Nothing you have to worry about. There has been a biological attack, but your station is as secure as it gets. If that changes, we'll evac your location. There's still a lot we don't know, but we have teams inbound to take control of the situation. The army has set up a quarantine line around the city to contain the outbreak."

"Outbreak?" Becca leaned forward. "What sort of outbreak?"

"It's some sort of pathogen. According to the army, it spreads fast but requires physical contact. So again, you're safe where you are."

"Sure, whatever." The back of Becca's neck started to sweat. "What are my orders? I can——"

"Negative, Crow's Nest. You're to remain on standby."

"I can't just sit here." She slapped her desk.

"Relax, we have troops inbound and they have drone personnel already assigned. We don't need you right now. Sit tight until contacted, and stay off the line." The connection abruptly terminated.

Becca let out an indignant scoff as if she had just been insulted.

"What an asshole." She chewed on her lip.

Finally, when she was finished stewing, she clicked back to

her browser and looked over a few sites. There definitely was something stopping the city's inhabitants from sending out any messages. There wasn't a single post from within Seattle, leaving her with no way to find out more. All she could find were threads and articles speculating about what could be happening.

Each theory she read was dumber than the last. There were posts claiming it was everything from the rapture to aliens. Becca let out a mirthless laugh. There was even one idiot repeatedly posting about the zombie apocalypse. Finally, she closed her browser and flopped back in her chair to stare at the ceiling whilst swiveling back and forth.

"Sit tight, my ass." Becca lowered her vision back to her display and started typing. "There has to be a drone pod somewhere near me."

Skyline had built up an impressive infrastructure all over the world. This included stations of ready-to-use drones in every major city; all she had to do was find one close enough to access. After searching her interface for a few minutes, she found a list of all of Skyline's remote addresses that were not currently in use. It was a list of thousands of GPS coordinates. Normally she would be assigned one, but there was technically nothing stopping her from logging in to any of them.

Becca checked her own GPS location and used it as a search parameter. With that she found a match. Actually, she found an exact match.

"There's a pod on this building?" She glanced up for a second before selecting the address. Obviously, the connection would be noticed, but she hoped she could at least find something out before Central Ops terminated it. She was sure to be yelled at, but she couldn't just sit there and play sudoku all night.

Drone pod connected.

Almost immediately, the green light next to her work

station's camera lit up. Her comm-line clicked on at the same time.

"What are you doing, Crow's Nest?"

Becca fumbled with her headset before giving the camera her most innocent smile. For a moment, she regretted the fact that she was still in her pajamas.

"I was attempting to launch a drone from the pod on the roof of my building." She decided to go with honesty.

"That isn't what was meant by 'sit tight.'"

"Yes, that's true. But I am a highly capable operator and my skills are going to waste." Becca looked straight into the camera. "I understand that we have a team inbound, but they aren't here yet. At the very least, I can help get a clear picture of what is happening out there. The more information we have, the safer our people are going to be when they land." She sat tall to present as much confidence as she could.

Several seconds of silence went by.

"Alright, that would actually help."

"Thank you." Becca let out a relieved sigh.

"Report back what you find in the text channel. You'll be contacted if anything important comes up. Just be prepared to dock your units and stand by when ordered to." The camera light went dark and the comm-line broke connection.

"That's more like it."

Becca ran her fingers across the keyboard and the whole screen went dark. The lighting of the room followed suit, blocking out the world around her other than the monitor. The sound of four propellers starting up was audible over her stereo headset. The noise faded to a near silent hum. The drone's HUD populated the screen, showing her battery life as well as a mini map of her location in her upper right corner.

She clicked to her armaments, finding her options empty. Apparently, the units on the roof weren't combat models. All she had was a few camera settings, facial recognition software, and optical camouflage. It was better than nothing.

Before reaching for the sticks mounted on the console, she

punched in the launch command into the keyboard. A warm glow spilled into the room from the wraparound monitor as the drone's lights bounced off the inside of its enclosed charging bay. Becca heard the familiar click of the pod's locking mechanism just before the lid popped open.

Seattle's cityscape filled her view.

"No sense hesitating."

Becca pushed forward on the stick, taking a look back as she climbed. The drone pod was round, like a UFO. The lid of the charging bay she had just launched from closed. There were five more bays around the pod's edge.

"Six lives," she noted, just in case she lost the unit she was controlling.

With a tap of the sticks, her view spun back around as she began her descent. She stopped to look into her apartment on her way down. Out of curiosity, she let the drone hover in place and peered over the monitor.

There it was, just floating outside the window.

It had been years since she'd seen a drone in person, not since training. It seemed smaller than she remembered, about the size of a sofa pillow. Its narrow body hung between four propellers, with two slender arms folded up underneath. Becca reached down to shut off the running lights and activated its optical camouflage. The drone shimmered for a second, then vanished as if it wasn't even there.

She looked down to watch herself on the monitor. Her black hair was tied back in a haphazard ponytail and she looked pale. The sight sent a chill down her spine as everything started to feel more real than normal. It began to make sense why Skyline never sent her on any local missions. There was something unnerving about being so close to the situation, even if she was safe in her apartment.

Becca took a deep breath and reached for the sticks as police lights flashed below.

"Here we go."

CHAPTER FIVE

"Not good!" Digby pushed past the roaming dead in the hall of whatever building he was in and hobbled his way up a flight of stairs. It was only a matter of time before someone showed up with the village guard to put an end to the curse before it spread further.

"I'm not about to be hunted down like a common zombie." He slowed, resting his hand on a railing to steady himself. "Actually, I'm not a common zombie."

That was right. He was a mage.

Digby tightened his grip on the rail. If he was captured, a much worse fate might befall him. An image of being burnt at the stake floated back to him, reinforcing the fear of what might happen to him if it was discovered that he was capable of witchcraft. Looking down at the tattered rags that he'd been wearing for the last eight hundred years, he realized he probably looked worse than the curse's more recent victims.

"I need to blend in better."

Digby crept up the stairs and pushed into the first unlocked room he found. The placard on the door read 'Restroom.' A row of strange booths filled one side of the tiled room, while several extravagant basins lined the other side.

He froze as soon as he saw a mirror hanging on one wall. The urge to run from his reflection surged through his body, begging his unsteady legs to get moving. Resisting the impulse to flee, Digby staggered forward until his deceased visage became clear. His unbeating heart sank.

"That's that, then." He pushed a lock of greasy white hair from his face. "I'm a corpse."

A pair of milky green eyes stared back at him. He touched the dark gray skin of his cheek. His face was gaunt, and his eye sockets were sunken deep into his skull. His collarbone and rib cage were visible under the skin that was stretched tight across his body.

He didn't even have a nose, just a hollow cavity in the middle of his face. It didn't hurt, but it wasn't pretty either. Digby lowered his head and leaned forward on the basin below the mirror. A sudden stream of water began flowing from a spout at its center.

"What's this?" Digby held his hand under the flow, letting the lukewarm water run through his fingers. It shut off just as suddenly.

"Huh?" He moved his hand about, unsure of what he had done to call the water forth. It flowed again when he held his hand under the basin's spout. He focused on the device, hoping Analyze would tell him more. It did, without taking several seconds to come up with an answer this time.

Sink: common, water source.

"Amazing. A lot must have improved while I've been gone." Somehow, water could be delivered indoors without even needing to pull it up from a well. Digby spent the next several seconds putting his hands under each of the basin's spouts to watch them activate. Getting carried away, he noticed a second smaller spout on each. This one released a small amount of white foam.

Soap: common, cleaning agent.

You could use a good scrubbing.

Digby wanted to back-talk the Heretic Seed, but it was probably right. He tried to smell himself but couldn't really tell if his odor was bad or not. It was like his senses were out of tune. He could still smell everything, but none of it really bothered him. Not that he had a nose to smell with anyway.

Trying his best to avoid looking at his reflection, Digby stripped off what remained of his clothes. He dropped his tunic to the floor, noticing a dark patch of blackish-green on his gray skin just over his heart. Veins spread out from it, reaching around his side. After examining the discolored area, he went on to remove his ancient boots. As he yanked his foot out of one, a scrap of folded fabric fell out, hitting the floor with an odd clink.

"What's this now?" Digby reached down and picked up the bit of cloth. It was stiff and crusty after eight hundred years of being stored in his boot. Unfolding it, he found a pair of black rings. Each simple band shined with a familiar obsidian gloss. He stared at the rings, feeling something in his mind shake loose as the Heretic Seed helped fill in the blanks.

Heretic Ring: rare, synchronizes the wearer with the Heretic Seed to assign a starting class.

Digby's fingers moved almost on their own, following the echo of his past. Raising his left hand, his eye fell to the line of runes that encircled his middle digit. He simply couldn't stop himself from slipping one of the bands down over his knuckle. The instant he did, a memory of his past came untangled. The room around him faded away to the dark stone walls of the castle where he'd been cursed.

Then, there was blood.

———

Trapped in his memory, Digby slapped a hand over the gaping bite wound on his wrist. It seemed like a good idea to hold his blood in. Behind him, the deceased inhabitants of the castle shambled closer, their pale eyes trained on him.

They smelled like death.

Digby ran, only looking back to throw his torch at the monsters, leaving him in the dim light of the moon that shined in through the windows.

At least they're slow. He picked up his pace, leaving the ghoulish creatures behind.

Why did I come here?

Alright, that wasn't a real question. The reason was obvious. He was bored. That was why. It had been a quiet night at the tavern when Henwick, one of the village hunters, rushed in with stories of witchcraft at Lord Axton's castle.

Digby had smirked at the claim. Despite his lack of belief, he'd followed along regardless. Henwick was well-liked, and the rest of the tavern had seemed to care about what he had to say. Torches and pitchforks had been handed out, and in the end, Digby hadn't argued. It wasn't every day he got to visit a lord's castle. With a little luck, he'd thought he might be able to liberate a nice coat or a bit of jewelry while no one was looking.

None of that mattered now. All the shiny things in the world wouldn't stop the bite wound on his wrist from bleeding. Thoughts of that moment flooded his mind.

How is this happening?

I'm not a fool.

I don't even believe in monsters!

Digby burst through the first door he came across. A candle flickered as he fell into what he assumed was Lord Axton's study. Scrolls littered the desk and tapestries hung on the walls. He scurried back to the door and bolted the lock. Then he waited, holding onto the hope that his pursuers would pass by. His heart sank when a steady pounding came from the door. He'd prayed for the lock to hold.

It did.

Oh, thank the Lord. Digby's attention returned to his arm. The creatures outside would have to wait. Within the memory, he was starting to feel faint and there was no way to know how much blood he'd lost.

Pressing harder on the wound, he had ransacked Lord Axton's desk. Scrolls and quills were thrown to the floor, but he found nothing that could dress his injured arm. In frustration, he shoved everything off the desk save for the lone candle.

An empty mug hit the floor along with a polished box of dark wood. The box lid fell open as it clattered across the stone. Digby ignored it and moved on to tear apart a nearby shelf. He didn't care what was inside it; he needed bandages.

That was when he noticed the trail of blood tracing his steps around the room.

"How…?" Digby remembered a cold numbness settling into his body. "How is there this much blood?" He'd tried to stand but fell over on his side, the castle growing dim around him.

This is it.

This is how I die… on the floor of a castle I shouldn't be in.

All because I wanted to steal a few trinkets.

Digby reached for the wooden box laying nearby, finding three rings tucked into a velvet pillow within. Delirious from the loss of blood, he plucked one up with his finger. It was just a simple band made of some sort of black glass. It was smooth to the touch. For a second, a spark flickered from within the material.

What was that?

At first, Digby had thought it had been his imagination, but as he held the ring, the flickering grew constant. A string of tiny glyphs had begun to streak across the ring's obsidian surface. One word had consumed his mind in that moment.

Witchcraft!

Digby had almost thrown the object away, but hesitated. Normally, sorcery wouldn't have been the first conclusion that he jumped to, but after being attacked by the creatures in the castle, well, witchcraft was the only explanation.

Digby stared at the ring, unsure what to do. It was clearly powerful; he could feel it pulsing in his hand. An implied offer of salvation willed him to put it on.

So he did.

Witchcraft or not, it was better than dying.

The obsidian ring had warmed his finger as soon as it was in place. Then it grew hot.

"Gah!" Digby flailed his hand in panic. The dark ring shrunk, tighter than any piece of jewelry should've ever been. It felt like it might sever his finger from his hand. His vision had begun to fade as the band sunk into his skin as if being absorbed by his body. A line of dark runes were left in its place.

The last thing he remembered was one word appearing in the air before him. Each letter translucent like a ghost.

SYNCHRONIZING

———

Digby opened his eyes, laying on the tile floor of the restroom after being released from his memory. He immediately looked for the ring he'd found in his boot. It was on his finger, right where he'd left it. Unlike the ring he'd found and put on back in the castle, this one didn't respond to being put on or held. He tried the second one to the same result.

"Perhaps they only work for someone that hasn't yet connected to the Heretic Seed." Digby thought it over. If that was the case, then the two rings he carried might be able to bestow magic on someone else. He let a grin creep across his face. That made the two obsidian bands quite valuable. "I bet someone would be willing to pay a king's ransom for power. Not to mention the Timeless passive ability that would come with it could stop them from aging. I might even be able to trade one of these things to someone in exchange for safety."

Digby wished he could remember more of what had happened in his past. Unfortunately, he seemed to have reached the limit of his recollection.

Maybe with some more intelligence, I might be able to remember more. He wondered, thinking back to what the Heretic Seed had said about intelligence being linked to memory and the processing of information. He would have to look into that later, but first, he needed to wash up.

Digby stood up and placed the two rings on top of an over-sized rubbish bucket for safekeeping before getting to work. It took a bit of time to bathe with the waterspouts on the basins turning off every ten seconds, but he made do. If he was going to pass for human, he at least needed to smell like he hadn't died nearly a millennia ago.

He soaked a sheet of paper that hung from a box mounted on the wall and scrubbed until his skin turned from a dingy gray to a somewhat cleaner gray. The paper sheet he used fell apart, but the box on the wall spat out another each time he tore one off. He threw them to the floor when they were no longer usable, then he washed his hair to remove the grease.

Finally, he looked down at his body. It was still a malnourished sack of skin and bones, but at least it was a clean malnourished sack of skin and bones. He took a long sniff, catching an earthy aroma.

"Not quite as fresh as a spring rain, but it's better than centuries of rot." Digby poked at his discarded rags with one foot and grimaced. "I probably need clothes now, don't I? Can't very well walk around with my knickknack out for the world to see."

Returning to the restroom door, he poked his head out,

finding another zombie wandering by. It wore a simple but well-tailored coat and pants that looked rather striking.

Unfortunately, the fronts of its garments were covered in blood. Apparently, the creature had eaten recently. Digby winced as a hungry ache from within reminded him that he was in the same boat.

A second, less fashionable zombie passed by. It had on some sort of a short robe with a hood and a pair of pants. Style aside, the clothes were at least clean, save for a red stain at the cuff of one pant leg. Digby gestured to the zombie.

"Hey."

To his surprise the unfashionable zombie turned.

"Yeah, you." Digby beckoned with one hand. "Come here."

For a moment, the zombie seemed to continue on its previous path, but then it turned back and came toward the door. Digby wasn't sure if it was obeying him or just happened to walk closer by coincidence. He reached out and grabbed the zombie by the sleeve to pull it into the restroom.

"I apologize for this, but I'm going to need your clothes." He promptly pulled the robe over its head as well as the shirt underneath, analyzing each as he did.

Zip-up hoodie: common.
T-shirt: common.

"Better than nothing." Digby tossed them across a sink and got to work on the zombie's boots. They were well-worn and looked to be the right size. He marveled at the soles, unable to recognize the material they were made from.

Hiking boots: common.
Tube socks: common.

"That's better." He tossed the boots aside and went for the pants, trying his best to ignore how awkward it was. "Can't say

I've ever stolen another man's pants while they were wearing them."

Now that he'd remembered a bit more from his past, it was clear that thievery came naturally to him. That must have been why he'd tucked the two rings into his boot. He must have come to the same conclusion about their value back then when he'd woken up after synchronizing with the Heretic Seed's system. He shook off the thought and continued with the robbery.

Jeans: common.
Briefs: common.

"Well, I thank you for your generosity, but if you don't mind." Digby opened the door and pushed the naked zombie back out into the hall. "I may not remember much, but that was probably the easiest theft I've ever committed."

Digby donned his new outfit, taking a bit of time to figure out how to work the fasteners. Fortunately, he had some clue after seeing how the zombie he'd stolen the garments from had worn them. The closure on the pants was the hardest part, requiring him to pull up on some sort of metal tab. He simply lacked the dexterity to make proper use of it without his fingers slipping.

Eventually, he gave up and left it open. The button at his waist seemed sufficient to hold the pants up, anyway. They were tight but comfortable once he had them on. Stepping in front of the mirror, he took in his new outfit. The words 'Seattle University' ran across his new shirt beneath the short robe that his Analyze ability had called a hoodie.

"Not a bad haul." He smiled back at his reflection, showing a mouthful of blackened teeth. If the mirror had cracked, it wouldn't have surprised him. Digby sighed and pulled up his hood, letting his shaggy white hair hang down to hide his face a little. He retrieved the two heretic rings from atop the rubbish bin and slipped them into one of his boots. The hiding place had worked well enough for the last eight hundred years, why change it now?

Suddenly, an empty feeling rumbled through his body, reminding him how hungry he was. Somehow, he could feel that there was more to be eaten out in the world. He couldn't help but wonder how he still had room in his stomach after eating nearly two whole bodies. The Heretic Seed chimed in with a message to answer his question.

RACIAL TRAIT
VOID: A bottomless, weightless, dimensional space that exists within the core of a zombie's mana system. This space can be accessed through its carrier's stomach and will expand to fit whatever contents are consumed.

Better get used to being hungry.

"That answers that, I suppose." Digby sighed at the realization that he may never feel full unless he devoured everyone and everything he encountered. The idea of eating anyone else didn't sit right. The two people downstairs had been an accident that he didn't care to repeat. He wasn't a monster, no matter what he looked like.

With nothing left to wash, he exited the restroom and walked past the naked zombie he'd stripped as he continued down the hall.

"Be seeing you."

CHAPTER SIX

Alright, you can do this.

Digby adjusted his pace to keep his gait as human as possible as he traveled down the hall of the unknown building that he'd woken up in. He slowed, realizing that the faster he moved, the more his lack of strength and agility revealed what he was.

Just stay focused and keep moving.

Eventually, the hallway let out to a room somehow even larger than the one he'd been in back downstairs. Three layers of walkways wrapped around the walls like extravagant balconies. Glass lined the floors as if forming a barrier to stop people from falling over the edge. Massive windows covered the front of the room with a set of three doors at the bottom.

Unlike the hall where he'd come from, only a few of the glowing tubes set into the ceiling were lit up. Beyond a few posts that held some sort of lantern, the area outside was dark as well. Strangely, the windows almost seemed to dim what little light there was, as if the glass itself was tinted in some way.

Letters ran along one wall, labeling the room he stood in as the Seattle Institute of Science and Technology, Public Exhibits.

A skeleton of a massive fish hung from the ceiling like a decoration.

Digby's mouth fell open for an instant before he snapped it shut. The future was bound to be full of surprises. He didn't know what sort of people would hang such a large skeleton as a decoration; but it wouldn't do for him to give himself away by acting like it was the first time he'd seen something like it.

That was when a frantic cry came from the other side of the room, where another hallway stretched off into the shadows. A moment later, a woman burst into the space, her heels clicking across the floor as she ran. There was a red axe in her hands.

She was alive.

The urge to give chase pushed Digby forward for an instant before he shoved the need back down. A second impulse to help the woman echoed through the human side of his mind. Again, he held back and ducked behind a case displaying a miniature scene of snow and water. There was a pair of zombies after her already.

The woman climbed over a circular desk labeled 'Information,' and started swinging. The red axe slammed into the first of her pursuers. Digby raised his eyebrows, impressed. She was doing better than he had back when he'd been in her shoes. That was when she noticed him peeking out from behind the display case.

"Don't just hide there, help me!"

Digby ducked back into hiding. He wasn't in any condition to fight and there wasn't anything he could do.

...or was there?

He'd absorbed enough mana to get back to full while he was washing up earlier, and his Cremation spell could set alight the flesh of the dead. He Analyzed his target.

Zombie: common, friendly.

Digby arched an eyebrow at that last word. It seemed that,

as one of their own, the creatures wouldn't fight back, though that might change if he attacked them first.

The woman sunk her axe into the head of the other zombie, reminding him what the living might do to him if he was to reveal himself. Not to mention that casting spells in front of a human would surely get him burned at the stake. He Analyzed her too.

Human: common, neutral.

Three more enemies shambled toward her from the shadowed hallway at the other end of the room. There was a limit to how long she could keep up the fight. With that, Digby stood, hoping that if he saved her, she might help him in return, if only to repay a debt.

"Get down!"

He focused on the group, being careful not to target his own hands like last time. Power flowed through him as his mana dropped.

MP: 78/93

A greenish glow shimmered over one of the zombies. Then, nothing happened.

"What?"

Cremation resisted.

He tried again.

Cremation resisted.

By all means keep trying, you might wear them down.

"Shut up." Digby ignored the Heretic Seed's taunt and did exactly that, casting the spell a third time. Finally, success; the zombie in the back ignited in green fire. The repeated casting must have weakened whatever resistance the zombie had. He'd have to look into the cause later.

"The hell was that?" The woman slammed her axe into another enemy as the Cremated zombie collapsed to the floor.

1 common zombie defeated, 30 experience awarded.

Digby checked his mana, finding forty-eight points left, just enough to take down the last zombie, assuming their resistance was the same as the first. He raised his hand toward his target, but before he could cast the spell, a sound like stampeding cattle came from the floor above.

The woman let out a scream that echoed through the room as a hulking form slammed through the glass barrier that lined the walkway. Shimmering fragments showered to the ground just before the creature landed on its prey with a meaty crunch. The woman's head cracked against the desk and snapped to one side.

Digby fell back in shock.

The mass of muscle that had leaped from the floor above could have been human, except for the fact that it was nearly twice his size. Even its clothing had split as if unable to contain the beast. The remnants of a shirt and pants hung in tatters.

Zombie Brute: uncommon, neutral.

The brute clutched the woman's body as it turned toward Digby and roared. A wave of intimidation penetrated deep into the core of his being. The beast hadn't formed any words but somehow its meaning was clear.

Mine.

Digby inched away from the monster until his back met a wall. The neutral relationship attached to the beast meant that he wasn't in danger, as long as he didn't do anything stupid like attack or get between the brute and its meal.

"How did a zombie get like that?"
The heretic ring answered the question.

RACIAL TRAIT
MUTATION: Alter your form or attributes by consuming resources of the living or recently deceased. Required resources are broken down into 6 types: Flesh, Bone, Sinew, Viscera, Mind, and Heart. Mutation path is determined by what resources a zombie consumes.

Happy hunting.

"Does that mean I'll get stronger if I eat?" Digby willed the heretic ring to show him his status again and focused on the line that read Mutation Path. The information ring flipped to show him a new list.

AVAILABLE PATHS AND MUTATION:
PATH OF THE LURKER
Move in silence and strike with precision.

SILENT MOVEMENT
Description: Removes excess weight and improves balance.
Resource Requirements: 2 sinew, 1 bone
Attribute Effects: +6 agility, +2 dexterity, -1 strength, +1 will
BONE CLAWS
Description: Craft claws from consumed bone on one hand.
Description: .25 sinew, .25 bone
Attribute Effects: +4 dexterity, +1 defense, +1 strength

PATH OF THE BRUTE
Hit hard and stand your ground.

INCREASE MASS
Description: Dramatically increase muscle mass.
Resource Requirements: 15 flesh, 3 bone
Attribute Effects: +30 strength, +20 defense, -10 intelligence, -7 agility, -7 dexterity, +1 will

BONE ARMOR
Description: Craft armor plating from consumed bone.
Resource Requirements: 5 bone
Attribute Effects: +5 defense, +1 will

PATH OF THE GLUTTON
Trap and swallow your prey whole.

MAW
Description: Open a gateway directly to the dimensional space of your void to devour prey faster.
Resource Requirements: 10 viscera, 1 bone
Attribute Effects: +2 perception, +1 will

JAWBONE
Description: Craft a trap from consumed bone within the opening of your maw that can bite and pull prey in.
Resource Requirements: 2 bone, 1 sinew
Attribute Effects: +2 perception, +1 will

PATH OF THE LEADER
Control the horde and conquer the living.

COMPEL ZOMBIE
Description: Temporarily coerce one or more common zombies to obey your intent. Limited by target's intelligence.
Resource Requirements: 5 mind, 5 heart
Attribute Effects: +2 intelligence, +2 perception, +1 will

RECALL MEMORY
Description: Access a portion of your living memories.
Resource Requirements: 30 mind, 40 heart

Attribute Effects: +5 intelligence, +5 perception, +1 will
Units of requirement values are equal to the quantity of
resources contained by the average human body.

Digby's jaw fell open at that last line. If he understood everything, most of the mutations required the consumption of one or more people. This meant that if the requirement was one bone, he would have to either eat an entire skeleton or enough bones from multiple people to account for the same quantity.

The only mutation that required less than a whole body's worth of any one resource was the Bone Claws listed under the Path of the Lurker. Though, he was pretty sure he didn't want to alter either of his hands permanently. Digby looked up at the zombie brute that was currently ignoring him.

That must be the Increase Mass mutation.

A shiver crawled across his skin. That would mean that the brute had already eaten at least fifteen people. It was another fact that reinforced Digby's theory that he had been sitting downstairs doing nothing for several hours before becoming aware of what was happening around him. That was the only explanation for how a zombie could have eaten that many people already. Even then, fifteen bodies was a lot to eat. The monster must have gorged itself the entire time.

Looking over the other mutations, Digby gained a new appreciation for the Heretic Seed. Without it, he would have lost all semblance of who he was, and from what the Path of the Leader said, the price to regain his memories was steep. Recall Memory was the most demanding mutation of the bunch. Forty hearts and thirty minds would be hard to come by without going on a murder spree.

Reading further, Compel Zombie seemed like the most useful and economical option. The ability to coerce other zombies would help if the curse had spread beyond whatever city he'd woke up in. Not to mention he was still lacking in the intelligence department, and an extra two points would go a long way.

The Heretic Seed showed him a new circle of information as he wondered what sort of resources were already in his void.

AVAILABLE RESOURCES
Sinew: .5
Flesh: 1
Bone: .2
Viscera: 1
Heart: 2
Mind: 2

Digby cringed at the knowledge of what he'd eaten. It had been easy to pretend like it hadn't happened, as if it had been someone else down there in that room. Seeing the list though, well, that was undeniable.

Digby searched his information for any other racial traits that he might have gained by becoming a zombie. There was always the chance that he'd missed something useful. A moment later, he found them. He was already familiar with his Mutation and Ravenous traits, but there were three more in the list that he hadn't seen yet.

BLOOD SENSE
Allows a zombie to sense blood in their surroundings to aid in the tracking of prey. Potency of this trait increases with perception.
GUIDED MUTATION
Due to an unusually high intelligence for an undead crea-ture, you are capable of mutating at will rather than mutating when required resources are consumed. This allows you to choose mutations from multiple paths instead of following just one.
RESIST
A remnant from a zombie's human life, this common trait

grants +5 points to will. Normally exclusive to conscious beings, this trait allows a zombie to resist basic spells that directly target their body or mind until their will is overpowered.

That explains why my Cremation spell took a few tries to stick.

Apparently, a spell could be resisted if his target possessed enough will to stop his mana from affecting their body or mind. Digby frowned, realizing the limitations of his spell. In comparison, Fireball had been far superior since it only created a throwable projectile, making it more of an indirect attack.

Cremation, on the other hand, needed to ignite necrotic flesh directly, making it near useless without squandering his mana to cast it multiple times to wear a target's resistance down. That was, unless his target was an inanimate corpse, or himself.

He sighed. There was no sense worrying about it now. Not while the brute was still eating in front of him. Digby couldn't help but notice blood dripping down the information desk. It swam through his senses like the song of a siren.

Too bad, it doesn't look like that brute is willing to share its prey. Digby recoiled at the thought, remembering that the prey in question had been a woman fighting for her life just a moment before.

"What the hell is wrong with me?" He pressed a hand to his forehead. "I'm not like them. I'm not a monster."

The brute roared at another zombie that had been drawn by the fresh blood on the floor. It shrank away in submission, passing by the scene and approaching Digby on the other side of the room.

He decided that was his cue to leave.

Pushing his weakened body up, Digby crept up a nearby stairway to avoid the brute. On the second floor, he headed down a hallway that read 'Climate Studies Exhibits.' The further he could get from that brute, the better.

A noise from behind him told him he wasn't alone. The

submissive zombie from below was following him. Digby Analyzed it to make sure it wasn't dangerous.

Zombie: common, friendly.

"Didn't want to pal around with that brute either, huh?"

Obviously, the zombie didn't answer.

"Well, you can't follow me." Digby hastened his pace, trying to lose the creature while looking a bit more like an uncoordinated corpse the faster he walked. "All I need is for someone to see us together and get the wrong idea. I'll be thrown on the pyre for sure."

The walking corpse ignored his complaint.

"That Compel Zombie mutation would really come in handy right about now." Digby stopped and turned to his unwanted companion. "Look here, if you don't stop following me, I'm going to cremate your head. At least that way I can get some experience."

The zombie only moved closer.

Digby groaned in frustration and focused on the harmless monster. That was when he felt something strange coming from his target. The zombie stopped beside him, somehow radiating waves of… not thoughts, but something else.

Even stranger, Digby understood what it meant.

Teeth.

Not tooth, but specifically teeth, as in plural. As in, the many.

Strangely, the meaning was clear to him. The zombie wished to remain together, because together, they were strong. A tooth alone couldn't bite much, but teeth, well, teeth could devour the world. Digby couldn't argue with the logic. There was safety in numbers. Maybe he'd been thinking of things the wrong way.

Digby turned away from the zombie and continued toward the climate exhibits. A second zombie entered the hall further down, only to turn to Digby and his new companion. It let out a hollow moan as a wave of intent hit him far stronger than the desires of the zombie beside him.

Teeth.

The thought was simplistic, but Digby found himself walking forward without meaning to. It was almost as if he couldn't stop. After a few steps he planted his feet and held his ground. A quick Analyze explained what had happened.

Zombie Leader: uncommon, friendly.

Maybe this one is smarter than you.

Digby doubted that was the case, but still, the Path of the Leader was powerful. The zombie at his side left him behind to obey the leader's intent.

That must be the Compel mutation. I have to be careful, it almost worked on me.

That was when Digby remembered that, unlike the brute he'd run into a moment before, the leader was listed as friendly. It made sense; a leader needed the cooperation of other zombies to survive.

Maybe it would behoove me to go with the flow here.

Digby started walking again, following the other zombies toward a room at the end of the hall. The leader stopped like he was waiting for him. As Digby approached, he noticed a silver crest emblazoned on the zombie's chest. The word security was written across the top in an arc. Just beneath that was a tag with the name, Carl, written on it.

"Well hello, Carl. Been eating some brains have you?"

Carl didn't answer. Instead, he gestured toward the room at the end. Digby shrugged and continued.

He wasn't even halfway there when he sensed the blood.

CHAPTER SEVEN

Digby froze the instant he followed Carl, the zombie leader, into the climate studies exhibit. His feet threatened to carry him forward against his will as the void inside him howled to be filled.

There was so much blood.

Bodies were piled at the center of the room beneath an enormous stuffed bear standing on its hind legs. Red spatters marred the white fur of the taxidermy beast. A dozen common zombies congregated around the bear's feet where the corpses were. It was a feast fit for a king.

Carl, the zombie leader, must have organized the small horde to take down the group that now laid dead on the floor. Now he was trying to grow his pack and make them stronger.

Digby wondered why the bodies hadn't reanimated like the others. Perhaps the curse didn't affect everyone at the same rate. Thinking about it, he figured it had something to do with their constitution values, since the attribute's description mentioned something about falling ill. Maybe the curse took longer to take hold in healthier individuals.

Shaking off the thought, Digby couldn't help but be

impressed by Carl's leadership. With only a couple points of intelligence, the zombie leader had accomplished a lot. In spite of that, every ounce of reason Digby had told him that he should be sickened by the sight. Of course, that raised the question, why wasn't he? Somehow it didn't feel wrong at all. Actually, it was pretty damn appealing, and there was plenty to go around.

Digby considered his situation. As strange as it was, he really couldn't pass up an easy meal. If he allowed himself to starve, he might fall back into his ravenous state, and that could be dangerous. He could hurt himself or someone else.

If anything, eating was the responsible thing to do. After all, it wasn't like he had killed any of the people in the pile. Other than those first two downstairs, he was innocent. Besides, that had been caused by the curse. Nothing he'd done so far was actually his fault.

At least, that was what he told himself as he moved closer.

Just forget they used to be people and pretend the bodies are something else. Digby did his best to convince himself that he wasn't a monster as his instincts took over. Before long, he was having a pleasant meal with some new zombie friends. They didn't have the best table manners but there wasn't a table in the room, so that didn't seem so important.

Digby tried his best to keep his stolen clothes clean, crouching on his feet so that his knees stayed off the floor. It wouldn't do to kneel in the blood like the others did.

His list of available mutations hung in the back of his mind to remind him what resources he needed most. Again he gave thanks to the fact that he'd put his additional points into intelligence. If he hadn't, he wouldn't have accessed the guided mutation trait that gave him more control over his options.

With it, he could pick and choose which mutations to take. Thinking it over, his priority was obvious. He'd already witnessed how powerful the Compel Zombie mutation was, not to mention it came with two points of intelligence. That would bring him up to where he had been before he'd died.

There was also the Silent Movement mutation. That one could give him back his agility. Maybe then he could walk or run normally without falling down. Granted, that would also lower his strength a bit, and he was already lacking in that department as it was. The rest of his mutations were out of the question. They either had ridiculously high resource requirements, or would alter his physical appearance too much to blend in with normal people.

Compel it is, then.

Of course, that would require him to get his hands on some hearts and minds. With the rest of the group grabbing at whatever they could, he didn't see how he could do that without being more aggressive. Not to mention he didn't know how to get through a human skull to begin with.

Digby looked to Carl, hoping he might give him a clue. Unfortunately, the zombie leader seemed content to grab what he could with the others for the time being.

There has to be a way.

Checking the contents of his void, Digby found that he must have figured out how to open a skull before because he had already eaten two minds while he'd been downstairs.

Maybe I just crack them on the floor?

A few minutes of trying went by with mixed results, gaining him two more brains to leave him short one. Digby looked around the room hoping to find something that might function as a tool.

There were numerous pictures on the walls and a few glass boxes housing various miniature landscapes, none of which looked like something he could use to crack a skull.

That was when he noticed something strange above him.

The hell is that?

A large blue ball hung from the ceiling. Blotches of green, brown, and white were scattered around the object in a way that made it look like someone had wrapped a map around its surface. It was even textured in some places to suggest mountains. It was strange, for sure, but what had drawn his attention was the human foot peeking out from the top.

There's someone hiding up there. Digby's eyes widened. *Oh god, there's someone hiding up there!*

A slow trickle of crimson streaked down the sphere's side. Whoever it was must have been hurt. Digby glanced at the zombies around him. None of them had sensed the blood, probably because there was already so much on the floor to hold their focus. It was only a matter of time before they caught on.

Digby stood up and walked a few feet away to get a better angle. Not wanting to frighten the poor bastard, he peeked over his shoulder to spot a young man clinging to a metallic rope that held the sphere to the ceiling. He couldn't have been more than nineteen or twenty.

Shame, there was no way the boy would make it down alive. Not with the feast going on below him. This brought up the question, what could Digby do about it? He shrugged. Nothing, really. All he could do was hope the unfortunate soul would be granted a swift death. That was when a voice echoed through his memory, hitting him hard like a slap to the face.

What is wrong with you, man!

Digby flinched. He recognized the voice as Henwick's, the hunter that had roused him and the rest of the tavern back home to attack the castle. He scowled. A part of him had always resented the man for his unabashed heroism. Digby reached for the threads of memory, hoping to trigger another immersive flash of information like before. This time, they simply slipped away from him, to drift back into the fog. Digby clenched his fists in frustration, cursing his useless mind. He must have reached the limit of what he could recall.

With a few more points of intelligence, I might be able to extend my reach.

Of course, even if he remembered more, he still couldn't do anything about the poor wretch clinging to the sphere above him. It wasn't like he could somehow convince the growing horde below to simply move along and let the boy go.

Or could I?

If he could compel them to leave, they might cooperate. Digby spun back to the meal on the floor. It seemed that claiming the Compel mutation could kill two birds with one stone.

But first, I need to get that last skull open.

More importantly, how many hearts were left? Digby stumbled his way back to the pile and gave up on keeping himself clean. He needed to be first in line. The other zombies let him through, still eating whatever was within their reach.

Come on, come on. Digby dug deep for a heart, realizing they must have been one of the first parts to go since they were easier to get at than others. He slipped and struggled but was able to find two. Shoving his prizes into the pockets of his stolen hoodie, he scrambled for one more.

Damn it.

There wasn't any left. The scraps were all starting to blend together into an unrecognizable mess of gore. That was when he saw one zombie at the edge clutching what he coveted.

"Mine!" Digby lunged forward, snatching the heart from the creature's hands. The zombie reached out to take it back, but Digby kicked it away as he squirmed around on his back.

"It's mine, not yours." Out of some juvenile impulse he licked the heart. "There, now you won't want it."

The zombie did, in fact, still want it. With no other option, he ate the heart right then and there whilst holding his rival back with one foot. It gave up and went back to the pile to look for another.

"Good luck, I've already picked it clean," Digby gloated as he devoured the two hearts he'd stuffed in his pockets. That was when he caught the eye of the boy hiding above as he peeked over the side of the hanging orb. No doubt he was curious about the fact that there was a talking zombie.

Digby could have said something to reassure the young

man, but he feared communicating with him might draw too much attention if the boy responded. Obviously, that would be stupid, but in all honesty, he had no idea how smart the tasty morsel up there was. The fact was, if the zombies noticed him, they wouldn't leave until he was dead. Digby decided to ignore him for the time being and seek out another brain.

One more to go.

Thanks to the difficulty of getting through the bony shell, there were still plenty left. After a couple more minutes of smashing things on the floor, Digby had what he needed. The heretic ring immediately responded.

GUIDED MUTATION
Requirements for the leader's mutation, Compel Zombie, have been met.
Accept? Yes/No

"Hell yes!"

As soon as the words left his mouth a wave of sensation crawled through his necrotic gray matter. Digby clutched his head as everything blurred. After a moment of writhing in the pool of blood on the floor, clarity cut through the fog that had clouded his judgement since he'd woken up.

Mutation, Compel Zombie, active. You may now coerce one or more zombies into following your intent. Limited by target's intelligence.

Try not to confuse them.

Intelligence increased to 18.
Perception increased to 10.
Will increased to 14.
Total Mana increased to 106.

"Finally."

Digby reveled in the knowledge that he was now just as smart as he'd been when he was alive. He let his thoughts wash over him, enjoying the ease in which they flowed. Of course, he soon realized that he might not have actually had much going on in his head when he was alive either.

Perhaps my original values were not that high in comparison to others. Eighteen intelligence seemed like a lot, but without a benchmark to weigh it against, then there was really no way to be sure. He might have been the village idiot, for all he knew.

Digby shook off the thought and refocused on the situation at hand. That boy was still trapped above. He made a point of checking his mana before doing anything rash.

MP: 93/106

He had absorbed some while he'd been eating, but with the added points in intelligence, perception, and will that his recent mutation granted, his maximum mana had increased, leaving him below full. Considering how fast he burned through his magic, it seemed prudent to wait for it to replenish. Since waking up, the rate varied, but for the most part he'd gained around ten points of mana every minute, as long as he didn't cast anything to cause a delay.

Wasn't there a way to speed things up? Digby willed the Heretic Seed to show him the details of his absorption.

MANA ABSORPTION
Ambient mana will be absorbed whenever MANA POINTS are below maximum MP values. Rate of absorption may vary depending on ambient mana concentration and essence composition. Absorption may be increased through meditation and rest.

Rest is out of the question. I'm pretty sure I don't sleep anymore, but what's this about meditation? From what he could remember, it was clear to Digby that he'd not been one for quiet reflection in his life. Meditation wasn't common back in England eight hundred years ago, after all. Nevertheless, he closed his eyes and held still, hoping to see an impact. He remained like that for ten seconds before growing impatient.

Damn… He had only gained two points. *Well, I guess that will take some more practice, then.* Giving up, Digby waited a couple minutes for his absorption to do its job before pushing himself back up. With that, he turned to the rest of the zombies in the room and clapped his hands together.

"Alright now…"

Every zombie in the room looked in his direction as Digby realized that he didn't know what to tell them.

"Umm, as you were."

It was obvious that he needed them to leave, but he wasn't sure how much they could understand. Would the Compel ability translate his meaning or would he have to dumb his commands down? Not to mention he had to think of a good reason for them to leave their meal behind. Would they even listen?

There was only one way to find out.

"Everyone," he tried again, "there is a brute zombie just down the hall from us. Now, I don't know if any of you have met one of these oversized beasts, but they don't exactly share their food and it's only a matter of time before it senses the blood in here. I suggest, nay, I insist that we move to a safer locale."

Confused moans echoed all around.

He definitely had their attention, but they apparently weren't getting his intent. Even Carl seemed lost. The only word that had gotten a reaction was brute. Digby let out a breathless sigh before dumbing his command down.

"Brute close, teeth follow."

To his surprise, the group stood. Sure, most of them were still eating whatever they were holding, but it was a start.

"Yes, yes, take that with you." Digby grabbed a scrap as well without really intending to. "Come along now."

The hungry group clustered up behind him. Even Carl joined him. Digby wasn't sure if his Compel had worked on the zombie leader or if they were just responding to the threat of a brute being in the vicinity. Either way, Digby appreciated the zombie leader's willingness to work together. From there, as Digby began to move, so did the rest of the horde.

I could get used to this.

Digby couldn't help but feel powerful with the group of zombies obeying him so easily. No one had ever followed him back when he'd been alive. He continued to direct the group away from the climate studies exhibit. Hopefully the boy hiding back there could get to safety.

Maybe I should lose my new friends here and circle back to make sure he gets away.

It seemed like the prudent thing to do. The boy might even be useful. At the very least, he might know something about the world Digby had woken up in.

"This should be far enough." He reached a flight of stairs further down the hall and pointed. "Go." The horde seemed to get his meaning, heading down the steps without him. "Keep 'em safe, Carl." Digby patted the group's original leader on the shoulder as it passed by, then he made his way back to the previous room.

Creeping back in through the door, he looked up to the boy on the hanging sphere. He was right where Digby had left him, apparently too scared to come down.

"Hello there." He waved in an attempt to break the ice.

The boy huddled closer to the metallic rope that held the structure up.

"Oh, come now, is that anyway to greet the one who just saved your life?" Digby made a point to declare a reason for a debt. A little guilt could go a long way to get what he wanted.

"You're one of them." The boy spoke without peeking down.

"No, I'm smarter than them." Digby beckoned to him. "Now, why don't you come down from there?"

"Hell no, you just want to eat me." His eyes darted around the room as if looking for an escape route.

"No, I don't." Digby hesitated, wondering for a second if he did want to eat the boy. He shook off the impulse. "I led all those zombies away so that you could get down from there."

"No, you just don't want to share when you kill me."

"I hardly think—"

"I saw you eating with the rest of them." The boy jabbed a finger at the mound of food below him. "You shouted, 'Mine,' and ate someone's heart. Then you bragged about it."

I did do that, didn't I? Digby lowered his head. "Alright, yes, I did eat a couple hearts. But that was only so that I could help you. I needed to eat enough to make the other zombies listen to me. That's how things work. You eat hearts and minds to win over hearts and minds."

The boy scoffed. "Yeah right, like I'm going to believe that. That's probably why you can talk, you ate enough brains to learn to speak."

"Now you listen here, you ass," Digby thrust a dead finger in his direction, "I was talking before you were born."

"I liked it better when zombies couldn't talk," he snapped back.

"Alright, alright." Digby rubbed at the bridge of what was left of his nose. "Clearly we have gotten off on the wrong foot here."

"You think?"

"What's your name?" Digby looked up at the boy, giving his most sincere expression.

"It's Asher."

"What kind of a name is that?"

"This is Seattle, my parents are hipsters."

"What the hell is a—" Digby stopped himself. "Wait, no, sorry. It's been a long night so far." He shook his head. "My name is Digby."

"What kind of a name is that?"

"A better one than yours," Digby growled up at the boy, forgetting about his apology from literally seconds before.

"It sounds like something out of Oliver Twist."

"I don't know who that is——"

Before Digby could say something snarky, Asher lost his grip and fell. The boy landed in the mound of gore with an audible squelch. He immediately scampered backward into the feet of the stuffed bear looming over him. With nowhere to run, he stared up in panic like Digby might pounce at any second.

The poor wretch looked terrible. His skin had a sickly pallor and he was drenched in sweat from head to toe. One of his sleeves had been torn off and tied around his wrist. Blood stained the fabric of his bandage.

"Are you okay?" Digby made his best effort to show concern without approaching the boy. "You look worse than me."

"I just felt a little weak all of a sudden."

"Then it's a good thing that someone cleared the zombies out of the room earlier, isn't it?" Digby gave him a smug grin.

"Are you seriously not going to eat me?" Asher took a short breath.

"Lord no, I'm not a monster." Digby folded his arms. "If you were already dead, I might have a bite, but not if you're still breathing."

"Okay. Good." Asher staggered back to his feet. "That's…" He trailed off mid-sentence. Then he threw up.

"Gross…" Digby waited for him to finish.

"Sorry, like I said, I haven't been feeling well." It had probably taken everything the kid had to keep himself together up until now.

"Were you bit?" Digby gestured to the bloody bandage around the kid's arm.

"Yeah." Asher deflated. "I'm an intern here, and these things just came up out of the labs downstairs. Everyone panicked. It spread so fast. I was bit about an hour ago, and I've been feeling worse and worse ever since." He let out a mirthless laugh. "I'm probably not going to survive the night."

"Maybe, maybe not." Digby tried to encourage the boy.

It occurred to him that offering Asher one of the two heretic rings he carried in his boot might help with whatever curse was surely working through his body. It wouldn't remove it, but the ring would at least allow him to regain his mind after he turned.

Digby shook his head, remembering that he had passed out for an unknown length of time after synchronizing with the Heretic Seed. If he gave Asher a ring here where the boy was vulnerable, he would simply end up as food before he had a chance to wake up. Not to mention the rings were valuable, and he wasn't sure he wanted to give one up so easily. He decided to give some positive words instead.

"I didn't turn into this until I died." Digby gestured to his corpse. "So if you can stay alive, you might live long enough to break the curse."

"Curse?" Asher arched an eyebrow.

Before either of them had a chance to elaborate, a loud groan came from the hall just outside, too loud to be a common zombie. Digby cringed as the lie that he'd told Carl and the rest of the horde came back to haunt him.

A meaty hand gripped the side of the doorway.

The brute downstairs had indeed sensed the blood.

Digby let out a breathless sigh.

"I really am cursed, aren't I?"

CHAPTER EIGHT

"How is this even possible?" Becca watched in horror as the dead milled about in Denny Park while her drone hovered just above the small area of trees nestled into the city.

It had all happened so fast.

According to the few reports she could find, the first incidents had happened around two in the afternoon, just before she had gone to bed. In the eight hours that followed, the outbreak had surged throughout the city like wildfire.

All it took was a bite.

Now, other than a few last vestiges of humanity fighting here and there, the zombies had taken over. Becca did her best to forget that she was locked in an apartment smack dab in the middle of it all, waiting for Skyline's troops to land and secure things.

Not that there was much left to secure.

At this point, the only thing her employers could do was investigate what happened and figure out how best to stop it from spreading beyond the city.

She hoped there were other survivors trapped inside the buildings like her, but it was hard to tell. Anyone with half a brain would be trying their best to stay hidden. This left nothing but darkened windows in all directions.

Even the stores and businesses had all gone dormant, with most of their interior lighting switching to nighttime settings. Other than the streetlights outside, the shadows were there to stay. It was hard to believe how dead the city had become.

That was when a voice came over her headset.

"Phoenix to Crow's Nest—"

"Yar!" Becca jumped out of her seat at the sudden interruption. Her headset clattered to her console in front of her. The view in the massive wraparound monitor shifted violently to one side, forcing her to stabilize her drone before picking up her comms. Once she was back in control, she shoved her headset back on.

"This is Crow's Nest, sorry. Go ahead, Phoenix."

"Oh good, for a second there, we thought the zeds got to you." The voice on the other end was masculine and sounded surprisingly friendly.

"No, no… I just dropped my headset. I'm a little on edge." Becca froze. "Wait, I thought the zombies couldn't get to me."

"Being on edge is understandable, you're probably not used to being this close to the action. Sorry for the zed comment, it was a joke. Nothing can get to you until your apartment's lockdown is disabled. You're the safest person in Seattle right now."

"That's… good."

"I'm Communications Specialist Easton. I'll be your primary contact with Phoenix Company. We've been assigned to the situation and will be here until it's resolved. I report directly to Captain Manning, and will pass on any information you have."

"I'm sorry, I haven't worked with Phoenix Company before." Becca searched her memory for any mention of the name. She came up blank.

"I should hope not. Our operations are usually classified. According to your file, you've only been running drones a few years for basic missions overseas. We usually work with more experienced operators. Nothing personal."

"But you're making an exception because I'm already here flying around," Becca added, hoping Easton wouldn't immediately order her to dock her unit and sit tight.

"That sums it up. Welcome to the big leagues." Easton clicked off the mic for a few seconds before returning. "Anyway, we just landed a few birds outside of the museum of pop culture and have begun setting up a field base in the main lobby there. It's prime real estate with monorail access so we can reach a secondary location if we need to evacuate. What observations can you tell us about the situation here?"

"From what I've seen, there are a lot of zombies out and about. My guess is in the tens of thousands and growing by the second. Whatever this is, it spreads like crazy." Becca relaxed, having avoided being benched for the time being. "The streets are problematic, but the creatures seem to be forming groups and congregating in some areas, which is leaving some streets clear." Becca pulled away from Denny Park and headed in the direction of the museum, passing over the heads of the dead below her drone. "As long as you have a drone to scout ahead you should be able to move somewhat freely. I can help with—"

"Negative, we have things covered. You're running a non-combat drone and we already have our own units active. Plus, let's just say that we've brought enough firepower to deal with almost anything we might run into."

"So what are my orders then?"

"For now, locate survivors and mark their locations. Once we have a better handle on things, we'll need to get those people out of there. If you observe anything new, just report in."

"Oh... I mean, understood." She was really hoping to do something more proactive, but at least he hadn't told her to stand down.

"Perfect. We'll keep you updated if anything we find in the city concerns your safety."

"Thank you, and please let me know if there is anything more I can do."

Becca slouched back as Easton clicked off the line, surprised that Phoenix Company didn't want her to do more. It felt like they were sidelining her. They probably weren't happy that she took over a local drone pod without orders to do so. Then again, they didn't tell her to disconnect so they could take it over, either. Maybe they really did want her to find survivors.

She shoved her doubts back down and checked her battery readout. It was still at ninety percent.

"Plenty of charge to make an impact."

She leaned forward in her seat and continued to fly through the dead city until she caught something flickering at the edge of her monitor.

"Is that... green fire?"

CHAPTER NINE

"What the hell? You led it right to me!" Asher frantically looked around the room, clearly searching for something to defend himself with.

"I did no such thing; it sensed the blood in the room," Digby spat back. At least this time he was telling the truth.

A hulking mass of necrotic muscle pushed its way through the door on all fours as if it couldn't balance itself on two legs.

Zombie Brute: uncommon, neutral.

As long as I don't get in its way it should leave me be. Digby stepped away from the dead bodies in the room and gestured toward the pile like a chef offering a meal. The brute hesitated, its eyes flicking between the pile of scraps and Asher.

"Can we fight it?" The boy froze as if waiting for the beast to decide his fate.

Digby considered the option, remembering how many times he'd had to cast Cremation to get it to take the last time he'd used it. No doubt the brute had the same resistance, or more.

Not to mention he might wind up angering and making it hostile toward him.

"You're welcome to try."

The brute sniffed the air for a second, then locked its sights on Asher. Apparently live prey was better than scraps. With a gravelly roar, the brute charged.

Asher leapt out of the way as the beast crashed through one of the glass cases, tumbling into a second case behind it. Fragments of shattered glass trickled from the brute's back as it pushed itself back up. It shook off the impact and began searching for the boy again.

Digby wasn't sure how well the oversized zombie could track his prey. Maybe if Asher could make a break for it while the brute was confused, he might stand a chance. That was when a few stray zombies peeked in through the door, blocking any chance Asher had for escape. They must have been drawn by the ruckus.

Maybe he doesn't have to escape. Digby knew what the brute's attributes were, or at least had a good guess. The beast's mutation path was all about strength and defense, but it lacked agility. Just the fact that the zombie had mutated told him that its agility was a flat zero. That was why it was using its arms to support itself.

Come to think of it, back when it had killed the woman earlier, the brute hadn't actually jumped on her. It was more like it had run straight off the walkway above and fell on her from there.

"Keep dodging. It's not as dangerous as it looks; it can't turn once it starts moving." Digby crept around the edge of the brute's vision. "Just stay away from it. It can't hurt you if it can't grab you."

"I can't just dodge it forever." Asher strafed around the room while the brute refocused on him. "Can't you call it off or something?"

"I can't..." Digby trailed off. "Actually, I might as well try."

He turned to the mass of muscle and took on his most commanding stance. "Stop!"

The brute turned back to look at Digby. It didn't look friendly.

"Ah, sorry." Digby gave it an awkward grin. "Never mind."

The brute let out its loudest roar yet, sending droplets of spittle in Digby's direction. The point was clear. They were not friends.

"Apparently we aren't on good terms." Digby scratched at the back of his neck, confirming that his Compels didn't work on an uncommon zombie. It was probably because he himself was also uncommon, after taking a mutation from the leader's path. It stood to reason that he could only compel the dead if they were less powerful. Perhaps there would be a way to increase the power later, but for now, it seemed the option was out.

"Well, do something!" Asher dove to one side.

Digby hesitated. Picking a fight with a brute might not be the best plan. Then again, watching Asher die when he could have done something didn't sit right with him either. That would truly make him a monster. If he didn't try to help, could he even claim to be human? Still, it wasn't like he had anything to fight with. Digby's eyes widened, realizing how wrong he was. It was true that his Cremation spell was too weak to cast directly at the brute, but he might not need to. There was dead tissue ready to ignite laying all around him.

He nodded to himself and reached down to pick up a bone that still had a bit of meat on it. He took a nibble, because, well, it was there, so why not? Then he cast Cremation to set it alight. Green fire engulfed the remaining flesh and blackened the bone. Digby held it up like a torch. Then he lobbed it at the brute. The bone spiraled through the air, hitting the beast in the rear. It bounced off, but some of the burning tissue transferred on impact to create a patch of emerald fire on the brute's backside.

"Ha!" Digby laughed. It served the brute right for not

sharing and being rude. It turned back again to let out another roar.

Zombie Brute: uncommon, hostile.

"Welp, that's to be expected." Digby got ready to leap out of the way, grabbing another scrap of meat from the floor and lighting it while he was there. His mana dropped to seventy-six.

The brute charged, only to crash into another display case. A model of some sort of imitation snow exploded around the monster as Digby threw himself to one side. He launched the burning chunk of corpse as he did. Unfortunately, he failed to remember that his agility and strength were still lacking.

"Damn!" Digby fell in the mess covering the floor.

In a panic, he scurried away. Reaching for whatever he could find, he snagged one of the skulls that he'd been unable to crack open earlier. With another Cremation, it went up in flames.

The remaining flesh burned away from the blackened bone as emerald fire licked across the surface. The flames glowed brighter around the eyes as the contents within began to burn as well. The effect gave the skull a haunting visage. It popped and screeched as if pressure was building up inside its brain cavity.

Digby threw the makeshift weapon as hard as his weakened arms could. The green flames roared through the air as a high-pitched whine came from the skull, sounding like a scream. It crashed into the brute's flank, exploding on contact. A burst of liquified gray matter covered the beast's back and side. It howled in discomfort, thrashing around in the wreckage of the display case.

Digby pushed himself up as fake snow drifted through the air around him.

"What the hell did you do?" Asher froze in place, slowly turning his eyes to Digby.

"Cremation, it's a spell." He avoided making eye contact

with the boy, not wanting to have to explain everything in the middle of a fight.

"A spell?" The kid's voice shot up an octave.

"Yes, I'm a magic zombie," Digby snapped back.

"What?" Asher staggered backward.

"No time for questions. You can burn me at the stake later."

"I might not have to." Asher gestured to Digby's hand, which was now on fire.

"Not again." Digby grabbed a discarded shirt from the floor and patted out his burning fingertips. "I really need to be more careful."

He examined his hand, finding blackened bone where his fingertips should have been. His first impulse was to cast Necrotic Regeneration, but the brute was still moving, and he needed his magic more than he did his fingertips. He glanced at his mana.

MP: 61/106

That low already? Digby stepped away as the brute rose back up, having put out most of the flames covering its body. It looked... angry.

"Listen," Digby kept his eyes on the brute as he called to Asher, "I need you to keep it busy for a bit."

"Why?" The boy tensed, getting ready to dodge.

"Because that spell didn't do nearly enough damage. And I'm going to need a weapon. I have one available, but I'm going to need to eat something."

"Whatever, just hurry." Exhaustion was evident in Asher's voice.

Digby sighed, realizing which mutation he needed to take next. Bone claw. He looked to the Heretic Seed's information ring and willed it to show the contents of his void. He focused on one line.

Bone: .2

The requirement for the mutation was bone, equal to a quarter of what the average human had in their body. Apparently, he had eaten a bit already, probably back when he was still a mindless zombie earlier that night. Now, he just needed a little more.

The brute charged, getting a face full of broken glass as Asher dashed away. The kid was doing his best. It was time Digby did too.

The reason mutations were rare amongst zombies became apparent as soon as he dug in. Most of the mutations required bone, and as Digby was figuring out, bone was hard to eat. He couldn't do much more than scratch the larger pieces. That just left the smaller ones like fingers and the like. He choked down what he could, the Heretic Seed rewarding him with a new message.

GUIDED MUTATION
Requirements for the lurker's mutation, Bone Claw, have been met.
Accept? Yes/No

"Fine." Digby held out his right hand with its missing fingertips as a jolt of sensation streaked through his body. It was like every bone in his skeleton was vibrating at once. Falling to his knees, he clutched his wrist to his chest. The blackened stumps protruding through his skin flaked off, leaving five sharp points of bleached bone.

Then, they grew.

The sensation was different from pain for his deceased body, but it wasn't comfortable. Digby gasped as the exposed bone elongated, each claw curling slightly as they became thicker and stronger. Gray skin knitted itself up around the base of each, leaving a talon protruding at the end of each digit.

Then suddenly, his hand just felt right. It was like it had always been that way. Digby flexed each finger, remarking on how easily they moved. Even his other hand felt stronger. Like some of the control had carried over.

Dexterity increased to 12.
Defense increased to 9.
Strength increased to 9.

"You ready?" Asher panted and gasped for air, still leading the brute around the room. Occasionally he threw something to keep the thing's attention.

"Almost." Digby grabbed the shirt that he'd used to snuff out the Cremation flames on his hand a moment before and scraped together every bit of loose flesh nearby. While he was at it, he found a discarded leather garment in the pile. "What's this now?"

Leather Jacket: common.

The coat was black and covered with more of those metal type fasteners with tiny teeth running up both sides of the front. A set of three short—but wicked-looking—metal spikes sat upon each shoulder. On the back, a rather striking crest adorned the leather. It bore the image of a bird holding a feather and arrow with a shield of stripes in front of it. The words 'HEY HO LET'S GO' ran around the edge with 'THE RAMONES' across the top. It looked sturdy enough to help protect his body.

"Every little bit helps." Digby pulled what was left of an arm from the sleeve and slipped the garment on so that his hood hung over the collar. The jacket was covered in blood, but so was he, so that didn't seem to matter. He had no idea how influential the Ramone family was, but he hoped they wouldn't mind him wearing their crest.

Plus, he liked their motto.

He returned to the t-shirt full of gore he'd been gathering and hefted it up like a sack, ready to throw. Then he grinned.

"Hey ho, let's go." As the words left his mouth, the sack of human remains burst into emerald flames.

MP: 46/106

Digby glanced down at his hand, grateful for the fact that his Bone Claws were less flammable than his bare fingers had been. He was now able to hold the improvised weapon without burning himself in the process. Lacking the strength to throw the bundle with much force, he swung it by a loose end to gain momentum.

"Hey big fella?" Digby cackled like the magical zombie he was as the flames roared through the air beside him. The brute turned to face the maniacal laughter. He let go, sending the bloody sack straight into the monster's face. Fire splashed like water into the brute, engulfing its head and showering the floor around it with burning chunks. It was a direct hit.

"Yeah!" Asher cheered as the brute panicked.

"Who's hostile now?" Digby taunted while his Cremation flames ate away at the beast's eyes and began to cook its brain.

It screamed and slapped itself in the face in an attempt to get the flaming tissue off. It actually tore some of its own flesh away in the process, leaving an exposed patch of skull. Flaming chunks spattered across the floor. Digby readied his claws and crept closer for a finishing blow as smoke drifted through the air. All he had to do was wait for the flames to take their toll and go in for the kill.

Just a few more seconds.

That was when a familiar alarm echoed through the room.

"Oh no…"

Digby raised his head, finding more of those silver spouts that had been embedded in the ceiling downstairs. A moment of dread passed. Then came the rain.

"Not again!" Digby dropped his vision back to the brute.

Steam wafted from its charred flesh as water ran down its face. Somehow it looked angrier than before.

"Please tell me you have something else planned." Asher stepped behind Digby.

That was when a light shined in through the window, casting the brute's shadow across the floor toward them. Digby pulled up his hood to hide his face as he shielded his eyes with his left hand. There was an object floating in the air outside.

"What the hell is that?"

CHAPTER TEN

"What the hell is that?" Becca stared at the rippling muscle of a massive creature's back. It took up nearly a third of her monitor.

That was when she realized there were two survivors standing on the other side of the room. They were both shielding their eyes as if staring into the sun.

"Shit!" Becca killed the drone's lights and switched to night vision. Green shapes took over the monitor.

The hulking beast charged at the pair of survivors, water splashing into the air with each heavy step. Becca arched an eyebrow. The fire that had caught her eye a moment before must have triggered the building's suppression system.

The creature slammed into a wall as the two survivors leapt out of the way. She couldn't make out much detail with the drone's night vision turned on, but they looked to be in rough shape. It was only a matter of time before their luck ran out.

She clicked over to her comms. "Easton? Is Phoenix settled in enough to send out a squad?"

"What, why?" the specialist responded.

"I have two survivors just a couple blocks from you. They're in danger and need rescue."

"Ah." Easton sounded unprepared for the request. "We're not really at a stage where we are beginning evacuations; we're still in the investigation phase."

"They don't have time to wait and there's something else here, something that needs investigation." She hoped the discovery of the creature would be enough to score her some points with Phoenix Company. Saving the two survivors wouldn't be bad either.

"Like what?"

"A monster." Becca cringed at her wording. "Or something, it's big. Definitely not a zombie. Anyway, whatever it is, your captain is going to want to check it out." Becca snapped a screenshot of the beast. "Sending you a still now."

Becca waited as a moment of silence went by.

"The hell is that?" Easton replied.

"That's what I said." Becca glanced back at the survivors on her monitor, making sure they weren't going to run and lead the monster away.

"Okay, yeah, that's something to tell the captain about. We'll check it out."

"Thanks. I'll see if I can help these two hold out." She let out a relieved breath at the fact that her information hadn't fallen on deaf ears.

"Sure, and try not to lose the creature."

Becca nodded to herself. She had guessed right as to what Phoenix Company's priorities were.

Minimizing her drone's feed, she clicked over to the area's network map. A screen of hundreds of interconnected access nodes flooded her vision. Her job didn't require much in the way of hacking but, occasionally, she'd needed to tap into other systems. She wasn't an expert, but what she lacked was compensated by Skyline's system, which could brute force its way into most civilian networks.

"There!" Her mouse streaked across the screen to select an

access point to the Seattle Institute of Science and Tech. A
window opened with a list of options.

"Damn."

The doors weren't networked.

"I need another way in." She scrolled through her options,
selecting a line that read security. "Or maybe I don't."

Becca cycled through the building's security cameras until
she found the right room. The angle didn't matter, she just
needed a working microphone so she could hear what was
happening inside. The shouting was audible as soon as she
switched on the audio.

"Do something, Digby, you goddamn freak!" a voice
demanded over the sound of a fire alarm.

"Oh, I'm sorry, Asher, was saving your life once already not
enough? You ungrateful sack of hog leavings."

Becca's brain hit a wall, unable to process what she had just
heard. The second voice, Digby, she assumed, had a thick
English accent and sounded like the villain of a Disney movie,
all gravel and spite. She blinked once to clear the confusion
their argument caused, then went back to the list of security
options. After overriding the fire alarm to shut it off, she tapped
into the institute's announcements system. Then she cleared her
throat.

"Hello, I have help on the way. Just hold tight." She smiled,
waiting for their grateful cheers. Her face fell an instant later.

"Who the hell is that?" Digby groaned.

"I think it's the drone." Asher pointed in her direction.

"What the hell is a drone?"

"Yes! This is the drone!" Becca shouted over the two of
them. "I'm outside the window." She flicked her lights on and
off to show her location.

"Well you're no help out there." The wicked-sounding
survivor stood up just after dodging away from the monster.
Digby moved awkwardly, as if he'd been injured and had
trouble walking.

Becca glanced at the camera feed, trying to get a better look at him. With his hood up, it was hard to see if he was hurt. He'd shoved his right hand under his leather jacket. Becca hoped he wasn't hiding a bite. Even with the sprinkler system showering him with water, he was still covered in blood. It looked like he'd been rolling in it. The other survivor, Asher, was just as filthy but moved better.

Becca searched the institute's staff listings for their names, finding an Asher Thomas under the interns.

"What sort of help is coming?" He scrambled away from the monster.

"I have a private military squad on route. They should be here in…" Becca cringed, hoping they were actually on their way. "…in a few minutes."

"Military? As in the authorities?" Digby shrieked, before settling down. "Ah, yes. Good, good. They'll be able to save us, right?"

"Yes, they are heavily armed and can take down whatever that thing is."

"Oh, thank god," Asher added, finally getting the point that she was there to help.

"Yes, perfect, just perfect…" The gravelly voice of the other survivor trailed off, before adding, "Is there a way out of here?"

Becca brought up the building's floor plan. "Yes. Just down the hall is a flight of stairs that leads to an emergency exit. But it will lock behind you once you go through it, and the streets aren't much safer. There's hordes of infected roaming the area."

"Good to know." The blood-soaked man backed toward the window, giving Becca a clear look at the Ramones logo on the back of his leather jacket.

She flipped her mic up to mute herself. "What is he, some kind of punk rocker? I didn't think that was still in style." She smirked. "He's probably faking the British accent."

Becca unmuted herself as the strange man dove out of the way. The hulking beast slammed its face into the window a second later. Cracks spiderwebbed across the glass, but it held firm.

"I'm going to scout ahead to the lobby to make sure there's a clear path for my squad. So stay alive." She pulled away from the window and flew up to the roof, glancing at the building's floor plan. "I know there's a skylight up here somewhere."

A moment later she found it.

"Oh damn..." The entryway wasn't packed but it wasn't empty either, with a couple dozen zombies wandering into the space. "I hope the squad can get through there."

Becca switched to Skyline's channel.

"What's your ETA, Phoenix?"

"Fifteen minutes," Easton responded.

"The survivors inside may not last that long." Becca pulled away and took a lap around the building, checking the emergency exit that she had told Digby and Asher about.

"Crap." There were another dozen zombies milling about out there as well. She switched back to the institute's speaker system to talk to the two survivors again. "My team is still fifteen minutes away. Can you—"

"Fifteen minutes?" Asher panted between words. "I can't keep this up that long. What about that emergency door?"

"The brute will only give chase." Digby strafed around the room.

"I'm sorry, I wish I could do more." Becca shrugged on her end of the monitor still safe in her apartment. "You're just going to have to—"

"Hang on?" Asher finished her sentence for her. Then he deflated. "I'm going to die here."

Digby gave a half-hearted shrug. "Probably."

CHAPTER ELEVEN

Water poured across Digby's vision.

At least the continuous rain spraying from the ceiling would wash some of the blood from his clothes. Glancing at the window, he caught that thing that Asher had called a drone floating around as if held up by magic. Maybe witchcraft wasn't as frowned upon in the future as he thought.

No. I can't take that chance.

He tugged his hood down and shoved his clawed hand under his jacket to keep his more monstrous features hidden. Revealing himself was still too big of a risk. Eight hundred years had passed, meaning whatever force made the little object outside the window fly could be anything. All Digby knew was that whatever a drone was, it was powerful. Just the fact that it was able to send foot soldiers to wherever it wanted was terrifying.

More importantly, he needed to make sure he wasn't there when the army of whatever country he was in got there.

I could just leave.

Digby glanced at the brute as it lumbered around after

Asher. Glass from the smashed display cases cracked under the beast's hands and feet. A few shards stuck out of its arms.

It's not like I'm helping that boy by staying by his side.

The zombies in the hall wouldn't stop him. He could just slip away while the drone wasn't looking. With a little luck, the authorities would make it in time to save Asher. Then again, they might not. The question was, could he abandon the boy and still live with himself?

The brute locked its sights on Asher, stomping its feet in a steady rhythm as if attempting to intimidate the boy. The steady pounding echoed through Digby's mind until, suddenly, another window of clarity opened to cut through the fog in his mind. A memory surged forth, spurred on by the recent increase in Digby's intelligence and the beast's continuous pounding.

No! Not now!

The brute vanished along with Asher. Digby's body tensed as the building morphed into the main hall of the castle from eight hundred years ago. As much as he needed to find out what had happened back then, the timing couldn't have been worse.

———

The sensation of suddenly needing to breathe flooded back, slamming Digby down into another immersive flashback.

Digby's mind raced, now remembering waking up on the floor of the castle's study where he'd found the heretic rings. In the time he'd been unconscious during the Heretic Seed's synchronizing, the zombies that had chased him there had begun to break down the door.

Somehow, the bite wound he'd received was gone, healed by the mana that coursed through his body.

Bursting through the door, five zombies gave him a frantic lesson in the abilities he'd gained as a living mage. The memory of learning how to use his spells repopulated his mind as he scrambled to escape the room. After slipping past the five zombies that poured through the door, he threw two Fireballs behind him to set the entire room alight.

With five enemies defeated, he remembered receiving his first experience message, followed by a level up. He ran into two more zombies on his way to the castle's main hall, using the last of his mana to leave another two burning corpses in his wake.

Trapped within the memory, Digby struggled to break free. To return his mind to the present before he or Asher—or both—ended up dead. Try as he might, though, he couldn't pull away from the events in his past, succeeding only in blurring the two moments in time together. A steady pounding thumped through his mind. In the present, the brute stomped its feet while back in the past, something slammed against a side door within the castle's main hall.

The memory solidified around him, rooting Digby in the moment. He raised his hand, ready to cast Fireball as the door cracked and splintered.

The pounding continued.

Whatever had been on the other side was coming through.

Finally, the door burst open as a familiar man exploded into the hall. It was Henwick, the hunter that had gathered Digby and the rest of the villagers to attack the castle. He lowered the axe he used to break through the door to his side while carrying a torch in his other hand. A spattering of dark blood covered the man's chest. Digby immediately shoved his hand behind his back as if he hadn't been just about to use witchcraft.

"Graves! Thank god you're alive." The man rushed over to him as soon as he saw him.

"Yes, I am still breathing." Digby released the tension in his shoulders, glad to find he wasn't the only survivor, even if the charismatic hunter wasn't his favorite person.

"Thank the Lord. I feared the worst when you ran off with those things chasing after you." Henwick gestured to the blood stains all over Digby's clothes. "I see you were able to fight them off."

"Oh, yes." Digby tugged on the glove he wore, making sure

the markings of his heretic ring were hidden. "I, ah, did what I could."

"Good man, good man." Henwick placed a hand on his shoulder. "I'm glad you didn't end up like the others."

"The others?" Digby's stomach turned as he noticed the absence of the rest of the mob he'd attacked the castle with.

"Yes, the others. Everyone we came to this hellscape with." Henwick lowered his head and clenched his fist around the handle of his torch. "Those things ate them. They're all dead."

"All of them?" Digby sucked in a breath, unsure if they could escape alone.

"Yes, man, all of them. We're all that's left." Henwick gripped his axe tighter as if he was about to slam it down in frustration. "We need to get moving."

"Say no more." Digby had spun toward the main doors as Henwick began to run the other way, deeper into the castle.

"Wait, where are you going?"

"I'm going home, or at least, anywhere but here." Digby thrust one finger at the door in protest.

"You can't go home." Henwick marched back to him, stomping his boots on the stone floor. "There's still a witch in this castle. We have to find her and burn her before whatever curse she has unleashed upon this world spreads."

"A witch?" Digby's voice rose an octave.

"Yes, a witch." Henwick put down his axe and swept a hand through the air. "That wicked woman appeared just after you ran off and began working magic the likes of which I've never seen."

"All the more reason to get out of here." Digby rolled his eyes, wanting nothing to do with the hunter's quest.

"What?" Henwick's face fell with a flash of anger. "Damn it, man, we're all that's left here. We have to——"

"Look, sir," past Digby planted one foot in an attempt to stand his ground, "if I had known that I would be dealing with actual witchcraft tonight, I would have stayed in the tavern. So no thank you, I'm leaving."

Shock and confusion washed over Henwick's face. "But I told everyone we would be facing witchcraft when I roused the village."

"Well, yes, but I didn't actually believe that." Digby folded his arms like a stubborn child. "And, to be honest, I wasn't listening all that carefully."

"Then why are you even here?" Henwick's eyes widened.

"Because I was bored!" Digby threw his arms out to his sides, leaving out his intent to steal from the castle.

Without warning, Henwick slapped him across the face. "Hold yourself together, man!" The burly hunter gripped Digby's shoulder tight enough to hurt. "I know you're scared, but this is your chance. God is calling you to stand tall. To be the guardian that this world needs."

"I don't think god has anything to do with what's happening here." Digby slapped his hand away.

"Maybe not. But either way, the castle grounds are crawling with those abominations, so you don't have a choice. Escape is no longer an option." Henwick picked up his axe and shoved his torch into Digby's hand. "You can stay here and perish alone, or stand up and fight alongside me."

Digby hesitated, stealing one last glance back at the castle's main door whilst debating on making a run for it.

"Let's go!" Henwick shouted, demanding Digby's attention. "Who knows, you might find that courage suits you."

With that, Digby finally nodded and followed the heroic hunter down into the depths of the castle.

That was when a scream tore him back to the present.

———

"Wake up, you asshole!" Asher knelt over him.

"Wha-what happened?" Digby glanced around, recoiling as the brute rolled through a display case nearby.

"You were just standing there like an idiot." Asher dragged him back to his feet so they could put in some distance. "I had to shove you out of the way of that monster before it plowed into you."

"Why didn't you climb back up to that sphere and leave me?" Digby looked the boy in the eyes, shocked that he had risked his life to help him.

"I don't know." Asher spat his words, showing his frustration with having to save him. "I didn't think of it."

Digby got his bearings and turned toward the brute. He couldn't abandon Asher now, not after the boy had protected him. Henwick's words echoed through his mind.

You might find that courage suits you.

Digby glanced at his mana.

MP: 46/106

Close to half left. Even still, all he had was his Cremation spell, which had been rendered useless by the water that rained down from the ceiling. Digby held his left hand out to let the liquid run down his fingertips. The sensation made his eye twitch.

"Would someone please stop this rain!"

"What?" Both Asher and the disembodied voice of the drone responded in confusion.

"The rain, damn it!" Digby swung his hand up to point at the ceiling, flinging water in an arc. "Can't you stop it?"

"The sprinklers?" The drone responded. "No, it's not on the building's network. It has to be turned off by hand, but there's no way to make it to the valve with all the zombies roaming the building. Right now, I think the only thing keeping them out of your room is the larger monster."

"Just tell me where this valve thing is," Digby insisted as he threw a handful of broken glass at the brute to draw it away from Asher.

"It's down on the lower floors." The drone hovered back and forth outside.

"Great, that's back where I started," Digby growled to

himself. With his agility what it was, he would never make it down there and back up to cremate the brute in time before the authorities arrived. Not much point in trying. Then a thought struck him.

Wait, I am still a zombie. Cremation isn't my only ability.

"Asher!" Digby stabbed a finger at the boy just as he was preparing to jump out of the way of the brute. "How fast can you get back up on top of that ball where I found you?"

"Pretty fast, if I can climb the stuffed polar bear." Asher leapt to one side. "But what about you?"

"Never mind about me, just be ready." Digby started for the hall. "I'll be back, and I'm bringing friends."

"Wait, don't leave me." Asher reached out.

"It's not safe out there." The drone added.

Digby ignored their arguments and pushed past the zombies that had been watching the fight from the hall. He made a point of making it look like he was trying to knock them down and run. He slowed as soon as he made it out of the room; he couldn't keep that pace up for long.

It's okay, I don't have to go far.

He hobbled his way back to the large room where he'd first run into the brute. If the drone was to be believed, it should be full of zombies. Friendly zombies, that was.

"Where are you going?" The drone's voice followed him through the hall as if it could still see him somehow.

"To get help." Digby kept his head down to hide his face and maintained his act of avoiding the zombies. They weren't even trying to attack him.

You all aren't helping me sell this. Digby groaned at his necrotic conspirators.

"Follow me, teeth," he whispered to the next few that he passed, using his Compel mutation. One by one, they began to obey. "Yes, that's right. The many teeth."

Digby kept it up all the way to the lobby where he not only found more allies, but Carl, the zombie leader from earlier. His previous group of dead friends must have circled back around.

"I am so glad to see you." Digby made his way down the stairs toward the floor, stopping a few steps from the bottom. Keeping in mind that the drone was somehow still watching and listening to his every action, he addressed the room.

"Listen up, zombies!" Digby put every ounce of intent he had into a Compel. Every head in the room turned toward him.

That worked better than expected.

"Are you insane?" The feminine voice of the drone echoed through the room. "There's a dozen already following you."

"Yes, but that brute back there is the bigger problem." Digby shrugged off the warning and beckoned to his zombie brethren. "Live prey this way, follow."

Digby continued down the stairs and circled around to the climate studies wing where Asher was hopefully still alive. He would have doubled back the way he'd come, but he couldn't get past the zombies following him without it being obvious that they were friendly.

Weaving between his monstrous allies in the lobby, he headed up the stairs on the other side. Carl joined him, following a few bodies behind. Digby almost felt bad for lying to the horde, since he had no intent to let them eat the poor boy. As long as Asher was able to get back up on that globe thing hanging from the ceiling, they wouldn't be able to reach him.

I just hope Asher is a tempting enough morsel to motivate the horde to attack the brute.

Alone or in a small group, they wouldn't dare, but with this many... Digby looked over his shoulder at the fifty or so zombies following his lead. The brute didn't stand a chance.

"This is a bad idea." The drone... droned on.

The thing was probably right, of course, but it was too late now. Digby made a show of struggling to stay in front of the horde as the many teeth packed the hallway behind him, filling all available space. Their arms reached out in anticipation, helping to sell the idea that they were after him as well.

Eventually they reached their destination.

"Told you I'd be back!" Digby stepped through the doors

with one arm held out toward his new friends, making a point of keeping his distance.

Snarls erupted from the door as jaws snapped at the air. The zombies poured into the room behind him, knocking over any display that the brute hadn't already smashed.

"What the actual fuck?" Asher recoiled in horror as he climbed up the stuffed bear to reach the sphere hanging from the ceiling.

The brute's response was similar, stopping its pursuit to face the horde that filled the other side of the room. The monster backed up to put itself between Asher and the zombies, but remained facing the horde as if it was afraid of turning its back to them. In a show of force, a roar, louder than before, tore through the room.

Mine!

The word echoed through Digby's mind like a blow to the head. He winced as the horde behind him shrank away in unison. Shaking off the threat, he marched toward the brute.

"Oh no, you don't. They aren't scared of you anymore."

Digby made his way around the brute to rejoin Asher, hoping the beast wouldn't turn its back on the horde to make a move on him. Throwing his left hand out toward the young man on the back of the stuffed bear, he sent out another Compel. "Here it is boys: food."

"What the hell is wrong with you?" Asher's breathing sped up to a rapid staccato.

"I can't watch this," the drone added.

Digby leaned toward the boy. "I suggest you get up to that globe fast."

Asher continued to climb the white bear, frantically grabbing at its fur for purchase.

The horde moved as one as the brute let out another roar to push them back. Both sides stood at a standoff like two armies afraid to destroy each other. The zombies had the advantage, but the brute wouldn't go down easy.

"He's nothing!" Digby moved to the side of the room, to

keep his distance from the conflict. From there, he beckoned to his allies. "That beast is just an obstacle to be torn apart."

The brute stomped and growled, to make itself as intimidating as possible, clearly sensing the danger it was in. Impatient snarls answered back but the horde remained where they were, unable to cross the line.

"Come on, damn it! You are the many! Not the few." Digby howled at the horde like a villain. "You are the many teeth that can devour the world."

"God damn it, what the hell?" Asher threw himself off the polar bear's head to grab hold of the globe's support rope. Digby tensed his entire body, unsure if the boy would be able to hold on with his injuries and the curse weighing on him. The sphere swung back and forth as he clutched the rope, struggling to get his feet up. The din of roars and snarls grew to a deafening cacophony below as he pulled himself up to safety.

"Yes!" Digby raised his hand to the sky and shouted out one word along with a Compel. He wasn't sure what made him think of the command. It had just appeared in his mind as the interpretation of his desire. Plus, it felt right on his tongue.

"Rend!"

Finally, the horde rushed forward all at once, like an avalanche set off by his murderous intent. The brute leaped into the wall of walking corpses, slamming its meaty fists into its attackers. Bones crunched and limbs were torn. Three zombies fell, their skulls crushed beyond recognition.

"Rend and tear!" Digby climbed on top of the broken displays for a better view. A wild cackle erupted from his throat as he got carried away in the moment.

"Holy shit!" the drone shrieked.

Digby paid it no attention.

The brute raged against the onslaught, throwing zombies clear across the room. Carl, the group's previous leader, snarled cooperatively, sending a second Compel that reinforced Digby's to drive the horde into a frenzy.

The tide turned in an instant, zombies piling over the brute in a cascade of bodies. Digby cheered them on from the side-lines as the brute's roars shifted into screams. Fistfuls of torn muscle flew into the air.

"Oh jeez!" Digby came down from his bloodlust as the horde literally tore the brute apart. "Gah, no, too much. Too much." He recoiled at the sight of the slaughter he'd caused and stepped back to where the polar bear and Asher were.

The brute's screams faded as the frenzy died down. Then, slowly, one head after another looked to Digby. Their eyes somehow different as if there was something new there.

1 zombie brute defeated, 230 experience awarded.

Carl stepped to the front of the group and moaned. A concept came along with the sound. The best translation Digby could come up with was *faith*.

Digby's mouth fell open.

The horde had faith in him. He'd led them against an enemy they feared and showed them what they were capable of. Silence filled the room for a moment before the entire horde started moving toward their next meal clinging to the globe hanging over Digby's head.

"Digby, you need to climb up to Asher," the drone called out, clearly afraid for his safety, unaware that he was as dead as they were.

He glanced out the window at the strange floating machine, realizing that his positioning beneath Asher had made it appear as if the horde was after him as they shambled toward him. He took a step back as the drone continued.

"My team just reached the lobby, but they won't make it up to you before that horde rips you apart."

Digby glanced up to Asher, then to the metallic rope connected to the ceiling. "Pretty sure that thing isn't going to hold both of us." He had no intent of sticking around until the authorities arrived. Instead, he tugged his hood down. At least running away would make him appear heroic, like he was willing to sacrifice himself to lead the monsters away from the boy. Hopefully, in the care of the authorities, Asher's wounds would be treated and the curse removed. "I'll lead the horde away. Just make sure your foot soldiers get the boy down safely."

That'll do nicely.

Digby had to stop himself from patting himself on the back for his performance. Stepping toward the horde, he strafed around them in an attempt to make it to the door. He just hoped that their newfound faith in him would trump their need to eat Asher hiding behind him. Giving the boy one last look, he held up one finger to his mouth and winked as they made eye contact. He hoped his point was clear.

Keep your damn mouth shut about me.

With that, he made a break for the door.

"Come on then, there's more food this way." Digby attempted to run. Surely, his shaky movements served to make him look more doomed in the eyes of whatever the drone was using to watch him.

The horde turned to follow as he stumbled into the wall of the hallway outside. He pushed off, using his hands to support himself with each seemingly desperate step. Reaching the stairs that the drone had said led to an exit, he threw his ragged body forward.

A sudden explosion of activity erupted from back in the building's entryway, like hundreds of muffled pops. The sounds blended together into one chaotic ruckus. Digby flinched. *That must be the authorities. Just what sort of weapons do they have?* Surely swords and spears couldn't make that kind of sound. He didn't hang around to find out.

"Run! They're right behind you," the drone shouted in a panicked voice before delivering information to whoever was back in the lobby. "There's a survivor upstairs and another being chased by—"

Digby didn't wait to hear the rest as the emergency exit slammed behind him.

"Finally." He panted on reflex despite not breathing or

feeling winded. A moment later, the door opened behind him as Carl led the horde forward.

"Gah!" Digby wondered if there was a way to explain that he had lied about there being more food elsewhere. Then he shook his head. "Whatever, follow me if you want, it's better than staying here and facing whatever weapons those foot soldiers have."

Foregoing any attempt to move like a human, Digby ran for everything he was worth. Buildings unlike any he'd seen towered overhead on both sides of a narrow alleyway. There wasn't time to stare in awe; he had to move. He had to put in some distance. Carl and the rest of the zombies began to fall behind, having attributes so far below his. He may not have been as agile or strong as a regular human but he was still faster than the rest of the dead. Digby glanced back over his shoulder, finding them a few dozen feet back. They may have been slow, but they were also persistent.

I should probably lose my friends here too. No telling if they'll be forgiving when they realize I'm not leading them to food.

Eventually, Digby came across a metal ladder leading up to a flight of stairs that ran up the side of one of the smaller buildings.

"Perfect. I should have just enough attributes to get up there." With a little luck, the horde would be stuck down below. Climbing was not their strong suit, after all.

Digby jumped to the first rung and reached for the next. His nine points of strength and eight of agility weren't much, but it was enough to get him up to the stairs above. He stopped to rest as the horde filled the alley below him. They reached up, attempting to climb the ladder. They only made it up a few rungs before falling back down.

"Look, I'm sorry, alright?" Digby steadied himself on the railing above with his clawed hand. "Now move along and find someone better to follow." With that, he turned his back on his faithful army and climbed.

Digby froze as soon as he reached the roof. The city of

Seattle stretched across the horizon with buildings so tall they made castles look like ant hills. In the middle, an impossible tower held up a plate surrounded by glass, with a spire pointing toward the heavens.

Mankind had moved forward.

"How?" Digby dropped to his knees. "How is it this beautiful?"

CHAPTER TWELVE

Becca watched through the window of the science institute as Skyline's men gunned down the few remaining zombies that had stayed behind after that survivor, Digby, had led the rest away.

"Zero-one to Crow's Nest," the squad leader stared out the window at her drone with one hand on his ear, "where is this monster you were talking about? All we have in here is a kid."

"Yes, that's Asher, he's an intern at the institute." Becca paused. "And, the monster is... sort of all around you."

"What?"

"There was a horde of zombies in the room a moment ago that tore the creature apart. It doesn't look like they ate any of it so its remains should be all over the floor."

"Well shit, it's all just scraps now." The squad leader kicked at a clump of something near his foot, sending water splashing across the floor. "Could someone turn off these damn sprinklers?"

"Sorry, the survivors didn't have time to wait. One of them used himself as bait to lure a horde of zombies in to kill the creature."

"Where is this horde now?"

"Gone, the same survivor led them away from the boy in there."

"They're probably dead then."

"Maybe." Becca sank in her chair, not sure if she was ready to write the man off.

"We're going to take whatever samples we can and head back." The squad leader walked away from the window.

"Is Asher alright?" Becca asked before the squad leader got out of sight.

"Yeah, he's fine." The line went silent, telling Becca that she was no longer needed for the time being.

Unable to let go of the possibility that Digby might have escaped somehow, Becca circled her drone around to the emergency exit at the back of the building. It was unlikely, but whoever the guy was, he seemed to have a strong understanding of zombie behavior. The way he had drawn a horde into a conflict with a larger monster, using both sides as threats to keep himself on the sidelines, was insane.

He had even shouted at them as if encouraging them to attack. The only explanation she could think of to explain what she'd seen was that Digby must have had enough interactions with the walking corpses over the last few hours to gain a detailed understanding of how to handle them. Becca could only imagine what it must have been like for the man, struggling to survive in a city overrun by the dead.

Digby was a jerk, but clearly, he had been a resourceful jerk. One that had risked his life to save someone else. From the way they talked, Becca assumed he hadn't even known Asher before tonight, yet still he saved the intern's life. From that, Digby was either the most selfless person she'd ever seen or completely out of his mind.

Both seemed equally plausible at this point.

"Okay, if I was being pursued by a horde of zombies, where would I run to?" She piloted her drone down the surrounding alleyways, sweeping the area for signs of a struggle.

The uncertainty was killing her. If she found him dead, she could at least forget about him like she usually did during a mission. Unfortunately, her training had conditioned her to leave no stone unturned. On top of it all, she couldn't shake the feeling that she was missing something. Her heart sank when she found the horde that had been following the abrasive survivor. They filled an alleyway a few blocks away. Digby was nowhere to be seen.

"They must have overtaken him and torn him apart." Now they were just hanging about with nothing to do. "That answers that, I guess."

At least the distraction had kept her mind off the fact that she wasn't that far away. She hopped up from her chair and grabbed a bottle of water from the fridge before returning to the controls. Taking a sip, she hovered over Digby's killers as one of the monsters attempted to climb a ladder leading to a fire escape. It fell back down after reaching the second rung.

Becca choked on her water, spilling a mouthful down the front of her hoodie.

"That clever jerk." Digby must have climbed the ladder to get out of reach. It was the only thing that made sense. Given what she'd already seen, she found it hard to accept that the man had just let himself be killed. She grabbed the controls and flew up toward the building's roof. Flight after flight of metal stairs passed through her monitor's field of view before she reached the top.

Then, there he was.

A man in a Ramones jacket leaned on the opposite side of the roof's edge, staring out across the cityscape like he had nothing better to do. A row of potted plants lay at his feet as part of a rooftop garden. Becca hesitated, not sure what to say to the possibly heroic, possibly insane man. He stood deathly still, as if trying not to draw attention to his presence. She pushed the stick forward anyway and flicked on her drone's external speaker.

"There you are." She tried her best to sound relieved. "I can't believe you made it."

The man flinched as she spoke but didn't turn around.

"Yes, yes, you found me. Now run along and do whatever it is you do."

"Ahh." Becca's mouth fell open, not sure how to respond to such a rude response. She decided to stay positive. "Asher is safe."

"That's nice." Digby continued to stare off in the opposite direction as if making a point to act casual.

"Now that I know where you are, I can have my team come rescue you as well." Becca pushed her drone forward to get in front of him.

"Thanks, but no." Digby walked away from the building's edge, keeping his back to her as if he was angry. "I'm not looking to get to know the authorities."

"Is that some sort of punk rock thing?" Becca followed him.

"What is punk rock?" Digby cocked his head to one side beneath his hood.

"Is that sarcasm?"

"What's sarcasm?"

Becca rubbed her eyes before responding. "Hey, I'm just trying to help you."

"Well, don't. I'm fine."

"That's too bad, my team will be passing by this building on their way back to their field base. They are going to want to know everything you can tell them about these monsters. So like it or not, you're getting rescued." Becca checked the location of zero-one on her map, finding the squad a block away after leaving the science institute. "Look, you can see them now."

Flying to the other side of the building, she adjusted her angle until she found Skyline's team walking through the street. At the back of the group was Asher struggling to keep up. They were on foot, with another drone hovering over their heads. Unlike hers, it was a combat unit. The drone even had some sort of ring attached on top that she didn't recognize. No doubt it was special equipment exclusive to Phoenix Company.

She muted herself for a moment to complain. "I guess they really don't need me."

"Where will they take Asher?" Digby interrupted her sulking.

She unmuted herself as he leaned over the side of the building to see. Becca glanced to her peripheral, trying to catch his face at the edge of her wraparound monitor. The side of his hood was all she could see. Keeping his face hidden was starting to seem purposeful.

"Where?" he repeated, pulling Becca out of her suspicions.

"Back to their field base, their medic will have to check him over. I assume they'll get him to safety after that."

"Do they have a way to remove the curse?"

"What?" The question caught her off guard.

"The curse," Digby's tone sounded serious, "as in witchcraft."

"I'm sorry, what?" Becca blinked, unsure of how to even comprehend that last statement.

Before she could get another word out, her attention was drawn back to the scene below where one of Phoenix's men grabbed Asher's wrist. Becca switched on her drone's directional microphone and dropped down to the street as the man forced the intern to his knees. Becca flew toward the conflict, only making it a few feet before they shoved their rifle in Asher's face.

"Wait! Don't—" was all the intern got out before they put a round in his head. Becca held her breath as the silenced shot echoed through her mind. Asher's corpse fell to the pavement a second later.

"He was hiding a bite," Asher's killer announced while lowering his gun.

"Could have taken him back to monitor the change," one of his squad-mates argued.

"Kid looked like shit, was probably going to turn before we made it back."

"True. Just make sure he's not coming back and get moving," the squad leader instructed just before another member of the group put two more rounds into the intern's head.

Becca's heart froze like ice in her chest. She had seen people shot before, but she'd never known their names unless they were already a target. This was different. She'd worked hard to help save Asher. That was when she remembered Digby was watching too. She reached for the controls, her hands shaking as she turned away from the scene and climbed up to the rooftop. Digby stood with his back to her drone.

"Why?" His voice was raspy and dripping with anger, sounding like tearing paper.

"He was hiding a bite…" Becca didn't know what to say other than to repeat the words of the soldier that had taken Asher's life.

"Why didn't they try to help him?" The strange man's body shook as if struggling not to shout.

"They couldn't; he was too far gone and we don't have a cure." Becca's throat began to ache, having no idea what to say that might make Digby understand.

"Did they try a priest? A sage? A healer?" He kicked one of the potted plants that sat on the rooftop. "Hell, did they try witchcraft?"

"No… Why would they?" Becca furrowed her brow.

"It's a curse, damn it, why wouldn't they?" Digby swiped his left hand through the air while keeping his back to her.

"There's no such thing as curses or witchcraft." Becca rolled her eyes, unable to believe the argument she was having.

"Says who?"

"The entire civilized world," Becca argued.

"Then the entire civilized world is wrong." Digby stomped on the remains of the plant that he'd kicked a moment before, grinding it into pulp.

"Look, they didn't have a choice." Becca changed the subject, not knowing how to argue with such insanity. "I understand how you feel, but Asher had been bitten. I know that seems—"

"Go away." Digby's tone fell to a spiteful whisper as he clenched his fists at his sides.

"No…" Becca started to argue before she noticed something strange about his right hand. It was hard to tell in the dark, but it looked larger. "What's wrong with your hand?"

"Go away!" Digby stormed off toward the door that led into the building below.

"What's wrong with your hand?" Becca pushed forward, ignoring his tantrum.

"Get away from me!" the man growled, almost sounding like one of the monsters in the alley below.

"What's wrong with your hand?" Becca insisted, raising her voice.

"What do you think is wrong!" Digby spun around and reached to his hood with his right hand. Bone white claws tipped each finger.

Becca gasped as he tore his hood down, her drone's camera taking in every detail of his ghastly visage in high definition. A pair of milky green eyes stared daggers at her through the monitor. Locks of ghostly pale hair fell across the ashen gray skin of his face as rage contorted his mouth into a vicious snarl. Becca nearly got up from her chair and ran before remembering that she wasn't actually there.

"How is this possible?" She fumbled her control sticks.

"How do you think?" Digby's snarl bent upward into a smug expression. "Witchcraft."

CHAPTER THIRTEEN

"What are you?" The drone backed away until it hovered just over the edge of the rooftop, like it wanted to make sure it was out of reach.

"A zombie." Digby stepped forward, hoping to intimidate the little thing. "And as you can see, I am in no need of rescue, so fly back to wherever you came from and leave me be."

"But how?" The drone glanced down at the street below with a single lens as if afraid it might fall. It flicked its glass eye back up and pushed closer to Digby. "How are you talking? Why is your hand like that? And why were you helping Asher?"

Digby flinched at the boy's name, a grimace taking over his face. He hadn't even liked the young man, but still, Asher had pushed him out of the way of that brute to save him. It was likely that he wouldn't have survived the curse, but still he didn't deserve what he'd gotten. Those men had just shoved some kind of weapon in the kid's face and shattered his skull.

"I helped the boy because he was there," Digby folded his arms, more interested in arguing than telling the truth, "and because I could."

"Why didn't you just eat him?"

"I don't eat everyone I meet." Digby turned up what was left of his nose. "And I can talk because I was a mage before I died."

"You were a mage, as in magic?"

"Yes."

"That's not possible."

"Why not?"

"I already said, magic isn't real." The drone sounded frustrated, as if its tiny metal brain couldn't fathom anything supernatural.

Digby enjoyed being the one with more knowledge for once. If he'd had a spell other than Cremation, he would've cast it just to make the drone squirm. Unfortunately, the only available target on the rooftop was himself. He had a good mind to cast it anyway and damn the consequence.

"If magic isn't real, then explain this." Digby slashed at his left arm with his claws to shave away a bit of necrotic flesh. Fifteen points of mana later and each scrap burst into flames, hanging at the ends of his talons where the fire wouldn't spread.

"Shit!" The drone darted backward and disappeared over the edge of the building.

That worked a little too well. Digby stood awkwardly with his claws burning like candles. A second later the drone peeked back up over the side.

"Put that away."

"What's wrong, scared of a little fire?" Digby waved his hand around before swiping it to one side with a flourish to extinguish the flames.

The drone ducked for a second but rose back up once the fire was gone. "I thought you might attack."

"Not likely. The only thing that spell can hurt is me."

"What?"

"It's called Cremation." Digby gave an exaggerated shrug. "It only sets dead things on fire."

"Hold up." The drone stopped short. "Did you just injure yourself to make a point out of spite?"

"Would you have believed me if you hadn't seen for yourself?"

"I don't know if I believe you even after seeing it."

"Bah." Digby brushed the drone aside and glanced at his mana to make sure he had enough for a Regeneration.

Mana: 74/106

He couldn't help but notice his absorption rate had increased a bit. There must have been higher levels of ambient death essence in the area due to the situation in the city. Digby cast the healing spell and watched as the damage he'd caused to his arm knitted itself back together.

"How the...?" The drone moved closer to watch the process.

"It's magic." Digby let out a breathless sigh. "Why is that so hard to accept?"

"It's hard to accept because magic is impossible." The drone moved away. "No matter how much we wish it was."

"What's that now?" Digby's ears pricked up. "Your people wish magic was real?"

"Sure, we've been telling stories and fantasizing about it since forever."

Digby tapped his claws on his freshly healed forearm, remembering Henwick's words about burning that witch that had started everything. "So what you're saying is that I wouldn't be burned at the stake just for having this power?"

"No." The drone let out a laugh. "This isn't the dark ages. We don't do that anymore."

"Thank god." Digby let go of the fear that had been hanging over him since waking up. "That has been worrying me all night."

"I'm glad to have put your mind at ease." The drone glanced back down at the street in the direction that the squad went. "Actually, if that power is real, it would make you valuable to my employers. I work for a private military contractor called

Skyline. I know you have no reason to trust us, but we are here to help, and I can guarantee your safety."

"You're right, I don't trust you. And what is a military contractor?" Digby didn't like the sound of it, especially after seeing them in action.

"It's a privately-owned company that sends combat forces on missions as part of monetary contracts that are negotiated with whatever country requires their services." The drone seemed to be dumbing it down.

"So they're sellswords?"

"What's a sellsword?"

"A mercenary, one who kills for whoever pays them." Digby sneered as he spoke, liking the drone's lords even less.

"Yes, they are mercenaries, but not in a bad way. They don't just work for the highest bidder. Mostly they handle peace-keeping missions. And they would be very interested in helping you." The drone seemed to be trying to push past the murder that its lords had just committed as if it hadn't happened.

"Mercenary or not, I'd rather these Skyline people stay away from me. Especially after that…" Digby stabbed a finger at Asher's body cooling on the street below. "If that's what they do to someone who has been bit, then I can only imagine what they would do to me."

"I wish things had gone differently, but they didn't have a choice." The drone sounded defensive.

"I don't really care." Digby swatted at the thing. "And I wouldn't expect a hunk of scrap like you to understand. You don't even have a body to worry about." Digby spat his words, hoping to make the drone feel inferior. The thing paused for a long moment before speaking again.

"Digby, what do you think you're talking to?"

He scoffed and repeated the word that Asher had used in hopes of sounding more informed than he was. "A drone."

"Not quite." The device lowered itself to the rooftop before the four spinning portions slowed to a stop. "You are talking to a person controlling this drone."

"Oh, so you're human?" He kept his tone even, trying to hide his surprise.

"I am."

"Do you have a name?" He glared down at the thing.

"I do."

"Will you tell me?" He beckoned with his clawed hand, trying to draw out more information that he might use to his advantage.

"No, but my call sign is Crow's Nest."

"So that's what I should call you?"

"Sure."

Digby crouched down to look at the strange machine. It made sense that there was a person controlling the thing. He'd actually found it unsettling that its voice sounded so human, like it was trying to mimic a person. Leaning closer, he stared into the eye-like lens on its front. The one thing he couldn't understand was just how a woman could fit inside the tiny thing.

"You think I'm inside it, don't you?"

"What? No…" Digby responded, understanding from the woman's tone that it had been a ridiculous assumption.

"I'm piloting it remotely. The camera on the front shows me everything."

"I see…" Digby didn't really understand, but he didn't want to look stupid so he played along, hoping the woman would explain it further.

"That means I am sitting in a room far away from where you are and controlling this machine from there. I can see what it sees through the lens on the front, and I'm talking to you through its speaker." An audible laugh came from the drone. "How do you not know how a drone works? Where are you even from?"

"I'm sorry, Crow's Feet." He got her name wrong on purpose to annoy and hopefully distract her from her question. "I can't be expected to be aware of every stupid invention that mankind thinks up."

"It's Crow's Nest. And you didn't answer my question."

Digby considered his options. He wasn't actually sure where he was, so if he said he was from England, then he might give himself away. After all, there was a chance he was still in England. Granted, no one sounded like him, so odds were that he was in a different country. Now that he thought about it, his homeland might not even exist anymore. With few options, he followed his instincts and lied.

"I'm from Seattle." He gestured to the text on his shirt. "See, the University of Seattle."

"Sorry, try again. This time with the truth."

"Fine, I'm from England," he snapped, annoyed at how easily she saw through him.

"That doesn't explain why you don't know what anything is. Honestly, it's like you're from the past."

"I, ah…" Digby faltered, finding few words to pull himself out of the hole he'd dug.

"Shit, that's it. Isn't it?" The drone lifted off the rooftop and rose to meet his eyes.

"What? No. I'm… ah."

"When are you from, Dig?" It moved closer.

Digby looked away toward the ground and mumbled under his breath, "Eight hundred years ago."

"What was that?"

"Eight hundred years ago." He rolled his eyes, unsure how the woman had been able to pull everything out of him.

"Holy shit." The drone hesitated as if the woman behind it was wrapping her head around the idea that she was talking to an eight-hundred-year-old magic zombie. Eventually, the drone continued. "How did you get here?"

"I was frozen." Digby shrugged. "Just thawed out, it seems."

"Are there any more like you?"

"No. I'm one of a kind." He stood tall with a hint of pride before he remembered that it wasn't anything to be proud of.

"That would make you the first zombie, and the likely source for this outbreak."

"Ahh…" Digby's jaw dropped, realizing that he just gave

away the fact that he'd started the nightmare that the world of the future was now living in. He gave the drone an awkward shrug in defense. "I didn't mean to…"

"What does that mean?"

"It means I wasn't in control when I woke up. It was this curse, damn it." He raised a finger as if to make a point. "It's not like I meant for any of this to happen."

"How many people did you eat?" The drone's tone grew more serious.

"Two." Digby looked the drone straight in the eye and abandoned any hope of hiding what he'd done. "And I bit a third. I think they were the one that spread the curse from there."

"Jesus." The drone went quiet for a moment as if trying to work through what he'd just said. "That… explains some things."

"But, like I said, I was not in control. My intelligence was no more than the rest of these mindless corpses. Obviously, I feel bad about hurting those people, but there was nothing I could have done to stop myself at the time."

"So you're saying that none of this is your fault?" The voice sounded suspicious.

"I am." Digby tried his best to sound sincere.

"Hundreds of thousands of people have probably died due to your actions, but it wasn't your fault."

Digby winced. He hadn't realized the number was so high. Clearly the world would have been better off if he'd stayed dead. His head drooped.

"I realize that I am the cause of what has happened here. But none of it would have started if I hadn't been turned into this." He gestured to his ragged body. "I am just as much a victim in all this as everyone else." The drone stared at him through its glass eye for a long moment before responding

"Okay, I get that." The machine raised up and approached him again. "But all things considered, the right thing to do now is to take responsibility for what's happened."

"And just how do you suggest I do that? Turn myself in to your mercenary lords?" Digby scoffed, as the conversation circled back.

"To my employer, yes."

"Not happening." Digby stomped away. "If you think I'm going to give myself to those sellswords, you have another thing coming."

"I can't apologize enough about Asher. I wanted to save him too, trust me. But it was already too late. As horrible as it sounds, the only thing the men down there could do was give him a merciful end." The drone's tone sounded honest. "That being said, there are far more people out there that we *can* save, and Skyline does have the world's best interest—"

"I don't care."

Digby's claws tensed, ready to smash the drone to pieces if it kept insisting on the same thing. He held himself back. Considering the information the woman had about this new world, finding a way to make use of her as an ally or accomplice would be beneficial. Then again, it was more than likely that she would sell him out at a moment's notice, probably out of loyalty to this Skyline organization of hers.

Unless... Digby suppressed a sly smile and turned back to the drone. "Tell me your real name and I might consider doing as you say," he lied.

The drone paused for several seconds before responding. "It's Rebecca."

"Ah, that's better." Digby steepled his hands, or at least tried to with one of them being tipped with claws. "Now Rebecca, I have a counteroffer for you."

"I don't think you have much to bargain with at the moment."

"You'd be surprised." He gestured for her to turn around.

"Seriously?" If the drone could have raised an eyebrow at him, it probably would have.

"Some privacy if you will." Digby continued to twirl his finger in the air.

"Fine, but don't even think about running away." The drone rotated with a huff. "I'm faster than you."

As soon as she was facing the other direction, he fished one of the heretic rings out of his boot where he'd hidden it. He promptly stood back up and hid the obsidian band in his hand, adding, "Let me ask you, how would you like to be immortal?"

"It hasn't worked out real well for you." Rebecca turned back around to face him.

"True, but that's just because I was cursed before I understood the power I had gained. You could be different." He left out the part about barely remembering anything about what had happened to him as a crooked grin crept across his face. Then he opened his hand to show her the ring. "This will give you the power to heal any wound, stop you from aging, and control over magic so powerful that you shall never fear death." He might have exaggerated a bit, but none of it was technically a lie as far as he knew.

The drone hesitated for a few seconds, then moved closer to the ring. Its glass eye rotated as if examining the glossy, black band in detail. "This is what gave you that power?"

"And it's the reason that I regained my intelligence as a zombie. Just think of all that you could become." He closed his hand around the ring. "All I ask is that you help me for the night. Once I'm safely out of this city, I'll hand this ring over to your drone and you can fly it back to wherever you are and claim it as your own. Or, if you so choose, you may bring it to the lords that you serve. Surely with it, they will have no use for me."

The hovering machine fell silent as if thinking his offer over.

"All you have to do is slip it on your finger, and immortality could be yours," he pushed once more, hoping the woman would give in to the temptation. If not, then at least the drone was close enough for him to strike.

Becca leaned on her console with both elbows, staring at the ring on her monitor. She muted herself.

"This is insane."

She glanced to Digby's dead face, where hundreds of points had been highlighted and analyzed by her camera's software. A line of text ran across the screen.

True, 77% accuracy.

She had activated her camera's *Veritas* function a few minutes ago when she'd realized how shifty Digby was. The software identified lies by monitoring micro-expressions. Normally it was more accurate, but the zombie's corpse-like appearance and missing nose seemed to be disrupting the analysis. Though seventy seven percent was still enough to go on.

Becca scrolled down the results of their conversation. The zombie had been lying on and off the entire time, but she was able to draw out plenty of information regardless. Magic was real, zombies were cursed, and she could become immortal.

It was all insane, but based on her software, it was the truth. At least, Digby certainly believed it.

In the end, it didn't matter. Even if she was to take the ring and fly it home, she couldn't get to it. She didn't have the unlock code to her apartment's front door.

Not that she would take the ring anyway. The thought of having magic was tempting but from what it did to Digby, she imagined that there were plenty of downsides. All she could do was make sure the ring found its way back to Skyline.

She unmuted herself.

"Okay, Dig, you have a deal. I'll help you escape." Agreeing was her best option to learn more.

"I knew you'd see it my way." The dead man tossed the ring up, clearly forgetting that he didn't have the coordination as a zombie to catch it. He ended up chasing the band across the rooftop as it rolled away. He snatched it up and rubbed it on his blood-stained shirt. "No harm done."

Becca shook her head at the ridiculous, talking corpse. It was obvious that he was trying to manipulate her, but he had so little knowledge of the world that he was ill equipped for the task. On the other hand, she had every advantage possible. The fact that he knew nothing of her drone's capabilities to track and inform on him made her job easy. All she had to do was stay by his side as long as possible.

"Okay, the first thing you need to do is get back down to the street." She pointed him toward the door to the rest of the building. "Head down and I'll meet you out front."

"Perfect." Digby sauntered over to the door and pulled it open, looking back to her. "Thank you for taking my side. I promise you won't regret it."

"I better not," she joked to set him at ease. "See you down below."

Becca pulled away and flew over the side of the building. She clicked over to Skyline's comms as soon as she was out of sight.

"Crow's Nest to Phoenix."

"Yes?" Easton responded immediately.

"You are not going to believe what I found."

CHAPTER FOURTEEN

Digby strolled along the street while Rebecca's drone followed behind. By exiting the front of the building he'd been hiding on, he was able to lose the horde that he'd gathered around the back. They would be fine without him. The rest of the zombies on the street paid him and the drone no mind. They had no interest in the device other than a few passing glances.

Digby made a note of where Skyline's forces were located and headed in the opposite direction. According to his new ally, the mercenaries had set up a fort of some kind near that strange space needle structure. He pushed on, keeping the spire at his back.

As they moved, he got a clearer idea of what sort of damage he had caused. Blood was smeared here and there, while horseless coaches littered the street, abandoned by their owners. Some even looked to have collided with others. The chaos that had taken place must have been intense.

Rebecca corrected him when he called the strange vehicles coaches. Apparently, there were a number of names for them. The drone rattled off terms like, cars, trucks, sport utility vehicles, and tractor trailers. Digby ignored much of the lesson, coming to his own conclusion that the smaller coaches were called cars and the bigger ones were trucks. Beyond that, having so many words just seemed superfluous.

The occasional fire burned with no one to put it out and papers blew through the air from the broken windows of the buildings above. He tried his best to put the damage out of his head, instead focusing on wrapping his mind around how much had happened while he was gone. He spent the next ten minutes asking about England.

"Explain this to me one more time." Digby rubbed at his temples. "You're telling me a bunch of religious zealots abandoned my homeland, piled into a few ships, sailed across the ocean, and colonized wherever this is?"

"Yes." The drone hovered beside him.

"Then they decided they didn't like the British?"

"It was more complicated than that, but yeah, they declared their independence to stop unfair taxation."

Digby walked in silence to let that sink in, then he cocked his head to the side. "So why did they throw tea in the ocean?"

The drone sighed. "You are getting hung up on the wrong details."

"Whatever." Digby shrugged off his curiosity. He didn't need to know everything right away. "At least I know how far I am from home."

"Is that where you want to go? Back to England?" Rebecca circled him before flying backward to face him.

"Probably not, there's nothing for me there." Digby scratched his head. "Right now, I just need to find somewhere safe. The way I see it, if I can find a place where I don't have to worry about being killed, I can focus on my magic. In time, I should be able to remove my curse. If I can grow stronger, I may find a way to regain my humanity and put all this behind me."

"How do you get strong—" Rebecca's words were cut off as

her drone backed into a roaming zombie. The device wobbled back and forth as if trying to regain its balance.

"Might want to watch where you're going, there." Digby gave her a smug smile.

"I know that. Shut up," she snapped. "Can't you tell your friend here to get out of the way?"

"Sure." Digby looked the zombie in the eye, feeling confident in his ability to control the monster after doing it so many times already. With one word he sent out a Compel.

"Move."

With no reason to refuse, the zombie stepped aside so that he and Rebecca could pass. Digby stopped short as a new message ran across the bottom of his vision.

SKILL LINK
By demonstrating repeated and proficient use of the non-heretic skill or talent, Compel Zombie, you have discovered an adjacent spell.
CONTROL ZOMBIE
Description: Temporarily subjugate the dead into your service regardless of target's will values. Zombies under your control gain +2 intelligence and are unable to refuse any command. May control up to 5 common zombies at any time.
Rank: D
Cost: 10MP
Duration: 10 minutes (+50% due to purity, total 15 minutes.)
Range: 10feet (+50% due to purity, total 15ft.)
Limitations: Commands are limited by the target's intelligence. Effective against common zombies only. Ineffective against the living.

You always did have trouble making friends, might as well enslave them instead.

"Hey now." Digby couldn't help but smile. "I just learned a new spell."

"You what?" Rebecca hovered in the air staring at him. "How?"

"Skill Link." Digby shrugged, trying not to give her the idea that the process was new to him. "I learn related spells by doing non-magic things well enough. I just learned a spell called Control Zombie from using my Compel mutation."

"How is that different from what you have been doing?"

"I can control them completely for fifteen minutes rather than just giving them suggestions." Digby rubbed his hands together. "I wonder what else I can learn."

"So do I," Rebecca added. "Can I see you cast it?"

"Definitely." His mana was back to full and he was itching to try it out anyway. Digby reached his hand toward the zombie he had just compelled and thought the word Control. A shimmer of green light passed over its body and just like that, it belonged to him.

A line appeared next to his mana value.

SUBJUGATED: 1 common zombie.

A timer of fifteen minutes appeared underneath the word for a moment before fading away. It returned when Digby looked for it, like it would only show him when he wanted to know.

That's convenient.

Digby appreciated the Heretic Seed's forethought in keeping his view from becoming overcrowded with too many numbers. He pumped his eyebrows and turned to the nearest zombie to repeat the spell.

SUBJUGATED: 2 common zombies.

Interesting. Digby tapped his chin with one claw as the second timer appeared and faded away. He beckoned to both of the zombies, his grin growing when they stepped toward him immediately.

"That is impressive." Rebecca flew closer to him. "Can you tell them to do anything?"

"Not anything." Digby sent the pair of zombies across the street and back again. "They don't have much intelligence, so they will only understand simple instructions." He pointed to Rebecca's drone. "Attack." The response was instant. Both zombies snarled and reached out for the hovering object. "Stop." Digby held up one hand just before they reached her.

"What the hell, Dig?" The drone's speaker crackled as Rebecca shrieked.

"Sorry, I wanted to know if they would actually do it."

"How about you not use me as a test? M'kay?"

"Oh, relax, I had them under control." Digby cast the spell on another three zombies, bringing his mana down to fifty-six. "There we go."

"Are you done gathering minions?" Rebecca seemed to be getting impatient.

"Yes, yes, I'm done." He beckoned to his zombies. "We'll be off then." Recruiting five might have seemed like overkill, but Digby couldn't shake the feeling that Rebecca had been a little too easy to convince earlier. It made sense to have a few extra allies around just in case she had any plans to double cross him. Not to mention the Heretic Seed's messages had said that using his magic often would help it to grow.

With his loyal band of undead in tow, Digby headed down the street, passing by several kinds of businesses on his way. It was nothing like the main throughway of the village where he'd come from. He could remember at least that much. Here in the future, there were so many goods available right at the people's fingertips that the sheer variety of what the future held was staggering. People could get a cup of tea, stop at the apothecary, and purchase clothing all on the same street.

Most of the shops were dark, with a few lights on here and

there. Just the fact that there were lights on at all was mind boggling. Digby had only ever used candles. As far as what made the devices light up, he had no idea. He just assumed it was another discovery made after the world had left him behind. Digby dragged his feet as a familiar melancholy settled in. The feeling was chased away by the display in a shop window.

"What... is... this...?" He pressed his hands against the glass, his claws scraping on the surface.

"That's a jewelry store." Rebecca continued down the street without looking back.

Gold, silver, and gemstones filled display cases beyond the window. It was beautiful. Digby's heart would have skipped a beat if it had still worked. He immediately turned around in search of something heavy, finding a satchel inside one of the open cars that littered the street. He fished through the bag and pulled out another one of those computer things that he'd seen back when he'd thawed out. This one, however, was thin and folded open and closed like a book.

The device might have been useful at some point, but right now, he just needed something heavy. Digby ignored the computer's intended purpose and slammed it into the jewelry store's window. It bounced off, throwing him back.

"What are you doing?" Rebecca flew back to watch his struggle.

"I'm breaking this window." He tried again, slamming himself into the glass.

"That's stupid." The drone hovered there as if judging him.

"You're right." Digby looked up at it. "I am being stupid."

"Okay then, let's—"

"I have minions!" Digby interrupted the drone. "Why am I breaking this window myself?"

"That's not what I meant."

Digby refreshed his subjects with another round of Control spells, noting that a second casting extended the time he had to command each of them back up to fifteen minutes. He handed one of them the foldable computer.

"Break it down."

A moment of cooperation later, and the window was no more. Digby hoisted himself through the opening and beckoned to the others. Rebecca hovered in behind them.

"Are we seriously robbing a jewelry store right now?"

"Indeed we are." Digby ordered his minions to knock over whatever display cases they could. "Once we get out of the city, we're going to need valuables to trade."

"You know what, I'm not even going to bother explaining why that's a bad plan." Rebecca landed her drone on one of the unbroken cases. "Go nuts. It really doesn't matter to me either way."

"Sounds like someone doesn't want this lovely necklace then." Digby placed the thickest gold chain he could find over the drone's camera, then proceeded to slip a ring on each of his fingers, only stopping when he got to his claws which were too thick to fit any of them. "That's a shame."

"Dig, get this off me. I won't be able to fly straight," the drone complained. "And if you're going to steal things, maybe you should go for something useful."

"Fine." Digby pulled the gold chain off the drone and stuffed it into his pocket along with several other trinkets. "Maybe we should find some weapons." He turned to his minions to give them a new command. "Head out there and bring back anything I can use to fight with. You have," he glanced at the list of subjugated zombies at the lower corner of his vision so that their timers appeared, "ten minutes."

The zombies each headed out the broken window in search of whatever their simple minds might perceive to be a weapon.

"Let's see what they come up with." Digby sat down in a chair to relax while his subjects did the heavy lifting.

"Fun." Rebecca's drone remained where it was, as if bored.

The first of his minions returned only seconds later,

carrying a rather large shard of broken glass from the jewelry store's window.

"This doesn't look promising." He took the glass from it and tossed it aside. The next zombie returned with a brick. Digby didn't even bother taking it. Another stepped back through the window holding a leather bag with a strap attached to it.

"A purse?" Laughter began emanating from the drone. "What are you going to do with that? Swing it around and beat people with it?"

"Maybe I will, Becky." Digby growled back, shortening her name in an attempt to annoy her, while he dumped the bag's contents on the floor and slung it over his shoulder. "I could use something to carry things in."

"Fine, then. Enjoy your purse." Rebecca groaned at the shortening of her name but continued to find the item funny regardless.

Finally, the fourth zombie came back dragging something useful. The end of a wooden baton was clutched in one hand. It was black and had a handle sticking off one side. From the other end dangled a leather belt with a number of pouches and objects attached to it.

"That's better." Digby removed the baton from where it was attached to the belt and tossed the rest on the floor. He wrapped his hand around the handle and took a practice swing.

Baton: common, melee weapon.

"I'm not very strong with my left hand, but I might be able to do some damage with this."

"Shit, Dig." Rebecca took flight again without warning.

"Gah, what?" He raised the baton at the sudden movement.

"Look at the belt."

"What about it?" He bent down and picked up the item.

"There's a gun in its holster."

"What's a gun?" Digby found something that looked like a handle sticking out from some sort of holder. "You mean this?"

"Yeah, that's more dangerous than anything else you've found."

Digby fumbled with the holster, eventually drawing the object and holding it in his left hand.

Pistol: common, ranged weapon.

Digby barely glanced at the Heretic Seed's description, overlooking the word 'ranged' in the text. He tossed his baton aside and held up the gun only to swing it through the air like a small club. "I'm not sure how that is better than the baton, but I'll take it."

"No, Dig." Rebecca flew closer. "It's a firearm, you don't club people with it. You pull the trigger."

"What?" Digby stared back at her.

"That little thing in the middle, you pull that back."

"Oh, this." Digby slipped the tip of one claw in and pushed on the mechanism.

"Wait! Don't!" The drone yelled just before a loud bang erupted from the weapon.

Digby let out a raspy scream as the gun flew from his grip, blowing a hole in the palm of his left hand that had been covering one end. At the same time, the head of one of his minions, standing further away, exploded against the wall.

1 common zombie defeated, 30 experience awarded.

"What the hell happened?" Digby jumped away from the weapon on the floor. "That was what happened to Asher."

"Whoa, calm down," the drone urged.

"Don't tell me to calm down. One of my minion's heads just exploded." He stared down at the smoking end of the gun. "What if that had been pointed at my head?"

"I didn't think you would just pull the trigger without a second thought."

"Clearly, I would."

"Okay, well, just don't do it again. Guns fire a projectile that can hit targets from range." The drone glanced back and forth. "It's like a bow and arrow. You know what that is, right?"

"Yes, I know what a bow and arrow is, Becky." Digby narrowed his eyes at the drone. "We had those in my day."

"Good, a gun is like that, but smaller and more powerful. You just point it at what you want to shoot and pull the trigger."

"So someone could just point one of these things at me and splatter me all over a wall?" Digby threw one hand out toward the remains of his minion.

"Sort of..."

"Why would you people invent something like that?" Digby covered the hole in his hand and cast Regeneration. "What is wrong with you people?"

"Humanity excels at war. It's not something any of us are proud of." The drone sank back down to the counter it had been perched on. "But we've gotten very good at finding new ways to kill each other."

"I see that." Digby kicked the gun away. "Apparently the future isn't any more civilized than the past. And that's coming from someone that ate a few people tonight."

"Are you done?"

"I suppose." Digby stared down at the gun, realizing that he should take the weapon regardless of if he liked it or not. There was no telling what he might run into, and having it was better than not.

"Good, then we should probably get go..." Rebecca trailed off before finishing her sentence.

"What?" Digby asked as he picked up the belt and gun and fastened them around his waist.

"Didn't you have another zombie out there searching for weapons?"

Digby glanced at the Heretic Seed's information.

SUBJUGATED: 4 common zombies.

Checking his timers, they all should have returned by now. Yet one of them was mysteriously absent. That was when he noticed a flickering glow reflecting in the broken glass that lay on the street outside.

Digby sucked in an unnecessary breath of air.

"I don't like the look of that at all."

CHAPTER FIFTEEN

Rebecca's drone let out an unhelpful snort as the source of the flickering light stepped into view.

"No, that's not what I asked for!" Digby shouted at his minion. "I asked you to bring me weapons, not…" He gestured to the zombie holding a flaming hunk of unrecognizable junk. "This!"

"Technically, you asked them to bring you anything you could fight with, and fire does fit that description," Rebecca defended his half-witted minion.

"Yes, but now this idiot is on fire too." Digby backed away as the flames spread to the zombie's clothing to engulf its body. Eventually the mindless creature collapsed to the floor.

1 common zombie defeated, 30 experience awarded.

"Hey now." Digby raised an eyebrow.

"What?" Rebecca turned away from the burning zombie.

"That just counted as a kill for me." Digby stared at the line of text at the base of his vision.

"What do you mean by—"

Digby leaped out through the broken storefront before Rebecca could finish her sentence. He scanned the street for the source of his minion's fiery demise, finding smoke pouring out from a broken window of another storefront. Digby hobbled his way down the street until he could see inside.

Perfect! A fire raged inside the building.

Glancing at the timers on his three surviving minions, he saw that they only had seconds left on their Control spells. He recast the spell then pointed to the fire inside the building.

"Alright minions. Head on in." The three zombies simply turned and climbed in through the broken window. "Hurry up, we don't have all night." The zombies hastened their pace until they each walked straight into the flames. Digby stood still and waited for another message to come.

3 common zombies defeated, 90 experience awarded.

"Yes!" He threw both arms up in celebration.

"Now what are you doing?" Rebecca caught up to him.

"I just found a way to get free experience points." Digby held out a hand to the nearest zombie and cast Control.

"Experience points?" The drone stopped short. "You mean like, to level up?"

"Yes." Digby flicked his eyes to the drone. "How did you know that?"

"It's a basic function in most games." Rebecca moved closer. "Hold up a second, how do you even know you're receiving points?"

"I get messages." He gestured to the air in front of him where the words usually appeared. "Right around here. And my information ring is floating over here while my mana sits down in this area." He pointed to the little circle hanging in the corner of his vision as well as his current mana, displayed in the opposite corner. "They appear whenever I look for them."

"Wow." The drone hovered without moving. "You have a HUD like my system does."

"What's a HUD?" Digby casually told his newest minion to enter the flaming store.

"It stands for Heads Up Display, it's a user interface that overlays what you see."

"Alright." Digby glanced at his HUD, finding it a good term for what he was seeing.

MP 56/106

1 common zombie defeated, 30 experience awarded.

"Okay, I'm curious now." The drone sounded excited. "You're a magic zombie from centuries ago, but you have a heads-up display and earn experience. Just what the hell is giving you this power?"

"The power comes from something called the Heretic Seed." Digby shrugged. "Beyond that, I have no idea what the thing is or how it works."

"Okay, so according to this Heretic Seed, what level are you now?" Rebecca probed him further.

"I'm level..." Digby paused. "Level twenty-five," he lied, hoping it sounded believable.

"Impressive." Rebecca sounded like she bought it. "I'm going to need to examine this system in more depth."

"We'll have to add that to the list of things to do once we get safely out of the city." Digby cast Control on another two zombies and sent them into the bonfire, ignoring the experience message that followed. "I do wish the Heretic Seed wasn't so rude, though."

"What do you mean?"

"Sometimes the messages I get seem to criticize or insult me. I don't remember if it had been like that before I died, but it has been sort of an ass since I woke up here." Digby sent another passing zombie into the fire. "I assume a demon is watching and taunting me."

"Umm, okay." Rebecca pulled back a little. "I don't know if I believe in demons."

"Why not? It makes sense." Digby sat down against the wall while he waited for his mana to regenerate. "I was cursed when I died and didn't make it to a church or anything to be exorcised."

"I didn't have you pegged as someone who went to church?"

"I'm not. Or at least I haven't exactly lived a life free of sin. But a priest might help get rid of the demons in my blood that are making me sick. And it's not like I can get them all out with a bloodletting as a zombie."

"Hold up a second." Rebecca dropped down to look him in the eye. "What's this about bloodletting?"

"Just look at me. I'm clearly ill, so the demons in my blood must be stronger than normal."

The drone stopped short. "Dig... do you think people get sick because there's demons in their blood?"

"What? No..." Digby brushed off the ridiculous idea. "Sometimes they're in your bones."

"Wow." Rebecca hovered back and forth. "Just wow."

"What?" Digby raised his head to follow her with his eyes.

"I don't even know where to begin with that insanity."

"What, why is that insane?" Digby growled at the drone.

"Look, Dig, I get it, you're from a time before we knew what things were. But suffice to say, there are no demons in your blood."

"Then how do you explain all of this?" He gestured to the street around them.

"Easy." The drone spun around as if taking in the scene. "You were infected with some sort of virus that you then brought here to the present-day Seattle. And before you ask, a virus is a parasitic organism that inhabits people's bodies and makes them sick."

Digby scoffed, having trouble seeing how that was any different from demons.

"How do you explain magic then?" He raised his hand and cast Control again now that his mana had been replenished a bit. "If you can explain everything so easily with your future knowledge, then how could I do that?" He sent his new minion into the fire.

"I don't know, but the more I hear about this Heretic Seed that you're connected to, the less magical it seems." Rebecca's drone watched his minion walk into the fire. "From what you've described, it sounds like you stumbled on some kind of unknown technology."

"Oh, whatever. None of that matters right now." Digby stood as he brushed off her words. "No, right now, I need to get stronger." He raised his hand to cast one more Control.

SPELL RANK INCREASED
Control Zombie has advanced from rank D to C. Base duration has increased to 20 minutes. Plus 50% duration due to mana purity. Total duration: 30 minutes. Total number of controlled zombies increased to 10. Mana cost reduced to 8. Target's intelligence bonus is increased to 4.

Oh joy, ten, slightly less stupid minions.

"It's working already. Now all I have to do is keep casting until this spell reaches its limit, whatever that might be." Digby grinned at an image of himself leading an army of loyal minions. He glanced at the line at the bottom of his vision.

SUBJUGATED: 1 common zombie.

"I do wish this HUD thing would call them something other than subjugated. It sounds rather cruel." As soon as the sentence left his mouth, the word subjugated disappeared.

"Huh?" Digby stared at the change for a second before suggesting, "Minion?"

The new label popped up where the other had been.

MINIONS: 1 common zombie.

Perfect!

Digby spent the next few minutes alternating between casting Control and waiting for more mana. Rebecca seemed content to wait for him to do as he pleased. After sacrificing another three zombies to the flames, he got the message that he'd been waiting for.

You have reached level 11.
1,958 EXP to next level.
Plus 1 point to all attributes.
You have 1 additional attribute point to allocate.

"Finally!"

A jolt of power passed through Digby's body, making him lighter, stronger, and more focused all at once. He looked over his new attributes.

Constitution: 9
Defense: 10
Strength: 10
Dexterity: 13
Agility: 9
Intelligence: 19
Perception: 11
Will: 15

As much as he wanted to put his additional point into strength, he needed to get back his ability to run. He had to be prepared for anything and, right now, agility seemed to be where he was left wanting. Digby focused on the value, watching it rise by one.

Not quite back to where I was before I died, but closer.

"I take it you just leveled up?" Rebecca hovered by behind him in a nonchalant manner.

"I did." Digby raised his hand to look for another sacrificial minion, finding two zombies wandering nearby. "And I'm going to level up again."

He fired off another Control spell and attempted a second. The first zombie stopped to wait for his orders, while the other let out a snarl. The green shimmer of his spell passed over its body, but the zombie remained unbound.

"That's odd." Digby eyed the zombie.

Zombie Leader: uncommon, hostile.

"What's up with them?" Rebecca stopped to watch the creature hobble away out of sight.

"That one was a leader." Digby brought up the description of his Control spell, realizing that it only worked for common zombies. For a moment he grew tense, realizing that the attempt to Control the leader had made it hostile. Then he shrugged. "Oh well, at least it had the good sense to run away. Which is more than I can say about the rest of these half-wits."

He sent his new minion into the fire.

"And look, I'm doing the world a favor by removing some of the zombies from the streets."

"Yeah, you're a real saint." Flames reflected in her drone's glass eye as it watched his minion burn.

1 common zombie defeated, 28 experience awarded.

"Huh? That's weird." Digby read the message a second time.

"What is?"

"The amount of experience I got went down by two."

"Maybe the amount decreases as you level to force you to seek out bigger prey. That would make sense if this Heretic Seed is trying to make you stronger."

Digby opened his past notifications and looked back all the way to the beginning to find one of his experience messages from back when he'd been alive and fought a few zombies in the castle centuries ago.

1 common zombie defeated, 48 experience awarded.

"Damn." Digby scratched his head. "It dropped almost twenty points after I reached level ten, and two more now that I've reached eleven."

"Sounds like you lose two points every level." The drone bobbed up and down. "Also, thanks for telling me what level you really are. I thought you might have been exaggerating earlier."

"Damn it." Digby cursed the drone for catching him in another lie.

"Ah, Dig—" Becca started to speak.

"And damn it again for the experience loss. If this keeps up, killing zombies will be near worthless soon."

"Dig—"

He slapped his left hand on his thigh. "As it is, I'll have to kill over sixty of them to level up again."

"Hey Dig!" Rebecca interrupted his thought process yet again.

"What is it?" He stared daggers at her. "Can't you see I'm thinking?"

"Yeah, but you might want to look behind you." Rebecca's voice shook.

"Fine," Digby groaned and reluctantly turned around. His jaw went slack a second later. "Oh."

"Yeah, oh…" the drone repeated.

The zombie leader that he'd attempted to Control had returned, and this time, it wasn't alone. Apparently, he wasn't the only one who could spur a horde into action.

CHAPTER SIXTEEN

"Hi there." Digby waved to the zombie leader as it stood with a horde of at least thirty at its back. The fire inside the building cracked and popped with the bodies of his sacrificial minions. "Alright, now I know what this looks like..."

The lead zombie took a step closer, sending a Compel out to their horde. Digby picked up just enough to get the point. They were marking him as an enemy just as he had earlier with the brute.

"I don't suppose you can cast Control on all of them, can you?" Rebecca ducked her drone behind him.

Digby glanced at his HUD.

MP: 28/113

"I can only Control ten at once, and I don't have enough mana to even do that." He took a step back. "I probably should have saved some for an emergency."

"Maybe make a note of that for future reference," Rebecca added.

"You're not helping."

"Think you could hand over that magic ring now, rather than later?"

"Not a chance." Digby held out both hands to the horde. "Let's all be reasonable. Together we're strong. There's no sense fighting amongst ourselves." He added a Compel on top of his words to spread a feeling of unity. If he couldn't control them, he could at least try to sway them as one of their own.

The horde seemed to back down, becoming more docile. Their leader wasn't having any of it, letting out a snarl that carried the word '*threat*' along with it. The hostility of the group returned, their jaws snapping as they reached out.

"Fine, you want an enemy? You have one." Digby puffed out his chest, remembering how hard it was to convince his horde to attack a stronger opponent. All he had to do was ensure that he was more intimidating than the brute. "I am Digby Graves, the heretic mage. I have lived for eight hundred—"

Rebecca interrupted him with a sudden snort followed by an inappropriate laugh.

"Do you mind? I'm trying to intimidate them," Digby snapped back at her over his shoulder. "Just what is so funny?"

"Is your last name really Graves?"

"Yes, what of it?"

"So you're a zombie named Dig Graves?"

"That is… unfortunate." Digby sighed at the coincidence before returning his attention to the horde. "Sorry, where was I… Oh yes. Fear me, for I am Digby, lord of the dead, devourer of minds, and the right hand of death." He held his claws as if holding a beating heart. "Turn back or face my wrath." He sent out a series of Compels to reinforce the leader's assessment that he was a threat.

The horde held back.

"That is an impressive list of titles that you just gave yourself," Rebecca added.

"Quiet you. They don't even know what I'm saying, they just need to understand that I'm dangerous."

"Oh." The drone hovered a bit higher as if trying to stay out of reach. "But are you dangerous?"

That was when the zombie leader let out a raspy howl that Digby understood far too well.

Rend!

Digby was running before the horde started moving.

"Where are you going?" Rebecca shouted as he blew past her.

"Running for my life." He still didn't have much in the way of agility, but he had more than the horde. All he had to do was keep ahead of them.

"Okay then." Rebecca caught up behind him. "I'll go scout ahead and try to find somewhere for you to escape."

"Yes, you do that." He jogged as the drone flew away. "Just make sure you come back for me."

Digby kept moving, weaving between passing zombies that had not yet joined the horde behind him. The leader of the group let out a snarl to each as they passed by, amassing more followers with each second. The horde's frenzy surged as their confidence grew along with their numbers.

A Compel of *rend* was repeated.

Digby knocked over a rubbish barrel behind him, tripping a few zombies in front and causing a wave of bodies to tumble over each other. The rest simply swarmed around them and continued on, reaching out for him without skipping a beat.

"I'm sorry, alright!"

The only advantage he had was speed. Not that he was that fast to begin with. He tried to control his pace, worried that he might fall down if he pushed himself too hard. Though, for once he was grateful for his deceased status, as his body didn't seem to fatigue the same as it had when he was alive. He could feel his legs burning under the strain, but they didn't seem to slow him down. Plus, not needing to breathe had its benefits.

Behind him, the horde spread out to take up half the street. The windows of the buildings cracked under the strain of so many bodies pushing against them. The same was true for the cars that littered the area. None of the dead had the coordination to climb over whatever lay in their path. Instead, they crashed into obstacles like waves in the sea. They weren't fast, but they were determined.

Digby was sure he could outrun them for a while, but he wasn't sure he could lose them completely. Not to mention, with his limited agility, all it would take was one bad step to trip him up. He still had an advantage, but it wasn't much of one.

The strange, horseless coaches in the street were pushed aside under the combined mass of the horde. Hundreds of feet trampled everything in their way like a stampede of cattle. The deep foreboding sound reached into Digby's chest to grip his useless heart. Occasionally, a zombie would trip and fall, only to be crushed under the feet of the rest. Apparently, tearing him apart was more important than their individual safety.

"Oh god, what do I do?" Then he remembered he still had a weapon.

The gun.

Digby fumbled with the holster attached to the belt that he'd found, his claws struggling to work the clip that held the weapon in place. After a few careful tries, he managed to draw the pistol.

"Damn!" He struggled to get his dominant hand around the grip, unable to fit his clawed finger through the loop that housed the weapon's trigger. He transferred it to his left hand, with a noticeable difference in capability.

Good enough.

He turned back, still jogging to stay ahead of the horde and praying he wouldn't trip. Then he pulled the trigger. The gun barked and kicked. An audible crack came from his hand as one of his bones snapped under the strain.

It didn't matter.

What mattered was that the bullet slammed into the shoulder of one of the zombies in front. Being thrown off balance, they fell and disappeared under the feet of the horde.

1 common zombie defeated, 28 experience awarded.

Digby flexed his hand, noticing a slight change in its movement caused by the broken bone; beyond that, his grip held firm. It must not have been important.

No sense wasting the mana to heal it.

Digby fired again, aiming for the leader. He couldn't see where the bullet went, but the sound of breaking glass came from somewhere above. Pulling the trigger again, he clipped a zombie several bodies away from the leader.

"Bah," he complained at his own aim, having trouble accomplishing anything with his left hand in the limited lamp light of the street. Not to mention he was using a weapon that he hadn't even set eyes on before.

He fired again and again. The invisible projectiles punched holes in the chest of two more of his pursuers. Neither of them fell, nor had they been the ones that he'd been aiming at. He continued to fire, his frustration growing with each shot until the top of the gun got stuck in a strange position. Afterward, the trigger only clicked. Digby growled at the weapon before throwing it at the leader, having no more luck at hitting it than he'd had before. He glanced at his HUD.

MP: 37/113

He'd gained almost ten points; still not enough to stop a horde. Or was it? Digby ran through his options. He didn't need to kill them all, just the leader.

Using Cremation was pointless. He would never be able to get it to stick on the leader with its resistance being higher than that of a common zombie. As it was, he would still need to cast the spell three times just to take out one of the lesser targets. The only spell he had that could bypass his target's resistance was Control. Even with that, it only worked on common enemies, so a leader was still out of the question.

But what if… Digby let a grin creep across his face and focused on the zombie next to the leader.

Control.

MINIONS: 1 common zombie.

"Keep running," Digby shouted to keep his new ally's cover from being blown. He focused on the zombie and layered a second spell on top of the first.

Cremation.

An emerald shimmer passed over the zombie just before it burst into flames.

"Yes!" Digby pumped his clawed hand in celebration. His gamble had paid off. By casting Control first, he had been able to wipe out the zombie's resistance to his other spells.

"Now grab the leader!"

It was only a matter of time before his minion succumbed to the flames, Digby just hoped it was enough to take down the leader with it. The fiery zombie obeyed without hesitation, turning to the leader beside it and tackling it to the ground. They both disappeared beneath the horde in an instant. The wave of the dead came to a crashing halt, unable to proceed against a dangerous opponent without a leader to spur them forward.

Digby slowed as well, trying to catch a glimpse of the leader's fate. Snarls erupted from the mass. Each carried a desperate Compel that Digby had difficulty understanding, as if they had been sent without any real intent behind them.

Suddenly, a chunk of flaming tissue was thrown into the air, just before the horde reacted in a frenzy. The sound of bodies tearing at another was all that could be heard over their moans. Then, they all went still.

"Hello?" Digby froze. "We alright now?"

The horde answered by parting to reveal a charred corpse.

Digby relaxed as smoke wafted from the body. Then, it moved.

"Oh no." The fact that no experience message appeared told him everything he needed to know. His zombie minion had been killed by the horde rather than his spell, invalidating the reward. A kill must have needed to result from his direct actions to be considered his.

A moan came from the blackened form just before it raised its head to reveal a half-burnt face. The zombie leader growled, a row of white teeth showing between its charred lips. The horde slowly turned back to Digby. Again he ran as the mob of the dead surged forward with renewed ferocity.

"Hey, Dig." Rebecca's drone flew in from the side.

"I'm a bit busy." Digby jogged as best as he could.

"Yeah, well, I need you to turn around and head back the way you came."

"Why would I do that?"

"Because there's a construction site back near where we met that I can use to get you to safety. All you have to do is lead your friends here to the top of what's being built. I can lower a crane for you to escape on. The rest of the zombies will just run off the edge."

"What?" Digby snapped his head back to the drone.

"It will be simple."

"No, it won't. That's about the dumbest suggestion I've heard. Plus, that would take me too close to where your mercenary friends are. You want me to get caught?"

"Ah, no." The drone looked back at the pursuing horde. "And why is my plan dumb?"

"It wouldn't be if that damn leader wasn't back there. Unfortunately, it's smart enough to stop the rest of the zombies from killing themselves."

"Oh…"

"That's alright, you haven't led a horde before. You don't know what they're capable of."

Digby glanced back over his shoulder to realize that the crowd behind him had more than tripled in size. He couldn't even count the number of zombies snapping at his heels anymore.

I can't keep running, the horde will just keep growing with every walking corpse I pass.

He scanned the area ahead of him for anything that might give him an idea. All he found was another one of those car things with one end crushed into a tall metal pole as if it had run into it. Several signs were affixed to the post and it leaned to one side. The angle was enough so he might be able to reach a sign at the bottom that read 4th Ave.

"Alright, new plan." He lunged onto the back of the car and leapt up to the sign plate. Leveraging his ten points of agility for all they were worth, he hooked a foot up and hoisted his body further to climb the pole toward the lamp at the top.

"That's your plan?" Rebecca flew up to hover at eye level as the horde flooded the street below him.

"Sort of. They can't climb up here to get me at least." The gnarled hands of the dead rose toward him, unable to reach.

"Is there a step two to this plan?"

"Actually, yes." Digby clung tight to the pole whilst standing on the sign plate.

"Care to fill me in?"

"Of course." Digby turned to look the drone straight in its glass eye. "I'm going to need you to save me."

"What?" The drone scoffed. "Has your brain started rotting?"

"No, I assure you my mind is still very much functional. And you don't have to do much." He glanced around the street below. "All you have to do is find something a bit heavy and pick it up with your little pinchers. Then drop it on that leader's head from up high."

The drone hovered in the air for a moment, not moving.

"Now that is the stupidest idea I have ever heard. Why don't you just use the gun you found?"

"I tried that, but I ran out of shots." Digby rolled his eyes.

"Well then reload it. You have two more magazines on that belt."

Digby's jaw dropped.

"You don't have it anymore, do you?" Rebecca hit the nail on the head.

"I threw it at the horde when it stopped firing."

"Somehow, that is not surprising."

"Yes, well, that's that then. Now go find something heavy and get on with crushing my enemy's skull. How hard could it be?"

"Pretty hard. Do you have any idea what the weight limit on this drone is?" Two small stick-like limbs snapped out from underneath the camera, each bore a tiny clamp that resembled a crab's claw. They opened and closed as if demonstrating their capabilities. "These things weren't made to hold anything heavy. Not to mention I've only ever used them to place small explosive charges. And those only weigh a couple pounds at most. How the hell do you expect me to hit the leader of the horde with something that small? I don't even know which zombie the leader is. They all look the same from this angle."

"Are you done?" A frown hung from his face.

"Yes."

"Good, because the leader is that burnt one down there." He gave the drone a grin of dingy teeth. "See, not so hard to find."

Silence answered him as the drone hovered in the air.

"Rebecca?" Digby's face fell. "Are you there?"

No one responded.

"Damn it, Becky, you best not have abandoned me here." Digby swatted at the drone, his hand falling short. "We had a deal, you treacherous wench! You best not be thinking of calling in your friends to take my ring after this horde tears me apart. I swear I'll haunt you 'til your dying day! You better—"

"I better what?" Her voice returned.

"What?" Digby looked back over his shoulder as if someone else had been shouting a moment before.

The drone's speaker groaned in his direction. "I was checking some information on the surrounding buildings, and I might actually have an idea."

"Ah, good." Digby attempted his most charming smile. "I knew you'd come through."

"…Yeah. Sure you did." Rebecca pulled away and climbed up toward the roof of the building across the street.

"Alright," Digby talked to himself now that he was alone. "Just stay calm." He glanced down at the zombies reaching for him. The combined sound of their jaws snapping shook him to his core. It was like the constant popping of a crackling fire ready to consume him. Digby winced as the sound dislodged something in his mind, sending a cascade of images flooding back to him and threatening to drag him back to the past again. Back to the events that transpired before his death.

"Not now!" Digby struggled to push away the memory, fearing that he might fall as an unrelenting haze swelled around him. When resisting proved impossible, he threw his arms tight around the sign post and hoped for the best. Darkness surrounded him a second later, the crackling flame of a torch being the only source of light.

Digby spun around with his head on a swivel, flailing a torch through the air as he moved. Stone walls surrounded him.

He was back in the castle.

Back on the narrow staircase he'd followed that blasted hunter down so long ago.

———

"Make haste, Graves!" Henwick turned back to look up at him as he traveled down the seemingly endless spiral of stairs. The firelight of Digby's torch flickered in the dull reflection of the hunter's axe.

"Why must we continue down into the bowels of this damned castle?" Digby argued. "Surely no good will come of it."

"Because if we don't, who will?" Henwick continued down the stairs. "That witch can't be allowed to live. People have been going missing from the village for weeks. I can only assume that this witch has something to do with it." Henwick grunted his words, as if accusing him of being a coward. "As a man, I can't stand by while a woman like that still breathes. She will burn at the stake before this night is through. I shall see to it, if it's the last thing I do. The survival of the weak requires good men to take action. Otherwise, the wolves will have their way with the flock."

Digby opened his mouth to speak, but closed it again, unsure what to say to a statement like that. He didn't like how the hunter had compared people to sheep, but he didn't want to argue either. Especially when Henwick's mind was set on burning people at the stake. Digby was pretty sure that him becoming a mage would cause a strain on their budding friendship. The conversation was cut short the instant they came to a narrow door.

"Be ready, Graves." Henwick placed his hand on the handle. "Now is the time to prove to the world what sort of man you are." He pushed open the door without giving him the chance to back out.

"Oh my god..." Digby nearly fell to his knees as the hunter marched into the cavern that lay beyond. A stone walkway stretched from the door, across empty space, to a column standing in the middle of the enormous area. Another spiral staircase twisted around the column up to a platform at the top. The entire cavern almost seemed to be carved from a single mountain of rock, like it had been shaped by magic alone from the cliff face that the castle sat upon. Doors and staircases littered the walls of the cavern, with more walkways reaching out toward the column at the center.

Looking over the edge of the walkway, Digby caught a

glimpse of the ocean sweeping in from a cave entrance in the wall of the cavern. The tide crashed against the base of the column that held the platform above. A small boat floated below, held to a dock by nothing but a bit of rope as it rocked in the rough waters.

"Don't look down and keep moving!" Henwick rushed across the walkway, urging Digby to do the same.

Digby tightened his grip on his torch and tore his gaze away from the dock below as the hunter reached the stairway. With no other options available, he followed, making his way up the stairs that spiraled up the sides of the column. His breath froze in his throat the instant he reached the top.

At the center of the platform, sitting high above the ocean waves that crashed below, was a black monolith. It was smooth and glossy, like a pillar of obsidian. It was terrifying and beautiful at the same time. Lines of white runes trickled across its surface like rain, the same runes he'd seen streaking across the surface of the heretic ring that had been absorbed by his finger.

Digby didn't need to Analyze the structure to know what it was.

The truth was obvious.

He did so anyway to be sure.

Heretic Seed: unique.

The rings he'd stolen were just a proxy, a key to access the Seed's magic. This monolith was the gateway. It was the pillar of power that had activated the mana within him and connected it to the world around him. Digby began to reach out, mesmerized by the runes that trickled down the Heretic Seed's surface.

"This must be it, the source of the witch's power." Henwick stepped closer to the monolith just as a door far below swung open.

"Stop!" A woman's raspy voice echoed up to them as a

gnarled form stumbled into the cavern. Her hair was white and matted against her grizzled face.

"That's her!" Henwick gripped his axe with both hands. "That's the witch."

"Stay away from the pillar!" The witch glared up at them, her eyes shining with a deep emerald glow. They were almost hypnotizing. Digby couldn't take his gaze off of her, triggering his Analyze ability.

Heretic: Level 24, Necromancer, hostile.

As the witch shrieked up at them, zombies surfaced from the waters below, each clawing their way up the walls toward the walkways that lead to the column that held the platform that Digby and Henwick stood on.

"There's so many of them." Digby clutched his torch and stared down at the horde as it converged around the column below him to cut off any chance of escape.

"They must be the people that have been disappearing." Henwick's hands shook for a second before finding his resolve again.

"What do we do?" Digby's voice wavered.

"We do what we came here for." Henwick threw a hand out toward the Heretic Seed. "We destroy that!"

———

Digby clung to the sign post as the memory faded away, rooting him again in the present. A horde of angry zombies surrounded him just like they had back in the castle as he stood on the Heretic Seed's platform. The only difference was that now he was dead. At least that meant the dead might not eat him. No, they would just rend him to pieces.

The voice of the witch that had cursed him echoed through his mind, sending a flare of anger through his body at the realization that she had been the cause of everything. Before his emotions raged out of control, the groans of the zombies below tore him back to the situation at hand.

"Just relax, Digby. The horde can't get to you up here." He clung to the signpost harder. "Rebecca has a plan. Surely she will come through and rescue you." That was when an object smashed into the head of one of the zombies near the back of the group.

"Gah!" Digby peered up into the sky in search of Rebecca's drone, having trouble spotting her.

Then another object fell. It hit a zombie with the sound of shattering glass. He cringed at her aim. "She's not even close to hitting the leader."

Another object fell, smashing into a zombie behind him. Thirty seconds later, another came down. Like clockwork, two fell every minute, each with the sound of breaking glass. Watching more carefully, he noticed some kind of liquid splattering with each impact. Most of the hits only damaged limbs, but a couple found their mark, crushing skulls.

"What in the world is she— Oh god, no!" The pole he was clinging to bent to one side as the sound of buckling metal hit the air. The combined strength of the horde below was more than he thought. If he stayed there much longer, they might be able to tear down his hiding place with the sheer weight of their bodies.

Another bottle slammed into a zombie just below him, nearly hitting Digby's hand on the way down.

"What are you aiming at up there?" he complained as a familiar scent climbed into what was left of his nose. He flicked his eye to the zombie that had just been hit. Its now-broken arm dangled at an unnatural angle, the limb dripping with a clear fluid.

Digby let out a raspy laugh. He had spent enough nights in the tavern back at his village to know alcohol when he smelled it. And from what he could tell, it was a great deal stronger than what he had been used to.

"I take back anything I ever said about you, Becky." He beamed up at the drone high above him. "You're a genius."

The woman was showering the horde in booze. Beautiful, flammable booze. He squinted at the next few falling bottles.

Vodka: common spirits.
Rum: common spirits.
Whiskey: uncommon spirits.
Bourbon: rare spirits.

"Huh, she's dropping the good stuff now." Digby didn't recognize the names of any of the drinks, but it seemed that the future had gotten something right. Not that he could drink any of it anymore.

After clinging to the sign post for several minutes, he checked his HUD.

MP: 97/113

Almost back to full. Digby waited for another few bottles to fall then he readied his attack. He needed to set the horde alight in at least four places. That would take sixty points of mana for the Cremations. Plus, he needed to control them first, which would take another thirty-two.

"That's cutting it close," he whispered to himself as he added two minions to his ranks.

Digby made sure to pick targets that were in the middle of the crowd. He chose two more near the car that he had climbed up from. They would need to cover his escape since he couldn't set the horde on fire while he was still above them. Burning himself at the stake still wasn't high on his list. Once he was ready, he cast two Cremations behind him, then dropped to the car below.

Chaos erupted as soon as he landed.

Digby crashed onto the vehicle's roof with a hollow thud as hands reached out for him on all sides. Fire lit up the street behind him, spreading faster than he anticipated. A hand snapped around his ankle, ripping him off his feet to land on the car's rear. More hands reached out.

"Protect me." His voice came out in a panicked screech as the heat behind him grew. The sudden bonfire spat and crackled around him and he frantically kicked at the hands hindering his progress.

"Let. Me. Go!"

Suddenly, one of his minions appeared through the crowd to shove their fist into one of the opposing zombies. His defender's hand continued to travel, punching across the faces of not one but two enemies in an uncoordinated blow. That was when a heavy hand slammed down on his chest. It closed into a fist to grab a firm hold on his shirt. Digby started to scream but stopped the moment he looked into the zombie's eyes.

Zombie Minion: common, loyal.

He'd chosen well. The zombie yanked back on his shirt, dragging him off the car to the ground before letting go and throwing itself into the horde to cover Digby's escape.

"Thank you!" He scrambled away on his hands and knees. "I'm sorry." His two remaining minions both went up in sickly green flames as his mana fell to near empty.

"Spread the fire." Digby stopped, kneeling in the street while his defenders pushed into the horde, igniting the alcohol that had showered across the crowd. It was plenty to help spread the spell. The heat grew until the pyre engulfed the horde. Nothing could've survived the flames.

"Rest in peace," Digby added out of respect for the minions that he'd sacrificed, unsure why he wasn't cackling in victory like usual.

A wall of text blinded him for an instant before being condensed into a couple lines.

171 common zombies defeated, 4,788 experience awarded.

1 zombie leader defeated, 228 experience awarded.

A sudden wave of power surged through him.

You have reached level 13.

1,546 experience to next level.

Plus 2 points to all attributes.

You have 2 additional attribute points to allocate.

"Holy…" Digby couldn't believe his eyes.

I skipped clear over level twelve.

That was when Rebecca's drone lowered itself down directly behind him.

"I take it you figured out what I was dropping up there."

"I did."

"Good, we were lucky there was a rooftop bar up on the top of the hotel across the street. It was well stocked, so there was a wide enough selection to have enough options with a high enough proof to burn. Plus, no one up there looked like they were needing it. The party scene was dead, if you know what I mean." The drone looked over the bonfire before them. "Someone should have warned them about the dangers of alcohol."

"What?" Digby was having some trouble focusing on her words as something new distracted him.

"I was just saying that… oh, never mind. The joke just gets worse if I repeat it."

"Sure." Digby didn't even pretend that he'd been paying attention.

"You with me here?" The drone circled to hover in front of him.

He walked past it, to put some distance between the bonfire and whatever was drawing his attention. It was as if the smoke was inhibiting his senses. As soon as he got further away, everything became clear.

"Hey, you could at least laugh politely at my puns." The drone followed behind him.

"Yes, yes, very funny, Rebecca." Digby stopped to look around the street. "Sorry. I just sensed something nearby."

"Sensed what?" She slowed to hover beside him.

Digby paused before answering, unsure of how he was picking up the trail.

"I sense... blood."

CHAPTER SEVENTEEN

Digby took a few steps forward, looking over the street as he moved. Flecks of crimson were scattered about. A splatter on the side of a building, a smear on the inside of one of the wrecked cars nearby, and a trail leading into a doorway a short walk away. More was scattered about even further. Most of the flecks were dull and dingy, but some were vibrant as if full of life. He blinked, unable to believe that he couldn't see the blood so clearly before.

"What do you mean you sense blood?" Rebecca's drone caught up to him.

"It's everywhere." He slowed to a stop.

"Well, yeah, it's a zombie invasion, there's going to be blood." She brushed off his discovery.

"Yes, but I can see it glowing all over the street."

"You can?"

Digby checked his attributes.

STATUS
Name: Digby Graves
Race: Zombie

Heretic Class: Mage
Mana: 5 / 126
Mana Composition: Pure
Current Level: 13 (1,546 Experience to next level.)

ATTRIBUTES
Constitution: 11
Defense: 12
Strength: 12
Dexterity: 15
Agility: 12
Intelligence: 21
Perception: 13
Will: 17

AILMENTS
Deceased

You have 2 additional attribute points to allocate.

"My Blood Sense trait must be interacting with the increase to my perception. Having higher attributes than a normal zombie must have some advantages." He focused on his agility for his two additional points, bringing it to fourteen and getting a sudden jolt of sensation throughout his body. Afterwards, he almost felt normal.

Digby took a step forward, then hopped to the side. Then he danced a poorly coordinated jig.

"Should I be impressed?" The drone hovered in the air, looking bored.

"I didn't fall down."

"Bravo." The sound of Rebecca clapping was audible through her drone's speaker.

"Mock me if you want, but my agility is nearly back to where it was when I was alive." Digby ran a few steps at full speed without stumbling or needing to support himself on a wall. "At this rate, I might be able to pass for human before the night is through."

"You would need a nose first."

Digby strolled over to a window and checked his reflection, grunting in dissatisfaction. He wasn't as scrawny as he had been the last time he'd checked, but he was still far away from appearing human. Especially in the nose department.

"I wonder what attribute is linked to a healthy complexion."

The Heretic Seed failed to answer his question like it had the last time he'd questioned his appearance, suggesting that there wasn't one. Or, at least, this was as attractive as he was going to get. His pale green eyes stood out, reminding him of the witch that he'd seen back in the cavern beneath the castle eight hundred years ago.

A spiteful part of him hoped that the woman had perished back then, though, without remembering more, he couldn't be sure. He would have to find out. If she was somehow still alive, hunting her down for information would be at the top of his list after escaping from the city. The curse had been her doing; at the very least, she might know a way to reverse it.

Staring harder at his reflection, he hoped to trigger another memory now that he'd gained a couple more points of intelligence. Sadly, none came. He was so close to recalling everything. All that was left was finding out the specifics of his death. He couldn't shake the feeling that the few details he was missing were important. Digby placed his claws against the glass and dragged them across his deathly visage before turning away.

That was when the Heretic Seed decided to change the subject.

WARNING: Void resources low. Starving status has been applied. If food is not found, the racial trait Ravenous will become active when in the presence of prey.

Happy hunting.

Digby froze, understanding what that meant. He must have consumed too many of the resources within his void to increase his attributes. Adding to his values meant refining his body. The added tissue had to come from somewhere, considering he didn't have a living body that could grow on its own.

If he didn't eat, he would fall into the ravenous state he'd awoken in earlier. There was no telling what he would do with his mind impaired like that. He might pick a fight with another brute over some scraps, or chase someone off a cliff. Not to mention he would attack the first person he saw.

No, he couldn't take that risk. He checked his resources.

AVAILABLE RESOURCES
Sinew .1
Flesh .2
Bone 0
Viscera .3
Heart 0
Mind 0

I don't have a choice then. Digby deflated and focused on his Blood Sense to find the brightest glow, assuming that meant it was freshest. Stepping down off the raised portion of stone that lined the edge of the street, he headed toward a trail that led into a building on the other side.

Rebecca began to follow, but he held up his hand to stop her. "Wait here."

"Umm, no." The drone ignored him and weaved around his hand. "I'm not letting you out of my sight."

Digby rolled his eyes, not wanting to explain to his one ally that the only reason he wasn't trying to eat her was that she wasn't really there. Not if he wanted to keep her as an ally. As it was, he didn't think she had much trust in him to begin with. Not that he trusted her either.

"I just need to check on something." He walked faster. "I'll be right back."

"Sorry, no. I just saved you. You're not ditching me now." The drone sped up.

"Don't worry." Digby gave her a smile, assuming she'd misunderstood what the problem was. She must have been worried he might run off with the ring he'd promised her. He could understand that. If someone, zombie or not, had offered him power and immortality, he wouldn't have taken his eyes off them either. Not until the deal was done. "I still need you to help me get out of this city and I will uphold my end of the bargain."

"Then you won't mind me staying by your side until the end." The drone eyed him.

"No, but the building I need to check out is an enclosed space." He shrugged. "I just don't want you to have trouble moving in there."

"I can navigate a building just fine." The drone turned away toward the building's door with a stubborn groan.

"Suit yourself." Digby stepped inside. He hoped the power of the Heretic Seed was tempting enough to make the woman overlook whatever she might witness.

Inside of the building was a wide hall with a desk situated at its center. Letters were affixed to the wall spelling out the words Enterprise Suites. Several glass doors lined the walls, each with a different name. Some had an icon or picture on the glass as well.

"It's an office building," Rebecca commented as he read the text on the windows. "Each one of these doors leads to a business."

"There's so many." Digby continued further into the room. "Why does this world need so many businesses?"

"It's a much bigger world than what it was back when you were alive." The drone made a pass around the space, shining a light on many of the doors. "A bigger world requires more businesses to take care of the people's needs."

"It truly is impressive." Digby couldn't help but stand in awe. "So many people running shops and businesses."

"Not really."

"You're not impressed?"

"No, I am." The drone returned to his side. "But I wouldn't say that these companies are run by people anymore."

"Then what are they run by?" Digby arched an eyebrow.

"Other companies, really." A sigh was audible through the drone's speaker. "Half of these businesses are owned by the same company that owns Skyline. The chain just keeps going and going. When you trace it all back, the same companies own almost everything."

"How is that possible?"

"Money is power in this world." Rebecca fell silent for a few seconds. "It can even buy people."

"Well, slavery is nothing new." Digby shrugged.

"What?" The drone spun around as if startled by the word. "No, I didn't mean…" Rebecca trailed off before starting again. "You didn't own slaves, did you, Dig?"

"No, slavery was pretty frowned upon in England when I was alive. Not to mention I wasn't exactly in the economic position to be afforded such things. Why, has the practice returned?" Digby approached several droplets of blood near the center of the room, feeling his void howl inside him.

"It came back for a time, but thankfully, it has been gone for a couple hundred years now."

"That's good. For a second, I was worried that there were monsters worse than me in your world. Though, still, the idea that one organization could own so much of the world's business now is scary in and of itself. In my day, local lords held most of the power, leaving the rest of us competing for scraps. It was a harsh system." Digby let out a needless sigh. "Honestly, I'm a little disappointed that the world hasn't grown beyond that struggle."

"I can't argue with that, even if I'm a part of it." Rebecca turned her drone so that Digby could see the word Skyline etched into the side.

"Ah, well, maybe that will change once you're an immortal mage."

"Maybe." A somber laugh came from the drone's speaker. "Anyway, what are we doing here?"

Digby crouched down and placed the tips of his claws in a few droplets of blood. They were still wet. Digby lifted a claw to his mouth, tasting what he could only describe as a spark. The blood had been spilled from the living.

They were close.

"You're hunting, aren't you?" Rebecca's tone grew serious.

"I have to." There was no point in hiding it. "I'm starving and won't be able to control myself if we run into anyone. I'll become ravenous."

"So you thought, why not go with it?"

"Would you rather I eat you?"

"No."

"Then stop worrying about it. I tried to leave you outside, didn't I?" Digby picked up the trail, sensing more blood at the back of the room. "Besides, I don't rightly think whoever is leaving this trail is long for this world."

With that, Rebecca held any further comment as Digby followed his Blood Sense. The sensation grew stronger with each passing step as he reached the stairs leading to the next floor. There was definitely something up there.

I just hope I get there first. The thought scared Digby the moment it passed through his head. As much as he hated to admit it, he didn't want to share whatever he found.

Reaching the next landing, he was greeted by a hall painted bright white, with perfectly smooth walls surrounding him. A wide smear of crimson marred the flawless surface. It all led to a glass door. A bloody handprint glowed on its handle as if beckoning him in.

The need for food began to cloud Digby's judgment.

WARNING: Ravenous trait active. While active, all physical limitations will be ignored in the pursuit of prey.

Try not to hurt yourself.

Digby stalked toward the door, cursing his Ravenous trait. It was so much worse, being aware of his actions, like he was a prisoner in his own body as it moved on its own, unable to hold himself back. He reached out and dragged his claws through the crimson smear on the wall, leaving deep gouges across the strangely brittle surface. He was running by the time he reached the door.

Then, there was relief.

A pair of bodies, a man and a woman, lay on the floor.

Thank god, they're already dead.

They had been positioned with their hands on their chests as if they had been laid to rest. One of them was dark skinned, like a man Digby had known back in his village, while the other was as pale as a ghost. Some sort of puncture wound had been inflicted upon them both. There was only one injury on the woman, but several on the man. Those were the only details that Digby took in before lunging toward the meal. They were both still warm.

"Oh god, you're just going right for—" Rebecca spun her drone around to face the wall. "I am not watching that." She let out an awkward, misplaced laugh entirely inappropriate for the situation.

Digby ignored her. There was nothing she could have said to stop him. After a few minutes of savagery, his Ravenous trait waned enough to return control over Digby's body back to where it belonged.

"At least they were already dead," he commented between bites, as soon as he was able to speak again.

"True. You didn't kill anyone," Rebecca added. "But you would have."

"Indeed."

"That's what you meant by ravenous. You lose control? And that's why you killed two people when you thawed out earlier."

"Yes." Digby slowed down, to eat like a more civilized

zombie. "My regeneration and leveling consume the resources I eat, so I should eat as much as I can now so that I don't starve again."

"Is that how you think of it, as a resource?"

"That's what it is." Digby shrugged.

"Doesn't it bother you?" Rebecca peeked at him for a moment, before rotating to look at him head-on as if unfazed by the display.

"Absolutely." Digby tore off a scrap like he was snacking on a rib of pork.

"Then why do you look like you're enjoying yourself?"

"Well, it's sort of like…" He chewed for a moment while he thought of the best way to explain his thoughts. "Obviously, the human in me is horrified by pretty much everything I've done since waking up."

"But?"

"But the zombie in me wants to eat the human in me." He swallowed. "It sort of evens out in the end."

"I see." Rebecca landed her drone on the floor. "So why don't zombies just eat each other?"

"Hmm." Digby paused mid-bite. "I think it's too late once someone has turned. I have no interest in eating a zombie." He chewed a bit slower, wondering what it was about live or recently deceased prey that he was drawn to. "I think it's life. Like there's a trace of something in their body that hasn't yet faded. Once it's gone, there's no point."

"So you eat the living because they have what you don't?" Rebecca asked, her voice sounding muffled in a familiar way.

"Are you eating?" Digby eyed the drone as a crunching sound came from its speaker.

"Ah, maybe," she responded, clearly through a mouthful of something. "I figured we would be here for a while, so…"

"So you thought you'd fix yourself a meal?" Digby furrowed his brow.

"Yes." A louder crunch came from the drone. "And it's just a cracker."

"Oh good, that's much less strange," Digby commented, making his skepticism obvious.

"I thought you didn't know what sarcasm was?"

"I do now." He nodded, understanding the concept through context. "Apparently, gaining a couple points of intelligence was more helpful than I thought. But more importantly," he pointed at the drone, using the severed hand he was currently eating, "what part of watching a zombie devour a corpse said to you, 'Gee, I feel like a cracker'? You were disturbed when I started eating."

"Most of my missions take place in war zones." Another crunch came from the drone. "So I've seen my share of blood and dead bodies. I was caught off guard when you started eating, but honestly, some of the things that humans do to each other are worse than anything you're doing now."

"I'm sorry." Digby stared at the drone, unsure how to respond.

"Don't be. I'm not any better." Rebecca sighed. "I've taken part in attacks and raids. Even directly placed explosives that have ended the lives of enemy combatants. I've followed orders, and I've seen the damage those orders have caused."

"Is that what you meant when you said money can buy people? That you had already sold off your own conscience?" Digby continued eating as he attempted to drive a wedge between her and her lords to exploit later.

"Yes and no. I've made compromises with what I'm comfortable doing, but they have been necessary. And if I didn't, someone else would have. War is never a positive thing, but Skyline is a force for good, even if it orders its people to get their hands dirty."

"And you would betray them for the power that I offer?" Digby kept his tone as nonchalant as possible, wondering where the woman's loyalty currently lay. He finished off the limb he had been working on and started on another in an attempt to make his question seem less suspicious.

Silence answered him.

"Becky, are you still there?" He half expected mercenaries to burst in through the door at any moment as if she had been leading them right to him. He wasn't sure what her capabilities were, but he was starting to understand that she could be informing on him at any minute.

Finally, she spoke. "I have my reasons."

"Like what?" Digby nearly choked on a finger bone.

"It's personal, but let's just say that working for Skyline doesn't allow me the freedom that most people have." Her voice sounded sincere.

"Alright." Digby returned to his food, letting the subject drop. Freedom was a powerful motive, after all. A bit of warmth swelled in his deceased chest at the thought that he might be helping her. With him, she might be able to shrug off whatever yoke her lords had on her.

After that, he avoided any serious topics and took the moment to ask the drone more about the world he had been dropped into. He had a hard time believing most of it, but at least he understood what electricity was and why people didn't need horses to get around anymore. In exchange, he answered a few questions that Rebecca had about the Heretic Seed. He still didn't know everything about it, but he told her what he could, while making sure to keep a few things hidden so that she couldn't get a complete view of his abilities.

To his surprise, it hadn't taken as long as he expected to finish off two whole bodies. Apparently having a near-human level of strength and dexterity made the process much faster than before. What must have taken him hours back when he had first woken up had taken less than one now. Granted, he still wondered how that brute he'd fought earlier had been able to eat enough to mutate in the same amount of time. Perhaps some zombies had higher priorities than others.

AVAILABLE RESOURCES
Sinew 2
Flesh 2

Bone .25
Viscera 2
Heart 2
Mind 2

Obviously, there were still some remains that he had been unable to fit down his throat, but everything else was gone. All that remained were scraps and large bones in a puddle of blood. Digby focused on the fluid, watching as it lit up his field of vision. The crimson glow was dimmer than it was before, making the remains that he had been unable to eat seem less appetizing.

That was when a new message appeared.

SKILL LINK
By demonstrating repeated and proficient use of the non-mage skill or talent, Blood Sense, you have discovered an adjacent spell.
BLOOD FORGE
Description: Forge a simple object or objects of your choosing out of any available blood source.
Rank: D
Cost: 20MP
Range: 20ft (+50% due to mana purity, total 30ft.)
Limitations: Can be resisted depending on target's will. Size of the object is limited by the quantity of blood available. Once forged, blood cannot be reforged.

Sounds like you'll need a donor.

Digby read over the spell's description a second time, then he checked his HUD.

MP: 127/127

His mana had reached its maximum while he ate. He sat

still for a moment, contemplating what he should forge. A weapon made the most sense.

Maybe a sword? Digby shook his head. He didn't have any training with a blade. He could remember threatening people here and there with a dagger back in his day, but that had been more of a bluff.

The only thing he felt comfortable using at the moment were his claws. The fact that they were a part of him seemed to make them easier to use. Their only limitation was how sharp bone could get. Not to mention they could break or chip, requiring a Necrotic Regeneration to repair the damage.

Maybe there's a way to improve them.

Digby placed his claws in the blood covering the floor and pictured a shape in his mind. The fluid responded, pulling toward his hand and climbing his claws. It coated each tip in a crimson shell that extended into a razor-sharp talon that looked like it could shred his prey to ribbons.

"Woah." Rebecca's drone took flight, moving closer. "New spell?"

"Blood Forge." Digby grabbed a discarded skull that he hadn't been able to eat. He'd cracked it open to get at the corpse's brain but beyond that, he had no need for the empty container. Now though, there might be a use for it yet. Setting the skull down, he cast another forge. Blood pooled around it, flowing up the bone's sides to fill the hollow cavity. Then, in an instant, a hard-outer shell formed over the top. Digby raised the skull and shook it next to his ear to listen to the liquid center slosh around.

"What's the point of that?" Rebecca examined his creation.

"Saving it for later." Digby stuffed the skull into the satchel that he'd been carrying. "In a pinch, I could crack it open and drink the blood to stave off my Ravenous trait. Or more likely, I can cast Cremation on it and throw it."

"Will that work?"

"Oh yes, I tried it against the brute I fought earlier with a skull that still had a brain in it." Digby grinned. "It was effective."

"I assume that was what set off the sprinkler system back at the Science Institute."

"Actually, that was a sack of gore that I threw, but the idea is the same." Digby repeated the Blood Forge spell with the second skull and stored it with the other in his satchel.

Once he was finished, the pool of blood had shrunk significantly. He shrugged and cast another forge, watching as the remaining fluid formed into dozens of small pellets.

"What are those for?"

"Waste not." He collected them up and stuffed them in his pockets, tossing a few into his mouth as he stood back up and got ready to leave.

"You've got red on you." Becca pointed to his shirt with a light.

"What?" Digby glanced down at the red stains that covered the front of his clothing. "Yes, I will have to find a change of clothes at some point."

"Probably a good idea." The drone flew over to the door and waited for him to open it. "Shall we, then?"

Digby fastened the closure on the front of his leather jacket to cover the blood on his shirt now that he had the dexterity to work the metal tab up and down. There was more blood on his pants but at least he didn't look as scary. He pulled the door open and waited patiently for Rebecca to pass by. "After you."

"Such a gentleman." She headed back toward the stairs to leave.

Digby took one last glance at the remains on the floor. There was no way to know how they died, but he hoped that the pair were in a better place.

Rest in peace.

Pulling up his hood, he left them behind and headed out the door to catch up to Rebecca. Together they passed through the building's main hall, talking about the world's current events on their way toward the exit.

They had nearly reached the door when the sound of footsteps came from behind him. He froze dead in his tracks as the presence of someone behind him became obvious. In his ravenous state earlier, he hadn't thought to check any of the other doors for survivors. He had just assumed the place was empty.

He was wrong.

The building hadn't been empty at all.

CHAPTER EIGHTEEN

"Please don't go."

Becca nearly crashed into the glass door of the building when Digby failed to open it for her drone. She glanced down at his hand, frozen on the handle, unable to move as a voice came from behind them.

"I'm sorry," the voice came again, "please wait."

Becca watched Digby check the reflection in the glass door, where two shapes stood near the reception desk at the other end of the room behind them. They were both short, though one was smaller than the other. Becca couldn't make out much detail in the reflection other than that they were both black. The voice was female.

Please no. Becca's whole body tensed. "They're kids."

"What do I do?" Digby whispered to her as she hovered beside him.

"Ah, I'm not good with kids," she whispered back. It was the truth; she'd never really interacted with them before.

"I don't want them to end up like Asher." Digby pressed against the door like he intended to leave them behind. That was when Becca got an idea. She spun around and cleared her throat.

She had been reporting Digby's position to Easton back at Phoenix's field base since she'd met him. The strange magical zombie was the source of everything so, of course, she had been working to bring him in for capture. It would have been irresponsible for her not to, no matter what he was offering. If they could study him, they might be able to stop the spread of whatever virus or curse he was carrying. Plus, whatever lost tech he was using to produce the abilities he had might be an important discovery.

Unfortunately, Digby's little run through the city had taken them off course. Phoenix didn't have all of its equipment or transport vehicles in place yet, and the hordes were slowing their squads down more than she expected. It was difficult for the living to move through the city, but if she could get Digby to come to them, then that could solve everything. All she had to do was get him to help these kids.

"Hi there." Becca greeted the two teens in a chipper tone that sounded fake even to her. "Do you have anyone that we could talk to—"

"They're dead," the girl answered, her voice cracking.

"Oh." Becca wasn't sure how to respond.

The girl's eyes were red and puffy, like the eyes of someone who had cried until they didn't have a tear left in them. A boy clung to her. He couldn't have been more than thirteen. He held her hand awkwardly, as if he was conflicted between the need for comfort and the newly discovered independence of his early teenage years.

The girl was older, around eighteen or nineteen, with her hair tied back. She looked just as scared as the boy. It made sense. They'd probably lost their parents. An ache echoed through Becca's chest. She hadn't thought of her own parents in years.

"What are your names?" Digby spoke up, pulling her out of her thoughts. He remained at the door, clearly aware that showing his face to a pair of frightened teens was the worst thing he could do.

"Lana. And this is my brother Alvin." The girl gestured to the boy beside her. Alvin stepped back behind his sister as she continued. "Look, I'm sorry to bother you. But you're with the army, or something. Right? That's why you have that drone with you. My dad…" She hesitated. "He flew drones with me sometimes, and that isn't a civilian model."

"You're right." Becca flew closer and rotated in the air so they both could get a good look. "I'm a Skyline surveillance drone. Have you heard of Skyline?"

Lana shook her head.

"That's okay." Rebecca stopped spinning. "What's important is that Skyline is here to help—"

"You haven't been bit, right?" Digby interrupted her.

"No," Lana responded.

"Alright, good." Digby got on board. "My accomplice, ah, I mean, partner, Rebecca, can let her friends know where you are and they can come to rescue you."

"Really?" Lana sounded hopeful.

"Ah…" Rebecca hesitated to answer, knowing that Phoenix Company wasn't starting rescue operations yet and was unlikely to make the pair a priority. There was no way that they were going to come all the way there just to save two teenagers unless they could take Digby with them. She doubted the magic zombie would be willing to wait with them. "Yes, my friends at Skyline would eventually be able to help, but it might take them a while to get here."

"Why does that not surprise me?" Digby grumbled under his breath, just loud enough for her drone's microphone to pick it up. "Alright, Becky, I'm going to turn around. Could you, maybe, prepare them for what they are about to see."

"Ah, yes, I think." Becca panicked for a second, unsure how to prep someone for meeting a member of the walking dead. She tried anyway. "Okay, you two, what I'm going to tell you is a little scary, but I assure you, you're safe." She flew back to

Digby's side. "This is my friend, Dig. He's very special and he can help you, but he isn't a soldier. He is, however, a zombie."

Both of the teens stepped back toward one of the glass doors, Lana pulling her brother by his shirt.

"But he's a good zombie," Becca added before they had a chance to run.

"Yes." Digby took that as his cue to turn around. "I'm nothing to be afraid..." He trailed off the moment he saw their faces, his jaw hanging open like an idiot. A moment passed before he spoke again. "Oh, stop your trembling." Digby walked halfway across the room. "I'm nothing to fear. Now tell me, what happened here to leave you poor wretches alone?" His overly casual, bordering on rude, tone seemed to set them at ease. It was just too absurd to process.

Lana's face shifted between a half dozen of confused expressions before she finally spoke. "We were with a group. Our dad and his girlfriend, as well as a few other men. They worked in the building across the street." Lana hesitated as tears welled up but she dried her eyes on her shoulder and held herself together. "They started arguing over food and—"

"Yes, yes, I get it." Digby surprised Becca by interrupting the young woman's story, skipping over the rest as if he didn't want to make the kids relive the loss of their father. "So you ran and hid in here, that right?"

"Yes, our father made it here with us..." She choked on her words. "He... died once we were inside. So did Jess, his girl-friend. They tried to protect us. But..."

"Fine, whatever." Digby put up his hand to end their story, sparing them the trauma of reliving the event. His words may have been callous, but his motives seemed clear. Then again, he might just be a jerk and she was reading too much into the situation. Becca remained quiet as he continued. "I don't need to hear about your tragic..." He trailed off as his eyes flicked up toward the stairs where they had found the two bodies. He immediately covered his mouth with one hand.

Becca's eyes widened as she remembered the way the

corpses had been positioned. Their arms had been crossed like they had been given a funeral. She tapped her microphone's mute button.

"Oh no… he ate their father."

Becca noticed Digby check his purse, like he was making sure the two skulls he'd kept weren't poking out. That would be bad. He glanced back to her, like he wasn't sure what to say. Becca simply tapped her control stick back and forth to imply that she was shaking her head through the drone. She hoped the meaning was clear.

"Shut up, Dig."

He promptly did as he was told, and she clicked her microphone back on. "What's important is that you're both safe now." She changed the subject. "Dig and I will help you get to safety."

"Indeed." Digby nodded for a second before spinning back to Becca. "Wait, we will?"

"Yes, we will." She forced her most chipper tone. "All we have to do is avoid the hordes and lead you both back to Skyline's field base."

Digby stomped a foot like a child. "I'm not going back there."

"Relax. You don't have to." Becca flew back to the door to look out into the street. "All you have to do is take over a few zombies and command them to protect these two as they head back. You can do that right?"

"I…" Digby hesitated as if considering the idea. "I can tell a small group to stay with them. With the added intelligence the Control spell provides, my minions should be able to tell any other zombies that the kids aren't food. As long as no one makes much noise or acts in a particularly tasty manner, they should be fine."

"Wait, no." Becca paused pretending to check her map. "I just did the math. You can only control your minions for a limited amount of time, right?"

"Yes, thirty minutes."

"That's not enough."

"What are you talking about?" Lana stared at them both, clearly confused.

"Magic." Digby brushed her question aside. "Keep up, child."

"I know, it was hard for me to believe at first too, but he can control other zombies." Becca turned back to Digby when the pair of teens seemed to accept a basic explanation. "Anyway, we've traveled over an hour away from Skyline's field base."

"Damn, we'll just have to leave them here then." Digby shrugged.

"Or we can go with them most of the way to refresh the spell when we get close. We can send them off on their own once we know they can make it before they run out of time."

"But that would still require that I go back the way we came." Digby poked at the obvious hole in her plan.

"Yes, but we have all night. It's not like another hour is going to kill us."

"Wouldn't it be safer for them to wait here, rather than running through the street with us? Some of these rooms might have food and somewhere to hide." Digby pointed to one of the glass doors.

He had a point. Becca felt a little sick that she had been thinking of endangering the pair of teens just to push Digby into Phoenix Company's hands. She flipped over to the area's network maps and slipped into the office building's cameras. Tapping up a few floors, she found her justification.

"Sure, they would be safer hiding here. But I'm looking at the camera feeds of a few floors up, and there's a horde of about thirty up there. Probably people who got stuck here during the outbreak after working late."

"What?" Lana's eyes shot up to the ceiling.

"Sorry, it was probably better not knowing."

"Sure, but knowing is better than walking up there and running into them. Jesus, I was going to search the upper floors for food just before seeing you both." Lana turned her gaze to Digby. "We need to leave."

"Fine." He folded his arms. "I'm not a monster. Well, I am, but I'm not evil."

Lana grimaced as she looked at his face.

"You could at least act grateful." He turned back toward the door and stomped through it. "I'll be back with some friends, just stay here and be quiet."

Becca dipped the front end of her drone as if nodding to the pair, before following him out. It didn't take long for the dead man to find new minions. They waited a few minutes for him to absorb enough mana to use his Control spell, since he'd used most of his magic on his Blood Forge spell upstairs.

Afterward, his new minions plodded their way over to them, one of which had a gash across their abdomen and was in the process of losing some organs. Digby told the injured one to stay where it was.

"Don't we need all the help we can get?" Becca asked while Digby gave orders to each of his new minions.

"Those kids just lost their family. They don't need to see more blood and viscera. It's better if that minion stays away."

Becca's mouth dropped open as Digby confirmed what she suspected. His words earlier were definitely meant to spare the two teens from being traumatized more than they already had been. It would have been nice if he'd chosen his wording with a little more tact, but still, it was surprisingly kind considering how abrasive his attitude had been so far. There was a chance that there was some good in him after all. She shook off the thought, reminding herself that he needed to be captured.

"How are the kids going to tell which zombies are safe and which are not, if we meet more on the way?" Becca wondered out loud, figuring that Phoenix Company might benefit from knowing which zombies he controlled.

"You can't tell?" Digby gestured to the bunch.

"Not really. Once a person stops looking alive, they sort of blur together."

"What would you have me do, paint them green?"

"Actually, yeah." Becca pulled up her map, finding a hardware store one block away. Zooming in with her camera, she saw that the window was already broken. "I'll be right back."

A couple minutes later, she returned with a can of green spray paint clutched in her drone's slender arms. With a little instruction, Digby painted a large X across the front and back of each of his minions. Once Becca was satisfied that there would be no confusion, she headed back toward the office building.

A part of her felt bad for deceiving the centuries-old peasant. He was beyond rough around the edges, but he did seem to care about the safety of the two teens inside, just like he had for Asher earlier. It seemed innocent bystanders were his one weakness.

She muted herself for a moment. "Maybe he isn't so bad, for a man-eating zombie."

That was when she realized he wasn't with her. Becca spun her drone around to find him talking to one of his new minions. It was the injured one that was losing some of their entrails. A moment of whispering later, Digby sent the creature off in the opposite direction.

"Where's that one going?" Becca probed at the suspicious behavior.

"That one has a different mission." Digby headed back to the office building where Lana and Alvin were waiting and held the door for her and the rest of his minions.

Becca watched as the lone injured zombie entered the building across the street, remembering what Lana had said about what happened to their father. The men that had attacked them were probably still in there. She snapped her camera back to Digby.

"I'm not evil," he kept his voice low, "but I'm no saint either. And men who steal a parent from a child are worth nothing more than experience points."

"But that's murder." Becca watched as a wicked grin crept across his face.

"I am a monster, after all." Digby clapped his hands and returned to the two teens. "Alright, I'd like you to meet your new friends."

They both backed away as five zombies wearing green paint approached.

"They're really safe?" Lana shielded her brother behind her.

"Absolutely," Digby gestured to the group. "Stand on one foot." The group all raised one leg, which caused two of them to fall over. Digby rubbed his forehead. "Alright, so they aren't the most coordinated, but you understand my meaning. They will only do what I tell them."

"Seriously?" Lana stepped closer to one of the zombies as it picked itself up from the floor. Alvin followed close behind.

"Alright then!" Digby spun back toward the door. "Let's get you poor souls out of here, and out of my hair."

Becca gave the group of zombies room as they gathered together with Lana and Alvin at the center. She couldn't help but notice a smug expression on Digby's face. Something about it felt cruel. She pushed his crimes out of her head, writing the victims off as an acceptable loss before heading for the door.

"I'll scout ahead to find a clear path." Becca flew over Digby's head and out into the street before switching over to her comms.

"Easton, the package is inbound, marking the rendezvous point."

CHAPTER NINETEEN

Digby watched for any sign of threats as he headed back to where he'd met Rebecca earlier that night. The newly-orphaned Lana and Alvin followed behind him, surrounded by his minions. The drone flew by in the distance, searching for the safest passage through the fallen city's streets.

Thanks to Rebecca's scouting, they were able to avoid running into much more than a few stragglers here and there. A few well-placed Compels sent most zombies away without consequence. The ones that stuck around got a Control spell cast their way, bringing his minions up to eight. The continued use of the spell rewarded him with another rank.

> **Rank increase: Control Zombie has advanced from rank C to B. Base duration has increased to 30 minutes. Plus 50% duration due to mana purity. Total duration 45 minutes. Total number of controlled zombies 15. Mana cost reduced to 6. Plus 6 intelligence will be applied to targets while under your control.**

The spell was quickly becoming the strongest tool in his

arsenal. Controlling just one zombie had made him stronger, so he could only imagine what he could do with fifteen. Not to mention, it seemed that the zombie he'd sent off on its own had been successful.

2 common humans defeated, 148 experience awarded.
Minus 75% due to distance. Total experience gained 37.

Digby stopped short for a second to reread the text. Apparently, he couldn't expect full points from kills that he was not around to witness. Still, thirty-seven points was better than none. A second message came in a moment later.

Minion: Common Zombie, Lost.

"Well that's to be expected."

One of the men that had murdered the children's family must have lived to fight another day. Digby grimaced at that fact. A moment later, another message ran across his vision.

1 common human defeated, 74 experience awarded.
Minus 75% due to distance. Total experience gained 18.

Ah, there we are. His minion must have gotten a good bite in before expiring. A pang of guilt nibbled away at his chest for the murder, but he shooed it away. Those men had stolen a parent from those kids. They deserved what they got. Still, he couldn't help but hang his head and avoid eye contact with the others.

To make matters worse, one of the side effects of gaining more intelligence was that he now remembered his own family, or lack thereof, more clearly. Perhaps that was why he felt so strongly about the men that he had just killed. His mother had died the day he'd been born and his father, well, the man hadn't been much of one. At least the memories explained why he rarely used his family name.

"Turn left in two blocks." Rebecca passed by overhead.

"What's a block?" He lifted his gaze from the ground.

"It's the grouping of buildings between streets." She kept moving until she was out of sight again.

Digby smiled at the drone. It was clear that, back in his time, most people couldn't stand him for more than a few minutes, let alone spend hours with him. He may have lost everything by dying, but at least he wasn't alone anymore. The thought made his dead chest feel a little warmer.

That was when a sudden snap came from behind him, like the sound of a stick breaking. Digby spun around to find one of his zombies grabbing Lana by the shoulder. Panic surged through his mind.

What did I miss? They were supposed to protect... wait.

Lana held a hand over her mouth, suppressing a scream as the zombie let her go. His other minions moved in step, pulling the girl and her brother away from where the first zombie stood. That was when Digby noticed something white clamped around his minion's foot. It looked like a bone, but in the shape of a mouth and filled with jagged teeth. A string of dark, fleshy tissue weaved through it as if pulling the object tighter.

Trap: Jawbone

Digby froze, looking to the children to make sure they were safe. Lana nodded back. Glancing at his HUD, he brought up his mutations list and focused on one.

JAWBONE

Craft a trap from consumed bone within the opening of your maw that can bite and pull prey in.

Digby furrowed his brow. The trap was only laying in the street, not within a zombie's maw. *Maybe it had been left there?*

Suddenly, a black shadow expanded beneath the trapped zombie's leg like a hole in the earth. A dark sludge seeped from the opening. His minion began to sink as soon as it grew wide enough to surround its foot. Then the trap yanked down. The zombie thrashed, splashing the sludge to the side. It mattered not. The force below it was too great, pulling down until his minion's other leg simply snapped to fit through. The shadow shrank as soon as the corpse vanished into the ground, leaving nothing but a spatter of black goo.

Digby checked his mutations list again.

MAW

Open a gateway directly to the dimensional space of your void to devour prey easier.

Both mutations were part of the glutton's path.

"We have an uncommon zombie here." Digby held up his hand to the others, signaling for them to stay back as he reached into his satchel and retrieved one of his blood forged skulls.

"What's that?" Lana asked, sounding curious rather than horrified.

"Nothing, don't worry about it." Digby checked his HUD to see what he had to work with.

MP: 103/127

He spun to scan the area, searching for a zombie that looked different from the others. If a glutton was anything like a brute, it would stick out. Then again, if it was similar to a leader, it might not. Either way, it was clearly after the kids.

"Rebecca!" Digby shouted in the direction that he had last seen the drone. "Need some help." She was nowhere to be seen.

Damn, bad time to wander off, Becky.

A block away, a couple zombies milled about. Digby sent out a Compel telling them to clear out. They both obeyed, understanding that a glutton being nearby was a threat. He waited and scanned the street for a clue. Almost a minute of silence went by.

Nothing happened.

"Maybe it gave up?" Digby hoped out loud.

As if to prove him wrong, another shadow, wider than the first, appeared on the side of a nearby building. Black sludge dripped down the wall just before a corpse was spat out onto the ground. It was covered in the same black fluid, though a green patch of paint near the shoulder told him that it was his missing minion.

"Apparently, the glutton can't eat other zombies." Digby relaxed for a moment. "At least I'm safe."

Lana and Alvin tensed up.

"Oh, don't look at me like that." He brushed their fears aside and turned away to address the empty street. "I know you're out here, glutton. How about you show yourself? I have a blood-filled skull with your name on it." He scraped his claws across the surface of his makeshift explosive.

An answer came in the form of another jawbone floating up from a shadow near Alvin's foot. Lana pulled him away just as a second trap came up closer to her. Several more rose up through the street to surround them from a dozen small shadows.

"Alright, no one move." Digby held out both his hands, backing away. "I'm going to find this thing and kill it before—" His words were cut off by the snap of serrated bone. He tore his foot free just before a jawbone that had appeared beneath him dug in its teeth.

"Gah!" He hopped on one foot until he was sure of a safe place to step then he jabbed a finger at the wicked thing. "Oh, you sneaky little…"

The glutton must have realized that he was an obstacle in need of removing before it went after the live prey he was protecting. Digby assumed that meant that he'd been labeled as hostile. A fight had been dropped in his lap whether he wanted it or not.

He tapped his claws on the skull in his hand before placing it under his arm to free up both hands.

"Alright then, if you won't come out, how about I make

you?" He grabbed the trap before it could sink back into the shadow around it. A sinewy cord tethered it to the glutton's open maw. It must have been what pulled his minion into the shadow. Just as he realized what it was, the cord yanked down.

"We'll have none of that." Digby slipped a razor-sharp talon around the trap's tether. It snapped as soon as he cut into it. A howl echoed from a structure across the street in response. He squinted in the direction of the source. The building was unlike the others that he'd seen so far. It had several layers of stone but with each level open to the elements.

"I'll be back." Digby pointed to a pair of his minions. "Keep them safe." He would have instructed a couple zombies to come with him, but he wasn't sure they would navigate the surrounding jawbones with their limited mobility. Instead, he crept into the new structure alone. Cars sat here and there as he stalked his way across the cold stone of the strange, layered building.

Must be some sort of vehicle storage.

It made sense. According to Rebecca, many people owned their own coach, so they would need a place to store them when they weren't in use.

"At least the vehicles don't need to be fed or have their leavings removed." Digby chuckled to himself.

A sign reading 'Parking Garage' confirmed his assumption. It had hourly prices listed, though Digby didn't understand enough to know if the rates were reasonable. He would need to familiarize himself with the currency of the land at some point, but that was a problem for another time.

Stepping carefully, he made sure not to set foot in another trap. Though a part of him hoped to find more of the glutton's jawbones, just so he could cut them loose. Making the creature scream seemed to be the fastest way to locate it. That was when a metallic clatter came from behind him.

Digby spun toward the sound, raising his blood forged skull. He stopped before setting it alight. The sound had come from a pair of zombies. An empty container rolled past their feet. On reflex, he sent out a Compel to send them away. Then he thought better. He could use all the help he could get. Even if they stepped in a trap, they would serve well enough as a distraction.

Raising his hand toward the first, he cast Control before it got away. His new minion stopped, awaiting his command. He focused on the second, casting the spell again. This time, it only shimmered across the zombie's skin.

"Shit! Grab it!" he shouted to his most recent minion. The zombie snapped its head to the side and reached for the glutton hiding in plain sight beside it. It howled in protest as his minion's dead fingers curled around its wrist. Apparently, this type of uncommon zombie looked normal.

Digby raised the weaponized skull he carried, casting Cremation as he let it fly. A sound like a screaming animal echoed through the parking garage as the pressure inside the skull increased. The glutton reacted by yanking his minion into the line of fire. A burst of liquid flame crashed into its body, covering the unfortunate zombie from head to toe while leaving the glutton unharmed.

"Damn it!" Digby rushed forward, his claws drawn back to strike.

Plowing into the pair, he kicked his burning minion aside and reached for the glutton. To his surprise, the glutton reached for him as well.

Snap.

Horror washed over Digby's face as the glutton placed a jawbone on his left wrist. Swinging at the monster's face, his claws came up short as the sinew connected to the trap yanked him to the side. He fell to the stone floor, only to be dragged up a ramp leading to the next level of the structure. A gaping shadow waited at the top, large enough to swallow him whole.

The glutton howled in victory.

"Shut up!" Digby shouted back as he flailed for purchase to stop his ascent. His claws scraped the stone of the ramp with a horrible screech. Unfortunately, he forgot that the blood forged tips were not only sharp, but also fragile. They shattered under the pressure, leaving crimson shards in his wake and his best weapon gone.

He tried to slash at the cord, but his Bone Claws alone weren't sharp enough. Finally, in desperation he focused on the black sludge seeping from the glutton's gaping maw. Digby hoped the viscous substance was what he thought it was as he cast Cremation. The wall burst into emerald flames, consuming what he now understood was the liquified remains of the glutton's previous prey.

The shadowed opening winked out, leaving burning puddles on the stone. More importantly, it also severed the sinewy cord that had been dragging Digby toward the glutton's open maw. Rolling to the side, he yanked the jawbone from his wrist, tearing the sleeve of his jacket and taking a layer of his own flesh along with it. Digby resisted the urge to cast a Regeneration. The wound looked bad, but it wasn't severe enough to impact his ability to fight.

The glutton howled as several traps appeared across the sloping floor between them. Digby reached for his second skull only to realize that he'd dropped his satchel somewhere along the way. Growling at his own clumsiness, he sprang up and rushed the glutton in desperation.

Jawbones snapped at his feet one after another. His near human agility was all that kept him free of their grip. The glutton snarled as he slammed into the monster and wrapped his left hand around its throat. Thrusting his claws forward, he buried them into his foe's gut.

"Swallow that!" Digby reached in to tear out whatever he could get a grip on.

The glutton screeched, the volume of its cry forcing Digby to wince as it wailed in discomfort. Its mouth stretched wider than a human's jaw should have been able to. A surge of panic streaked through Digby's mind as the creature's cheeks split open to reveal more teeth lining the sides of its head. At the same time, its jaw unhinged with a sickening pop, creating an opening large enough to bite off his head. A sinewy tongue slithered from its massive jaws, reaching out for his neck.

"Holy hell!" Digby struggled to pull his claws free, but the monster gripped his wrist. That was when he realized he hadn't Analyzed his opponent.

Zombie devourer: rare, hostile.

"What?" Digby struggled to hold the creature's jaws back as his mind tried to process what he'd just read. There hadn't been a devourer listed anywhere on his list of mutation paths.

The creature's mouth clicked and popped as if bones were snapping into a different configuration. Suddenly, its lower jaw split down the middle. More teeth lined the divide to snap at Digby's outstretched hand. A shadowy hole formed in the depths of the devourer's throat.

Fighting the urge to pull his hand back, he kept his grip firm to hold the foe at bay. Black fluid seeped from the creature's maw, filling its mouth until it dripped from between each jagged tooth. Digby's hand slipped as its lower jaw snapped shut, ripping off one of his fingers and splattering the liquified remains of past prey all over his arm.

The wound didn't hurt, but the terror of what was happening drew a scream from Digby's throat. He struggled to adjust his grip to keep his hand away from the creature's jaws, only to lose another finger. His knees shook and buckled, allowing the monster to push him back over an abandoned car. Fluid dripped and spattered as the vile creature screeched in his face. Glancing behind him, Digby caught the edge of another jawbone rising from a shadow on the car's hood.

No!

He pushed back but whatever physical attributes a devourer had were close to his own. All he was able to do was postpone the inevitable as he was lowered closer to the oozing puddle below him.

Think, Digby, think! His frantic mind searched for a way out.

Then it hit him. The puddle behind him was made up of the remains of the monster's victims. There had to be some blood in there somewhere. He focused on the revolting sludge, picking up traces of old blood. It was good enough. Without even checking to see if he had enough mana left, he pictured a shape in his mind and cast Blood Forge.

"Eat this!" Digby jerked his head to the side as a spike of black blood surged up from the puddle. It shot past his neck to pierce the devourer's eye, bursting from the back of its skull until it slammed into the ceiling. The creature's body thrashed and spasmed as the jawbone on the car clamped onto Digby's elbow, pulling down for a moment before going slack. Then the devourer fell limp.

1 zombie devourer defeated, 1,224 experience awarded.

"What the hell is a devourer?" He dropped his head back to rest on the car as the creature's body slid down the spike to lay across his chest. He hoped that the Heretic Seed might have an answer, but no message came.

There must have been more mutations available than just the ones on his list. A second tier of sorts. That would explain why the creature had been worth so much more experience than the brute he'd fought earlier. The next tier must have needed to be unlocked by completing the first before he could see it on his list. If that was the case, his guided mutation ability may have hurt his potential. It might have been a mistake to pick and choose from multiple mutation paths instead of committing to one. There was no way to know what he'd passed up.

"What's done is done." He didn't want his jaw unhinging anyway.

Although, that Maw ability was intense. If he could gain access to his own void like that, he could make use of the blood within as a weapon in combination with his forge spell. Not to mention he could eat without choking down bones. He checked his resources, finding that he still needed to consume close to eight bodies worth of viscera to unlock the mutation.

"I've got to keep that one in mind for later." Digby wriggled out from under the devourer's corpse and got back to his feet before plucking his missing pointer finger from between the creature's teeth. "I'll take that back, thank you very much."

He searched for his missing pinky as well, but was unable to find it. The digit must have fallen down the devourer's throat to be swallowed up by its maw. He checked his mana.

MP: 37/127

"Plenty to fix this."

He held his severed pointer finger in place and cast a Regeneration. The bone and flesh knitted back together to attach the severed digit. The torn skin on his wrist and arm regrew at the same time. To his dismay, his absent pinky finger didn't grow back, leaving a bony stub in its place.

"That is less than ideal." Digby groaned, then thanked whatever god or demon that might be listening that his middle finger hadn't been lost as well. He wasn't sure if he would be able to cast magic without the digit that bore the Heretic Seed's runes. Digby shrugged and returned to lamenting the loss of his pinky finger as well as the diamond ring that he'd stolen from the jewelry store that he had been wearing on it.

After finding his missing satchel and making sure the remaining skull was still inside, he headed back to where he'd left Lana and Alvin.

"I hope my minions haven't gotten hungry while I was away."

CHAPTER TWENTY

"What the hell, Dig?" Rebecca hovered in the street near Lana and Alvin.

"What did I do?" Digby stumbled his way out of the parking garage where he'd nearly been killed a minute before. Again. The children seemed none the worse for wear in his absence. His modest horde surrounded them like well-behaved minions, following his commands not to eat the pair.

"Did you seriously leave two unaccompanied minors in the middle of the street during a zombie invasion?" The drone's lens eyed him in a way that he perceived to be accusatory.

"They're not alone." He gestured to his minions as they stared hungrily at the children.

"Those are zombies."

"Well-behaved zombies," Digby added just as one reached for one of the children's shoulders. "Hey, stop that."

"Thus my point." Rebecca flew back over to shoo the zombie away. "I've had to keep your minions in line for the last couple minutes. What the hell were you doing in there?"

"I see, maybe they have trouble resisting their base urges without me around." Digby gave them a new order to keep them in line. "And for your information, I was fighting for my life in there." He gestured behind him with a claw.

"In that parking garage?" Rebecca glanced over his shoulder. "I thought I heard some screeching."

"Yes, it was a rare zombie hell bent on eating these two." He continued walking down the street in the direction they had been traveling before being interrupted. "But don't worry, I handled the foe. Even lost a finger for my trouble." Digby attempted to layer in some guilt while he patted himself on the back.

"Gross." Lana averted her eyes from the bony stump on his hand.

"Indeed." Digby shoved the offending appendage into his pocket.

"Maybe you can find a replacement?" Lana offered.

"Good idea." He beckoned to one of his minions. "You there, give me your finger."

The zombie simply cocked its head to the side before attempting to bite off its own finger. A moment later, it handed him a mostly crushed digit, clearly lacking the intelligence to do a better job.

"Thanks." Digby shook his head and dropped the destroyed finger to the ground.

Brushing off his minion's cognitive limitations, he continued down the street, asking more questions about the vehicles that littered the road. The idea that people had found a way to travel long distances so fast was intriguing. It was a luxury that someone of his standing couldn't dream of. Now though, these vehicles had become plentiful, even vital for employment according to Lana, whose father traveled in and out of Seattle every day for work.

The young woman explained a bit of her situation, having taken something called a train into the city to meet her father and his lover. They stayed with the man for part of the week while their mother lived elsewhere. It was a small comfort that one of their parents might still be alive outside the city's limits.

Alvin remained quiet, but no longer clung to his sister. Apparently, the child was becoming more comfortable with the idea that Digby wasn't about to eat him.

The conversation came to a halt when they reached another vehicle leaning on its side against a building with only two wheels on the ground. It was larger than the others and colored black. The letters S.W.A.T. were spelled out in bold letters on the side.

"It's an armored truck." Rebecca circled around the boxy thing.

"Is that good?" Digby stared at her blankly.

"It's a police vehicle," Lana added, looking a little wary of the truck. "There might be something inside that we can use."

"Oh, then by all means." Digby called his minions to the vehicle and instructed them to tip it back over. They were good at simple tasks like that where they could work together. Digby stood to the side with Lana and Alvin while Rebecca hovered by his shoulder.

"Shouldn't you help?" Rebecca rotated to stare at him.

"They look like they have it under control." Digby folded his arms before adding, "Put your backs into it, fellas."

The vehicle began to rock before tipping. It landed upright and bounced on its wheels. To Digby's surprise, the beast of a machine wasn't even dented. The remains of a couple bodies were inside, along with a lone zombie dressed the same as the corpses. It ignored Digby and the others outside as it ate what remained of the men inside the vehicle.

"Nice, we can use some of that." Rebecca peered in through a window.

"Yes, there seems to be some scraps left to eat." Digby rubbed his hands together without thinking.

"What? No!" She spun back to him. "I'm talking about the equipment. They have body armor and weapons."

"Oh yes, that's what I meant." Digby scratched at his head, realizing he shouldn't eat anyone in front of them anyway. He returned his attention to the vehicle and reached for the door handle. "It's locked."

"Damn, we might as well keep going then." Rebecca continued on her way down the street, stopping as Lana spoke up.

"Can you get that zombie to let us in?" The young woman peered inside, clearly trying her best not to look at the zombie enjoying its meal.

Digby shrugged and cast Control, getting the zombie's attention. "Hey, you, unlock the door."

To his surprise, his new minion did as it was told, popping the lock's mechanism. Apparently the six intelligence that his Control spell added to his target made a big impact. They couldn't remove a finger cleanly, but they could at least perform mundane tasks even if Digby himself didn't know how to operate something. It was as if the mana of his Control spells stimulated their dead minds into motion so they could think for themselves to some degree. He wondered if it would remain when the spell wore off.

Once the door was open, Digby instructed his minions to remove the corpses from the vehicle and lay them against the building. Alvin turned away, understandably. Lana took a few deep breaths as if suppressing the urge to throw up. After a few seconds, she seemed to be fine.

"They must have taken a turn too hard and tipped the truck." Rebecca floated over the remains.

"That's horrible." Lana stared at the corpses.

"Looks like they were already dead when this guy started eating them." Rebecca shined a light on a wound on one of their heads.

"What killed them?" Digby crouched down nearby.

"They did it themselves." The drone pointed its light at a gun clutched in one of their dead hands. "Must have been trapped inside."

"Why would they—"

"To prevent becoming like him." Rebeca turned to Digby's

new minion. "Better to die fast than turn slowly, or be eaten alive."

"Fair enough." Digby started to remove their equipment just as Lana crouched down beside him to help. "You don't have to—"

"It's okay." She glanced back at her brother. "Stealing isn't my first choice, but this stuff will help us survive."

"They don't need it anymore." Digby shrugged. "Nothing wrong with looting them now."

"You speak as if you've robbed the dead before." Rebecca floated past his head in a casual manner.

"Like I said, they don't need it." He winked in her direction.

"That how you got that jacket?" Lana eyed the Ramones crest on his back.

"Maybe."

"Looks like you're going to need a new one."

"You might be right." Digby glanced at his torn sleeves before shrugging the garment off. The rest of his clothing bore various red and black stains. "I'm due for a change anyway."

"Probably zip your fly this time." Rebeca shined a light at Digby's crotch to highlight the opening he'd been unable to get closed earlier when he'd first stolen the garment.

"My what?" Digby looked down at his trousers.

"The zipper." Lana gestured to her own pants and pulled a metal tab up and down to make an example. "How do you not—"

"Oh shush, like you're an expert on everything." He cut her off before having to explain anything more about being several centuries old. Telling the pair that much would only serve to confuse them. Afterwards, he glanced over a few new items he'd collected.

Uniform: common.
Knee Pads: common.
Chest Armor: common.
Helmet: common.

Tactical Gloves: common.
Combat Knife: common.

"Not bad at all." He picked up everything but the helmet and headed toward the nearest building with an open door to change. It was some sort of fancy clothing shop.

"I suggest washing up in the bathroom." Rebecca followed him to the door. "I can't smell you thankfully, but I imagine being around you isn't pleasant."

Digby frowned back at her, then leaned to the side as if to ask Lana for her opinion.

The girl shook her head.

"Well then, I shall be back." He waved to his minions. "Don't eat anyone while I'm gone."

After a moment of wandering the shop, Digby found a room with a basin and faucet in the back. He washed what he could and threw on the uniform he'd found. It took longer than he expected to get himself put together. Having claws on one hand made it difficult to get dressed; though, after regaining more of his dexterity, he was at least able to work the zipper on his pants.

"There, all clean and fresh."

Inspecting himself in the mirror, he found that he was getting used to his deathly appearance. The fact that he was missing a nose barely registered anymore. He pulled a glove onto his left hand and discarded the other. With that, he headed back outside, only stopping to liberate the most expensive looking coat in the store.

Faux Mink Coat: uncommon.

Digby pulled the extravagant garment on over his new SWAT armor. Then, for good measure, he snatched a new satchel from a shelf on his way by. The letters L and V adorned the leather in a pattern that seemed to express wealth.

"I'll be a lord yet." Digby smiled as he slung it over his shoulder.

Laughter met him as soon as he emerged from the shop.

"What's so funny!" he snarled as Rebecca landed nearby, like she couldn't laugh and fly at the same time.

"What are you wearing?" Lana leaned on the SWAT truck holding her sides, now wearing one of the chest protectors and a pistol strapped to her thigh. Even Alvin added a few chuckles.

"It's a fur coat, and it's lordly." Digby stomped one foot.

"It's something alright," Rebecca added.

"Why did you steal a purse?" Lana asked.

"I need to carry things in something, don't I?" He checked his rather fluffy reflection in the storefront window. "Alright, so the coat might not be that practical."

"That's one way to put it." Rebecca laughed.

"Like you look any better." He swatted at the drone. "No one even knows what you look like. You could be covered in stains and we would never know." The drone promptly shut up. "Eh? Struck a chord, did I?"

"Hold on, Dig." Lana entered the store returning with a long, black garment made of heavy leather. "This should work better for the look you have going."

Digby grumbled but took up the item she offered anyway.

Leather Duster: uncommon.

"Fine." He dropped his fur to the ground and pulled on the new coat before turning to the window. His mouth fell open as soon as he saw his reflection. "Oh wow."

"Much better." Lana held out her hand to make an odd gesture with one thumb raised.

"No it isn't." Rebecca flew closer to look at him. "He looks like he's going to a cosplay convention."

"Quiet, you." He ignored her and spun around, not caring enough to ask what cosplay was as he let the leather garment fan out around him. "It's like a cape."

"Plus, it works with the black SWAT gear underneath to make you look badass." Lana handed him a black bag she'd found in the truck. "And this will hold more than that purse."

Duffle: common.

"Is looking badass a good thing?" Digby accepted the item.

"It's better than looking like a pimp from the seventies." Lana kicked at the fur coat on the ground.

Digby didn't bother asking what a pimp was either, opting to toss whatever he could use into the duffle. He ignored the guns, knowing full well that his aim was terrible with his left hand and that the claws on his right couldn't fit through the loop on the handle to operate the trigger. Once the bag was full, he slung it over his shoulder where his satchel had been.

"Wish I could do something about this." Digby held up his hand and flicked the empty finger of his glove where his missing pinky should've been.

That was when he realized he had found a knife.

He cast Control on each of his minions to refresh the spell. It had ranked up since recruiting them, so recasting should've brought their intelligence up to six. Then he handed his knife to the nearest one.

"Would you be so kind as to cut off a finger." He pulled off his glove and held up his pinky stump. "This one please."

The zombie complied, this time using the tool to execute the command without confusion. With a crunch of bone, the zombie offered up the severed digit.

Lana immediately threw up.

"Gross…" Digby stared at the young woman, unsure how something so small had pushed her beyond her limit. She had seen so many horrors already.

He turned away from her and took the offered finger. Holding it in place, he cast a Regeneration and grinned as his bony stump accepted the new body part. It reconnected with a disturbing squelch.

Then Alvin threw up.

"Oh, please, it's not that bad." Digby wiggled his new finger at the pair of teens before grabbing a helmet from the ground and shoving it on his head.

"Hey, Dig." Rebecca flew up beside him.

"Not now," he pulled his glove back on, "I'm helping these two adjust to the horrors of zombification."

"That's nice, but you might want to turn around."

Digby was getting sick of the drone repeatedly telling him there was something behind him, even if it was true and he needed to know. A sound came from behind him, sending a flood of fond memories back through his necrotic mind.

It was familiar.

CHAPTER TWENTY-ONE

"Is that what it looks like?" Rebecca drifted backward to hide behind Digby.

"Why yes, Becky, I think that it is." He grinned as the familiar clip-clop of hooves came from a midnight-black form wandering through the middle of the street. The majestic beast met his eyes with its own milky white orbs. "Yes. That, right there, is a zombified horse."

A saddle sat atop its back as if it had simply lost its rider.

"I thought there was no need for horses anymore?" Digby gave the drone a sideways look.

"It's a police horse. They use them on occasion in the city."

Digby took a step toward it.

"What are you doing?" Rebecca pulled back to where Lana and Alvin stood.

"I'm going to claim it." Digby kept his voice low to avoid frightening the dead animal. "What does it look like I'm doing?"

"Why?"

"Because the streets are too cluttered to get any of these cars moving. With this fella, we can just ride our way back to your Skyline friends in half the time of walking." He nodded to himself. "Then we can drop these brats off and get back to running away like we are supposed to."

"Hey," Lana complained.

"Quiet, brat." Digby dismissed her with a wave of his hand and stepped closer to the horse before attempting a Control spell. Green light shimmered across its fur, but the magic failed to take hold.

"Damn, I really need to start analyzing things before wasting mana."

Zombie Horse: rare, neutral.

"And that would be why it resisted. Control only works on common zombies."

The horse reared up in protest to his spell.

"Hey, hey." Digby held up both hands and sent out a Compel. *You're safe.*

The horse calmed, but still seemed wary. His Compel didn't carry much weight for the creature, but at least it sent out a positive feeling.

"Easy now." He kept his Compels going in an attempt to sooth the animal. "It's alright, I won't hurt you. We're the same you and I, just a couple out of place corpses."

The horse let out a deathly whinny that sounded like a sheep being slaughtered as it stomped its hooves in a threatening manner. It seemed to be telling him to stay back. Digby didn't listen. He had finally found something that reminded him of his time. Letting it go wasn't an option.

"Dig, stop," Rebecca whispered over her drone's speaker. "I don't think it wants to be friends. And we don't have time for this."

"Shh." He held up a finger to his lips. "I just have to win it over." Digby crept closer and sent out another Compel.

He reached into his pocket for a few of the blood beads he'd forged. Holding them out in the palm of his hand, he offered them to the animal like a carrot. The horse eyed the treat greedily. It must have had a difficult time finding food, considering it was built for grazing rather than chasing prey.

As for how it got turned into a zombie, he had no idea. Could the curse have passed on the same way as it did with humans?

Maybe… but if that was the case, then what made the creature so rare? Maybe because there are less of them compared to people? Or that it was unlikely that a zombie would bite a horse to begin with?

Digby shrugged off the question; it didn't matter now, he was so close. He held out his hand, keeping his palm as flat as possible. To build trust, he ate a few pellets.

"See, perfectly safe." He emphasized the word safe with a Compel.

The horse took a step toward him.

"That's a good…" Digby leaned to the side to glance at the animal's underside. "…girl."

The horse sniffed the contents of his hand before pressing her mouth into his palm. Her lips flapped at the blood forged kibble, dropping a few to the ground. Once they were gone, Digby refilled his hand and offered more. Eventually, when he thought it was safe, he patted the animal's neck. The horse stood still as he stroked her fur.

"There we go." He stepped closer until he could rest his shoulder against the animal's neck. "We are the many, strongest as one." The words soothed him as well as the horse, sending a sudden wave of worry through his mind. He was starting to feel more like a zombie than a human. A feeling of appreciation radiated from the animal as if she was grateful for the meager food that he provided.

"You poor thing." He gave her another handful of blood pellets while continuing to send out soothing Compels. "You haven't eaten anything since you turned, have you?"

Lana stepped forward. "Is it safe?"

"I think so. She doesn't seem to know how to hunt, and didn't go ravenous. Maybe horses don't have the trait." Digby stroked her neck "I'd keep your hands away from her mouth, though. Just in case."

That was when a message came from the Heretic Seed.

SKILL LINK
By demonstrating repeated and proficient use of the non-mage skill or talent, Compel Zombie, on a non-human target, you have discovered an adjacent spell.
ZOMBIE WHISPERER
Description: Give yourself or others the ability to sooth the nature of any non-human zombie to gain its trust. Once cast, a non-human zombie will obey basic commands.
Rank: D
Cost: 10MP
Duration: 10 minutes
Range: 10ft (+50% due to mana purity, total 15ft.)
Limitations: Obedience may not be consistent due to a target's animalistic nature.

Just don't go building any undead arks.

"Not bad." Digby raised a foot to the stirrup just as a massive object passed by overhead. The horse bolted at the sound, catching Digby's boot in the foothold hanging from the saddle. He fell back and cracked his head on the street. The world blurred for a moment as he forgot about the spell he had just learned. The horse ran free, too afraid to remember his soothing Compels from a moment before.

The sound of hooves exploded all around as Digby found himself being dragged along the street. He raised his hand to cast his new Whisperer spell on the horse to get her back under control. Before he could focus on anything, his face slammed into a wrecked car, yanking his foot free from the stirrup. The familiar clip-clop of the horse trailed off into the distance as he waited for the stars to clear from his vision. He was just glad he was wearing the helmet he'd found earlier.

"Dig, are you okay?" Rebecca flew in to hover over him. Lana and Alvin followed with his minions in tow.

"What in the bloody hell was that?" He searched the sky for the offending thing that had frightened away his new pet.

"I think it was a transport carrier." Rebecca flicked her lens up to the sky.

"A what?" Digby snapped.

"An aircraft carrying heavy armor vehicles. Skyline must have called one in to help them push through the streets."

"You could have warned us something like that was coming." Digby shoved himself up and cast a Necrotic Regeneration to repair whatever was out of place.

"I didn't know." The drone spun back to him. "They didn't tell me they were bringing anything else in."

"Great, even more reason to be worried about them." He flexed his limbs to make sure nothing else was damaged. "The sooner we get away from here, the better."

"Then we should stop taking detours and get these two to safety." Rebecca drifted toward Lana and Alvin.

Digby settled down, satisfied that he was in one piece. He stared off in the direction the horse had gone. Then he let out a breathless sigh and turned back to the road leading to Skyline's base.

"Yes, I suppose we should get going."

CHAPTER TWENTY-TWO

Digby muttered a complaint to himself as he cut through a small park, almost back where he'd started the night. His modest horde followed behind, guarding the two youths in his charge.

"Damn brats," he cursed the pair under his breath before a smile forced its way back to his face. He couldn't have left Lana and Alvin to fend for themselves. That would have been heartless.

True, his heart might not function anymore, but he still had one. After watching Asher die in the street, it was good to know he'd at least helped someone. Besides, Lana and her silent brother were good kids that certainly didn't deserve to have their father's corpse eaten by the likes of him.

Despite his more altruistic impulses, the frustration of the situation was still maddening. Like it or not, he needed to send the young lady and her brother on their way soon.

Looking to the side, he noticed a building that he recognized from earlier. It had been near where he'd met Rebecca. He groaned. Somehow, he had gone in a gigantic circle and accomplished nothing.

Well, not nothing.

He had leveled up and gained quite a bit of knowledge about the world. Walking and even running came natural to him again. He glanced at his HUD.

MP: 127/127
MINIONS: 15 common zombies.

Not so bad, he nodded.

The trees in the park swayed gently in the night air. It was like a tiny patch of wilderness tucked snug into the heart of the city. Digby wondered how much of this new world was developed in the same way. Were there still forests and small villages? Or was it all cities the size of Seattle?

I'll find out soon enough. Thinking about how much the world had changed, he couldn't help but notice how much he'd changed as well. He placed his hand to his chest, still unsure how he had died. *I'll have to figure that out soon too.*

He walked on as a few zombies wandered aimlessly across the grass, though they kept their distance from his minions. In fact, the larger his horde grew, the further the other zombies stayed away. Digby looked back at his followers, each with a green X painted across their chests.

Not a bad bunch. He puffed out his chest at the sight of his loyal horde.

A greenish, metal figure of a man riding a horse loomed over the scene. The statue sat upon a stone block the size of one of the cars that littered the street. Seeing it set off his complaining again.

"Stupid Skyline and their stupid flying contraptions scaring away my stupid horse."

"Are you still complaining about that?" Rebecca flew past Lana and Alvin to hover beside him.

"Indeed I am." He swatted at the drone only to have it dodge. "With that horse, we could have been there and back by now."

"Maybe, but we're almost there now, so it all worked out."

"Bah." He pouted like a child. "I think this is far enough. My minions can see them the rest of the way."

"Not if you want to make sure none of them get munchy on the way." Rebecca flew around him to look him in the eye. "You remember how your zombies got while you were fighting that devourer. I'm not sure how long we should leave them alone with the living."

"Do we get a say in this?" Lana spoke up.

"Of course, dear." Digby clasped his hands together in a 'isn't that precious' sort of way. Then dropped them to his sides to add, "Provided you agree with me."

"I do, sort of." Lana glanced around the park. "I get that we're slowing you down, and you have done plenty for us already. So, I never thought I'd say this, but I trust your undead minions."

"Perfect, on you go then." Digby shooed them forward without hesitation.

"Hey, you can't just—" Rebecca chased after him. "We need to stay together, just a little further—"

Digby turned to argue just as something spattered across his neck. Reaching back, he pulled his hand away covered in blood. It was too cold to have come from the living. Alvin made a sound like that of a frightened animal. Digby spun back to find Lana's hair covered in black ichor.

"Oh god, are you hurt?"

He reached out for the girl as she shook her head and pointed at his minions ahead of them.

MINIONS: 14 common zombies.

Digby froze as a member of his horde dropped to the ground with half of its head missing. Then, the skull of a second zombie burst.

MINIONS: 13 common zombies.

"What the—"

"Get the kids." A voice yelled from behind a tree as another two zombies' heads shattered.

"Don't shoot!" Lana dropped to her knees without hesitation, throwing her arms up above her head as if making sure they were as far as possible from the pistol strapped to her thigh. Her brother dropped as well.

Three men dressed in the same uniform as the ones that had killed Asher rushed forward, aiming a weapon that Digby hadn't seen up close before. It looked like a pistol, but larger, with a thick cylinder attached to the firing tube at the end.

Silenced Rifle: uncommon, ranged weapon.

The weapon flashed with a rapid flicker accompanied by a dozen muted pops.

Digby's shoulder fragmented into scraps as several unseen objects slammed into his body. His chest armor absorbed several impacts, but his arm hung limp. He spun to the side, losing his balance and dropping to the stone walkway that surrounded the statue at the center of the park.

What happened? Was that a gun? Have I been shot?

Questions streaked through his head. He rolled over just in time to see one of the men grab Lana by the arm. Another picked Alvin right up off the ground to carry the boy away. Lana looked back as she was yanked out of the park. A drone similar to Rebecca's, except with a metal ring floating above it, followed the young woman and her brother until they were out of sight.

Digby's eyes flicked from one detail to another in panic, catching a patch on the mercenaries' arm. Letters arched over an icon of a bird in flight.

Skyline.

"They haven't been bit!" Rebecca's drone darted in between where he lay and the mercenaries. "I repeat, the children are clean."

"What is the meaning of this?" Digby struggled to get back to his feet, casting a Necrotic Regeneration to regain the use of his arm.

"Stay calm." Rebecca urged. "They're going to take the kids to safety. So just stay calm."

Digby glanced at his HUD.

MP: 117/127
MINIONS: 11 common zombies.

"Stay calm, my deceased ass." He ordered his horde to scatter, then turned to run.

"Don't!" Rebecca shouted. "They're here to help. I told them you're special. That you can help them stop all of this from spreading."

"You what?" Digby stopped and stomped one foot as three of the armed men approached. "That wasn't the deal!"

"I know." The drone lowered its camera to the ground. "But we need to learn what caused this and how to stop it."

"You lied." Digby's mouth grew into a snarl.

"It was my mission. I had to bring you in. You'll be safe with us." She looked him in the eye. "Trust me."

Digby's chest burned as he growled at the drone. Every instinct he had told him to run.

"The target is secure." Rebecca spun to face the rest of Skyline's sellswords. "Lower your weapons."

The group of men kept their guns raised, taking aim at Digby's head. "Take him out!"

"Wait, no!" Rebecca darted to the side to block their shot. "He isn't dangerous. He's just scare—"

Flashes of light lit up the park accompanied by a discordant chorus of muted pops. The drone's frame shattered in an instant, sending fragments of the device flying in Digby's direction as Rebecca's voice cut off mid-sentence.

His head whipped back with a violent jolt. The helmet he'd looted absorbed an impact, sounding like someone had dropped a bucket over his head and beat it with a ladle. Oddly enough, that had happened more than once back in his village.

Digby hit the ground again, shoving down whatever memories the sound had dragged up. His village didn't matter anymore. No, right now, all that mattered was survival.

Scurrying away on all fours, he lunged for the cover of the statue nearby. Bullets filled the air, showing him the devastation that the future was capable of. The mercenaries' guns barked like a dozen feral hounds as chips of stone and dust exploded from the statue around him.

What do I do? What do I do? What do I do?

Digby ducked down and pulled his knees up to his chin. Clasping his head he found the clip on the side of his helmet shattered, and part of his ear missing. How could he have been so wrong? Just moments before he was patting himself on the back for becoming more powerful in the last few hours. Now, there wasn't anything he could do.

Magic was nothing compared to the weapons the future had created.

Digby checked his HUD again.

MP: 117/127
MINIONS: 7 common zombies.

I have to fight back. What other option was there?

He reached into his duffle and pulled out his last blood forged skull. It had belonged to Lana and Alvin's father. Digby clutched it to his chest. He had to make it count. The Cremation spell needed to ignite it cost too much to waste. At least he'd thought to forge a new set of blood claws earlier. If he moved fast, he might be able to kill one of the men before his talons broke. All he needed was an opportunity.

That was when the gunfire stopped.

Digby's eyes widened, remembering what Rebecca had said earlier. Guns needed to be reloaded.

That's it. He cast Control on the nearest zombie and shouted a command loud enough for the rest of his minions to hear.

"Attack!"

With that, Digby sprinted in the opposite direction as his newest zombie, hoping the sellswords might lose track of him with the distraction. The rest of his minions closed in as well, dividing his enemies' attention. He cast another two Control spells on a pair of passing corpses as he ran, bringing his horde back up to ten.

The group of Skyline's men inserted something into the underside of their weapons and opened fire. His minions were cut back to five in an instant.

Digby flicked his eyes around the park, counting seven of the uniformed sellswords, not including the ones that had dragged off Lana and her brother. He hoped they wouldn't end up like Asher.

His thoughts were ripped back to the fight as a bullet struck his body armor. He turned in the direction it came from. One of the mercenaries stood, aiming a rifle straight at him. Digby winced, expecting another bullet just before the man lurched to the side and screamed. A zombie with a green X painted across its body reached around his neck. Stray bullets peppered the ground by Digby's feet as his minion set upon the unfortunate man. A message of gained experience passed through his vision.

1 armored human defeated, 124 experience awarded.

An instant later, another enemy was overtaken near the other side of the park. Digby ignored another experience message as he started running toward the next threat. Drawing back his claws, he readied a thrust aimed at the edge of the man's body armor.

Then, he choked.

What am I doing? The question echoed through his mind, dredging up an instinct from the life he'd had before his death.

This man was human.

Digby had killed the three men earlier that had attacked Lana and Alvin's family. Though, then, he hadn't been there to watch it happen. He'd only given an order and let a minion hunt them down. Now, he was the one wielding a claw of bone and blood. A second impulse surged from the depths of his necrotic gray matter to silence the first.

This man was human... and humans were food.

Digby retreated into the comfort of his hunger. He wasn't human. Not really. Not anymore. These men were trying to destroy him. Not only that, but they had killed members of his horde. They had severed their connection to the many, and the many should remain whole.

The choice had already been made.

Before he knew what he was doing, he was rushing forward. Swinging his left arm, he slammed the skull of Lana's father into the mercenary's jaw. He followed the attack with a second, this one snapping two of his blood talons off deep in the man's side. His prey cried out as Digby's teeth tore into his throat. One of his minions joined in to help bring the threat down. A message of more experience ran across his vision, followed by the familiar surge of power.

1 armored human defeated, 124 experience awarded.
You have reached level 14.
2,595 experience to next level.

Digby ignored the rest of the message as the urge to stay and eat his prey nearly overwhelmed him. Fighting his instincts, he tore his teeth and attention away from his victim and willed the Heretic Seed to drop his extra attribute point into agility. It wasn't a moment too soon. A bullet slammed into the back of his helmet, sending it flying from his head. It hit the ground and rolled to the base of the statue at the center of the park.

Digby spun without hesitation, grateful for his choice in attributes as he found a pair of Skyline's men ready to fire. One word formed in his mind.

Cremation.

He tossed the skull from his left hand to his claws to keep from lighting himself on fire as emerald flames spread across its bony surface. Then he let it fly. The men attempted to shoot the screaming ball of fire out of the air only to rupture the skull at the last second. Burning blood showered the man on the left, engulfing his face in a choking inferno. The poor soul let out a scream, only to inhale a lung full of emerald flames.

The mercenary on the right did his best to put out the flames as the other collapsed. Digby glanced at his mana.

MP: 91/134

Plenty left.

Without the resistance of the mercenary's living mind to keep Digby out, the body's blood was his to do with as he pleased. Waiting for the burning body on the ground to stop moving, he visualized a shape in his head and cast Blood Forge. The angle had to be perfect.

In an instant, the entire blood supply of the charred body exploded from its chest, impaling the man beside him with a crimson spike. He never saw it coming.

2 armored humans defeated, 248 experience awarded.

Digby turned in pursuit of the remaining two gunmen. Apparently their modern weapons weren't as powerful as they seemed. That was when a round, black object landed at one of his minion's feet nearby. At the same moment, the two men dove behind a pair of trees as if hiding from something.

Digby stared at the egg-shaped object on the ground.

Did they throw that?

The answer hit him along with a concussive blast as the black egg exploded. Dirt and grass filled the air along with pieces of an unfortunate minion. Flying several feet, Digby slammed into the base of the park's statue. His head cracked against the stone, feeling like something was out of place. He ignored it.

Digby pushed himself off the stone and dashed through the cloud of dirt at the center of the recent explosion. An earthy aroma flooded his senses. Using the debris drifting in the air as cover, he searched one of the fallen mercenary's bodies. His effort was rewarded with another of the strange black, egg-like object.

Grenade: uncommon, explosive.

Excellent!

Without hesitation, he threw it in the direction of the men, bouncing it off one of the trees. It landed dead center between where they were hiding. Digby cackled in victory.

They should know better than to show me their weapon's capabilities. I'll just toss them right back.

A moment went by where nothing happened. It continued longer than expected. Digby's celebratory cackle trailed off into an awkward chuckle as one of his enemies poked their head out. They glanced at the object on the ground. Then they laughed.

Uh oh. Digby watched in horror as the man picked up the explosive and pulled a metal ring from the top before tossing it back in his direction.

"Damn!" Digby dropped his eyes to the item as it landed at his feet. He turned to run, the device detonating behind him no more than seconds later. Jumping, he landed against the stone, this time planting his boots on the surface. Digby kicked off with all his strength to launch himself into a sprint back toward the explosion's origin. He wasn't about to waste an opportunity.

"Rend!" Digby rallied his four remaining minions into action as he raced through the falling dirt. The sellswords were still laughing when he appeared from the cloud of debris.

They raised their guns, one firing at his meager horde while the other leveled his weapon at Digby. He darted to the side, taking a bullet to his left shoulder, feeling the bone shatter. It didn't stop him. He didn't need it.

The mercenary struggled to adjust his aim, but Digby was already too close. Ducking low, he drew back his claws and sprang up. The razor-sharp edges of his three unbroken blood talons streaked through the man's exposed throat. In the same motion, Digby turned and buried his crimson claws into the second man's side. Pulling them back out with a flourish, he leapt away to watch the pair fall.

His minions would eat well.

"Who's laughing now?" Digby leaned forward to gloat, his voice falling to a spiteful growl. He didn't expect an answer, but to his surprise, he got one.

They both let out a labored laugh.

Digby froze as a shimmer of magic swept over one enemy, followed by the other. He stepped back as the shock of what was happening registered. Both mercenaries' wounds were closing, the flesh knitting back together.

That was when he noticed a patch on each of the uniformed sellswords' shoulders, bearing an emblem of a golden ring. Digby hadn't seen it on any of the other mercenaries.

He took another step back, realizing that, again, he hadn't bothered to Analyze any of his opponents. Responding to his thoughts, the ring at the edge of his vision snapped out and multiplied to encircle the heads of both men. Digby's eyes widened as soon as he read the text at each ring's edge.

Guardian: Level 14 Mage, hostile.
Guardian: Level 13 Fighter, hostile.

CHAPTER TWENTY-THREE

Becca jumped in her seat as her monitor went black, her speakers crackling with distortion.

"They shot me!"

Her mouth fell open in indignation. "They actually shot me. What kind of operation is Phoenix Company running?"

Becca unzipped her hoodie and ripped it off, realizing she was sweating. Who cared if she had a stain on her tank top? She was pissed, and there wasn't anyone around to see her anyway.

All she had done was follow orders and reported what she'd found. She'd even made it clear to Easton that Digby was valuable and not a target. Sure, the zombie lied constantly and thought there were demons in his blood, but he hadn't seemed evil. Plus, he was wielding some form of technology so advanced that it was indistinguishable from magic.

"Why the hell would they attack him?" She couldn't understand what they were thinking. "Only one way to find out."

Becca clicked over to her comms, pressing her mouse button much harder than necessary.

"Easton, pick up." She couldn't help but growl her words.

"I hear ya, Crow's Nest. What's the problem?'"

"Your squad just attacked the package I was escorting. That's the problem." Becca stood up and paced around her living room as she spoke into her wireless headset.

"Oh, ah… yeah, Manning didn't want to take chances with bringing a zombie into custody."

"I thought I made it clear that Digby is not like the others." Becca forced herself to lower her voice, trying her best not to shout. "He may be a zombie, but his value is undeniable. He needs to be taken alive… or undead… or whatever he is."

"I completely understand." Easton sounded sincere. "But the situation is complex, and Captain Manning has a lot of additional information to consider. What I do know is that we're doing everything we can to protect the two youths that were traveling with you. As long as they haven't been bit, I can assure their safety."

"Okay, sure, that's something." Becca unclenched her jaw. "But you need to talk to Manning again and get him to understand. We can't let Digby be destroyed; he might be our only hope of stopping the spread of this outbreak."

"Look, I can talk to him again, but I don't have any new information. Manning has a lot on his plate, and I don't know how nagging him again will help."

"Fine, I'll talk to him myself." Becca slapped her mouse button to cut the line. Her chest heaved like she had just run a mile as the frustration of being dismissed gnawed at her.

Bringing up her drone interface, she accessed the pod on the roof. She still had control over five more units. There was nothing she could do to help Dig, but she could at least try to talk some sense into Manning. She tapped the launch button and pushed forward, stopping the drone just outside the charging pod.

"They might not appreciate me barging into their field base with a drone that I wasn't officially ordered to operate." She landed the unit on the roof next to the pod a second later. Skyline was sure to order her to stand down and release control if she made too much noise. They might even forcibly disconnect her. Actually, she was surprised they hadn't already. If they did that, reconnecting to the pod would be impossible. Their security was far too strong to hack into the pod from the outside.

"But if I'm already in…" She trailed off as her fingers attacked her keyboard. A moment later she'd severed the link between the drone she controlled and the charging pod that acted as a secure access point. From there, she assigned the unit a new address separate from Skyline's system, just in case. At least then she couldn't be disconnected.

Wasting no time, she launched a second drone only to land it immediately next to the first and complete the same procedure. She did the same with the third and fourth. It wasn't until she tried to access the last unit that an error message ran across her monitor.

Drone pod disconnected…

"Shit!" Becca slapped her desk as Skyline cut her access. "They must have noticed the rapid launches." She flicked her eyes to the camera embedded in the monitor, expecting the light beside it to flicker to life. It didn't. Almost as if she wasn't worth the trouble of an explanation. She blew out a long breath and slumped forward over her consol. "I am in so much trouble."

A second later she sat up straight.

"Fuck it." She launched one of the four drones she'd severed from the network. "What are they gonna do, fire me? Not after all the time and money they've already put into me."

With renewed determination, she pushed the sticks forward. There was no time to hesitate. Instead, she flew straight for the Museum of Pop Culture that Phoenix Company had claimed as their base.

Becca cocked her head to one side as the oddly-shaped building came into view. Silver paneling covered two thirds of the structure, placed in a way that it curved like the folds of fabric draped over a table. A giant magenta cylinder sat in the center, just as shiny as the rest of the building. The monorail line passed through its upper floors.

It was definitely an interesting choice for a base of operations.

Corpses littered the stairs as she approached the entrance. Three automatic turrets had been set up at the top near the doors. They must have been exterminating every zombie that approached the building. Phoenix Company seemed to be leaving the mound of dead to rot, as if the corpses served as a warning to the rest.

It wasn't a bad idea actually.

If there was one thing that Becca had learned from spending time with Digby and his horde, it was that zombies were surprisingly timid creatures. They only attacked if the numbers were on their side and kept their distance while alone. The only exception had been the mutated zombies that didn't need the support of a horde. Among the corpses of the dead were two brute types. Not even they were a match for Skyline's fire power.

A row of three black kestrel aircrafts had been landed off to one side. The futuristic machines were made up of an aerodynamic body, with two arms sticking out on each side to hold a vertical rotor, just like a drone. The propellers were encased in circular guards to keep them from being damaged. They weren't as fast as a jet but they were ideal for urban areas where landing zones were hard to come by. Plus, their maneuverability allowed them to move between buildings with ease. Becca had piloted a couple overseas since they operated almost identically to a standard drone, only bigger and heavily armed.

Each kestrel could carry around twelve combatants and was capable of near silent flight, including optical camouflage. Becca couldn't help but notice that the numbers didn't add up. She wasn't sure how many men Phoenix Company had brought, but three aircrafts weren't enough to have carried all of them. There had to be more landed somewhere else.

The transport carrier that had passed overhead while Dig was messing with that horse had been a pelican dropship. An aircraft that size wouldn't be able to land, so it must have dropped Skyline's ground vehicles nearby. Becca hoped that meant a few squads would be securing the cargo so that she would find less opposition between her drone and Captain Manning.

Descending toward the auto-turrets, Becca headed straight for the front doors of the museum. Her screen went black an instant later.

Unit lost...

"Shit, they freaking shot me again." Becca flared her nostrils, realizing that the auto-turrets must have labeled her as a target. She had assumed they would ignore her since Skyline's defense system was capable of recognizing her drone as one of their own. That was, unless they had marked her non-combat models as targets when she severed them from the network. A chill ran down her spine.

"No sense stopping now." She immediately connected to one of the three drones she still controlled, making a point to hide it on the roof of another building just in case Phoenix sent one of their drones to destroy hers. Once it was safe, she did the same with the rest of her units before taking control of the last one.

Again she flew straight for the museum. Upon her arrival, she engaged her optical camouflage and kept her distance to avoid being shot down. There would be no point in trying to go in the front this time. It was unlikely that the squads inside would politely hold the door for her.

Looking for a better option, she cursed to herself. She had wasted too much time already. Digby could already be dead for all she knew. With nothing left but to throw a Hail Mary, she flipped over to her comms.

"Easton!"

"Wa! Hey, what?" The man sounded like he had nearly fallen from a chair while leaning back.

"Get your ass to a back door or something and let me in." She wasn't even trying to be polite anymore.

"Sorry, no can do. You are to release control of your drones ASAP, and stand down."

"I'm not doing that." Becca wasn't about to take no for an answer.

"I mean it. You weren't supposed to be assigned to this operation. I can't just let someone without clearance into a field base. I could be demoted, or worse."

"I get that, I do. But I have information that Manning needs to hear. You have to agree that if there is even a chance that my intel is vital to the operation, then you have to at least hear me out. What's more important? Your career, or stopping this outbreak? Because I'm pretty sure the needs of the many outweigh the few here."

Several seconds of silence answered her, followed by a heavy sigh. "I don't disagree, but I'm not going to let you in no matter what you say."

Becca opened her mouth to argue but he continued speaking before she had the chance.

"That being said. One of the squads is securing the tram that's sitting up in the monorail station on the second floor, just in case we need to use it to evac. They have some gear to move around, so I'm willing to bet they've got a door propped open up there while they work. If you hurry, you might just be able to slip in before they're done."

"Thank you." She let out a relieved sigh.

"Obviously, leave my name out of things if someone asks who told you."

"Will do." Becca took off for the monorail station, finding the tram parked, just peeking out from the side of the building near a science fiction themed sculpture. A picture of Doc Brown and Marty McFly was plastered on the wall outside. Becca slipped in close to the roof of the train and did a quick scan of the station to find one door propped open with a small bag. A few men in tactical armor moved in and out.

"Thank you, Easton." Becca kept her distance waiting for the monorail station's occupants to enter the tram. Her optical camouflage could keep her mostly hidden, but it wasn't perfect. Plus, the sound of her propellers might give her away if she got too close.

Once the coast was clear she slipped inside and ducked into a shadow near a series of display cases, each containing costumes from various sci-fi and fantasy movies. She nearly jumped out of her seat when she accidentally rotated her camera to look at the xenomorph from Alien right in its extra mouth.

Hovering up to the ceiling, she followed the hallway to the atrium near the museum's entrance. From what she'd seen through the front doors, that was where Phoenix Company had set up shop. It was a large space with a couple stairways leading down from the second floor.

Equipment had been set up and stored through the room, including a seemingly endless supply of ammunition. Tables had been dragged from a small cafe to support it all. Most of the men wore Skyline uniforms and body armor, making it hard to tell who Captain Manning was. Zooming in on their uniforms, Becca didn't recognize most of their patches or rank markings.

Off to the side, a communication station had been set up. A man wearing fatigues without any armor sat behind it. His hair was cropped short and a pair of black framed glasses sat on his face.

"Nice to see you, Easton." Becca ducked behind a flying car from Bladerunner that hung from the ceiling by a series of wires that made it look like it was hovering.

Easton glanced around before raising the pair of head-phones he wore around his neck to his ears and flipping down his mic. "I assume that means you're inside."

"Yes, I'm over by the Bladerunner car." She raised her

drone up a hair and disengaged her camouflage for a second so he could see her from where he sat. "Now, you wouldn't happen to know what Manning looks like, would you? I'm trying to get a look at their uniforms, but Phoenix Company seems to have a unique way of marking rank."

"Yeah, we do things a little differently." He gestured to one side with his head. "Manning is over by the Star Trek display. Just look for the biggest guy there, you can't miss him."

"Got it." Becca switched off her comms and over to her drone's speaker, flipping up her mic to mute herself. Afterward, she zoomed in on the area, finding only what could be described as normal-sized people. Then, a giant of a man walked out from behind a display to give an order.

"Oh shit, that is big."

Captain Manning was close to seven feet tall and covered in muscle like he had been chiseled from stone. His hair was matted as if he had been wearing a helmet and an intimidating beard covered his face. Becca couldn't help but notice a broadsword resting against one of the display cases nearby. For a second, she thought it was movie prop, but zooming in, she found it locked into some sort of tactical sheath that matched some of the other gear that was nearby.

"That's... odd." Becca shook her head, ignoring the detail as she flew out of her hiding place to head straight for him. She disengaged her camouflage as she flipped down her mic. "Excuse me, Captain Manning?"

"Aw, Christ." He glanced at her drone before turning back to what he was doing. "Who the fuck let you in?"

"Ah, I." She struggled to reform her thoughts, not expecting such a dismissive attitude. "This is Crow's Nest. I need to have a word with you about your handling of the package that I was escorting."

"I know who you are, Rebecca. I requested your file as soon as I was told you were active in the area. And no, we don't have anything to discuss other than why the hell you are controlling a drone after having your access revoked."

Becca decided to go with honesty. "I had to sever the link to this unit. I realize how inappropriate that sounds, but I'm not sure you fully understand our situation, sir. The zombie I was escorting is intelligent, capable of conversation, and—"

"I am aware what the zed is capable of." Manning walked past her as if done with the conversation.

"Again, I'm not sure you are." Becca followed him across the room. "Digby is the source of this outbreak and has a connection to some sort of technology that we know nothing about. He must be taken in and studied if we are to have any chance at stopping this thing before it spreads. And like I said, he is intelligent. I believe he can be convinced to cooperate."

"This thing already has spread." Manning turned to face her. "Haven't you looked at the news and media feeds you have access to?"

"What?" Becca's blood ran cold. "No, I have been focused on bringing you a valuable subject."

"Then how about you take a look at literally any website. There are outbreaks popping up all over the west coast." Manning pointed to the bodies piled up outside. "This situation is no longer contained."

Becca opened a browser at the edge of her monitor, and clicked on her social media bookmark. She didn't need to look further. Most of the country was still asleep, but the world was already in a panic. Zombies had been sighted in over a dozen cities, as if spreading outward from Seattle at an alarming rate.

"How?" she mumbled, forgetting to mute herself.

"I take it you just checked the news." Manning's expression turned smug. "People are going to wake up in a new world in the morning."

"This is impossible." Becca closed her browser. "How could a virus spread so fast? Zombies can't even run. How could they get hundreds of miles from here already?"

"The curse is more potent than we anticipated—"

"What did you just say?" Rebecca thought she'd heard him wrong.

"I said curse." Manning turned to look directly into her camera.

"But it's a virus. You can't actually—"

"I mean exactly what I said." He dropped into a chair to sift through a few papers. "Which is why we need to see to it that this zed of yours is destroyed."

"You mean you already know about the abilities he has." Becca leaned forward in her chair.

"Of course we do. We assume he is connected to something called the Heretic Seed. It's a system that allows the user to tap into the world around them and manipulate it in ways that could be described as magic." He pulled off one of his gloves to reveal a gold ring around his middle finger. Carvings of intricate runes covered its surface just like the markings around Digby's hand.

"Fragments of the Seed were discovered on the coast of England by Skyline's parent company long before either of us were hired. Whatever the thing was, it had been destroyed centuries ago. After studying and experimenting with the fragments, they were deemed too dangerous to activate. Instead, the Heretic Seed was reverse engineered into a new system that could be managed more responsibly. We call it the Guardian Core and it was the reason Skyline was formed. We use it to ensure the survival of the human race." Manning stabbed a finger down on the table. "And that's why we're here. Why do you think we're so secretive and manage our employees so carefully? We have to make sure that this system stays out of the wrong hands. You just haven't reached a rank that would let you in on that knowledge."

Becca's eyes bulged enough to hurt as she stared at the golden band on the man's hand. A part of her didn't want to believe it, though another part felt that it was the only thing that made sense. If Digby had been exposed to the Heretic Seed's system over eight hundred years ago, then it stood to reason that it hadn't been well hidden. Someone would have come along and taken control of it.

She dropped her head into her hands and ground her palms into her eyes. It had been hard enough to reconcile that zombies and magic were real, but now she was working for a company that used the same power. Even worse, she'd never even had a clue. She raised her head and forced herself back to the conversation.

"Whatever, all that just makes Digby more important. If he is connected to the original system that created this outbreak, then he is still our best chance at getting the situation under control."

"Do you have any idea what that abomination is?" Manning's voice grew cold. "Your friend out there is a catastrophe waiting to happen."

"He's just one zombie," Becca argued.

"That's only half the problem." Manning slapped the table beside him. "That thing is also a heretic, which means that it absorbs ambient mana to power its abilities."

"I know that much."

"Sure, but do you know that mana is made up of multiple types of energy and that being dead is causing him to suck in nothing but death essence?"

"And that's... bad?" Becca had no frame of reference to fall back on.

"Yes, it's bad." He stood up and leaned forward so that his face took up her entire monitor. "Having a pure mana balance is practically unheard of, and if we don't destroy that zed now while it's still stupid and weak, we might not be able to later. I shudder to think what it could turn into if it was allowed to roam free. This curse would be nothing compared to the death god that monster could become if given enough time."

Becca had trouble seeing Digby as the threat that Manning did, but if everything he said was true, then maybe destroying him was the right choice. She shook her head and flicked on her camera's veritas software, watching hundreds of dots appear on the Captain's face.

Accuracy 97%.

If she was going to let Digby be destroyed, then she needed to be sure Manning was telling the truth. "Okay, I understand. If you really think he's too dangerous to let exist, I'll stand down."

"I do." Manning relaxed his shoulders and sat down again to go through his papers.

Becca glanced to the side of her monitor.

True, Accuracy 97%.

"Alright, then what are my orders?" She backed down.

"Nothing. You aren't an official member of this operation."

"But I'm here now and I can still help."

"I know." Manning gave a sympathetic sigh. "I imagine this is hard to hear, but you need to respect the chain of command here. You don't have clearance for anything I just told you. I'm definitely going to catch hell for showing you this." He gestured to the ring on his hand before pulling on his glove.

True, Accuracy 97%.

"I'm sorry if I've made trouble for you." Becca let go of the anger she had been holding onto and decided to be polite to preserve whatever reputation she had left.

"It's alright." Manning gave her a smile that looked odd coming from the bear of a man. "I don't blame you for wanting to help. I can only imagine how you must feel being stuck in a building in the middle of all this. That would be enough to make anyone a little crazy."

"I guess so." Becca grimaced in spite of her words, not appreciating being called crazy.

"Don't worry about all this. We know what we're doing here, and we're good at it." He chuckled.

"I'm sure you all are."

"Excuse me, sir." Easton stepped into the view of her camera to interrupt the conversation. "I can't get a response from zero-one."

"Shit." Manning waved her away. "I have to deal with this. Just head back and return that drone to where it belongs. When this is all over, I'll put in a good word for you. We need more operators with your initiative."

False, Accuracy 98%.

Rebecca sank into her chair. That wasn't a surprise. She had probably annoyed the guy enough that he would never want to work with her again.

"I appreciate that." She didn't know what else to say other than to lie back and make her exit.

"Good, and we'll have a kestrel sent to your building to make sure you get out safely. So just sit tight."

Becca's mouth went dry and her eyes welled up.

False, Accuracy 99%.

She pulled away toward the door that she'd entered through. Then she muted herself to keep anyone from hearing her hyperventilating. Manning may as well have lied straight to her face.

No one was coming for her.

That was why he'd told her everything about the Guardian Core. It didn't matter if she knew, because she wasn't going to survive.

She looked away from her monitor and turned to the blast door that stood between her and freedom. Then she looked to her kitchen. There was only a few days' worth of food. The zombies outside may as well have been kittens. She would starve before they could ever get to her.

Flying back out into the night air, she stopped to hover over the museum while she struggled not to throw up. Getting fired was the least of her concerns. She was already dead.

"No." She clenched her jaw and pulled back up to her console to grab the sticks. With her drone severed from the system, Skyline couldn't track its location. There was no way she was just going to put it back in its charging pod and give up. Not while there was still one person on her side. He had been right about Skyline all along. She just hoped he was still alive, or whatever passed for alive to a zombie.

Becca sped off in the direction of the park where Digby was last seen.

"Where are you?"

CHAPTER TWENTY-FOUR

How?

Digby read the text hovering in his field of vision a second time.

Guardian: Level 14 Mage, hostile.
Guardian: Level 13 Fighter, hostile.

"How?" Digby repeated, this time out loud.

"Wouldn't you like to know." The mage grinned just before thrusting his hands downward. Cold filled the air as a layer of blue light flickered across the ground. Ice followed, coating the grass with a solid sheet in a flash.

Digby scrambled away, slipping backward to land on his bony rear. The rest of his minions continued forward, falling as soon as they set foot on the ice. They didn't stand a chance with their agility so far below human standards.

The mage lowered himself to the ground and pushed his hands down as if working some unseen force into the earth. Digby scurried back just before shards of solid rock erupted from the ground in a circle around both guardians. His minions were not so lucky, each being impaled by the sudden spell.

"No!"

His horde, the many, was gone in an instant. He was alone again. Panic threatened to consume him before he shoved it back down.

Think, man, think!

He searched his mind for anything that might give him an edge, remembering that all of his attributes had been reset to zero when he'd passed away. Even with his mutations, that meant that both mercenaries had at least twice the values that he did since they hadn't died and had their attributes reset to zero. The only questions were, did these guardians level up the same as a heretic, and if so, where did they choose to put their additional points?

The mage would've had to put most into intelligence. That much was obvious. He didn't know what would be most important to a fighter. Strength, maybe? He assumed he was right. The math didn't look good. Plus, the mage could heal everything he threw at them.

Digby's unbeating heart sank. It was hopeless.

That was when he realized their one weakness.

They were alive and being alive meant they couldn't ignore their injuries like he could. Not only that, but they also felt pain. For him, a wound was simply uncomfortable. To them, it was much worse. Even a good scratch would require a spell to heal.

Digby glanced at the blood that dripped from his claws. He had forced a couple Regeneration spells out of the mage already. With that, he had a chance.

I wish there was a way to see how much mana they have left. Unfortunately, that was more information than the Heretic Seed could Analyze. Digby crawled away on his hands and knees and glanced at his HUD.

MP: 71/134

240

Forcing them to use the rest of their mana was going to be difficult. Especially with only half of his own to work with. That was when he remembered the bodies of his minions were right behind the mage. He thanked them for their service. It seemed even in death they were helping him. Twenty mana was steep, but now wasn't the time to be stingy.

He pictured a shape in his mind and cast Blood Forge on the fluid remaining in his minion's corpses, sending a black spike straight for the mage's back. To his horror, Digby watched as the man simply stepped to the side, letting the attack pass by harmlessly.

Damn, he really is smarter.

"I was wondering if you would try that again." The mage continued toward him. "Can't believe you thought it would work a second time after showing us what you can do."

Digby clenched his jaw, grinding his teeth as if they had wronged him. More than half his mana was gone. The knowledge sent jolts of fear down his spine. He forced himself to relax.

"Alright, alright, I may have been a bit hasty here." Again, Digby found his back against the stone base of the statue at the center of the park. He pushed himself up to his feet and held out his hands in a submissive gesture. "I apologize for…" He gestured to the scene around him littered with bodies "…this. I assure you; fighting was not my first choice. I was only defending myself. And you all had thrown the first punch, so to speak. Besides, the wounds I inflicted on your men could have been healed by your magic. So really, I wasn't the end cause of their deaths. It's more like you let them die."

"I'm not going to waste mana on fodder." The mage confirmed what Digby had already suspected. He didn't have enough MP to use his magic frivolously. On top of that, the man's attitude toward his fallen comrades was disturbing. The idea that regular people weren't worth saving seemed wrong, even to Digby's questionable moral compass.

"Yes, yes, by all means, let the normal humans die." Digby

shook off his disgust in favor of keeping up appearances. "Us magic users should stick together. So how about we call a truce here?"

"We're not here to negotiate." The fighter leaped forward without warning, throwing a punch aimed at Digby's chest.

"Hey!" He dropped to his knees getting his head out of the way as the stone cracked behind him. A shockwave of force hit him from the side, throwing him to the ground. Whatever abilities the fighter had must have been powerful.

A second punch came for his head, slamming into the statue's base. Digby let himself fall flat on his back to dodge just as a hole the size of his skull fragmented from the corner of the stone block. The fighter's fist continued straight through without so much as a scratch.

"Quit falling down and fight back." The man grabbed Digby by the front of his body armor and tore him off the ground. The fighter placed him back on his feet to punch him square in the stomach.

Pain wasn't a factor for Digby's necrotic flesh, but everything felt wrong. It was as if his bones had been reduced to splinters and his organs beaten to liquid. His legs simply gave out as his control over the lower half of his body was severed. Digby grabbed at the man's chest, catching hold of one of the pouches on his armor. Yanking forward, he lunged at the fighter's neck, his teeth snapping at empty air.

"Nice try." The mercenary shoved him to the ground with one hand and gripped his arm with his other as he pinned him down. The sound of bones cracking came from Digby's wrist as more of his body snapped out of place.

Digby shoved at the fighter on top of him with his other hand in a frantic attempt to push him away as the mage behind approached to stand over them. There was nothing he could do. The only thing he had left was the blood in his own body and enough mana for one or two forge spells. Even with that, he had no idea how he could kill both enemies with that little. Then his left hand felt something familiar through the material of one of the fighter's pouches.

It was worth a try.

Digby focused on his intent, like he had with the skulls back in the office building, telling his forge spell exactly what he wanted. It felt different, like he had more control over the blood in his own body. Then he set it in motion.

It wasn't like he needed his blood anyway.

A black spike erupted from his chest armor before impaling the fighter's abdomen. The column of blood shot upward through the mercenary toward the mage standing behind. The second sellsword stepped aside with ease like before, letting the spire extend past him harmlessly. Digby let out a raspy laugh, feeling like his entire body had been broken.

"You think that's funny?" The fighter squeezed his throat as if toying with him. He gestured to the blood spike extending through his abdomen. "I'm a fighter, this is nothing."

"I can't believe you tried the same thing a third time." The mage added. "You're as dumb as the rest of these mindless zombies. I'm just going to heal him once you're dead."

"Are you now?" Digby forced a cracked grin. "I wonder about that…" He let his one functioning limb fall to the stone, his hand open to reveal a metal ring attached to a pin.

The mage drained of color as his eyes flicked around in search of the grenade that Digby had found in the fighter's pouch. The realization on the mage's face was clear the instant he figured it out. He turned his head to the side to peer into the hollow spike of black blood that had passed by his head.

"Shit—"

Digby ducked beneath the fighter's body just as the world went white. The air was torn apart with a sound like thunder. The fighter fell flat against him, inadvertently shielding Digby from the blast. The mage didn't stand a chance, no matter how much mana he had. Not when Digby had made sure to position the grenade as close to the man's head as possible. That was one injury that a healing spell wasn't going to fix.

"You…" The fighter twitched as he choked out a word as his comrade's headless corpse hit the ground. "You think this can kill me?" There were dozens of cuts across his skin. "It's going to take a lot more than that—"

"Good." Digby pulled what was left of his body close and sank his teeth into the man's throat. He cast a Necrotic Regeneration to gain back the use of his other arm and drove his claws into the fighter's side. Feeling the spell return some of the function to his body, he pulled his head back.

"Go ahead." Blood poured from the man's throat. "Fucking eat me."

Digby looked the dying man in the eyes, resisting the urge to give him what he wanted.

"I think not." He ran a clawed finger down the side of the fighter's face in an almost loving manner. "Welcome to the horde."

Digby dropped his head back to the stone as the fighter breathed his last breath. The swell of clarity and power that accompanied a new level followed as he stared up at the deep black of the night sky. The obsidian darkness above reached out for him, pulling his mind back into his memories to give him the last answer he sought.

Digby smiled as his past flooded back to him to lock the final piece of the puzzle into place.

"It's about damn time."

CHAPTER TWENTY-FIVE

Again, Digby found himself back in the castle to relive a vivid memory of his past. The event that had caused his death was mere minutes away.

The rough, stone walls of the cavern that housed the Heretic Seed surrounded him as he stood on a platform high above the waves. Below, the ocean crashed against the column that held him aloft as the water flowed in through a cave entrance in the wall. The rough sea tossed a small boat to and fro as zombies emerged from the surf. Cold, dead hands clawed at the stone steps that circled the column up to where Digby and Henwick stood.

There was no way out.

"Help me, Graves!" Henwick rushed to the Heretic Seed, unaware of the power he was tampering with as he drew back his axe to strike. "This cursed monolith must be destroyed."

Digby hesitated, unsure how destroying the Heretic Seed would affect the mana that flowed through him.

"Stop! You know not what you do." The witch that had been the source of everything screamed up from one of the doors below, her gnarled body climbing the stairs that lead up toward the walkway that bridged the gap to the column Digby stood on.

"Hurry, you fool. Before she reaches us." Henwick slammed his axe into the side of the obsidian monolith, sending a ripple of white runes spreading out across its surface from the impact like ripples on a pond during a rainstorm.

"But…" Digby froze as a message flashed across his vision.

WARNING: Heretic Seed stability in jeopardy.

"For god's sake, help me, man!" Henwick pleaded at him. "We must destroy the source of the curse; it is our only chance."

With the dead climbing the column below, Digby didn't have a choice. It was his life or the Heretic Seed. He didn't need to do the math to know which was more important to him. Digby rushed to Henwick's aid, swinging his torch into the glossy black surface of the monolith again and again. Embers exploded into the air around him with each impact.

"It's working." Henwick continued to swing.

WARNING: Heretic Seed stability in jeopardy.

Committing to the act, Digby ignored whatever entity was sending him messages as a dead hand slapped onto the surface of the platform behind him. He glanced back, just in time to watch a snarling form pull itself up into view. With a panicked yelp, he swung his torch harder, each blow becoming more frantic than the last. All he could do was pray that if they destroyed the Heretic Seed, the zombies would fall along with it, like Henwick seemed to believe.

The brave hunter beside him chopped faster as well, chipping away fragments from the monolith with his axe. They jingled like bells as they fell to the ground. Sparks flew with each strike as more white glyphs lit up the dark shape in discordant patterns. Cracks spread with each blow.

WARNING: Heretic Seed stability critical.

A chip burst from the side, shattering into the air with a wave of power.

Then another.

"I don't know if this is a good idea." Digby swung only to miss when a cold hand curled around his collar and yanked him back. He watched as Henwick's face fell just before teeth clamped down on Digby's shoulder. To his horror, Henwick merely refocused on his task, clearly writing him off as a necessary sacrifice for the greater good. A second arm wrapped around Digby's leg. He let out a panicked yelp as more teeth bit down.

That was when the hunter's axe cleaved deep into the center of the monolith. Unable to pull it back out, Henwick looked up in panic just before the entire Heretic Seed exploded in a blast of unstable energy.

Fragments of shattered obsidian peppered Digby's body, shredding the skin of his face and hands. Pain burst through his ribcage as a large shard pierced his chest. His heart seized, the obsidian shard driving itself in like a nail as his body was thrown from the platform by the explosion. Flesh tore away from his neck along with the zombie behind him.

Digby lost track of Henwick, cursing the hunter's name as he plummeted toward the water beneath the platform.

He never should have listened to the man.

He should have argued.

He should have run away.

Now it was too late.

That was when his body slammed into something solid. His leg snapped on impact with an audible crack. Stones fell all around him, splashing into the water as the motion of waves lifted him up and down. He reached to the side, smearing blood along the edge of the boat that had been tied up below. Somehow, he'd landed aboard the small craft.

"Regenerate, regenerate, regenerate!" He coughed out the

words to activate one of the two spells he had as a living mage. He could feel the mana within his body, but he couldn't control it. With the Heretic Seed destroyed, could he even use the magic it granted him?

A moment of unbearable agony went by, as if his connection to his new found power had been severed. Then, after what seemed like an eternity, his mana flowed. For a moment, the pain throughout his body began to fade. His leg and God knew what else were broken, but at least his heart was beating again.

It pumped at an uneven rhythm, sending jolts of pain through his chest with each ragged thump. The wound on his neck continued to bleed. It would take more than one spell to bring him back from the brink. He cast Regenerate again and again, until his limbs snapped back into place. The spell ran out of power before healing everything, as if there was too much damage to repair and its attention was being drawn to something more important.

Blood continued to trickle from the bite wound on his neck as Digby pulled himself up to the side of the boat and clawed his way toward the dock. If he could untie the mooring, maybe he could row his way to safety. He just needed a few minutes to absorb enough mana to cast another regenerate and keep himself breathing.

Henwick was surely dead, and even if he wasn't, Digby wasn't going back for him. For that matter, he couldn't see the witch either. He hoped she perished along with the hunter.

Fumbling with the rope that tied the boat to the dock, he let out a hoarse scream when it refused to come loose. That was when an ear-splitting crack drew his attention above. Stone chipped away from the column that held up the platform above as it buckled under its own weight. The blast must have been more powerful than he'd thought, causing the entire structure to lean to one side.

"No!" Digby kicked away from the dock, landing at the back of the boat just before the falling platform pulverized the post his craft was tied to. A chunk of rock landed on Digby's other leg, pinning him to the bottom of the craft. Waves crashed up over the side, chilling him to his core and filling his mouth with seawater.

Salt burned his nostrils as the boat drifted toward the entrance of the cavern and out to sea. Pain accompanied every frantic heartbeat, even after his recent Regeneration had mended what it could. Confusion washed over him, unsure why the spell hadn't helped more. He clutched at his chest in desperation just as he realized the horrifying reality of what was wrong.

I never pulled it out.

A shard of the Heretic Seed had pierced his chest when it had exploded, and he'd cast Regeneration without bothering to remove it. Digby tore at his clothing in search of the wound, only to find it gone.

Realization surged through him.

The reason his Regeneration spell couldn't heal all of his wounds was because it was taking everything it had to force his heart to beat despite the obsidian shard impaling it. He clawed at his chest, trying to tear at his skin.

He failed.

Drained of strength, Digby fell back into the seawater that sloshed around in the boat, clutching the wound on his neck. All warmth left his body as the Regeneration spell's effect crawled to a stop. Looking back over the edge of the boat, the castle burned as it shrank away from view.

The tide swept him away, further into the distance as he cursed the world for his fate.

"Damn... you... all..."

CHAPTER TWENTY-SIX

Digby lay with the corpse of a level thirteen fighter on top of one of his legs.

The memory of his death retreated to the back of his mind after answering the question that had plagued him since waking up eight hundred years in the future. He had a shard of the Heretic Seed nailed through his heart.

That was it.

He'd made the mistake of casting regenerate back there in that boat, without having the forethought to remove the shard first. With that, he'd healed the wound and trapped the obstruction inside his heart where it was sure to kill him.

That was how he'd died.

He let out a mirthless laugh at his own stupidity. Granted, he had also been cursed, so odds were he wouldn't have survived that night, anyway. As for how his connection with the Heretic Seed was still stable, he had no idea. The thing had been destroyed eight hundred years ago; he was sure of it. The Seed had exploded before his very eyes. Perhaps he would figure it out in time, but right now, he had bigger problems.

Digby pushed the fighter's corpse off his legs, rolling it to the side to lay next to the body of the mage who'd had their head blown clean off by a grenade.

"Sorry, you don't get to be one of my minions." He chuckled to himself, then cast a Necrotic Regeneration to regain the use of his legs. Afterward, he looked back through the Heretic Seed's messages to see what he'd missed.

> 1 level 13 Fighter defeated, 1,272 experience awarded.
> 1 level 14 Mage defeated, 1,372 experience awarded.
> You have reached level 15.
> 2,663 experience to next level.
> You have 1 additional attribute point to allocate.
> **NEW CLASS DISCOVERED**
> You have satisfied the level and mana balance require-
> ment to unlock the specialized mage class, Necro-
> mancer. Accepting this class will severely limit what
> spells can be learned but will also make more powerful
> spells available within your specialty.
> **Advance to necromancer? Yes/No**

Ooooo, decisions, decisions.

Digby read over the text a few times. Apparently killing the fighter and mage had been worth more than anything else that he had fought so far. As for the choice of advancing to necromancer, well, it didn't seem like much of one. It was likely that the spells he would be losing access to wouldn't even work with his deathly mana balance anyway. He thought the word 'accept' and was rewarded with a new message.

> **NEW SPELL DISCOVERED**
> **ANIMATE CORPSE**
> Description: Raise a zombie from the dead by implanting
> a portion of your mana into a corpse. Once raised, a
> minion will remain loyal until destroyed. Mutation path of
> an animated zombie will be controlled by the caster,

allowing them to evolve their follower into a minion that will fit their needs.

Rank: D

Cost: Variable

Range: 10ft (+50% due to mana purity, total 15ft.)

Limitations: Mana required to animate a corpse is dependent on the amount of experience that would be gained having killed the target corpse in its living state. Mana used to animate a zombie will remain with target to manifest a bond between master and minion. Implanted mana will initiate a self-sustaining mana system forming within the targeted corpse. Because this spell implants a portion of your mana into a target, it will decrease the caster's maximum mana by the amount spent. Mana used will not be reabsorbed by the caster until the animated zombie is destroyed.

Hope you aren't afraid of commitment.

NEW SPELL DISCOVERED

DECAY

Description: Accelerate the damage done by the ravages of time on a variety of materials. Metal will rust, glass will crack, flesh will rot, and plants will die. Effect may be enhanced through physical contact. Decay may be focused on a specific object as well as aimed at a general area for a wider effect.

Rank: D

Cost: 10MP

Effect Radius: 2ft (+50% due to mana purity, total 3ft.)

Range: 10ft (+50% due to mana purity, total 15ft.)

Limitations: Decay may be resisted by a target's will, making it difficult to damage a hostile target directly.

Bad time to start a garden.

"Wow." Digby couldn't believe how powerful the animate zombie spell sounded. Granted, it would also lower his maximum mana with each minion he created, but still, it might be worth it. Out of curiosity, he focused on the corpse at his feet, wondering how much mana he would have to give the dead fighter to bring him back. The circle at the edge of his vision snapped out to hover over the corpse just like it did whenever he used Analyze.

Corpse: Human Fighter, 1,270 MP required to animate.
Unable to cast due to mana deficiency.

"Gah!" He jumped away from the corpse, afraid he would accidentally sacrifice all of his mana to the fighter without even animating them successfully. Digby turned to one of the other random corpses on the ground and focused on it.

Corpse: Human, 70 MP required to animate.
Animate corpse? Yes/No

"No." He frowned; seventy was too much to spend if he wasn't going to get it back until the zombie was destroyed. The fresh corpses would be better off as food. Digby shrugged and checked his attributes.

STATUS
Name: Digby Graves
Race: Zombie
Mutation Path: None
Heretic Class: Necromancer
Mana: 21/141
Mana Composition: Pure
Current Level: 15 (2,663 Experience to next level.)

ATTRIBUTES
Constitution: 13

D. PETRIE

Defense: 14
Strength: 14
Dexterity: 17
Agility: 17
Intelligence: 23
Perception: 15
Will: 19

AILMENTS
Deceased

Digby dropped his extra point into strength. His claws still took a lot of effort to do any real damage with and he needed the boost. That was when a pair of stray zombies wandered into the park and approached one of the dead mercenaries that littered the ground.

"Hey! You there, get away from that." Digby hobbled his way over to them, still struggling with the damage he'd taken in the fight. "Those are mine. I killed them; I'm going to eat them."

The zombies both backed off, clearly picking up his Compel.

"That's better." Digby paused to think. "On second thought, there's plenty to go around. But if you want handouts, you're going to have to work for it." He cast Control on them both. "Now, pick that up. We can't stay here. I'm sure Becky's friends will be checking in once they figure out I wasn't such easy prey."

The two zombies struggled but managed to pick up the corpse enough to drag it. Digby beckoned them to follow before heading toward one of the store fronts across the street from the park. The establishment looked to be some sort of apothecary. Finding a place out of sight between a few racks of bottles, Digby had his new minions place the body on the floor before sending them back out for the rest of the corpses.

Encountering a second pair of zombies near the back of the

store, he took them under his wing as well and sent them out to help gather the corpses. Around ten minutes later, he had the spoils of the battle safe inside the store. He didn't want to stick around too long, even hidden away, but for now it was as good a place as any to hide and eat.

Digby instructed his new minions to prioritize the bone and sinew, while he gorged himself on as much viscera as he could. It made sense to work towards the glutton's Maw mutation after witnessing how strong it was earlier. Not to mention it would make eating faster and less messy in the future. He looked over his available mutations anyway to make sure he hadn't missed something.

AVAILABLE MUTATIONS:
SILENT MOVEMENT
Description: Removes excess weight and improves balance.
Resource Requirements: 2 sinew, 1 bone.
Attribute Effects: +6 agility, +2 dexterity, -3 strength, +1 will.

INCREASE MASS
Description: Dramatically increase muscle mass.
Resource Requirements: 15 flesh and 3 bone.
Attribute Effects: +30 strength, +20 defense, -10 intelligence, -7 agility, -7 dexterity, +1 will.

BONE ARMOR
Description: Craft armor plating from consumed bone.
Resource Requirements: 5 bone.
Attribute Effects: +5 to defense, +1 will.

MAW
Description: Open a gateway directly to the dimensional space of your void to devour prey instantly.
Resource Requirements: 10 viscera, 1 bone.

Attribute Effects: +2 perception, +1 will.

JAWBONE
Description: Craft a trap from consumed bone within the opening of your maw that can bite and pull prey in.
Resource Requirements: 2 bone, 1 sinew.
Attribute Effects: +2 perception, +1 will.

RECALL MEMORY
Description: Access a portion of your living memories
Resource Requirements: 30 mind, 40 heart.
Attribute Effects: +5 intelligence, +5 perception, +1 will

Other than Bone Armor and jawbone, his Maw mutation still seemed like the most useful. Digby grimaced, wishing he could see the hidden tiers that he assumed could be unlocked by committing to a single mutation path. That was the only way he could explain the capabilities of the devourer that he'd fought earlier. Unfortunately, he suspected that he had probably doomed his chances of reaching any of his mutation paths' upper tiers.

Eventually, Digby's attention was pulled away when one of his zombies motioned to start on the fighter's corpse. He shooed them away, still having plans for that jerk. It didn't take long for the curse to raise the new undead guard. Once the fighter was up and about, Digby instructed it to start eating the bone and sinew as well.

Unfortunately, the fighter seemed to have lost whatever prowess and abilities it had when it was alive. Digby couldn't help but wonder if that was why the cost to animate the corpse had been so high. Maybe sacrificing that much mana would allow the zombie to keep its abilities and attributes. He shook his head. It would have to remain a question for another time. Besides, there were other ways for zombies to get stronger.

The Path of the Lurker was the fastest to reach. Digby hoped he could retain control over his minions after they mutated as long as they were already under his spell to begin with. To his satisfaction, two of the zombies, including the fighter, developed Bone Claws, while another two gained the Silent Movement mutation. His remaining minion just stood there looking dumb.

Digby shook his head at the lone common zombie.

Fortunately, his assumption had been right that he would retain control of his horde even after they mutated into uncommon zombies. It was worth the risk to gain more powerful minions. He looked over his HUD, making sure to check his resource levels while he was at it.

MP: 141/141
MINIONS: 4 lurkers, 1 common zombie.

AVAILABLE RESOURCES
Sinew: 3
Flesh: 3
Bone: 3
Viscera: 7
Heart: 5
Mind: 5

He still lacked enough viscera to claim the Maw mutation, but his horde was becoming a force to be reckoned with. With their feast taken care of, Digby went through the armor and clothes that he'd stripped off his enemies' corpses. Tearing off the SWAT armor that he was wearing, he stared down at his chest where the shard of the Heretic Seed was embedded. Dark veins spiderwebbed across his skin, reaching from his impaled heart to cover the left half of his chest.

"At least I know what these lines are coming from now."

Digby shrugged and changed into fresh clothes, finding that Skyline's body armor had better coverage than the SWAT equipment he'd had on before. Once he was armored up, he found the new gear was more form fitting and easier to move in.

Satisfied with his attire, he pulled his leather trench coat off the shelf where he had left it and slipped it back on. The shoulder was ripped where he'd been shot, but it was nice not to be covered in blood and who knew what else again.

Finally, crouching down to the floor, Digby placed his right hand in the puddle of blood and reforged a coating around his claws to increase their damage. He instructed the fighter zombie to do the same and formed it a set of crimson talons as well. With the rest of his mana, he refreshed his Control spells and forged three more skulls full of blood to use as Cremation bombs. After making use of most of the blood, Digby noticed something shiny and gold on the floor.

"What have we here?"

He snatched it off the floor with a claw and examined the object. It was a ring, bearing similar runes to the ones that were etched into the skin of his left hand. For a moment he wasn't sure where it had come from, then he glanced at the fighter zombie standing behind him. A band of gold sparkled on its finger as well. Unfortunately, it was on the same hand that had since mutated into a set of claws, causing the metal to stretch and bend into misshapen scrap.

Digby returned his attention to the golden band in his hand, realizing it must have belonged to the mage he'd killed. One of his zombies must have stripped it off while eating the man's fingers.

Apparently, there were more differences between heretics and guardians that he realized. Digby glanced at the black runes that marked his skin where the obsidian band he'd placed on his finger eight hundred years ago had been absorbed into his body. As it seemed, becoming a guardian was a less invasive process, meaning the rings that connected them to whatever system granted them power could still be removed. He rubbed a bit of dried blood from the golden band he'd found.

"It's mine now, I suppose." Digby grinned and closed his left hand around the ring just as the Heretic Seed sent him a new message.

Compatible spells detected.
ICICLE
Gather moisture from the air around you to form an icicle.
Once formed, icicles will hover in place for 3 seconds,
during which they may be claimed as melee weapons or
launched in the direction of a target. Accuracy is depen-
dent on caster's focus.
TERRA BURST
Call forth a circle of stone shards from the earth to injure
any target unfortunate enough to be standing in the
vicinity.
Choose one spell to be extracted.

Digby did a double take at the text. Could he really be able to learn a new spell off the ring of another mage? He hadn't received any messages when he'd held his heretic rings earlier. Maybe there was some sort of difference between the obsidian ones he'd stolen back in the castle and the gold bands that the guardians wore?

He wondered for a moment if this new ring would allow him to create a new guardian, just as the ones he carried created heretics. With his intelligence climbing a few points higher than it had been when he'd been alive, he found each question more interesting than the last. It was as if the nature of his mind had become more curious. Eventually, he shook his head and pushed his pondering aside for later, opting to focus on the question at hand. Which spell should he extract?

Digby reread the description of each spell before letting out an annoyed groan.

"Oh…"

All of his excitement at the new discovery faded away when he remembered that both spells would almost certainly require a mana balance other than the pure death essence that he was filled with. Some of the details of both spells were still hidden, but from the descriptions, it sounded like he'd need fluid and soil.

Although, he might be able to force one to evolve into something new by casting it anyway. It had worked for Fireball and Regeneration, after all. There was some risk to it, but the Heretic Seed had said that creativity and risk taking might be rewarded.

With no way to guess the outcome that he might get, he opted for Terra Burst. Icicle was too similar to Fireball so it made sense to pick something more unique. Ultimately, what he needed most was something that could do some damage. With a little luck, the earth spell might become something strong. The ring crumbled to dust the instant he made his decision.

Spell, Terra Burst, extracted.

What a waste of perfectly good gold.

Digby ignored the Heretic Seed's complaint and immediately attempted to cast the spell. He received the same warning as before when he tried to use Fireball with his deceased mana balance.

Terra Burst cancelled due to incomparable mana composition. Minimum 10% soil essence required.

He forced it regardless, getting a new spell in return.

Terra Burst has evolved into Burial.

"Yes!" Digby flicked his eyes around the store, looking for the result of the spell. Then, nothing happened.

Burial cancelled due to environmental limitations.

"What?" Digby read over the new spell's description.

BURIAL

Description: Displace an area of earth to dig a grave beneath a target. The resulting grave will fill back in after five seconds.
Rank: D
Cost: 20 MP
Grave Size: 4ft (+50% due to mana purity, total 6ft.)
Range: 10ft (+50% due to mana purity, total 15ft.)
Limitations: Requires access to bare earth to cast.

"Are you joking." Digby sat down and frowned at the description. Leave it to him to discover a spell that he couldn't use. With the city of Seattle being covered in streets and man-made structures, there was hardly anywhere left that had access to bare earth. Other than the park he'd just left, he hadn't come across anywhere that might work.

"Stupid death mana."

When he was finished sulking, Digby ordered his zombies to gather up the rest of the equipment. They would probably take a while to get all the armor on, so he thought it would be best to move before someone came looking for him. They could finish getting ready once they were further away.

They left behind the rifles since he still couldn't fire one properly with his claws and he had his doubts about his minions' capability to aim the weapons. He did, however, find two grenades that might come in handy later, especially if he ran out of mana. He tossed them into his bag along with the three skulls he'd forged.

Searching the rear of the store, he located a back door and guided his new, more dangerous horde through an alleyway. It seemed prudent to stay off the main streets until they put in some distance from Skyline's base. All that mattered was that he made a clean getaway.

As soon as he was convinced he was safe and hadn't left a trail, he ordered his minions to stop in an alley. He patrolled the length of the space to make sure there was no one around, then ordered them to strip and change into their new gear. Digby had to help a couple zombies that struggled with their Bone Claws.

"No, you'll never get those trousers off like that." He slipped one of his talons down the front of his minion's pants and slit the uncooperative garment all the way down one leg. "There. Now get this on." He tossed them one of the mercenaries' pants just as a familiar voice came from the other end of the alley.

"What the hell are you doing?"

Digby spun to find a drone hovering in the space. He narrowed his eyes the moment he saw it.

"Hello, Becky."

CHAPTER TWENTY-SEVEN

"Everybody run!" Digby grabbed whatever he could and bolted for the other end of the alley.

The rest of his horde got moving as well, each still in various stages of undress. Two of them were still missing pants and another was wearing nothing but a pair of black and yellow undershorts with the silhouette of what looked like a bat on them. One of his zombies tripped and fell while the others simply shambled forward. The only ones that were able to manage a brisk jog were the two lurkers that had gained the Silent Movement mutation.

Digby grimaced at their performance but kept running regardless. He couldn't risk staying back to help them now that Rebecca had found him again. It was only a matter of time before the traitor called in her mercenary friends.

"Wait!" The drone chased after him.

"Not a chance in hell, you treacherous wench!" Digby kept running.

The drone scoffed. "Did you just call me a wench?"

"Indeed!" Digby scooped up an empty can from the ground and lobbed it over his shoulder in her direction.

"Whatever, just stop. I'm alone and I'm on your side." Rebeca's tone came out sounding exhausted.

"That's just what a treacherous wench would say," he shouted back over his shoulder. "And if you think you're getting your mitts on the ring I showed you, then consider my offer rescinded."

"Please, Dig, I don't care about the ring. Just stop." The drone caught up beside him. "I didn't know they intended to kill you. I thought they would take you into protective custody if you cooperated. I didn't know how dangerous they thought you were."

"Nonsense. I'm not dangerous. I have no intention of hurting anyone."

"Dig, you just killed an entire squad."

"They attacked first!" Digby stopped short and spun on the drone while pointing to himself with a thumb. "If I hadn't defended myself, your lot would have killed me."

"I realize that, and I don't blame you for fighting back." Rebecca stopped to hover in front of him.

"I don't care if you blame me. As far as I'm concerned the blood of those men is on your hands." He jabbed a talon at her camera. "If you hadn't thrown me to the wolves, your people would still be alive."

"I was only doing my job. I didn't know——"

"You didn't know. You didn't know." Digby threw up his hands. "That's all you keep saying. Just playing dumb to confuse the eight-hundred-year-old-zombie." He dropped his arms back to his sides. "I suppose you also had no idea that your friends have magic."

"I... just found that out as well." Rebecca drifted forward. "I swear, I didn't know any of that. I'm not a high-ranking operator. They don't reveal that kind of thing to just anyone."

"Sure, sure, I believe you."

"You do?"

"Yes, I do."

"Are you sure?" The drone tilted to one side as if skeptical. "Because you sound like you're being sarcastic."

"Of course I'm being sarcastic!" Digby slapped the drone on one of its propellers, causing it to veer off to the side. "I'm smarter and know what sarcasm is now, remember?"

"Sure, and this coming from the guy that, just a few hours ago, thought people got sick because there were demons in their blood." Rebecca stabilized her drone.

"Bah, that may as well have been a lifetime ago." Digby folded his arms and turned up what was left of his nose. "I'm not ashamed to admit that I was a simpleton back when I woke up. That's the nice thing about leveling, it gives you the clarity to understand just how bad off you were. I'd love to see what your intelligence values are."

"Fine, whatever, you're a genius." The drone spun in a circle as if frustrated.

"That's right, I am." Digby gave her an exaggerated shrug. "Which means I don't need you anymore."

"I'm sorry, okay?" The tension in her tone was unmistakable. "I'm sorry you were attacked, and I'm sorry I lied to you. I thought I was doing the right thing."

"The right thing? The right thing!" Digby couldn't help but release a wicked cackle at her words. "My dear Becky, you didn't just lead me into a trap back there, but you put Lana and Alvin in danger too."

"I did no—"

"You did!" Digby cut her off. "I thought it was strange that you were so dead set on bringing those orphans into Skyline's care but—fool that I was—I wanted to believe that you were really on my side. To me, it seemed safer for them to find somewhere to hide and wait for help to come to them. But no, we just had to escort them through a city filled with the blood-thirsty dead. For heaven's sake, Becky, they were attacked by a devourer. They could have been killed."

"I never meant to—"

"What?" Digby stomped toward the drone. "You never

meant to endanger the lives of a child and young lady?"

"Of course not."

"Do you even know where they are now? Because I don't."

"They were taken in safely."

"And I'm supposed to take your word on that. They might be dead for all I know. Maybe murdered in the street, like poor Asher." He spat his words with as much venom as he could muster, angrier at the fact that she had betrayed his trust than the ambush that had nearly killed him.

"Okay. I get it." Rebecca shifted her camera away, clearly unable to look him in the eyes. "You're right, I used them. I didn't think about their safety. They were nothing but civilians in a war zone to me. I would've liked them to remain safe, but the mission took priority. That is what I was trained to do."

"Then I'd say that makes you more of a monster than me." Digby turned away from the drone. "And I eat people."

"I can't help what I am." She floated downward so she could look up into Digby's eyes. "All I can say is that I am on your side now, and I want to help you." Rebecca paused before adding, "And I need you to help me too."

"What are you on about?" Digby rolled his eyes.

"Skyline abandoned me."

"Oh, I'm so sorry." Digby gave her another dose of sarcasm, which was quickly becoming his favorite mode of expression. "Did they really? Did your murderous employers abandon you?"

"You don't have to be a jerk about it." The drone drifted away from him.

"Actually, I do. I gave you my trust and you tore it to pieces. You deserve whatever you get."

"I know, and I really am sorry. I mean it." Rebecca's voice cracked a bit. "And yes, Skyline has turned on me, so we're in the same boat here."

"Same boat, my necrotic ass." Digby raised his voice. "I am stuck here, running through this godforsaken future while people that I don't even know are trying to destroy me. I have to kill and eat the living, just to survive. How would you under-stand anything about that? You only see the world through the lens of this thing," he swatted at the drone, "all the while you sit at home, safe and sound."

Rebecca dodged his swipe and remained silent for a moment before finally adding, "I'm in Seattle."

"What?"

"I'm not safe at home. I know I told you before that I was somewhere far away." She flew closer. "But I am stationed here. I'm currently locked in an apartment a few blocks from the field base. And I just found out that Skyline will not be rescuing me. I can't leave, and I only have enough food for a few days."

"Why can't you leave?" Digby gave her a sideways look.

"Skyline keeps some of its personnel in controlled spaces. Mine is an apartment with a locked door that only they can open. I don't have the key."

"That would make you a prisoner." Digby scoffed, having trouble believing such an outlandish story.

"It's a requirement of my job." The drone drifted closer as if trying to reform a bond with him.

"That's your plan then?"

"My plan?"

"Yes, your plan. Your plan to trick me." Digby spun on the drone, baring his teeth. "You failed to destroy me the first time. So now you're spinning this new story of desperation. A princess in a tower in need of saving. Do you really think I'm that simple?" He stomped toward her.

"It's not a story." She backed up to avoid him.

"Do you really expect me to believe that anyone in their right mind would willingly work for an employer that keeps them in a prison? That you would just throw away your freedom in service of Skyline?"

"The world is a different place than it was when you were alive and opportunities are few and far between. I was never given a choice."

"Enough!" Digby snarled at the drone. "All you do is lie.

Now go away and leave me be."

"I'm not leaving." She hovered in place, like she was putting her foot down.

"That's what you think." Digby raised his hand and focused on the drone. "Decay."

"You son of a—" A sudden spark shot from the device before it spun off to one side and crashed into a wall. It plummeted into a pile of refuse bags a second later.

1 common drone defeated, 10 experience awarded.

He growled at the fallen drone for a full ten seconds before letting it fade to a quiet sob. His throat ached. Digby swallowed the pain.

"I should have done that minutes ago." He knocked the scrap aside with a halfhearted kick. "Good riddance."

It would have been easy to fall for another of Rebecca's ploys, after spending a few hours with the woman's mechanical puppet. She was a bit rough around the edges, but he'd be lying if he said he hadn't enjoyed having her as an accomplice earlier. It was the longest that anyone had spent with him before brushing him off. In the end, he'd suppressed his suspicions about her loyalty in hope that she might have truly been an ally. If he hadn't seen the treachery the woman was capable of with his own eyes, he might have believed her lies this time as well.

He was just glad he knew better now.

"I don't need her anyway." He held up his hands, his crimson talons gleaming in the dim light of the alleyway. "I don't need anyone."

Behind him, his collection of minions finished equipping the gear that they'd stripped off their last meal. Once they were done, they stood together to await new orders.

"I really don't need anyone." Digby fastened the chin strap of one of his lurker's helmets. "At least not anyone human. The dead are honest. The dead, I can trust."

Digby bent down to pick up the smoking remains of the

drone. There was rust coating every piece of exposed metal, showing him how powerful his Decay spell could potentially be.

"Not so smart now, are you?" He tossed the scrap aside, where it clattered across the ground to rest in a heap. Staring down at the drone, Digby noticed a familiar shape poking out from underneath.

"Is that a feather?" He pushed the scrap aside. Sure enough, a collection of black feathers lay poking out from under the ruined device. Digby knelt down and cleared away the trash.

"What do we have here?"

The corpse of a large, black bird rested on the alleyway cement. It looked like the remains of a raven, though its head was twisted backward as if it had flown straight into a wall.

"Poor thing."

The unnaturally tall buildings must have claimed the unfortunate creature. Digby made a point to sneer at the high rises above.

"Well, let's see if we can fix you up now, shall we?" Digby focused on the raven, getting a message from the Heretic Seed a second later.

Corpse: Raven, 5 MP required to animate.
Animate corpse? Yes/No

"Now that's a cost I can deal with."

Digby thought the word 'yes' and watched as a familiar green light shimmered across the avian form. His mana ticked down, decreasing his maximum value at the same time. A few seconds passed where nothing happened. Eventually, Digby got impatient and poked the corpse.

"Come on, you, wake up."

That was when a strange sensation swelled from within him. It was as if he had suddenly become aware of a presence other than his own. He could sense his mana within the bird.

First there was a twitch, followed by another. Then, slowly, the muddy black color of the raven's feathers began to drain, replaced by a pale white. Even its beak shifted to a light gray. The newborn avian zombie opened its dusty, green eyes and cracked its mouth, still unable to move any part of its body below its neck.

"Oh, sorry!" Digby panicked as he realized that the injury that had ended the raven's life was still disrupting the control it had over its body. Without thinking, he reached out to scoop up the poor creature and attempt a Necrotic Regeneration.

> **Spell ineffective. Unable to repair damage due to a lack of void resources.**
> **WARNING: Due to an attempt to repair damage without compatible resources to work from, your spell has activated the target's Ravenous trait.**

"It's just like when I woke up. The poor thing has nothing in its void." Digby glanced down the alley, realizing that he and his horde were still a little exposed. He lowered his head to the bird in his arms. "Let's get somewhere safe and patch you up. Sound good?"

With that, he dashed off, making sure that his minions didn't lag too far behind. It didn't take long before he found another open building. Ducking inside, he found the empty dining room of an oversized tavern. Tables were set about around a bar while garish pictures and objects hung all over the walls. He ignored it all and returned his attention to the newborn zombie he carried.

Digby sat down at the bar and reached into the duffle he'd instructed two of his minions to carry. He retrieved one of his blood forged skulls that he intended to use as weapons, hoping that the blood was still fresh enough to provide a decent meal. Banging it on the counter a few times, he opened a crack in the hardened outer shell. He dipped the tip of one of his claws into the skull's liquid center and brought a droplet of fluid to the raven's beak. Its tongue lapped at the blood eagerly.

"Good girl."

Digby wasn't sure how he knew that the raven had been female, but somehow the connection he'd created told him so. When he focused on the newly-formed bond, the circle at the edge of his vision spun out to display a new list of information.

STATUS
Name: None
Race: Zombie (Avian)
Mutation Path: Unspecified
Mana: 5/5
Mana Composition: Pure

ATTRIBUTES
Constitution: 0
Defense: 0
Strength: 2
Dexterity: 0
Agility: 8
Intelligence: 0
Perception: 0
Will: 0

AILMENTS
Deceased
Severed Spine

Digby cracked a fragment of bone from the skull and ground it into bits using a nearby spoon. The nameless raven chomped it down. After a few minutes of feeding the helpless zombie, he attempted another Regeneration spell. Watching closely, he waited for a reaction.

A moment passed. Then, all at once, the bird's wings spasmed and its head rotated back around to face the right direction. After that, it settled down and began to move normally. Digby placed it on the bar to watch as the unsteady zombie staggered back to its feet.

"Good job."

He reached out to help balance the raven, remembering that the majority of its attributes were still nonexistent. The only ones that weren't were its agility and strength. Digby focused on their bond, finding that the bird had a number of zombie traits as well. Some, like Ravenous, Blood Sense, and Mutation, were the same as his, but there seemed to be a couple new traits that were unique to her.

FLIGHT OF THE DEAD
As an avian zombie, the attributes required to maintain the ability to fly have been restored. Agility + 8, Strength +2.
BOND OF THE DEAD
As a zombie animated directly by a necromancer, this creature will gain one attribute point for every 2 levels of their master. These points may be allocated at any time. 7 attribute points remaining.
CALL OF THE DEAD
As a zombie animated directly by a necromancer, this minion and its master will be capable of sensing each other's presence through their bond. In addition, the necromancer will be capable of summoning this minion to their location over great distances.

"Interesting." Digby considered how the raven's abilities might come in handy. Then he clasped his hands together. "First thing's first. What should I put your seven points in?"

The raven stared at him, clearly confused.

The creature's agility had been taken care of for now by its flight trait. She could probably use more, but that would have to wait. No, right now, intelligence was where she was falling short. At least, that was what Digby assumed from her blank stare. Beyond that, some resistance was also a priority. If he was going up against other magic users, he didn't want them catching her with a basic spell that targeted her body directly.

The bird hopped once, then pecked at her own reflection in a nearby drinking glass.

Digby winced, then dropped four points into intelligence. He set the other three to will. Once he was finished, he fed the raven the rest of the blood from the skull to make sure it was clear of its Ravenous trait. The change was apparent a moment later as the bird hopped over to him with an attentive look in her eyes.

"That's more like it." Digby clapped his hands just before the bird took flight and dove for a piece of silverware that was on one of the tables. A thought resonated over their bond that translated into one word.

Shiny!

"I guess some more intelligence will be necessary at some point. Maybe the leader mutation path would be best for you."

She picked up one end of a piece of cutlery and began to drag it back to him like it was a gift.

Shiny!

"Can't argue with that." Digby accepted the present, then pocketed a few more eating utensils into one of the pouches on his body armor. Back in the time he'd come from, only the wealthy had the luxury of metal cutlery.

"I think we'll get along just fine." Digby bent down and scooped up the bird to place her on his shoulder. "Though, you're going to need a name."

The albino raven settled in.

"I hope you don't mind, but I'd like to call you Asher." Digby scratched her chin as he thought of the boy he'd tried to save earlier that night. Somehow, the name fit. The bird gave an indifferent caw, as if leaving the decision up to him.

"Asher it is, then." He stole a few more pieces of cutlery from the tavern for good measure. "Now let's see about finding someone to eat. I bet Skyline has a few more squads out searching for us. After what they've done tonight, they deserve to be added to the menu."

CHAPTER TWENTY-EIGHT

"This will work nicely." Digby stepped into the shadows of a partially constructed building with his new pet Asher perched on his shoulder.

The bottom floors were empty save for piles of building materials clearly meant to be used to erect the upper levels. Translucent sheeting hung throughout the structure as the night shrouded the place in darkness. It was the perfect place for an ambush.

He glanced at his HUD, taking a count of his horde.

MP: 136/136

MINIONS: Asher, 4 lurker zombies, 10 common zombies.

"Room for one more." Digby cast Control on a zombie that was wandering the street outside, bringing his total number of minions to sixteen, including Asher. He beckoned to the new zombie and instructed his horde to gather on the first floor.

"Alright, listen up, teeth. I can't guarantee that you'll all survive, but for the good of the horde and your benevolent master," he gestured to himself before making a fist, "we must eat."

The zombies seemed happy to follow his orders. They weren't strong, but the numbers were in their favor. With a little luck, they could take down one of Skyline's squads as a buildup to larger prey.

Hopefully, he could find more of their guardians. The fighter and mage from before had been worth so much experience, he couldn't pass up the opportunity to advance. Not to mention he might be able to extract a new spell from their rings like he had with Burial.

It was worth a try.

Digby familiarized himself with the building's layout, making note of convenient places to hide that would still give him a decent vantage point. On the first floor, there was an entry hall just inside the main doors and more rooms beyond there. The layout reminded him of the office building where he'd found Lana and Alvin.

The second floor was less finished and missing most of its walls, leaving much of the space open. With few obstacles, Digby cast Decay on the floors to weaken them here and there, making a note to remember where. He couldn't help but smile, imagining the faces of Skyline's mercenaries as the floor crumbled beneath their feet.

On the third level, he cast Decay enough times to collapse the floor all together, creating several holes that lead to the level below. If he needed to, he could retreat up there and toss Cremation skulls down on whoever failed to fall through the floor. He was rewarded for his efforts with a new rank for Decay.

The spell's mana cost remained at ten, but its area of effect increased from three feet to six. The range also doubled to thirty feet. It seemed he had a choice between focusing on a specific object for a more potent result, or hitting everything within the spell's area of effect, but causing less damage. Decay was useful either way.

The floors above didn't even have windows yet, exposing the building to the elements outside. Digby didn't think he would need to retreat that far, but it was good to know what was up there, just in case he had a need.

When his preparations were complete, he guided a pair of minions into position near a doorway just after the building's entry hall and directed the rest to wait in a stairwell at the other end of the building. His plan was to take as many of Skyline's mercenaries by surprise as he could to minimize his losses.

Once he had his minions where he wanted them, he ascended the stairs to the open floors above. He stopped to look out over the street below and lifted Asher from his shoulder to place her down on a barrel of discarded materials.

"You're still a little weak to be helpful in a fight right now." He scratched her chin. "And let's face it, you're a bit dumb."

He pulled a fork from his pocket and offered it to his pet, getting an enthusiastic caw in return as Asher clasped the utensil in her beak.

Shiny!

"Indeed." Digby watched her fiddle with the fork, using her foot to hold one end as she pecked at it. "You stay here and keep hidden until I come back for you."

Once he was satisfied that she would be safe, he headed back downstairs. He had just animated the bird and didn't want to lose her before he was able to get any use out of the creature. At least, that was what he told himself. The reality was that, having a pet made the silence a little more bearable, just as Rebecca's company had, prior to her betrayal.

He pushed the memory of the traitorous woman from his mind, balling his claws into a bony fist. She was just as bad as the sellswords he intended to eat. Actually, she was worse, pretending to be on his side just to throw him to the wolves. After that, she had been downgraded to food like the rest of Skyline.

Reaching the building's front door, Digby bid his minions a temporary farewell and headed out into the street to make a ruckus. It seemed the fastest way to lure prey into his web. Having reached the limit on his Control spell, he resorted to using his Compel ability to bring in some back up.

A group of five zombies followed his intent to gather in the street. They would have to be sacrificed, obviously. Though, unlike the zombies he'd commanded into a fire earlier, he wasn't just killing them for his own personal gain. No, Skyline was a menace. The more of them he killed, the safer the rest of his kind would be, even if he had to sacrifice a few of the dead in the process.

Finally ready, he spun on the compelled group and started the performance.

"No, don't just stand there!" Digby stomped over to them and shoved one to the side. "Hey, pay attention. You're all I have, and I won't have you staring off at nothing."

He raised his voice, straining his deceased vocal cords as he berated the group. Of course, they only responded with vacant stares. He hit them with another Compel to keep them in the street when they began to wander off. The display continued for a solid ten minutes.

"You lot are just about the worst excuses for undead minions I have seen all—"

He stopped mid-shout when his Blood Sense picked up something new. Digby glanced back over his shoulder and squinted down the street. He had gained another couple points of perception, so it stood to reason that his Blood Sense had increased in strength as well.

Scanning the area, he found only faint traces of blood, but still, there was something calling to him. It felt like power. No, that wasn't quite right. It was mana. He arched an eyebrow.

What the hell am I sensing?

Whatever it was, it was growing. Suddenly, the sensation flared up, coming from a few hundred feet away. Digby dove to the side just before a bolt of power streaked past him. He hit the ground, watching an arrow slam into the chest of the zombie closest to him.

D. PETRIE

The unfortunate creature stood awkwardly for a moment, staring down at the bolt sticking out of its chest. A second later its skin around the wound began to swell and bubble. Digby scurried away as the zombie's body jerked from side to side. Its confused moans grew into a steady howl in seconds. The noise swelled until the zombie exploded in a burst of heat, steam, and gore.

"What just happened?" Digby flicked his eyes in the direction that the arrow had come from, finding a man stepping out from behind a ruined car. In his hands was some sort of heavy crossbow.

Guardian: Level 14 Enchanter, hostile.

A group of mercenaries stepped out from cover behind him as he loaded a bolt into a slot on his weapon. Digby Analyzed the rest, finding them all to be armored humans. Seven enemies in total. The enchanter raised his weapon and tapped a mechanism on the side, causing the bowstring to pull back on its own.

Digby sensed the same phenomenon as before, like mana flowing through a body that wasn't his own. That was when he realized he was sensing a spell being cast. With his heightened perception, he must have been picking up the mana flowing through the man's blood.

Crap...

He scurried behind one of the other zombies just as a bolt hit the corpse with a solid thunk. Digby didn't look back as the poor monster began to howl. A wet sounding explosion came from behind just before gunfire lit up the three remaining zombies. The windows of a car nearby shattered as bullets peppered the vehicle behind them. Metallic pings filled the air.

Digby ran for all he was worth, not expecting something dangerous right from the start. Skyline wasn't taking any chances with him anymore.

Reaching the front door of the half-finished building, he darted inside to take refuge in the darkness. He sprinted past the pair of minions positioned at either side of the inner doors and slid behind a pile of building materials. Then, he waited.

Sure enough, his pursuers were right behind him.

A light shined in through the door as the end of a rifle peeked inside. The beam swept across the room, clearly searching for hidden threats. Digby suppressed a laugh as two men raced inside to secure the room. There was no stopping the zombies hiding against the wall on either side of the door before they tore into each of the mercenaries' necks.

Screams filled the air as another two enemies entered next. They were firing before they were even inside. Digby clenched his jaw as they cut down both minions. Bullets shredded the unfinished walls of the building. Clouds of white dust erupted from each impact.

2 common zombies lost.

To his surprise, the men didn't try to help their squadmates. Instead, they opted to secure the room. The enchanter with the crossbow came in behind them.

"Hang in there." He knelt down next to one of the fallen men as he bled out on the floor and pulled a small flask from a pouch. "Stay with me." The enchanter held out the container, letting his mana flow. The flask glowed for an instant before fading back to normal. Digby wondered what the man had cast, unsure what sort of spells his class was capable of.

The enchanter poured a clear liquid from the flask into the wounded man's mouth before dumping the rest on his bleeding throat. Digby's eyes widened as the wound on his neck began to heal. The man coughed and choked but settled down seconds later, taking normal breaths again. The enchanter turned to the other wounded enemy and reached for another pouch. His hand stopped before retrieving another flask. He let out a sigh as the man choked on a mouthful of blood.

"Shit. He's too far gone." The enchanter stood back up and aimed his crossbow at his fallen comrade. The dying man raised a hand in defense, but the enchanter pulled the trigger, pinning his head to the floor. "Sorry. Can't let the heretic get the kill."

Digby waited for a message telling he'd gained experience, but none came.

Did that bastard just steal my experience?

It was possible. The Heretic Seed seemed to require kills to be a direct result of his actions or commands. As the rest of the squad entered the room, he cursed the enchanter for taking what was rightfully his.

"Stay alert." Their leader loaded another bolt and tapped something on his weapon. A quiet whine came from the crossbow as the string pulled back into a firing position. "These two zeds were waiting for us. So I'm thinking this necro we're after was leading us into a trap."

"Are you sure?" One of the other men helped the healed mercenary to their feet. "It looked more like he was running for his life."

"Can't be sure. According to Crow's Nest, this guy is a liar and not afraid to fight dirty. Sounds like someone that would lure us into a trap by acting like a moron to me."

Digby narrowed his eyes at the mention of Rebecca's moniker. Of course she had reported back to Skyline on him. She had been in contact with them the entire time they'd been allies. He suppressed a growl, not appreciating the fact that she had called him a liar, even if it was true.

And that moron comment was just uncalled for.

That was when a sound came from the floor above.

"What was that?" One of the mercenaries raised his weapon.

"Proceed with caution." The enchanter stepped toward the stairs. "This guy might not be as dumb as he looks."

Would a moron have instructed one of his silent lurkers to randomly bang a hammer against the walls upstairs to draw you lot away from them? Digby mocked the group as they moved to the second floor.

Once they were out of sight, he crept out of his hiding place and headed for the stairwell on the opposite side of the building where the rest of his horde waited. He sent his common zombies into position near the entrance of the building. Then he beckoned his two clawed lurkers to follow him.

Skipping over the second floor where Skyline's squad was, he made his way to the third. Upon entering, he saw light shining up through one of the holes he'd made earlier. Digby stalked closer to peer down, finding the squad below.

Three enemies stood on a weakened section of the floor. It creaked under foot, sending an excited chill down Digby's spine. Any moment, they would drop back to the first floor where his common minions were waiting. Several seconds went by, then, nothing happened. Rolling his eyes, he cast another Decay at the floor.

Still nothing.

Casting the spell twice more, Digby frowned when again nothing happened. He checked his HUD.

MP: 106/136
MINIONS: Asher, 4 lurkers, 8 common zombies.

He couldn't waste the mana for another Decay that might not work. As it was, he'd already lost two minions and only taken out one of Skyline's people. He stepped away from the hole.

Looks like we're going to have to improvise. Digby beckoned to one of his clawed lurkers and instructed them to leap into the hole to land on the weakened section of flooring. He waited for two of the mercenaries to walk across it and gave his minion a gentle shove.

"Try to do some damage while you're down there."

The clawed lurker stepped off the edge, landing on top of one of the men. The mercenary shouted as the zombie pushed its claws into his guts beneath his chest armor. The floor gave way the instant the extra weight hit, opening a new hole that three enemies fell through, including the lurker's victim. More screams came from below as the men dropped into the room where the rest of his horde waited.

Digby let out a wild cackle as his improvisation paid off.

3 armored humans defeated, 360 experience awarded.

"The target's upstairs!"

A crossbow bolt shot up through the hole to hit the ceiling above Digby's head with a crack. A barrage of gunfire tore up the floor near his feet. He leaped back as bullets shredded the area. Rolling to where his duffle waited, he snatched up both of his blood forged skulls.

"Get to the stairwell!" The enchanter shouted from below.

Digby raced to the hole in the floor closest to the stairs and cast Cremation, hurling one of the skulls downward. It exploded against the floor to block the path up to where he was.

SPELL RANK INCREASED
Cremation has advanced from rank D to C. Ignition area
of effect is increased from 10 to 20 inches. Cremation
flames will now spread to materials other than necrotic
tissue faster.

Digby ignored the message, and threw his second skull for good measure, setting it alight as it burst against the doorframe below. His mana dropped to seventy-six and he lost another two common zombies. Fortunately, the clawed lurker he'd sent into the fray seemed to have survived the fall.

"Good enough." He turned away from the hole as another shout came from below.

"Head for the other stairwell!"

"Cut them off." Digby pointed to a hole on the far side of the floor, sending his silent lurkers into the fight.

Gunfire erupted below, along with cries of pain. One of Digby's minions howled as the number of lurkers under his control decreased by one. The sounds of combat ceased all at once, a moment of silence taking over. Digby watched the door on the far side to make sure none of his enemies had made it through.

2 armored humans defeated, 240 experience awarded.

Before he could gloat, a now familiar sensation surged from behind. Digby spun as the enchanter burst from the nearest stairway. Cremation flames climbed up the man's leg, turning from green to orange as they spread.

"You think a little fire is going to stop me?" The enchanter slapped out the flames with a gloved hand and raised his crossbow. The arrowhead protruding from the end glowed a threatening crimson.

Acting fast, Digby raised his hand and focused on the weapon to cast Decay just as the enchanter pulled the trigger.

A sudden crack struck the air.

The enchanter recoiled as the bowstring snapped and the bolt popped out of the end of his weapon, only to drop to the floor with no momentum behind it. A line of blood trickled down his forehead where the bowstring had lashed his face after snapping. He dropped his eyes to the glowing arrow on the floor before leaping away. Digby took that as his cue to do the same.

A concussive blast hit him from behind as the crossbow bolt exploded. He landed in a roll, nearly falling through one of the holes he'd made in the floor. Something in his chest felt out of place, probably broken a rib or two. Digby scrambled to his feet just as the enchanter got to his. The man reached for a gun holstered to his thigh.

"I think not!" Digby shouted as he raced to beat the man's weapon to the kill. The pistol barked twice, putting a bullet through his thigh while lodging a second in his chest armor. It wasn't enough to stop him from dragging his claws across the man's throat.

For good measure, Digby plunged his talons into his stomach before pushing him toward the hole that his lurker had leaped down a few moments before. With a swift kick to the behind, Digby shoved the struggling enchanter over the edge. He howled in victory as the man fell headfirst with a satisfying crack. His minions took it from there.

1 level 14 Enchanter defeated, 1370 experience awarded.

Digby let a celebratory howl fade to a quiet chuckle as he read over the last message a second time. With enough preparation, Skyline's squads didn't stand a chance.

"Not a bad haul."

That was when he remembered he still needed the ring from the enchanter's hand. He leaped back to the hole and leaned over the side.

"Hey minions, save some for me!"

CHAPTER TWENTY-NINE

The scent of smoke filled the hollow of Digby's nasal cavity.

"Oh yes. The building is on fire." He promptly remembered the blaze he'd started on the floor below him just before tossing Skyline's enchanter down to his minions. "I should probably do something about that."

With that in mind, he made his way to the far stairwell that was not on fire and backtracked to the source of the smoke. His Cremation flames had spread to the unfinished walls. Fortunately, the skeletal building didn't provide much to feed the fire, slowing its consumption of the rest of the floor. Digby glanced at his HUD.

MP: 66/136
MINIONS: Asher, 3 lurkers, 6 common zombies.

"Plenty of mana left." He raised his hand to the ceiling and cast Decay. It took two tries before the material collapsed to dust and smothered the flames.

"There we are." He brushed his hands together. "Now, about that meal."

Feeling pretty good about himself, Digby sauntered down to the first floor with a bounce in his step. He even gripped the railing at the bottom of the stairwell and swung into the empty space below with style.

At least, it should have been empty.

Digby froze as the silhouette of an armored man stood in the front doorway.

"Who—" He started to ask before the figure spun on their heel and bolted into the street outside.

Oh no you don't. Digby sprinted out the front door after the shadow.

Clearly, one of Skyline's men had waited outside as a guard. He must have intended to escape and call for reinforcements. That was the last thing Digby needed. There were still things to do in the building. People to eat and all that. Checking his mana, he found thirty-five measly points. It would have to do. He couldn't let a lone enemy escape to ruin his plans.

I just hope my minions behave while I'm gone.

Digby refocused on the fleeing mercenary as he weaved between wrecked vehicles like a rabbit running from a wolf. It wasn't enough. Digby wasn't the same bumbling zombie that he had been back when he'd thawed out in the basement of the science institute. No, he was stronger, faster, and much smarter. Vaulting over the hood of a car, he made use of the stats he'd gained throughout the night.

His prey scurried ahead, rushing past a trio of zombies without looking back. Digby cast Control on each of them before they had the chance to pursue the meal.

He's mine!

Digby blew past them as they awaited his orders. The mercenary ducked behind a car before darting into an alleyway, keeping low to avoid being spotted. It was a maneuver that might have confused a less intelligent zombie.

Futile. Digby scoffed and followed him in. He beckoned to his new minions for back up, just in case.

In the alley, the man tripped and fell in panic, only to pull himself up and rush to the nearest door. It was locked. A menacing laugh bubbled up in Digby's throat as the poor creature tried another door.

Again. Locked.

Metal fencing cut through the middle of the alleyway, severing any route of escape and trapping the unfortunate man in a literal dead end. Digby stalked closer, dragging his claws against the brick of the wall beside him just as he had the last time his Ravenous trait took over. The only difference was that this time, he was in full control.

The mercenary struggled to climb the fence, slipping with each frantic attempt. Light shined down from a broken window above to illuminate the meal as if serving him up on a platter. There was nowhere to hide.

Unlike the sleek black of Skyline's body armor, his uniform was covered with tiny, rectangular shapes, each of varying shades of gray to blend in with the city around him. Even stranger, his helmet lolled to one side like it was a size too big. He was even missing his gun, as if he'd dropped it along the way.

Digby didn't care. He wasn't passing up a free meal. The mercenary fell with his back against the fence and raised his hands to defend himself.

"Time to die!" Digby darted forward and drew back his claws. Then, he stopped.

"Did… you just talk?" The man lay frozen on the ground, mid-wince, like he expected to be killed as much as receive an answer.

"Who the hell are you?" Digby stood, also frozen, but much more confused.

The mercenary wasn't a mercenary at all, but a boy, no older than the intern that Digby had named Asher after. His frame was too slender for the equipment he wore to have belonged to him, leaving his armor hanging loose. One hand was even missing a glove as he trembled, shielding his face.

"Ah, my name is Alex," the boy answered his question, adding an awkward, "Sir," afterward.

"You're not one of Skyline's sellswords, are you?" Digby kept his claws raised, ready to strike if he didn't like the answer that came next. Though he did call off his minions, telling them to wait by a trash bin near the entrance of the alley.

"What's Skyline?"

Digby let out an instinctive snarl as the urge to attack hung in his over-excited mind. "Why are you dressed in that armor?"

"I found it on an army guy. They were dead, and, ah, it was better than what I was wearing."

"And why did you run when you saw me?" Digby narrowed his eyes.

"You're a zombie," the boy peered up through his pale fingers, a pair of black-rimmed lenses perched on his nose, "aren't you?"

"Sort of…" Digby trailed off before asking, "Why did you enter the building I was in?"

"It seemed like somewhere I could… um, rest and no one would mind." Alex began to lower his hand as his voice shook. "I'm alone. I didn't really have a plan. Everyone talks about their zombie apocalypse strategy, but it all kind of fell apart in the real thing."

"You've been planning for this?" Digby furrowed his brow.

"Yeah… I mean no."

"Which is it?" Digby stepped closer, getting annoyed with the boy's wishy-washy answers.

"Both." Alex flinched at the sudden movement. "I'm kind of a nerd. Fantasizing about the zombie apocalypse is standard."

"What is a nerd? And why would one fantasize about this?" Digby gestured to the world around him.

"I'm not sure how to—" Alex lowered his hand a bit more. "I guess, a nerd is a kind of outcast. And, the world kind of sucks." He looked down at the ground. "It's messed up, but sometimes it helps to imagine it ending."

"I'm starting to get that feeling too." Digby found the boy's explanation juvenile, but it resonated with him, nonetheless. Back in his village, people like Henwick were revered, while he was ignored and left to drink alone.

"Are you from Earth?" Alex pulled him out of his thoughts.

"Of course I'm from Earth, where else would I be from?" Digby snapped at him.

"Sorry." The boy shrank away and raised his hands again. "You just didn't know what a nerd was, so I thought this might be an alien invasion kind of situation."

"Well it's not." Digby folded his arms. "I'm eight-hundred-years-old, excuse me if I'm not up to date with all of your inane human words."

"Holy shit..."

"Yes, yes, it's all very surprising." Digby rolled his eyes. "Magic is real and you're talking to a zombie, so on and so on." He stared down at the boy. "Why are you out here roaming around alone like a half-wit?"

"I, ah, sort of lost my job today. I'd only had it for a few months." Alex's voice shook. "After that, I had nowhere to go, so I just wandered around trying to figure out what to do with my life. I stopped for a coffee and the next thing I knew, a dead woman attacked the barista. I've been running for my life ever since."

"Your employment situation probably doesn't matter anymore."

"That's true." Alex nodded. "My boss is probably dead." They both fell silent for a moment before Alex spoke up again. "Are you going to eat me?"

"I haven't decided." Digby surprised himself with his answer.

"Oh..."

"It's not like I want to eat you." Digby thought for a second. "Well, actually I do. Eating you would mean growing stronger, after all." He tilted his head to the other side. "Though, there are other people to eat and you don't seem like you have much meat on you to begin with."

"That's accurate." Alex inched away a little. "Also, I don't want to die like that if I can help it."

"You have a point. Being eaten doesn't sound fun." Digby let out a breathless sigh. The boy reminded him of himself. Well, a less hateful version of himself, at least. Having nowhere to go was something he could relate to. Before he knew what he was doing, he sat down beside the young man.

"Hey!" Alex scooted to the side, his eyes darting around like a frightened animal.

"Relax, I'm not going to eat you." Digby rested against the metal fencing. "I don't know what to do either. I didn't ask to become this, nor did I intend to wake up in this twisted future that your people built." He took a moment to rub at his temples, feeling exhausted mentally now that he had a moment to think about it.

"Can't argue with that." Alex finally stopped trying to inch away from him. "I'm only twenty-four, and I can already see how messed up things have gotten."

"That's just because you lost your job. You're a bit too young to be that cynical." Digby elbowed Alex. "Me? Well, I died. I have reason to be."

"At least you're not alone." Alex gestured to the zombies waiting by the trash bin. "You have plenty of friends."

"Sure, but they don't make for much conversation." Digby shrugged. "I am unfortunately one of a kind. A zombie with a human mind. It's actually difficult to know where I belong. Mostly, I just feel lost. I suppose I could eat you and cast aside my humanity. Just become a roaming monster and be done with it."

Alex tensed up.

"Oh stop, I already said I'm not going to eat you." Digby lowered his voice before adding, "Probably."

"At least you're honest about it. That's more than I can say for any of my coworkers and cheap-ass boss." Alex's tone grew harsh.

"What did you do, steal something?" Digby looked at the boy sideways.

"At work?" Alex rubbed at his eyes, clearly trying to process the conversation. "I can't believe the zombie apocalypse is happening and I'm having a heart to heart with a zombie."

"Indeed. Not what I expected either."

"And no. I didn't steal anything. There weren't enough employees in my department, and it was hard to handle the workload when you're running on a skeleton crew. No breaks or time off. I couldn't keep up, so I was cut loose."

"You should have been stealing," Digby commented.

"Nah, I was a copywriter. Nothing to steal there."

"Shame." Digby reached into his boot with one claw and fished around for a moment.

"So, why aren't you eating me, by the way?" The boy's voice shook a little, clearly uneasy.

"Because I'm not hungry right now."

"Oh…" Alex's eyes widened. "So you might want to later?"

"That answer depends on you." Digby found what he was looking for, feeling one of the two heretic rings next to his ankle. He had learned his lesson back when he'd met the intern back in the science institute where he'd woken up. If he hadn't been so stingy, he might have been able to save the boy by granting him the power of the Heretic Seed. Now, sitting next to another young man that might prove useful, he wasn't going to make the same mistake twice. Despite Rebecca's betrayal, he still needed allies.

"Do you know what this is?" He pulled the obsidian band out and held it before the boy.

Alex shook his head.

"It's a magic ring." Digby watched Alex's face, catching something akin to desire in the young man's eyes.

"Like actual magic?" He'd leaned forward slightly.

"Indeed. Curses, Fireballs, and all that." Digby pulled off

his glove to show him the string of black runes that encircled his finger. "I found one of these just before I died. Without it, I'd be just like the rest of these mindless drones." He smiled.

"And it gave you, what?" Alex swallowed. "Some kind of power?"

"Of a kind, yes." Digby scooped up the ring with the tip of one claw. "Though it may give you a different power. One that could make you strong enough to survive this night. One that may make you powerful enough so that the job you lost won't ever matter."

"And you would give that to me?" Alex reached out for the ring.

"Maybe." Digby snatched it back with his left hand, closing his dead fingers around it. "That's the part that depends on you."

"What would I have to do?"

"Help me," Digby answered with a grin. "I want you to help me navigate this new world. I intend to escape this city, and I will need someone that understands this future if I'm to remain hidden while I grow stronger. In time, I will be powerful enough to carve out a place for myself in this world. Having a loyal apprentice at my side would be quite helpful in my endeavors." He made a point of making the boy's job sound easy.

"That's it?"

"I should also mention that there is some sort of mercenary group called Skyline that seems to want me dead. Or, at least, more dead than I already am." Digby tilted his head from side to side. "They have magic of their own, and they don't seem shy about hurting their fellow humans to get what they want."

"So taking that ring means I may have to fight for you?" Alex added an upward inflection at the end, as if he wasn't sure if he should be asking a question or not.

"Possibly." Digby gave a nonchalant shrug.

"Shit." Alex rubbed at his forehead. "This is a villain's apprentice situation. Like at the start of a movie when the bad guy recruits a random, sad nerd to do their bidding."

"Oh, I'm hardly a villain." Digby rolled his eyes.

"You eat people." Alex added matter of factly.

"Only sometimes."

"Is that better?"

"I can still change my mind and eat you." Dig pointed a claw in the boy's direction.

"Point taken." Alex backed down.

Digby began shoving the ring back in his pocket. "And I can find another apprentice, so there's no obligation to accept my—"

"Wait." Alex reached out. "I'll do it."

"Why?" Digby leveled his eyes on the boy. He wasn't sure why he'd asked the question. It may have been something as simple as curiosity, or maybe he just wanted to test the boy's character.

Alex lowered his head. "Mostly because I have nowhere to go."

"That's not a good reason."

"I think it is. I have nothing to live for. I gave up most of my dreams and fantasies when I graduated college and started work to pay off the debt. Since then, I have only done what I was told. So yeah, when a zombie tells me magic is real and offers a chance at power, I'm going to take it. I have nothing to lose, and life has done nothing but push me around—"

"And now it's time to do the pushing? That's an answer I can understand." Digby turned the ring over in his hand a few times then flicked it into the air in Alex's direction. "Don't make me regret it."

Catching the ring, Digby's new apprentice began to slip the obsidian band over his finger.

"Hold on." Alex stopped just before it passed his knuckle. "I don't even know your name. What do I call you?"

"My name is…" Digby went silent for a moment before standing up. "I am known as Lord Graves." Sure, no one else called him that, but the boy didn't know and it was about time he stopped hiding from his family name. His father might not have ever given him much, but a name was at least something. Besides, he wasn't the same man that died all those centuries ago. No, he wasn't a man at all anymore.

"Okay." Alex stood up beside him. "Ah, my lord?"

Digby nodded at the sound of his self-given title.

"What happens now?" Alex slipped the ring the rest of the way on to his finger.

"Now, you pass out." Digby shrugged, remembering what had happened to him all those years ago. He wasn't completely sure that the ring would even work considering the Heretic Seed had been destroyed and only existed as a broken shard lodged in his heart, but if it did, then losing consciousness was likely.

"I'll pass out?" Alex's face turned white.

"Probably." Digby shrugged again.

"Probably?" Alex's voice jumped up a few octaves just as lines of runes streaked across the surface of the ring. The band began to shrink a second later, tightening around his finger. Alex flailed his hand and fell back against the fencing. Then, the ring simply sunk through his skin, becoming a part of the boy's body. All that remained was a string of black runes that encircled his middle finger.

A wave of exhaustion fell across the face of the new heretic as he slid down the fencing to where he'd lain a few minutes before. Alex stared up at Digby, his eyes full of a mix of fear and desperation.

Digby knelt down as if to comfort the boy. Then he grinned. "Let's hope I don't get hungry before you wake up."

Alex's eyes shot opened in panic for an instant before he succumbed to the Heretic Seed's influence and slumped to one side. Digby let a smile more befitting of a mentor replace his villainous grin.

"Don't worry, I won't let anyone touch you, be they dead or alive. It's no fun being alone." He focused on his new apprentice, telling his Analyze ability to read what it could.

Heretic: Level 1 Enchanter.

CHAPTER THIRTY

Digby guided his minions down an alleyway in search of another open building. It was dangerous to remain where they had ambushed Skyline's men earlier. Surely, another squad would come looking for them. With that in mind, he'd refreshed his Control spells and ordered his horde to carry the corpses and his new apprentice while he searched for a more secure location.

Several blocks away, he found an unlocked door that led into another office building. A large entryway greeted him, with two floors of walkways overlooking a desk in the middle.

"Set him down over here." He gestured to the three zombies carrying Alex's unconscious body, and they dropped him to the floor with a hard thud. "I probably should have told them to be gentle."

Once he was sure none of his new minions were going to get bitey with his apprentice, he had the rest of his zombies make a pile with the bodies of Skyline's men that had been killed in the ambush.

Making sure to take off his coat to keep it clean, he dug into another meal with his horde. Actually, calling it a meal wasn't quite right. It was more of a chore. He struggled to get down what he needed for his next mutation as fast as possible. He didn't want Alex waking up to such a sight if he could help it.

As he ate, he focused on a new line of text on his HUD.

Allies: Alex Sanders (Enchanter) MP: 117/117

He wondered if the boy would be able to see his status as well when he woke up. Not to mention he was also curious about why he would have access to another heretic's information. Maybe there was a reason the three rings he'd found back in the castle had been stored in the same box. It was possible that there was an intentional link created between them that carried over to the heretics that bore them, as if the three rings had always been meant for a trio.

Digby returned his attention to his HUD and made a mental edit to the display to remove his apprentice's class and surname. It seemed like information he could remember without it cluttering up his field of vision. He also changed the word Allies to Apprentices, then again to Coven, after deciding that sounded better. Lastly, he moved Asher into his Coven, feeling the need to separate the raven from the rest of his minions. There was something special about the bird, since it was his first truly loyal follower.

Nodding to himself, he read over the new display.

COVEN
Digby: MP: 64/136
Alex: MP: 114/114
Asher: MP: 19/19

MINIONS: 3 lurkers, 9 common zombies.

"That should do it." Digby scratched Asher's head as the raven pecked at a human heart beside him. He wasn't sure what she could do with her nineteen mana points but was glad to know she had them all the same. Deciding to think about it later, he glanced back to where Alex lay, still unconscious. "Now, I wonder what his attributes are?"

Digby focused on his apprentice's name, hoping the Heretic Seed would show him what he wanted to know. The little circle at the edge of his vision responded in an instant, flicking out and expanding to show a list of values.

Name: Alex Sanders
Race: Human
Heretic Class: Enchanter
Mana: 114 / 114
Mana Composition: Balanced
Current Level: 1 (230 Experience to next level.)

ATTRIBUTES
Constitution: 17
Defense: 14
Strength: 12
Dexterity: 14
Agility: 16
Intelligence: 17
Perception: 14
Will: 18

AILMENTS
Unconscious

"Hmm, quite a bit of will on this one." Digby scratched at his chin, glad that the boy didn't have more intelligence than him. That would have been embarrassing. He couldn't help but compare the new enchanter's numbers to his own from back when he'd been alive, finding that some were below while others were above. The new information left him even more curious of what the average person might have.

Looking the boy over, he seemed rather scrawny. Which

certainly would account for his low strength and defense values. Considering the muscle mass on most of the mercenaries he'd killed, their attributes must have been higher, giving him a rough idea of what a benchmark might be for a human in top physical shape. Taking his past-self and Alex into consideration, he estimated that most of Skyline's sellswords had around twenty strength. If all values were measured in similar increments, then it stood to reason that both he and Alex had been a good deal below the majority of the population.

He cringed, remembering how he'd bragged to Rebeca about being a genius when the evidence pointed to him being closer to average. "I may have exaggerated there."

Digby shook off the concern, wondering what it was about Alex's attributes that had decided that he would start out as an enchanter. The Heretic Seed answered the question as soon as he thought it.

> **ENCHANTER: The starting class for those who have a will attribute that is higher than the rest. This class specializes in imbuing inanimate objects and materials with magical effects. Physically weaker in close combat than other classes, but excels at ranged combat, support, and crafting.**

> *Try to keep this ally, alright? Last thing you need is another betrayal.*

Digby agreed with the Heretic Seed's snarky comment. Skyline's enchanter had been a problem at range. In fact, if he hadn't had time to prepare a few traps prior to the ambush, he might not have won. Digby shook off the thought and searched for the ring that enchanter had worn. Finding the gold band on the corpse's finger, he plucked it off and closed his hand around it.

> **Compatible spells detected.**

ENCHANT WEAPON

Infuse a weapon or projectile with mana. An infused weapon will deal increased damage as well as disrupt the mana flow of another caster. Potential damage will increase with rank. Enchanting a single projectile will have a greater effect.

PURIFY WATER

Imbue any liquid with cleansing power. Purified liquids will become safe for human consumption and will remove most ailments. At higher ranks, purified liquids may also gain a mild regenerative effect.

Choose one spell to be extracted.

Digby hesitated, glancing at Alex. What sort of lord would he be if he didn't take care of those that depended on him? Not only that, but Alex's class matched the ring's previous owner. Meaning there was a chance that he could access more from the item than a necromancer could. Digby shoved the ring into his boot, along with the remaining obsidian band that he already carried. With that, he continued to eat his fill until he reached his next goal.

GUIDED MUTATION

Requirements for the glutton's mutation, Maw, have been met.

Accept? Yes/No

"Yes." Digby snapped his fingers in confirmation.

Mutation, Maw, active. You may now open a gateway directly to your void for faster consumption of resources.
Perception increased to 17.
Will increased to 20.
Maximum mana has increased to 141 points.

Time to overindulge.

"Indeed." Digby immediately attempted to open his maw by holding out his hand and focusing on a space on the floor like he would with any of his spells. When nothing happened, he remembered the ability wasn't a spell. Thinking about the mutation would never work, not when it was meant to be used by a near mindless zombie.

Sitting down, he folded his arms and tried to put himself back in his own shoes from earlier that night, back when he barely had the intelligence to process a thought more complex than, *I'm hungry.* How would he have activated an ability back then?

Digby went over the concepts that he knew zombies understood. Rend, feed, the many teeth. It was all so simplistic. He tried concentrating on the satisfied feeling that came along with feeding, but it got him nowhere.

After a few minutes of trying, he kicked at one of the corpses on the floor in frustration. Then he laughed. It was a bit funny in a backward sort of way. Thinking about the problem was pointless. He was too smart to understand the perspective needed.

"Well, that was a big waste of time and corpses." Digby groaned and checked his resources, to see what he still had to work with.

AVAILABLE RESOURCES
Sinew: 3
Flesh: 3
Bone: 4
Viscera: 0
Heart: 5
Mind: 5

"Could be worse." He waved away the information. "But it could also be better."

That was when a sound like rolling thunder swelled in the distance. Digby arched an eyebrow at the doors of the building as Asher raised her head from a bit of gray matter she was pecking at. The rest of the horde stopped eating in unison as a strange tension filled the room.

"That can't be good." Digby stood up and crept over to the door to peek out. "What the hell?"

In the distance down the street, something was speeding forward.

Something big.

Cars were tossed to the side by an enormous metal form. It was three times as long and nearly twice as wide as the SWAT truck he had found earlier. Mounted on the front was a giant version of a plow, like what was used to till the fields back in his village.

The monstrosity rammed through a roaming group of zombies without even slowing down. Bodies burst on impact, their corpses vanishing underneath the massive wheels that stuck out on either side. Whatever the contraption was, it was larger than any vehicle he had seen so far. Behind it, a line of trucks followed, each bearing the same word: Skyline.

The bottom dropped out from Digby's stomach.

"We must leave, now." He spun to his horde. "Leave the bodies, we'll find food later." Then he froze.

What about Alex?

Digby flicked his vision to his unconscious apprentice. There was no way his minions would be able to carry the enchanter fast enough. Come to think of it, it was improbable that his common zombies would be able to escape in time even without carrying the boy. The only ones that stood a chance were his silent lurkers, Asher, and himself. The choice was obvious.

I have to leave them.

Asher flew up to his shoulder as if sensing his intent to flee over their bond. He took one step toward the rear of the building, where a red sign that read 'Exit' hung. He stopped dead in his tracks as his own words echoed through his head.

I won't let anyone touch you, be they dead or alive.

"I'm sorry." Digby glanced back at his unconscious apprentice. "Things just didn't work out." He started running for the exit again, slamming his clawed fist into the wall as soon as he reached it.

"Damn it." Digby ground his knuckles into the painted surface before turning back to Alex. The rumbling of engines in the distance grew to a roar. "I'm going to regret this."

He turned back to his confused horde. "Scatter! And bring back any zombie who will listen. Be they gluttons, leaders, or even brutes! There's about to be more food here than they can imagine, but it's not going to go down without a fight. Carry this message, for the many, Lord Graves calls on all. We must rend our threats asunder! Only then can our teeth devour the world."

The words didn't really matter, just his intent. Food was coming, and it would take many to consume it all. He hoped his common zombies could get the attention of a horde that was interested in the meal.

His minions acted without hesitation, scattering out the back door like rats. All except for the undead fighter that Digby instructed to stay behind. With his minions in motion, he pulled Asher off his shoulder as soon as they were gone and placed her on the desk in the middle of the room.

"You need to eat." He grabbed a half-empty skull, and shoved it to her beak. "I need you to mutate. You need to be smarter."

Asher did as she was told, looking like a chipmunk stuffing its cheeks with nuts. Digby tore a heart into bite-sized pieces while she ate. He couldn't see the raven's void contents but he hoped she was close to reaching two mind and two heart. With that she could gain the leader's Compel Zombie mutation and the two intelligence points that came with it.

"Yes!" Digby raised his pet into the air as a message came in.

Animated zombie, Asher, has gained the mutation Compel Zombie. She may now pass on their master's

**intent to any common zombie. Intelligence has increased
to 6. Perception has increased to 1. Will has increased to
4. Maximum mana has increased to 30.**

Setting her back down on the desk, Digby pulled the gold
and obsidian rings from his boot and slipped one over each of
Asher's feet, so they hung like bracelets.

"I need you to take these and hide." He glanced over his
shoulder as the din outside came closer. "I only told Rebecca
about one of the heretic rings, so they don't know I had two. If
we get caught, I don't want any of those goons from Skyline
getting their hands on it." Asher admired her jewelry.

Shiny.

"Yes, good girl." He ordered his remaining zombie to hold
the back door open before turning back to her. "Now go and
Compel every zombie you find to gather and attack. Then I
want you to hide when the fighting starts. I'll call you if I
survive."

The monstrous vehicle screeched to a stop just outside,
throwing a pair of random cars into the street. They skidded by
just outside the doors. There was only a minute left at best
before the mercenaries came for him.

"Go." Digby pushed Asher off her perch. "And if I don't
call for you by sunup…" He scratched her chin. "Just fly away."

Asher locked eyes with him for a moment, then bobbed her
head up and down before taking off for the back door.

"Did she just nod?" Digby watched her go before heading
back to the front door and peeking outside. "Gah!" He ducked
back as the guns for hire poured out of the vehicles. There must
have been over fifty.

A man the size of a truck jumped from a hatch on the side
of the lead vehicle. He wore a pistol at his hip and a broad
sword on his back. Digby's jaw fell slack at the weapon, finding
it out of place in the futuristic world that he'd come to know.
He scrambled away from the door as the beast of a man turned
toward the building he was hiding in.

"Surveillance has the zed in there. The trackers for the squad we lost contact with are there as well, including one from a previous engagement. Expect opposition. He has at least some of our men under his control."

"Captain?" A second voice chimed in. "Do we really think the zed is dumb enough to try to use our own forces against us? Doesn't he realize we can track them?"

"That's our saving grace here," the man in charge responded. "Our analysts have him pegged somewhere around level fourteen to sixteen based on what we know he's killed so far. That means he may have already gained access to the necromancer class, if so... well, let me just say I'm glad he's uneducated."

"Uneducated, my deceased ass." Digby scowled as he dragged one of the uneaten corpses from the pile through the room and dropped it beside the entrance. He did the same with another two partial bodies. "I'll show them what an uneducated idiot can do."

He paused, realizing that no one had actually called him an idiot. Digby shook his head, then hefted up Alex's unconscious body. He directed the zombie fighter that had stayed behind to help.

"Come on now, we need to hide." He dragged his limp apprentice to the nearest stairwell and ascended to the second floor where he could watch the door from the walkway above. "Feel free to wake up any time now, Alex."

The sound of boots reaching the building's entryway met his ears just as he got a vantage point of the doorway. He dropped Alex behind a large potted plant and beckoned to the fighter's corpse.

"When I say so, I want you to jump down and attack." He glanced at the zombie's Bone Claws. "And don't stop, no matter what happens. Tear into them with everything you've got. We just need to buy time for Asher and the rest of the horde to find whatever help they can."

Digby ducked down as light shined in through the door. He

gestured for the fighter to do the same. A beam swept around the room below like it was searching for threats. Digby checked his mana to make sure it was full.

MP: 141/141

"Time to hit them hard."

Digby waited for the first few mercenaries to set foot in the room before acting. Then he cast Blood Forge on the contents of the three corpses near the door. Needle-like spikes shot out from the bodies, using what little blood remained inside them. Most of the crimson forms shattered as soon as they came in contact with his enemies' armor, but a couple pierced flesh.

No matter, it was just a distraction.

"The fuck?" One of the men brushed his hand around his waist, snapping the slender blood forms to clear them away. That was when Digby sent in his minion.

With a little help, the fighter turned lurker climbed up onto the walkway's railing and jumped with its claws drawn back, ready to strike. Its arms burst into flames as Digby cast Cremation. He cast the spell again on each of the bodies near the door. His fiery minion howled as it slashed its burning claws into the first of the mercenaries' necks.

The men shouted in panic, not expecting a multilayered attack all at once. The fighter didn't stop, ignoring the flames as they climbed up its arms. Gunfire erupted from the mercenaries. Blackened viscera sprayed the desk in the middle of the room as bullets tore through the fighter's gut.

One of Skyline's men rolled on the floor, struggling to put out the fire that had spread to his clothing. The flames changed from green to orange as soon as they began consuming something other than dead flesh. Digby suppressed a snarl as three of the men expired, sending a line of text across his vision.

3 armored humans defeated, 360 experience awarded.

Unfortunately, that was as much as the fighter could do before a torrent of gunfire from outside claimed it. The body of Digby's only protector slumped to the floor in a burning heap as the Cremation flames consumed the corpse to block the entryway.

A din of shouts erupted from outside, though it was too difficult to make out anything that was said with so many voices speaking at once. One thing was certain, they wouldn't try a direct assault again. Eventually, the chaos subsided, and silence fell upon the building. Digby sat still, unsure what they would try next.

The silence didn't last long.

The windows lining the front of the building shattered all at once as bullets filled the floor below. The flash of dozens of rifles chased away the shadows as the walls fragmented into powder.

Digby scrambled away from the edge of the walkway and retreated behind the potted plant where Alex lay. Fortunately, Skyline's focus was only on the first floor. The barrage continued for a full minute before stopping all at once. Then a voice came from outside.

"Graves, are you still in there hiding on the second floor?"

Digby ducked lower as a drone passed by the nearest window. He cursed Rebecca, assuming she was informing on him even now.

"This is Captain Manning. As you can see from the state of the first floor, you're not going to be able to fight all of us. So what do you say you come on out and talk? I promise that no one will lay a finger on you if you cooperate."

Digby arched an eyebrow. It had to be a trick. They had definitely been trying to kill him earlier. There was no reason that they would suddenly change their minds. As soon as he poked his head out, they would shoot it off. They just didn't want to send in any more men to be slaughtered.

Digby held his ground, huddled behind the potted plant with his unconscious apprentice. How Alex had been able to sleep through the noise was beyond him. The Heretic Seed's synchronization process must have been more draining than he thought.

That was when the familiar hum of a drone returned to one of the windows. It looked just like the one that Rebecca had controlled, except this one had a pair of boxy attachments mounted on each side. He hoped the extra attachments meant that it was a different operator. That traitor was the last person he wanted to hear from at the moment.

With a mechanical click, one of the compartments on the side of the drone opened and a strange, circular device slid out. The hovering machine shifted its position to touch the attachment to the glass. As soon as it made contact, a high-pitched whine swelled, seeming to come from all around. Dust fell from above the window as the pane of glass vibrated. Digby covered his ears to drown out the noise just as the window shattered.

The drone slipped through the opening and swept its lens around the second floor. Digby kept his head low, waiting for the thing to turn around. The instant it looked away, he hit it with a Decay. Just as before, sparks shot from the stupid machine as it veered to one side and crashed into the wall. It spun and clattered to the floor, where it died.

1 combat drone defeated, 30 experience awarded.

"Nice try." Digby sat and folded his arms as smug as he could. A moment later, a second drone drifted through the window.

Not ready to give up then?

Digby hesitated, noticing that this new drone sounded different. Actually, it didn't make any sound at all. There was also a ring of metal hovering just above it like a halo. He'd seen one like it before on the drone that had helped take Lana and Alvin away.

"Whatever." Digby ignored the detail and cast another

Decay, expecting to turn the new drone into a pile of scrap like the last.

Spell resisted.

"What?" Digby's eyes widened as the drone beneath the floating ring flickered like a mirage, winking out of existence for a moment before returning back the way it was as if nothing had happened. Digby attempted to Analyze the strange drone, but it darted out of sight as gunfire came from the street outside.

Shouting followed.

Digby held his position, unsure what had happened. It sounded like a fight had broken out in the street beyond. The gunfire grew as more of Skyline's forces joined in. Opting to risk a peek, Digby crept to the window. A wicked grin spread across his face as soon as he did.

A horde of at least three hundred had entered the scene. Amongst it was a pair of his minions. Searching the crowd, Digby spotted a few leaders as well. His zombies must have relayed his message of food and the leaders had taken care of the rest to sway the many into action. With over three hundred teeth on their side, the numbers were in the horde's favor.

The mercenaries fell back to their vehicles, firing into the mass of walking corpses. Zombies fell one after another, but the horde was large enough to give the dead the confidence to push forward.

"Yes!" Digby threw his hands in the air before leaning against the side of the window to watch the chaos.

Skyline's forces continued to fight, lighting up the night with flashes of gunfire. Their aim proved deadly as one zombie's skull shattered after another. The horde hadn't even reached them yet.

From the other side of the street, a second horde poured onto the scene, taking a few of the mercenaries by surprise and dividing the focus of their forces. Digby caught a glimpse of

Asher flying above for a moment before disappearing behind a building. A pair of brutes joined the fight next, clearly drawn by the noise. The beasts simply plowed through the first horde to reach the feast beyond.

Grenades flew through the air, landing throughout the crowd. Explosions followed. Necrotic limbs and debris flew into the air with each earth-shattering blast. The devastation rattled the building Digby hid in.

Cackling like a madman, he cast Cremation on three of the fallen zombies near the front of the horde on the side closest to his window. A spark of green fire lit up the night, just enough to add to the chaos of the battle. It was almost a pity that he didn't have Rebecca with him to drop alcohol on the crowd like before.

On the other side of the battle, one of the brutes snatched a mercenary from the ground. The poor man was torn in half before his squad-mates could free him. As it was, it took at least a dozen men, all firing at once, to bring the brute down.

"That's right!" Digby scraped his claws against the wall. "Show them what the dead can do." He had a good mind to retrieve the two grenades he left in his bag sitting near the desk downstairs, but opted to stay where he was. The first floor was a little too exposed for his liking.

The hordes pushed forward even without his help, converging on Skyline's front line. Mercenaries fell screaming under the wave of shambling corpses. Digby's only regret was that they weren't all working off his direct orders or Compels, rendering the rewards of each kill invalid. Not one experience message appeared.

"No matter." Digby snarled through gritted teeth. "All that matters is that they die, and I live."

That was when the tide changed.

Skyline's men suddenly stopped firing, many spreading out to the sides of the battlefield. The engine of the enormous vehicle that had plowed its way through the street roared to life. Without warning, it rolled forward. The plow-like blade on the front slammed down to splatter the front line of the horde across the street. When it came to a stop, nearly half of the zombies were no more. What remained piled against the plow, their hands reaching up to pound against the unstoppable machine.

The burly man, Captain Manning, appeared from a circular hatch on top of the vehicle. At the same time, a section of its roof opened to reveal what looked like a rifle, but larger, mounted to a support structure. Manning held out one hand as light flowed toward his palm. It grew brighter, shining like a star in the dark of the street.

Digby had to shield his eyes.

Once the light stopped growing, the man closed his fist around it and thrust it into his own chest. His entire body glowed for a moment before fading back to normal. Without hesitation, he grabbed ahold of the enormous firearm mounted to the vehicle and opened fire.

The sound that followed was unforgettable. It was like a drum, thumping inside Digby's head. Bullets of white light shattered the night as they tore through the horde. Whatever spell the man had used, added a property to his shots that turned the walking dead into nothing but corpses. It didn't matter where they were hit, it simply ripped the curse right out of their bodies.

Digby focused on the man.

Guardian: Level 27 Holy Knight, hostile.

"Oh god." His jaw fell slack as the carnage ensued.

A brute attempted to rush the weapon but was reduced to a useless heap of dead muscle in seconds. Manning continued to fire, cutting a swath through the horde before rotating to the other side to do the same to the second mass of zombies. There was nothing they could do.

"Run, you fools." Digby dug his claws into the windowsill. "Run."

The hordes, coming to the same conclusion, lost the confidence that they'd had a moment before. Zombies turned to flee one after another, the dead scattering into alleyways and side streets to make their escape, each shambling away as fast as their meager attributes would allow. The holy knight continued to fire, picking them off a dozen at a time, reducing the majority of the fleeing horde to inanimate corpses, or smears on the cityscape.

"No." Digby pulled away from the window, only now realizing what sort of force Skyline was. They hadn't even lost half of their numbers in the fight. "How can I survive against that?"

The answer was simple.

He couldn't.

Digby glanced at his mana.

MP: 3/141

His feet froze as if nailed to the floor. If he'd still needed to breathe, he would have hyperventilated. A second later, he was running for the stairs. He sprinted toward the exit, only to stop halfway down to the first floor. He slapped the wall, gouging the surface with his claws in frustration.

"Damn it."

Digby turned and raced back up to grab Alex. Without the dead weight of his unconscious apprentice, he might have been able to escape before Skyline's men raided the building. Guilt gnawed at his chest having even considered it.

"Come on," Digby grabbed his apprentice by his shirt and slapped him, being careful not to use his claws. "Wake up, you useless sack of—"

"Wha... what?" Alex cracked one eye open.

"Oh really! Now you wake up?" Digby shook the confused enchanter just as the strange drone with the halo from before shined a light on them both. It darted back out the window as fast as it had appeared. A rumbling from outside followed.

"What's happening?" Alex struggled to get his feet under him.

"Nothing good." Digby let go of his apprentice's shirt and stood to face the window. He flexed his claws.

The rumbling grew to a roar as two massive shards of stone crashed through the window to create a ramp down to the street. Earth magic of some kind, Digby assumed without thinking about it further. Any window that wasn't already broken blew inward with a gust of wind that launched shattered glass through the room. Digby ignored the debris as sparkling fragments peppered his body, dealing a dozen minor cuts and scratches. He glanced back to make sure Alex was still safe behind the potted plant.

Skyline's forces came next.

Dozens of boots hit the floor as men ran up the stone ramps to leap into the room. More came running up the stairs as a dozen rifles shined beams of red light in Digby's face. He shielded his eyes with his claws.

Then, the holy knight, Captain Manning, walked up the ramp of stone and squeezed through the window into the building. He was huge, even larger up close. Shards of broken glass cracked and squeaked under his boots. He reached for the grip of his sword as he walked across the room. Its sheath split open down the center with a mechanical snap to allow him to draw the weapon from its position mounted on his back without reaching at an awkward angle. The knight stopped and pointed his sword in Digby's direction.

"Ready to talk yet?"

Digby answered with his most hateful snarl.

"What is happening, damn it?" Alex struggled as a man yanked him out from behind the plant where Digby had left him.

"You remember those men that were after me…?"

"Oh…" Alex nodded while staring at the enormous man before them.

Manning opened his mouth again to speak, but Digby

leaped forward without waiting to hear what he intended to say. He drew back his claws only to feel his feet fall out from under him. A gun barked from somewhere behind him as the bones in his shins shattered. Digby hit the floor an instant later.

"You really aren't the brightest, are you?" Manning crouched down to where he lay.

"Get on with it then." Digby spat his words. "Just kill me, I'm done running."

Manning gestured to a pair of men off to the side. They dropped down, each placing a knee on Digby's back so he couldn't get up. Grabbing his arms, they wrenched them back. Something cold and metallic closed around his wrists with a snap.

Then, just like that, his HUD vanished.

"Sorry, but destroying you is no longer our mission." Manning locked his sword back in its sheath on his back.

"Why?" Digby twisted his neck to look up at the massive knight.

Manning leaned closer.

"Orders changed."

CHAPTER THIRTY-ONE

"Ey! Fair are eew faking me?" Digby shouted through a leather muzzle that had been placed over his mouth as a pair of armored men dragged him out of the building he'd been hiding in. His legs were partially broken, his hands were bound behind his back, and his HUD was nowhere to be seen.

"Lord Graves?" A visibly confused Alex was being escorted in front of him. A chain bearing some sort of rune work connected a pair of manacles that were clamped to his wrists. "What do I do?"

"I'll fink os somethin." Digby shouted before being thrown into a truck at the end of Skyline's caravan. Without his hands to support himself, his head hit the floor. A heavy door slammed behind him. The sound of a latch being engaged came from the lock.

That could have gone better.

Digby rolled over by pressing his head against the cold metal plating of the floor, leaving a diamond pattern imprinted in his forehead that he could feel. Laying on his back, he found himself in a long space lined with benches on either side. No doubt the vehicle was meant to transport Skyline's troops.

There were a few narrow windows on each side and a slot at the front covered in metal grating.

With a bit of effort, Digby got to his feet, hoping what was left of his shin bones wouldn't snap under his weight. Once he stopped wobbling, he dropped down onto one of the benches. Pressing his face to the slitted windows, he caught glimpses of Skyline's people running back and forth, getting ready to leave. They'd lost some of their number in the battle with the hordes, but it didn't seem to faze them. Instead, they moved right on as if they had expected such an outcome.

Digby turned away from the window and focused on himself. He searched his field of vision for the little circle that had floated there since his connection with the Heretic Seed. It was nowhere to be seen. Nor was his coven's status.

I hope Asher made it somewhere safe.

Digby's thoughts were interrupted by the sound of the door's latch disengaging. He slid away to back up against the opposite wall of the compartment as the door swung open.

The bear of a man, Captain Manning, turned to the side to fit his massive body through the opening. It had clearly been designed without taking a person of his stature into account. He even had to duck his head once inside. He left the door open as if there wouldn't be enough room for him in the compartment if he closed it.

"You have caused quite the disturbance, Mister Graves."

"Fats Rord Grades to you," Digby growled through his muzzle.

Manning gave an annoyed groan before reaching behind Digby and securing his manacles to a ring mounted on the wall to limit his movement. Afterward, he unclasped the straps that held on the muzzle and pulled it off.

"What was that now?"

"I said, that's Lord Graves to you!" Digby snapped his jaws at the man's meaty hands while they were still in range.

"I'm not calling you that." Manning scoffed as he casually

pulled his fingers away like he wasn't even in danger. "Do you know why I haven't destroyed you?"

"Your orders changed, that it?" Digby added a scowl. "So what, I'm a prisoner now?"

"That will depend on you." Manning sat down on the opposite side of the truck, the bench bowing under his weight.

"What is that supposed to mean?"

"Do you know what you are?" Manning answered his question with a question.

Digby shook his head, not wanting to say anything that might give away information.

"You're an anomaly. A rare combination that defies the rules. Your death gave you an ability that under normal circumstances would be impossible." Manning relaxed into his seat. "I'll be honest, I was worried you might have grown too powerful for my men to handle."

"Who says I haven't?"

"Those handcuffs you're in say otherwise." Manning let out a gruff laugh. "Look, I'm going to level with you. You're dead, and that's filtering out all the ambient essence around you except the death essence that makes up your mana pool. Anyone else would have to work for lifetimes to reach a pure balance like yours." He sat back against the wall. "Now this wouldn't be an issue if you were a normal zombie, but you're still capable of magic through whatever connection you have with your Heretic Seed. And that makes you special."

"So what? You lot have the same power, can't you figure out—"

"Power yes, but not the same." Manning held up a hand to cut him off, displaying a familiar gold band on his finger. "The Heretic Seed is dangerous. It has no restrictions. It just gives anyone power and lets them do what they please with it. There's no approval process to verify the character of its champions. Case in point, you." Manning gestured to Digby.

"I never claimed to be a saint."

"Yes, and you've demonstrated that fact repeatedly. Just how many of my men have you eaten tonight?"

"A few." Digby rolled his eyes.

"If it were up to me," Manning's face shifted to a hardened stare, "I'd have you incinerated down to your last necrotic cell."

"But it's not up to you." Digby began to see where the conversation was heading.

"Unfortunately, no." Manning averted his eyes. "Apparently you are uniquely suited to aid in the casting of a spell that the higher-ups are looking to get done."

"What sort of spell?" Digby arched an eyebrow.

"That much, I have no idea." Manning shrugged. "It's above my pay grade. But if they need someone with a pure death balance, then it's something big and lethal."

"Why would your lords want to cast something like that?"

Manning chuckled. "My lords know what they are doing, and I trust that they have mankind's best interests at heart. Sometimes sacrifices are necessary for the good of us all."

"And what if I don't want to be a party of something like that?"

"You've already killed a city." Manning gestured to the street outside as one of his men gunned down a roaming zombie. "Everything happening out there is your doing. Not just that, but there are new outbreaks starting up throughout the world at this point."

"None of that is my fault." Digby lowered his eyes to the floor. "I didn't ask to be turned into this. And I haven't attacked anyone by choice."

"Except my men. Or are they somehow an exception?"

"Do you really think I had a choice in that?" Digby raised his head back up.

"You could have died and let this curse end with you." Manning cut right to the meat of it. He wasn't wrong. "That being said, there is another option open to you now."

"So what? I just join you and all is forgiven?"

"In a way." Manning relaxed his shoulders. "You will be

transported to a new home where you'll live in luxury and have all your needs taken care of."

"So I'd be a prisoner then? A lord locked away in a dungeon of gold?" Digby scoffed, finding the suggestion uncomfortably similar to what Rebecca had described her situation as.

"You'd be allowed to exist and be safe."

"Is that what you do with your people? Lock them in a comfortable prison and tell them they're safe?" He rolled his eyes.

"You have to understand, you are still dangerous." Manning's tone grew more sincere. "We would still have to take precautions to protect others from you."

"Maybe there's some truth to what that treacherous wench said, after all." Digby wasn't sure why he threw in the comment. It had just slipped out. His body tense as he waited for a response.

"Wench?" Manning tilted his head to one side. "Oh, that drone operator. Yes, Rebecca is stationed in an apartment here in the city where she has little to worry about besides her work. I apologize for her betrayal earlier. I've read her file, and she isn't exactly our proudest achievement."

"That sounds about right." Digby's chest tightened as a mix of pity and resentment surrounded his thoughts of his one-time ally. "What's wrong with her?"

"Rebecca was part of a mostly successful program that offers a second chance to the children of less fortunate households. Families are paid a large sum at signing and the children are put into Skyline's education system. From there, they're trained from their early teens to fill important roles within our organization. For most, it's an opportunity that would simply be out of reach."

That sounds an awful lot like buying children to use as servants. Digby suppressed the urge to spit at the man, instead saying, "Sounds like a good way to aid the peasants of your world."

"It's certainly better than the alternatives. I myself entered Skyline through the same program and it made me the man I am today." Manning shrugged. "But nothing is perfect, and sometimes the program fails. Rebecca has had every opportunity afforded to her, but even with that, she still slipped through the cracks."

"And that's why you've kept her here, alone in Seattle."

"Yes, though that part is unusual." Manning nodded. "Rebecca should have been moved to one of our bases long ago, where she could interact with the rest of our personnel where it would be determined if she was right for our Guardian Core."

"But?"

"But she has underperformed at her position. The seclusion that our trainees are housed in allows them to dissociate with the outside world but maintain a dependent bond with their superiors."

"Clever." Digby complemented the strategy, hoping to keep Manning talking. "And that breeds loyal servants?"

"Most of the time, but in Rebecca's case, she doesn't respect the chain of command and thinks she knows better. Those are not good traits for an asset, even if they are seeing the battlefield through a monitor. We can still use her for basic missions overseas, but anything beyond that is out of the question."

"Ah, so she's not worth the money that you all paid for her?"

"That's a harsh way to put it, but yes." Manning folded his arms.

"Not much in the way of incentives for your lot to come rescue her any time soon, then?"

"Right now rescue operations for anyone in Seattle are on indefinite hold until the higher-ups say so. The only people that have been evacuated so far were the two teens that were with you earlier. The girl is a little old for our training program but the boy, Alvin, is the right age to start. As for the rest of this city." Manning returned his stare to Digby. "That will largely depend on you."

"I think I understand." Digby lowered his head as he lied.

In truth he had no idea what to do. Whatever Skyline's

lords had planned didn't sound good. Even worse, it seemed like Rebecca had been telling the truth when she'd asked for help. She was imprisoned by an organization that had stolen her from her family. Skyline had used her, only to cast her aside when she didn't prove loyal enough. A dull ache echoed through his dead chest. She was just as much a victim as he was.

"What about Alex?" Digby looked up.

"Your accomplice?" Manning glanced back over his shoulder as if unconsciously looking to where they were holding him. It was toward the front of the caravan from what Digby surmised. "He will be safe. Just as you will be."

"When can I see him?" Digby looked Manning in the eyes. "He's a new heretic and will need some guidance. I'll need him brought to me as soon as possible."

"That's fine." Manning nodded. "I can have him sent to you once we have you settled into one of our properties."

"I see." Digby remained silent for a moment. "It appears that I should cooperate with you then."

"That is your best option. I'm glad you've come to see things our way." Manning gave him a warm smile that sent a chill down his spine. It was condescending and fake, as if the man wanted nothing more than to tear Digby's head off, but was playing nice for the moment. Digby suppressed the urge to spit in his face. There was a good chance that every assurance the man had given him had been a lie.

Manning kept his head ducked as he stood up. "We'll have to muzzle you again later, but I'll let you relax a little on our way back to the field base."

"Does that mean you'll take these off?" Digby turned to display the manacles binding his hands.

"Sorry, those are all that's keeping you from getting any other ideas. We'll get them off you once we get you out of the city. Just try to sit tight until then." Manning ducked lower and squeezed himself through the opening at the back of the truck, latching the door behind him.

"Like hell I'm sitting tight." Digby immediately started trying to break his own wrist.

It stood to reason that the manacles binding his hands were the reason he couldn't see his HUD or cast any spells. All he had to do was get them off. He pulled away from the wall, feeling something tear in his shoulder.

I'll rip my damned arm off if I have to.

That was when the familiar click of a speaker turning on came from below him. An even more familiar voice followed.

"You won't get them off like that. They secured the cuffs as tight as they go, and the chain is enchanted. I overheard someone talking before slipping in here to hide."

A strange blur floated out from under his bench where it had been hidden. The air rippled as if bending around a shape. With a sudden shimmer, the ripples cleared, leaving a drone hovering in the space.

"How many of those things do you have, anyway?" Digby turned away from the camera, not wanting to look Rebecca in the eyes.

"I still have one more."

They remained silent for a moment as it became apparent that she'd heard everything that had been said, leaving it all out on the table.

"So I'm not worth the money that I was purchased for, huh?" Rebecca lowered her drone to the bench opposite him.

"Oh, please. I didn't mean it. I was just trying to keep him talking."

"I figured; you lie more often than not. Manning is just as bad considering the amount of lies I've caught him in tonight. Though, I suspect what he said about me is true. That certainly stings. I thought I was good at my job. Anyway, I bet you feel bad for not believing me, earlier?"

"Yes, yes, I do, alright?" Digby finally looked at the drone. As much as he wanted to be angry at her for her betrayal, he understood why she had done it. Not to mention, he didn't want to be alone anymore either. "Can we move past the part where you say I told you so and skip to the part where we go back to being accomplices? I don't trust that your lords will keep my apprentice alive like they said. And I'd like to rescue him before he ends up dead in the street. Also, since when do you turn invisible?"

"Since always. It's optical camouflage, I just didn't use it in front of you in case I needed to deceive you at some point." She paused to let out an awkward laugh at her confession. "But more importantly, you're right. From what I heard outside, they don't intend to keep your friend alive once they have your cooperation." Rebecca laughed again. "I can't believe they think you'll play nice."

"You sound like you approve of the idea of me fighting back."

"After what I just heard? That's a yes. Plus, the amount of aircrafts they have doesn't add up. I counted earlier and there seems to be some missing. I had assumed they were using them to carry survivors earlier, but now, I'm pretty sure they are transporting zombies."

"Why?" Digby raised his head.

"Like Manning said, there have been new outbreaks all over, even in a few other countries at this point. I don't see how the curse could spread that far without help. It just doesn't math out unless someone is helping it along. I don't know why Skyline would want to plunge the world into a full-on zombie apocalypse, but they're definitely up to something."

"Well that gnaws my hide." Digby scowled in the direction of the rest of the caravan. "I don't like the dead being used by someone other than me."

"That sounds a little villainous of you."

"Too bad." Digby yanked on his manacles again. "I don't have time to play hero. Right now I need to get these things off and rescue my apprentice." The truck's engine fired up as if to add severity to his words. Digby glanced down at the drone, feeling the ache in his chest fade. "Now, how do I get out of here? You must have had a plan when you hid in here."

Rebecca floated off the bench where she'd landed so that she could look him in the eyes. Digby waited for her to reveal whatever she had up her sleeve that would free them both. An uncomfortable silence went by before she spoke.

"I have no idea."

CHAPTER THIRTY-TWO

"What do you mean you have no idea?" Digby stomped a foot on the metal flooring of the truck he was imprisoned in.

"Shhh." Rebecca flicked her camera to the slot that connected the rear compartment to the driver's cabin. "You want someone to hear you?"

"Don't shush me." Digby lowered his voice despite his words and leaned toward her. "Why would you let yourself get locked in here without a plan for escape?"

"What do you think, I can just blink my eyes and just magically open the door?" Rebecca's drone pulled away as if she was worried he might try to bite it.

"Can't you just do that... network thing... that you do to find a way out?"

"If this was a networked vehicle I could, but it's not."

"Why did you even come in here then?" Digby pulled on the manacles binding his hands behind him.

"I don't know. Maybe I just wanted to talk to you." The drone tilted back and forth. "Now that we're both on the same side, I thought it would be nice to let you know you're not alone."

"Oh yay, friendship." Digby lowered his head. "Lot of good that does us while trapped in here."

The truck started moving to remind him of his predicament. It wasn't traveling fast, but that almost made it worse. There would be plenty of time to curse his helplessness before they reached Skyline's fortifications.

He tugged on his chains again, wondering how they were blocking his magic. The power wasn't gone. He was sure of that. The familiar chill of his deathly mana was still flowing through him just as strong as ever. He just couldn't use it for some reason.

That was when he had a thought.

What if the chains only block the Heretic Seed?

Digby turned to Rebeca and said, "Rend." The surge of power that accompanied a Compel flowed from him just as it had before.

"What?" The drone drifted away, eyeing him as it reached the far side of the truck. "What are you trying to—"

"I got it." Digby laughed. "I can't cast any spells, but I still have control over my zombie abilities. Now if I can just get some of the dead to heed my Compels, I might have a chance at slowing this truck." He twisted his head to press it against the vehicle's narrow window.

"Do they need to hear you for that to happen?" The drone tapped on the wall with its camera. "Because I don't think anyone outside can hear. Not over the noise of the engine and the other trucks at least."

"They…" Digby trailed off. "I actually don't know. It might be a mixture of senses that allows them to pick up my intent. The words represent simple concepts that a normal zombie can understand, but I think they just carry the power rather than convey the instructions."

"That sounds like they still need to hear you."

"You're probably right." Digby lowered his head again. "And even if that wasn't the case. I don't know how to convince them to attack our captors. They aren't the bravest bunch, after all. They only attack if they have the numbers on their side. And even then, they take some convincing."

Clearly, compelling a horde of zombies from inside the truck was a fantasy at best. Beyond that, his claws were bound, leaving him with just one mutation that might help.

The Glutton's Maw.

Unfortunately, he still hadn't figured out how to use it.

"Rebecca?" Digby looked up to the drone. "If you were a near mindless corpse capable of opening a gateway to a bottomless void inside you, how would you go about doing that?"

The drone stared at him in silence for a second. "Yeah, you're going to have to explain that a little better."

Digby gave her a brief explanation of how his void worked and what opening his maw meant. Rebecca went silent for another few seconds before coming up with a suggestion.

"Have you tried eating something that isn't in your mouth?"

"No." Digby arched an eyebrow at her. "I'm dead, not stupid."

"Yes, but the rest of these zombies are. And they aren't having trouble figuring out their abilities." She had him there. "Think about it like this: you're able to fill this void space by eating. That means that there has to be an access point to it somewhere between your throat and stomach, right?"

"Most likely." Digby nodded.

"But that access point probably isn't open all the time. So it must only open when you eat. My guess is it's triggered when—"

"When I open my mouth." He finished her sentence.

"Exactly." The drone dropped down to land on the seat across from him. "So you've probably had the ability to open your maw all along. The mutation you've unlocked might only be the ability to relocate your access point from inside you to somewhere else."

Digby opened his mouth for a moment, paying attention to his body. It didn't feel the same as when he'd eaten anything. He closed his eyes and imagined one of Skyline's mercenaries running from him. Opening his mouth again, he bared his teeth to strike. To his surprise, something did feel different. The need to feed swelled inside him. He snapped his mouth shut to quell his sudden hunger.

"Alright."

Digby searched for something in the empty truck that he could try to eat. Unfortunately the space was bare, save for Rebecca's inedible puppet perched on the bench across from him.

Well, it's better than nothing. He stared at the drone, trying his best to pretend it was something more appetizing.

"What are you doing?" Rebecca eyed him as he opened and closed his mouth a few times.

"Nothing, now be quiet and act like a severed limb." He opened his mouth again just as a six-inch shadow formed beneath the little pegs that stuck out from the bottom of the drone like feet. It wasn't nearly as large as the gateways that the devourer had been able to create, but it was something. The ability to make it bigger must have been part of a higher tier.

"Hey!" Rebecca attempted to take off the moment she began to sink into the shadow. "Don't eat me."

Digby snapped his mouth shut, causing the shadow to vanish before the drone could escape fully. His closing maw sheared off one of its feet as easily as his teeth could take a bite of food. Black fluid dripped from the drone where it had dipped into the shadow.

"Sorry, I just needed something to target." Digby shrugged off her complaint.

"How about you not test your abilities on my drone? I only have one of them left besides this one." Again she flew as far away from him as she could get in the truck's compartment.

Digby ignored her and focused his attention on the chain binding his wrists. If he could somehow get the links to dip into his open maw, he might be able to snap them right in the middle. Rebecca fell silent as he closed his eyes, clearly under-standing what he intended to do.

He scooted his rear away from the wall and let the chain fall slack on the bench behind him. Then he opened his mouth and let his predatory instincts take over. Again, he felt the emptiness that came along with accessing his maw. There was no way to see the shadowed portal, but he could sense the blood within it enough to know where it was. He snapped his mouth shut.

With a metallic crack, his HUD flickered back to life.

COVEN
Digby: MP: 141/141
Alex: MP: 114/114 - SILENCED
Asher: MP: 30/30

He grimaced at the fact that his minions were gone. They must not have survived the attack that led to his capture. At least Asher and Alex were safe. His shoulders relaxed, if only a little. Though he wasn't sure what the word silenced next to his apprentice's name meant; probably that his magic was being blocked.

Digby cast a Regeneration to repair the damage to his legs and arm. Then he moved himself away from the wall of the truck and pulled his arms out from behind him. The chain connecting the manacles dangled from each wrist, no longer connected. He flexed his hands to work the sensation back into his limbs.

For a moment, he focused on the door, ready to Decay the lock into submission, but he thought better of it. There was a chance he might break something he didn't intend to and jam the lock instead. Trapping himself inside didn't sound like a good plan. There had to be a better way.

"How do we get out of here?" He turned to the drone for help.

"There should be a lock control for the back door up in the

cabin of the truck," Rebecca mentioned, unable to do much else without being there in person.

"I see." Digby turned his attention to the slot covered in metal grating that led to the driver's compartment.

Creeping closer, he grabbed the knob to the side of the slot and worked it open as slow as possible to keep anyone from noticing. The metal was thick, but it moved little by little. Once it was cracked enough for him to see through, he took in the scene.

Two men were sitting in the cabin. The one on the left was driving. Digby looked around the cabin, wondering where the door release mechanism might be.

Maybe one of the men up front knows.

Digby debated asking them before opting for a more tactical approach. He focused on the wall just behind the driver. This time, he didn't need to open his mouth to call forth his maw. Once he felt the emptiness swell, he cast forge to send a barbed spike of black blood into the man's back, making sure to pierce his heart.

The unfortunate driver lurched forward, unable to pull away from the barbed form. A gurgled cough erupted from his throat, followed by a brief moment of flailing limbs before he expired. The vehicle began to slow.

1 armored human defeated, 120 experience awarded.

"What the fu—" The passenger turned to the driver, catching Digby's eyes through the slot in the back of the compartment. His face turned white as he grabbed the wheel. Digby didn't waste any time, focusing on his recent victim.

Corpse: Human, 70 MP required to animate.
Animate corpse? Yes/No

"Absolutely!" Digby ducked to one side as the passenger in front pulled a pistol with his free hand. The gun barked, ringing his ears like a bell as the bullet tore through the metal grating. Sparks flew from where it ricocheted off the ceiling before it punched a dent onto the bench mere inches from Rebecca's drone.

That was when a line of text was added to Digby's HUD.

Common zombie animated: Minion has 7 attribute points to allocate.

The dead driver began to twitch, and Digby dropped all seven of the zombie's points into intelligence. Hopefully that would give them enough brain power to unlock the rear door. Unfortunately, the passenger was still a problem.

"Kill him!" Digby snarled through the grating just as the passenger reached for a device attached to the vehicle's controls near the steering mechanism.

"He's going for the radio!" Rebecca shouted, hovering at an angle so she could see through the slot.

Digby's new minion acted fast, lunging to tear into its prey. The passenger screamed for an instant before being cut off. Another experience message flashed across his vision as the truck swerved. He slammed his shoulder into the wall. Rebecca's drone did the same, taking a moment to stabilize itself. Digby clawed his way back to the slot.

"Keep it straight," he ordered, hoping his animated minion was smart enough to keep the truck on the road.

The zombie snatched the wheel and pulled back. Swerving in the other direction before straightening out. The vehicle continued to fall behind the rest of the caravan, apparently needing something from its deceased driver.

"Tell it to step on the gas!" Rebecca shouted through her speaker.

"What?"

"It's the pedal on the right."

"Oh yes." He didn't know what gas was or how it would

make the truck speed up, but at this point, Rebecca had no reason to lie. "Step on the gas."

The zombie looked pained for a moment, glancing at the perfectly good meal in the passenger seat beside them. Fortunately, its master's words carried more weight than its appetite. The zombie slammed a foot down as the truck lurched forward with renewed vigor. Digby hit his head on the ceiling.

"Alright, now follow that truck and unlock the door back here." Digby trusted his minion to understand his words. It seemed that seven intelligence was enough to help it remember how to perform everyday activities well enough. A sudden noise from the lock at the rear of the truck told him he was right.

"What do we do now?" Rebecca floated toward the exit as Digby kicked open the door.

"We make our way to the front of the caravan and get my apprentice." He leaned out the opening to find a small ladder on the back of the vehicle. "I gave Alex a heretic ring after only knowing him for ten minutes. He knows less about what's happening than I do, and he's been thrown into the middle of it all. He's going to need help."

"Why would you give him a ring after knowing him for ten minutes?" Rebecca sounded irritated.

"He was sure to end up dead before the night was through without it. I learned my lesson back at the science building. The ring wasn't doing anyone good rattling around in my boot when it could help someone survive." With that, Digby pulled himself onto the ladder. Ignoring the ground passing by beneath him, he climbed until his claws slammed down on the roof of the truck. From the edge, he peered over at the convoy ahead.

The rest of the trucks followed the behemoth of a machine at the front, clearly unaware that anything was wrong yet. The lead vehicle plowed on through all that was in its path. No doubt that was where Manning was riding. He hoped Alex was in one of the trucks behind. He didn't want to face off against Skyline's captain again anytime soon. Whatever a holy knight was, he wanted no part of it.

Digby pulled himself onto the roof and crouched down to crawl toward the front. His leather coat flapped in the wind behind him like the tail of a dragon. That was when he realized there wasn't much room between his truck and the next. He sighed.

"I guess I never told my minion how close to follow the other vehicles. So much for being capable of everyday tasks."

Almost as soon as the words left his mouth, the zombie driving below sped up to ram the vehicle in front of them. The sound of twisting metal filled the air as Digby slid forward to tumble down the front window of the truck. He came to a stop leaning against the back of the next vehicle as his minion continued to push forward against it. The zombie driver looked pleased with himself.

"Yes, yes, you're doing a great job." Digby groaned at his animated minion.

"What the hell is going on back there?" A voice shouted from inside the rear compartment of the next truck as someone attempted to open the door. They pushed it a crack before Digby's minion rammed it shut again.

Thinking fast, Digby hooked his claws along the top rung of the next vehicle's rear ladder and shouted at his minion to back off. The hood of the rear truck slid out from beneath him, leaving him hanging from the next vehicle. Digby clung to the ladder as the gap between both trucks widened. Dust and debris flew up from the wheels.

"There's eight mercs inside that truck." Rebecca's drone caught up.

"You see through walls now?" Digby snapped at the drone.

"I can see heat sources. It's not much, but I can tell how many people are inside by the temperature of their bodies." She explained matter of factly.

"That would have been good to know earlier." Digby shook his head as he clung to the ladder.

"Sorry, I didn't want to tell you then." She ended her sentence with an almost cheerful laugh.

"Whatever," Digby rolled his eyes. "Just go see if you can tell which carriage they're holding Alex—"

The door beside him popped open to reveal one of Skyline's men brandishing a rifle. They opened fire the moment they saw the zombie driving the truck behind them. Bullets peppered the window, cracking the glass without breaking through. Digby flattened himself against the opposite side of the ladder to keep from being noticed while their focus was on the truck at the rear.

"Hold your fire!" another voice yelled from inside the compartment. "That transport is carrying the prisoner."

"Not anymore, it's not." Digby grabbed a grenade from a pouch on the mercenary's armor and tossed it into the truck's compartment. He made sure to remember to pull the pin this time. Shouts of panic erupted from inside along with the sound of boots hitting metal. Six terrified men leaped from the truck just before the vehicle was rocked by an explosion.

More experience flashed across Digby's vision as he struggled to hold on. The now familiar surge of power that accompanied a level up followed.

You have reached level 16. 3,043 experience to next level.
All attributes increased by 1.
You have 1 additional attribute to allocate.

Digby placed his extra point into strength without a second thought. Five of the men that had escaped rolled to the ground, while one landed on the hood of the rear truck, face to face with its deceased driver. His legs hung over the front.

"Keep pushing forward as hard as you can." Digby shouted to his minion before climbing up the ladder to the roof. The sound of an engine roaring told him that the zombie had understood. Well, that, and the screams of the enemy that had been caught between both vehicles.

Digby clawed his way across the second truck to reach the third. Preparing to jump, his minion rammed the vehicle he stood on. The train of vehicles slammed into each other as he kicked off, only to land on the third truck in an uncoordinated crouch, nearly rolling off the side. A terrible screech cut through the air as his claws scraped the roof of the truck for purchase

Catching himself at the last second, he glanced back to make eye-contact with the driver of the truck behind him. The man shouted into an object connected to the vehicle's controls by a wire. Probably the radio that Rebecca had mentioned. There was no way to know what he was saying, but there was a sense of urgency in his expression.

"Trying to call for help, are you now?"

The driver's face went white as Digby extended a hand toward them.

"Goodbye!"

Focusing on the left wheel of the vehicle, he hit it with a Decay. Rust spread across the metal covering at the center, flaking away around the bolts that held the thing together. The truck rumbled and shook as the wheel wavered back and forth, trying to rip itself off. It didn't take much. A sudden crack sounded, and the entire wheel fell off. The front of the vehicle slammed into the road, scraping the ground with a cloud of sparks and debris before the corner stopped hard. With unyielding momentum, the rear of the vehicle continued forward regardless, flipping end over end.

Chunks of stone and scraps of metal flew into the air as the transport crashed into the ground upside-down with its wheels still spinning. The distraction didn't stop Digby's minion driving the rear truck from continuing forward in a single-minded attempt to follow orders. The engine roared as the vehicle and its deceased driver plowed into the wreckage.

More messages hit Digby's HUD.

Animated common zombie lost.
Maximum mana returned to 148.
3 armored humans defeated, 354 experience awarded.

It was a pity about his minion, but at least his maximum mana had returned to where it belonged. Losing seventy MP had been a steep price to pay to animate the zombie. His attention was torn away by Rebecca as she darted past him. "Alex is in the truck below you, along with four guards."

"Good to know." Digby crept his way to the ladder on the back of the truck as a white light streaked past his head. The sound of a drum-like gunshot echoed off the buildings above. His body tensed the instant he looked back. Manning had climbed up through the top hatch of the lead vehicle, and was now standing with his hands gripping the massive gun mounted to its roof.

"Not good!"

Digby rolled off the back truck to drop onto the ladder just before the air erupted in a hail of curse-killing bullets. As he dropped out of view, a single shot grazed his wrist, sending an odd numbness spreading through his arm like his limb was somehow returning to that of a common corpse.

Digby flailed his hand as the feeling subsided, like his will was reasserting its dominance over his body. He thanked every deity in existence for the fact that his attributes were so much higher than a common zombie's. If his Will value had been any lower, his night might have ended right there. As it was, that spell had still proved particularly lethal to him. Who knew what getting hit a few more times would do?

Digby flattened his body to the ladder as Manning continued to fire. White streaks carved up the side of one of the passing buildings, shattering windows and showering the street in broken glass. A group of three unfortunate zombies were caught in the debris.

"I think that was a warning shot." Rebecca's drone ducked down beside him.

"I'd hate to see what he does when he's trying to hit me."

Digby clung to the ladder with one hand and grabbed the handle of the truck's rear door with the other. Throwing caution to the wind, he cast Decay. There wasn't time to come up with a better plan. Metal creaked and groaned as the paint on the door flaked away. Rust spread out from his hand faster than every Decay spell he'd used before, as if it grew stronger with physical contact.

"Don't you dare break off." Digby cursed the handle as it began to move. A horrible grinding accompanied the motion just before the lock popped open. A wave of relief washed over Digby's body.

It was short lived.

A mercenary thrust a rifle out the instant the door opened. On reflex, Digby snapped his hand around the man's wrist and yanked, sending him tumbling to the street. Once the door was clear, he leaned in the opening.

"If you value your lives, you'll release my apprentice."

Digby opened his maw and cast Blood Forge to make his point, sending a narrow pillar of black fluid up from a shadow on the floor. The shape punched a dent into the armored vehicle's ceiling. The spell left him with just twenty-one points of mana. He was glad he'd used it, finding the three remaining guns for hire cowering at the back of the compartment.

Alex sat with his wrists bound in front of him by the same enchanted manacles that had been used on him. The boy raised his hand in a gesture that resembled a confused wave. "You came for me?"

"Of course I did." Digby beckoned to his apprentice. "Now, come along and jump from this moving vehicle."

"Ah, okay." Alex got up and slipped around the pillar of blood near the door. The ground flew by beneath them.

"Try not to die when you hit the ground," Rebecca commented as she drifted by.

"You're not helping," Digby snapped.

"This is not how I thought this day would go." Alex swallowed hard before hopping from the truck. The boy landed on his feet and tumbled back onto his side. Having his arms bound almost seemed to help him tuck his body for the impact.

Digby shrugged and followed, though his landing was less

than ideal. He rolled to a stop on his face with one arm twisted in the wrong direction. Nothing a Necrotic Regeneration couldn't fix.

He cringed when his mana dropped down to eleven points remaining. No matter, they were free once again. Digby pushed himself off the ground and shook his fist at the caravan as it left them behind. "Try to capture me, will you!"

"Yeah, keep running," Alex joined in, caught up in the excitement of the moment.

In response, the truck screeched to a stop, clearly realizing that their prisoners had escaped.

"Oh shit." Alex's face fell.

"Indeed." Digby spun on his heel and started running.

"This way!" Rebecca's drone poked out from an alleyway. "Run."

"Way ahead of you." Digby bolted past her, only turning back to make sure Alex was still with him.

"Keep up, boy. We have a city to escape."

CHAPTER THIRTY-THREE

"I am so not dying right now." Alex sprinted past Digby as he ran through the alleyway.

"That's the plan, my boy." Digby picked up his pace to keep up.

"Seriously, I just found out that magic is real and that I'm an enchanter." The chains binding his wrists jangled as he ran. "I don't know what that means or what I can do, but there is no way I'm getting killed without casting at least one spell."

"Agreed. We'll become a force to be reckoned with yet." Digby couldn't help but grin. "If Manning and the rest of his sellswords think I'm so dangerous, then I feel like I have no choice but to prove them right. After we escape the city, of course. All we need is some time and I'll see to it that we become so powerful that those fools at Skyline won't dare cross us."

"I can live with that." Alex gave an approving nod.

"Wow, that is some tough talk coming from two people that are literally running for their lives right now," Rebeca added from her place leading their escape. "And don't call people 'fools.' You sound like a villain."

"Bah, I say what I want." Digby puffed out his chest as he ran.

The shouts of Skyline's troops were still audible, but they were falling behind. With so little mana left, he couldn't believe they were actually going to escape. He'd been sure they were doomed back in the truck, but now, he was running free with his apprentice by his side and Rebecca guiding the way. Somehow, everything was falling into place.

"This way!" The little drone stopped beside the entrance to a building. "I hacked the lock. We can cut through and keep moving."

"Good work." Digby skidded to a stop, grabbing the door handle. His body felt lighter than it had the last couple hours. Rebecca was a better accomplice than an enemy. "I'm sorry I called you a treacherous wench."

"I bet." The drone ducked inside as soon as the door was open.

"Not to sound needy here, but how did you get your hand-cuffs off?" Alex jogged with his hands bound in front of him. The enchanted chain shimmered in the dim glow of the build-ing's after-hours lighting.

"Technically, I ate them." Digby glanced down at the severed links that had tethered his wrists together after being captured. "Or at least, I ate a couple links of the enchanted chain."

"Do you think I'll be able to make things like these cuffs once I get them off?" Alex looked at his manacles with eyes wide.

"Someday, maybe. Right now, let's just worry about making our escape."

"Right." He shook his head, refocusing on the task at hand, clearly excited about having any kind of magic.

"Over here." Rebecca's drone sped down a hallway, only to stop short as soon as she rounded the corner into the building's entry hall. Alex caught up to her first, skidding to a stop beside her.

"What are you stopping for…?" Digby's words trailed off as he stumbled around the corner. "Oh, that."

The building's extravagant lobby was enormous, complete with beautiful hanging chandeliers and gold painted accents lining the walls. Its opulence put anything Digby had seen before to shame. Interior design aside, the room was also home to around two hundred zombies.

One by one, hungry eyes turned toward them. Digby relaxed for a moment. It wasn't like they would do anything to him. He was dead and off the menu. Then he remembered his very edible, human apprentice standing beside him.

"Ah, Lord Graves? You can control them, right?" Alex took one shaky step backward.

"Not this many." Digby glanced at his HUD to find that he hadn't absorbed much MP back on the run there. "Also, I only have twenty-three mana."

"There's a footbridge up on the fourth floor that leads to another hotel across the street." Rebecca drifted in the direction of a bay of golden doors at the back of the lobby.

"Yes, that works." Digby spun on his heel and ran for the strange metal doors.

"Wait, what?" Alex turned to run just as the horde let out a collective moan.

"Run for your life, my boy." Digby caught the meaning of the moan, alerting the room full of dead that prey was close.

"Okay, and stop calling me boy. I'm twenty-four." Alex sprinted toward Rebecca.

"And I'm over eight hundred, so respect your elders." Digby caught up, finding no handle to open any metal doors in the hall. A sign with the word 'Elevators' hung off to the side.

"Come on, come on." Alex frantically tapped a circular button bearing an arrow pointing up. He flicked his eyes back the way they'd come as the horde spilled into the hall behind them.

"How do we open the doors?" Digby clawed at the seam that ran down the center.

"They'll open on their own once the elevator gets here."

"What's an elevator?"

"It's a..." The drone spun around in frustration. "You know what, you'll see in a moment."

Alex continued to tap the button while the horde surged forward. "Where's the stairs?"

"On the other side of those zombies. So, not an option." Rebecca sounded annoyed. "And tapping that button is not going to make the elevator move any faster."

The horde packed in to fill the hall behind them, forming a wall of slathering teeth that crept forward with every passing second. Making a run for it was out. There was no way past them and they were only ten feet away.

"I can't help it, this is scary." Alex jabbed the button again.

Rebecca hovered by the door. "Trust me, the doors will open right. About. Now..."

Nothing happened.

"Okay, I really thought that was going to work." Rebecca began to drift away from Alex.

"Where are you going?" His voice climbed to a panicked shriek.

"I don't want to be hovering next to you when that horde reaches us."

Alex's face turned white. Then a quiet ding came from behind to announce the opening of their escape route.

"Move." Digby sprinted past the drone to race through the open doors. He immediately slammed his face into a wall and fell to the floor. "What in the hell?"

"Get in!" Rebecca entered with Alex right behind her. The horde closed in.

"Come on, close, close, close." The enchanter jabbed at a button on the inside of the tiny room that the three of them now occupied.

"I repeat, what in the hell?" Digby grabbed a railing that ran along the interior of the space and pulled himself up. "This is just a box."

The zombies at the front of the horde reached out as another ding came from above. The doors closed with a quiet thump, the bony fingertips of the dead falling short.

"Holy shit!" Alex heaved a deep breath like he'd been holding it for the last few minutes. He slammed a finger into another button with the number four on it before looking down and letting out a relieved sigh. "Oh thank god, I didn't pee my pants."

"That's actually impressive," Digby commented, glancing down at his apprentices' surprisingly dry pants. A second later, a strange sensation of movement made it clear the box they were standing in was rising up. Glancing around the elevator he put two and two together. "Oh, elevator, as in elevate. I get it now."

"Yes, Dig. This will bring us up to the fourth floor." Rebecca sounded relieved that she didn't have to calm him down and explain the mechanism.

"That's clever." He nodded, appreciating the ingenuity of modern society. "What happens if we press more buttons?"

"Don't!" Both Alex and Rebecca spoke up in unison.

"I wasn't going to." Digby crossed his arms and looked away despite the fact that he was definitely going to press them all if they hadn't stopped him. "Whatever, let's get those mana-cles off you, boy." He changed the subject and opened his maw, creating a wet looking shadow on the floor. "Just dip the chain in there."

"Sure." Alex crouched down and did as he was told.

The elevator doors opened a moment later. Digby flicked his eyes to the empty fourth floor to make sure there wasn't another horde waiting for them before closing his maw and severing the chain.

"Oh wow." Alex's eyes widened the instant the link broke. "This is so... cool."

"Indeed," Digby agreed, understanding the context of the use of the word, cool. He was starting to appreciate his height-ened intelligence more by the minute. It certainly made thinking and making connections easier, even if his estimate of his current values were that he was only about average.

Alex walked forward at a snail's pace, clearly enthralled by the Heretic Seed's HUD that must have filled his vision after removing his manacles. The moment he stepped off the lift, another ding came from above.

"What?" Digby looked up. "I didn't press anything."

"The zombies downstairs must have hit the call button." Rebecca zipped out as the doors began to close.

"Wait, what?" Digby froze, unsure if the doors would crush him or not if he got in the way. His indecision cost him as he watched the elevator shut with him still inside. The last thing he heard was Rebecca's voice.

"Just stay in there, we'll—"

"Well, that was unhelpful." Digby tapped his foot as the box traveled back down. The elevator dinged again, and the doors opened to a wall of zombies.

"Oh no…"

The horde surged into the tiny space. Digby tried to Compel them to get out, but he couldn't reach the zombies further back that continued to push. The result shoved him into the back wall of the lift, unable to reach the buttons. It didn't matter, one of the zombies had apparently pressed most of them anyway. The doors began to close, bumping into the walking corpses that blocked the entryway before opening back up.

Digby cursed himself for not reaching out to stop the elevator from closing when it had been upstairs. He had not been aware they would simply open back up in the case of an obstruction. He checked his mana.

MP: 26/148

He'd only gained a few points. It was going to have to be enough. He cast Control on the zombies blocking the doors, gaining three new minions as well as a new message.

SPELL RANK INCREASED
Control Undead has advanced to rank A. Number of
zombies capable of being controlled has increased to 20.
Duration of spell has increased to 40 minutes, plus 50%
due to mana purity. Total duration 60 minutes. Mana cost
is reduced to 4. Target's Intelligence bonus is increased
to 8.

"Get clear!" He shouted at his new minions, sending out a
Compel at the same time to imply the lift was dangerous. Eventually, with some pushing, the doors slid shut, free of obstruc-
tions. The elevator rose up a moment later, leaving Digby's new
minions behind in the lobby. The lift came to a stop, one floor
up, before opening its doors again. An empty hallway greeted
him and the eight zombies that had fit inside the elevator
with him.

"Get out!" Digby shouted, adding a Compel to get them
moving. He didn't want the lift's passengers chasing after his
apprentice when they reached the fourth floor.

The zombies obliged, still under the impression that the
elevator was dangerous. The doors closed and the lift continued
on its journey. Unfortunately, Digby noticed too late that the
fourth floor was the one of the few buttons that hadn't been
pressed by whichever zombie had mashed their rear into the
elevator's control panel. This left him riding the irritating device
to half the floors in the building before it returned back to
where he wanted to go. A group of four zombies moaned at
him when he reached the twelfth level.

Digby glanced at the buttons, finding one that bore the
word 'close.' He tapped it and waved to the group before they
got any ideas about getting in with him.

"Sorry, no room."

A couple minutes later, he let out a breathless sigh as the lift
slowed to a stop at the fourth floor.

"Lord Graves, duck!" Alex appeared as soon as the doors
parted. He held a bottle of what looked like water above his

head, ready to fling its contents all over anyone still in the elevator. His arm jerked back, realizing that it was only Digby inside.
Fumbling the bottle back and forth, he spilled half its contents
down his front. "Shit, damn, sorry."

"What the hell are you doing?" Digby stepped out of the lift
before the horde below had a chance to call it back down to the
first floor again.

"I thought the elevator might have picked up more zombies
down below, so I was going to throw purified water at them.
Thought it might help."

"I did pick up a few passengers down in the main hall, but I
left them on another floor before returning, to avoid putting you
in any danger." Digby tried his best to sound like he'd behaved
responsibly before changing the subject. "What's this about
purified water?"

"Oh, it's a spell I have." Alex held up what was left in the
bottle. "Purify Water. It cleans liquids and gives it the ability to
cleanse status ailments from a person when they drink it. I
found a water bottle in a vending machine up here and I
thought I could use it to hurt zombies like holy water does in
video games." He flicked his eyes to Digby. "Or, you know, I
thought I could hurt other zombies. Not you…"

"Give it here." Digby snatched the half empty bottle and
poured a few drops on his claws to test the theory. A sudden
surge of real pain answered the question. "Gah!" He threw the
bottle across the hall, spattering the wall. A quiet sizzle came
from his claws.

"Okay then, that answers that." Rebecca drifted back down
the hall, shining a light in the direction they needed to go. "We
should keep moving. Skyline is still in the area."

Digby squinted at his apprentice before following her.

"Sorry." Alex fell in line, sheepishly. "I have magic, I had to
use it."

"That's understandable. And the more you use it, the
stronger your spells will get." Digby gave him a playful elbow.

"Thanks, Lord Graves." The boy seemed to appreciate the

gift he'd been given more than Digby had anticipated.

"What's with this Lord Graves stuff?" Rebecca's drone spun around as it drifted into the footbridge that connected the building to the one across the street.

"That's my title." Digby held his head high.

"Yeah, I'm not calling you that." She switched off her lights as they traversed the bridge to avoid giving away their position from the windows. "I'm going to stick with Dig."

"Why does she call you Dig?" Alex asked.

"His first name is Digby." Rebecca snorted through her speaker.

"Wait." Alex stopped short. "You're a zombie necromancer named Dig Graves?"

"Yes, the irony has already been pointed out, thank you." Digby crossed his arms and snarled at the drone for bringing it up. Their conversation was interrupted when a familiar high-pitched sound came from further down the footbridge. "Everyone get back."

The glass of one of the windows shattered just like back in the building he'd been captured in.

"They found us." Rebecca ducked back, letting Digby take the lead as another drone floated into the footbridge.

Digby hit it with a Decay, hoping it wasn't one of the ones that could resist the spell. It sparked and veered back out the window.

1 combat drone defeated, 30 experience awarded.

He spun back to Rebecca. "One of Skyline's men said they could track their people earlier; can they track you?"

"No." The drone shook its camera. "I took my drones off network earlier when they first attacked you in the park. I thought they might disconnect me if I questioned Manning, so I took precautions."

"Just bad luck then." Alex looked down on the street outside. "Maybe they saw us through the windows when we entered the footbridge?"

"Whatever the reason, they know where we are now." Digby let out an annoyed growl. "Let's move."

From there they sprinted the rest of the way across the bridge. There was another bay of elevator doors, but Digby opted to take the stairs. He'd had enough of lifts and didn't want to get stuck riding up and down again. Alex held the door for Rebecca, and they made a break for the ground floor.

"We have to get clear of the area before the ground troops reach our location." The drone darted out into the building's entrance hall. Fortunately, there were no zombies in this one. Unfortunately, there was something else waiting.

A metal shape glinted in the dim glow of the room's after-hours lighting. It shot across the space, hitting Rebecca's drone with a hard crack. Her mechanical puppet clattered to the floor and slid into a reception desk.

"I've lost a propeller." The drone struggled to get off the ground, only succeeding in spinning around in circles.

"What hit you?" Digby rushed across the room, hefting her up and tucking the drone under his arm.

"I don't know. I didn't get a good look."

"There!" Alex pointed to a metallic object. The shape slipped into the light, revealing a ring of silver hovering in the air. It was the same as the one that had floated over the strange drone that had resisted Digby's Decay spell.

The object floated just as the outline of a person flickered into existence below it. The figure solidified into a man bearing Skyline's insignia. Unlike the others, he wore no armor.

Digby readied his claws, knowing he was nearly out of mana. Without warning, the man called forth a Fireball and lobbed it in his direction. He dove out of the way just before the spell crashed into the reception desk behind him. The orb burst on impact, engulfing the area in flames. Digby rolled to the side before he realized something odd. There was no heat coming from the flames.

"What the?" He locked eyes with the mage blocking their path and willed the Heretic Seed to find out what it could.

Guardian: immaterial projection, Illusionist, level unknown, hostile.

"He's not real." Digby sprang back up.

"Then what is he?" Alex ran to the other side of the room.

"Some kind of illusion. He's just trying to slow us down."

The projection held out a hand again. The metal ring floated over its head like a halo as a white glow began to form in his palm. Motes of light swirled toward him, so bright that Digby had to shield his eyes. Real or not, the illusionist was a problem.

The light winked out a second later, revealing Alex slamming his fist into the projection's face. An undignified cry erupted from the illusions' confused mouth for a moment before it vanished. Without its master, the silver ring dropped to the floor with a metallic clang.

"What did you do?" Digby stood wide-eyed.

"Yeah! Eat enchanted fist." Alex punched at the air in victory before turning to his lord. "Oh, I infused my glove with mana. It's my other spell. Enchant Weapon. It lets me transfer some of my mana to an object to make it deal more damage. The description said that it can disrupt the mana flow of a target. Figured that might mess up whatever that guy was."

"Looks like you were right." Digby glanced back at the desk that had been on fire a moment before, finding it back to normal. Apparently, disrupting the projection's mana flow wiped out its illusions as well. He turned back to Alex, realizing that recruiting the boy was turning out to be the best decision he'd made all night. He certainly had a knack for understanding his capabilities.

"We have to keep moving," Rebecca reminded him from her place tucked beneath Digby's arm.

"Agreed." He walked forward and placed his hand on the door before turning back to the others. "Right now, we just need to get somewhere safe."

CHAPTER THIRTY-FOUR

"This will have to do." Digby stood over a round metal plate embedded in the street a few blocks away from where they encountered Skyline's illusionist. Rebecca called the plate a manhole cover. It reminded Digby of a giant coin.

"We just have to get that open." Rebecca gave directions the best she could, no longer able to fly after having one of her propellers damaged.

Digby set the drone down and helped Alex pry the manhole cover open. It took some time, but they made it work. He might have tried to use Decay to break through it, but that could just as easily get it stuck and he didn't have enough mana anyway. He really needed to rest and replenish his MP. It seemed like hours since he'd been at full. He might even try meditating again if he could just get five minutes where he wasn't running from enemies.

Once the opening was clear, and they were inside, they moved the manhole cover back into place. With a little luck, Skyline's troops would walk right by it. From there, they took to the sewers for refuge, finding the tunnels accommodating. Though, Alex had a few complaints about the smell. Digby didn't really notice. His undead senses were more tolerant to strong odors.

Rats scurried this way and that as they traversed the underground walkway. A stream of murky water ran to the side of the raised path where they stood, and several pipes lined the ceiling. After thinking about the functionality of the tunnels, Digby assumed the pipes carried human waste and the stream was mostly storm water.

The tunnel was a fascinating solution to a basic problem. It was also something that he would never have noticed before his intelligence had increased. When he'd been human, he didn't care to think about how things worked or why they were needed. Now though, he was noticing interactions and picking up on context to a point where he didn't need to ask so many questions.

Maybe adjusting to the future won't be as difficult as I assumed. He smiled at the thought, though he was still glad he'd gained companions to help him understand the things he couldn't figure out on his own. Alex had proved useful already. Digby focused on his apprentice's name as he walked. The circle at the edge of his vision snapped out and expanded to show the boy's attributes and spells.

Name: Alex Sanders
Race: Human
Heretic Class: Enchanter
Mana: 114 / 114
Mana Composition: Balanced
Current Level: 1 (200 Experience to next level.)

ATTRIBUTES
Constitution: 17
Defense: 14
Strength: 12
Dexterity: 14
Agility: 16

Intelligence: 17
Perception: 14
Will: 18

SPELLS
ENCHANT WEAPON
Description: Infuse a weapon or projectile with mana. An infused weapon will deal increased damage as well as disrupt the mana flow of another caster. Potential damage will increase with rank. Enchanting a single projectile will have a greater effect.
Rank: D
Cost: 15
Duration: 1 minute or until infused mana is consumed
Range: Touch

PURIFY WATER
Description: Imbue any liquid with cleansing power. Purified liquids will become safe for human consumption and will remove most ailments. At higher ranks, purified liquids may also gain a mild regenerative effect.
Rank: D
Cost: 10
Duration: 1 minute
Range: Touch

Not much to work with there.

Digby couldn't argue with the Heretic Seed's comment.

Alex had the same spells that were available to be extracted from the ring he'd lifted from the enchanter he'd killed earlier. The only difference was that his spells had a slightly lower casting cost. It must have been because they matched his starting class closer than Digby's.

He could only hope that, in time, Alex might unlock something more useful. Though, thinking back to the enchanter he'd fought earlier, the class clearly had its uses. The arrows that the man had fired were destructive, and the flask he carried was able to heal the wounds of others. From the description of Alex's spells, Digby assumed they would gain more functionality as they increased in rank, just as his own did.

Digby shooed away Alex's information as he reached a storm drain. It was as good a place as any to call Asher back to his side. Concentrating on his avian friend, he felt a presence in the distance. For a moment, the sensation of wind flowing across his face and arms washed over him. It felt like he was flying. An affectionate warmth came with it.

With Asher finally on her way back, Digby relaxed a little. The recently animated raven had been on her own for too long.

"So what do we do now?" Alex placed Rebecca's drone down to wait.

"I can guide you to a sewage treatment facility that dumps into the ocean," she responded. "You'll have to follow the coast-line and find somewhere to break through the military quarantine. It won't be easy, but with the power you both have, you should be able to."

"I'm not keen on attacking your military's quarantine line." Digby considered the option before another idea hit him. "We already have Skyline after us, I'd rather not go picking fights I can't win. If we're on the coast, couldn't we just steal a boat and escape to the sea?"

"Probably not. By now other survivors have probably taken every boat available. Not to mention the Coast Guard is watching the harbor."

"What's the Coast Guard?" Digby arched an eyebrow.

"It's a branch of this country's military that guards the coasts," Rebecca stated the obvious. "You might be able to get past, Dig, since you don't need to breathe and don't get tired. You could potentially swim your way to freedom. You would have to leave Alex behind, though."

Alex flicked his eyes to Digby as if worried he might be abandoned.

"Nay." Digby pretended that he didn't notice his apprentice's unease. "He's proved himself too useful."

Alex let out a sigh of relief.

"Not to mention I'd be forgetting something else," Digby added.

"What?" Rebecca asked through the speaker of her broken drone.

"You're still trapped here in Seattle."

"You're here in the city?" Alex stared down at the drone.

"Yes, she's back near Skyline's base." Digby locked eyes with her camera. "Didn't you want me to help you escape?"

"Ah, that…" Rebecca trailed off. "I do, but that might not be possible now."

"Why not?"

"Because, one, a horde has moved into the area surrounding my building. It's been growing for the last hour and it's around a thousand zombies deep. And two, Skyline is too close, and bound to be watching me. I'm sure they're hoping you'll come for me after seeing us together. Especially considering you just attacked a full convoy to rescue Alex. With me trapped in a location that they control, I am already the perfect hostage to draw you out."

"So, maybe I can use the horde to hold them off while we get you out."

"You can't control that many zombies. And as Manning already demonstrated, a horde is nothing compared to whatever power he has."

"I can't just leave—"

He was interrupted by the happy cawing of a raven landing at the mouth of the storm drain.

"Asher!" Digby reached up as his pet fluttered in to land on one of his claws. The bird flapped her white wings and hopped to his shoulder. "Who's a good girl?" He nuzzled the bird's head and removed both rings from her legs. Scratching the raven's chin for a job well done, Digby turned back to the drone laying on the stone.

"As I was saying, Becky. I can't leave you here." He held up the obsidian band he'd retrieved from his pet. "Not when I promised you immortality."

"You still have a ring?" She sounded surprised. "I thought you gave it to Alex."

Digby tried to act casual. "I had a second one."

"You said you only had one." Her tone went flat.

"I lied." He pumped his eyebrows. "I do that. Much like you neglected to inform me of your drone's capabilities."

Her speaker emitted a sigh. "That's fair."

"So let me ask you, are you going to just sit in your tower and wait to die? Or will you fight those who imprisoned you, and earn the power that you're owed?" He dangled the ring on the tip of one claw.

The drone remained quiet, sitting there on the stone.

"Your lord is waiting for an answer," Digby prodded.

"Shut up, I'm thinking!" she snapped. "And I'm not calling you Lord Graves, so you can stop trying to make that happen."

"That sounds like a yes." Digby let a crooked smile slide onto his face.

"Sure, why not. If you can get past the horde, break through a six-inch steel door, and defeat a group of mercenaries armed with magic, then be my guest. I'll be right here waiting. But keep in mind that doing that is exactly what Manning expects."

"What if we create a diversion?" Alex chimed in.

"Yes, that could work." Digby paced back and forth as he thought. "I could gather a horde and send it after those sell-swords while I sneak in. If I go alone, the thousand zombies out there won't stop me." He turned to Alex. "Sorry, you would have to stay out of this one and meet us later."

He lowered his head for a second before raising it back up. "Okay, I'll hold down the fort here and practice my magic."

"Sure, let's say you make it into my building and distract Skyline's people, that still leaves the fact that there is a blast door locking me into my apartment," Rebecca argued.

"Lord Graves can try his Decay spell?" Alex offered.

"Six inches of steel?" She scoffed. "I don't think so."

"What if I just Decay the lock?" Digby held out a hand. "That sometimes works."

She groaned. "It's an electric lock. If you try that, you'll just kill it and trap me in here forever."

"Fine then." Digby dropped his hand to his side before raising it back up with one claw pointed in the drone's direction. "What if we don't use the door?"

"Well I'm not jumping out the window," she answered in a flippant tone.

"Obviously, that would be stupid." Digby folded his arms as he continued. "What I mean is, if we can't get through the door, we can just go around it. Back in the building I attacked that last squad in, I had no trouble decaying a hole in the floors, so why can't I head for the floor below yours and go up from there?"

"That's..." She went silent for a moment. "That's actually not terrible."

"But how would you both get past the horde outside on the way out?" Alex poked a final hole in the plan.

"We shouldn't have to." Digby tilted his head from side to side. "If I use my smaller horde to draw the larger one into a fight with Skyline's men, then we should be able to slip out the other side of the building without too much of a problem. Once your former masters kill off my zombies, I can just control a bunch more and use them to secure our escape."

"That sounds a little risky." She still seemed to be on the fence.

"Well, it's a jailbreak, not a bloody walk in the park." Digby locked his gaze on the drone's camera. "It's supposed to be risky. And besides, if you don't survive the escape, then you're no more dead than you will be when you starve in a week or so."

"Oh, well if you put it that way, sure, let's go." Her tone dripped with sarcasm.

"I'm serious." Digby knelt down. "There's no hope if you give up."

She let out a long sigh. "Fine."

"Excellent." Digby clapped his hands together and stood back up.

"But if we're doing this, we're doing it right." Rebeca grew serious. "I want you to gather the strongest horde you can."

"I wouldn't try this any other way. I shall do everything in my power to make sure we come out of this victorious." Digby turned back in the direction they had run from and marched forward, only to immediately step on the tail of a rat. "Gah!" Both he and the rodent stumbled to the side.

"Yeah, this is going to go great." Rebecca let out a defeated sigh through her speaker.

"Don't quit on me now, Becky. You'll become my apprentice yet." He shoved the ring he'd promised her back into his pocket.

"Yay." She feigned excitement.

Digby ignored her sarcasm and continued his march, nudging rats out of the way with his foot as he went. Spinning back to give her a manic grin.

"Just imagine the look on Manning's face when we all slip out of the city, right under his nose."

"Yeah…" She paused. "I'm going to go pack a few things. I'll give you a couple hours before connecting to my last drone. We can meet up then."

"Where?"

"How about the alley behind the building I found you on, back when you ran from the science institute? That's close enough to my place."

"That'll do." Digby steepled his fingers just as her speaker clicked off.

Alex stood next to the now inactive, broken drone, looking like he wasn't sure what to say or do. Digby immediately marched off down the tunnel with Asher perched on his shoulder, only to stop and beckon to his apprentice with a claw.

"Come along, we have preparations to make."

CHAPTER THIRTY-FIVE

"What are we doing?" Alex jogged behind Digby as he turned down a branching tunnel in the sewers beneath the streets of Seattle.

"I'm looking for minions." He skidded to a stop near a storm drain and pulled Asher from his shoulder. The bird had been jostled enough already. He dropped her into Alex's arms for safe keeping while he climbed a few of the pipes that lined the wall of the tunnel to peek out onto the street above. "Hmm, empty. I was hoping for a few stray wanderers."

"You mean zombies, to join your horde?" Alex struggled to keep Asher steady as she flapped her wings in his arms.

"Yes. If I can recruit a few and find some corpses for them to eat, we might be able to get a couple to mutate into something stronger." Digby dropped back down, disappointed with the lack of potential minions out and about.

It seemed like the longer the night went on, the more the dead converged into larger hordes, leaving less stragglers for him to take under his wing. He considered trying to steal a few away from one of the larger hordes, but was a little afraid that he might make the entire group hostile if he tried to steal too many away.

"Is there anything I can do to help?" Alex stepped forward as Asher finally settled down in his arms. "I could maybe lead a handful away or something."

"It's probably safer for you to stay hidden." Digby surmised without looking at the boy.

"Oh." Alex's voice sounded defeated, catching Digby off guard.

"I thought you were afraid of being eaten." He gave his apprentice a sideways glance.

"I am, but…" Alex's mouth dropped open for a second. "I can't just stand around doing nothing. Not now. I mean, you've already rescued me twice tonight."

"Once." Digby held up a claw as he corrected the enchanter.

"No, you saved me twice."

"I did?" Digby furrowed his brow, having trouble thinking of a second rescue effort besides the caravan he'd freed the boy from less than an hour ago.

"The first was when we met. When you gave me this." Alex raised his hand to display the line of dark runes that encircled his finger.

"Well, sure." Digby let out a self-satisfied laugh. "But you're lucky I didn't decide to eat you. I wasn't too keen on you humans at the time."

"True, but I would be dead if I hadn't walked in on you in that construction site." The boy lowered his head. "I, kinda, didn't go there to hide like I said. I went there because it was a tall enough structure that I could get into easily."

"What does that have to do with—"

Alex's next sentence practically fell out of his mouth all at once. "I was planning on jumping."

Digby flinched as the obvious truth came out. Of course, Alex had to have known he wouldn't survive the night. If Digby had been human, he wouldn't have made it either. No, he would have been devoured by the first group of teeth that wandered by. He reached out for the enchanter in an attempt to comfort him, but stopped just short, realizing that a clawed hand was not the tool right for the job.

Alex shrugged. "The crazy thing is, I was actually excited when this all started. When the first few people got attacked and it was looking like the city wasn't going to recover, I was thrilled. It felt like a weight had been lifted. People were dying around me and all I could think of was that it didn't matter that I had been fired. I was free. It was like a game. It wasn't until later, when I witnessed a group of a dozen people get torn apart screaming, that everything started to feel real."

"That makes sense." Digby tilted his head from side to side. "All of this is so absurd that it's near impossible to accept it's really happening. And that's coming from a man that spent the last eight hundred years frozen with a shard of the Heretic Seed nailed through his heart."

"What?" Alex snapped his eyes to Digby's chest.

"What do you think killed me?" He pulled down his collar to show some of the dark veins that marred his gray skin. "Honestly, sometimes there are times where none of this seems real, even now."

"That's for sure." Alex stroked the zombified raven in his arms. "I think that made it worse when I finally figured things out. I couldn't believe how stupid I'd been. It was like I thought I was special, like I was the protagonist of a survival story. Once I saw the agony those people died in, I knew it was only a matter of time until the same happened to me. A few close calls later, and it just didn't make sense to push my luck. I saw that construction site, and figured jumping off something high was my bet to end things as quick as possible." Alex looked up for a second before dropping his eyes back down to the deceased bird he held. "Sorry, you probably think I'm an idiot."

"A bit." Digby let out a laugh. "But you were alone then. That's something I understand well enough. Being trapped with your own thoughts and hopelessness can sometimes be what does us in."

"That's why I want to help." The enchanter cracked a smile.

"Bah, you just want to use your magic." Digby brushed the uncomfortable conversation aside. "I've seen the look in your eyes. You're like a child with a new toy."

"Okay, that too." Alex held up his hand, staring at the Heretic Seed's mark. "But it's more than that. I feel like my life has meaning now. I wasn't just doomed before I stumbled into you, I was nobody."

"Ah, yes, but notoriety also comes with unwanted attention." Digby skulked further down the tunnel, looking for another storm drain.

"I think I'm okay with that." Alex followed behind. "I don't know what's going to happen after tonight. Maybe the world will somehow pull through this, and the curse will stop spreading. Or maybe it won't, and everything will fall apart. All I know is that I haven't done anything with my life so far, but now, I have a chance to change that. I realize my spells aren't the most powerful, but I want to do what I can, even if all I can do is support others. And hiding here in the sewer isn't the best way to start. Not when there's a group like Skyline screwing around out there. I mean, if this isn't a call to adventure, I don't know what is."

"I'm glad this has turned out to be a positive experience for you." Digby rubbed at the side of his head.

"Yeah, I know, it's weird. But honestly, screw it. I'm a goddamn enchanter, and I aim to make the most of it." Alex ran a hand down the back of Asher's neck to stroke her feathers. "So if there is anything you need, I'm game."

"Good, because I do actually have a task for you." Digby fished the gold ring he'd taken off one of Skyline's enchanters earlier out of his pocket and offered it to the boy. "Hold this trinket in your hand and tell me if the Seed tells you anything."

"Ah, okay." He awkwardly placed Asher on Digby's shoulder

and took the guardian ring, closing his fingers around it. "You mean like…" He trailed off as his eyes widened.

Digby watched the enchanter's pupils move from side to side as if reading. "Well, what's it say?"

"It says I'm unable to extract spells because I have either already discovered them or I have not met the level requirement."

"What?" Digby stepped closer. "I never ran into a level requirement before."

"So does that mean I can learn a new spell from this ring if I level up?" Alex opened his hand again.

"That's what it sounds like. I must not have hit the restrictions because I was frozen for my first ten levels. I have been behind on everything since then." He flicked his eyes back to Alex. "I'm glad I saved that for you. When I tried extracting a spell from it, the only options it gave me were the two spells you already have. It seems that being the same class as a guardian ring's previous owner is giving you access to more."

"So all you can extract from one of these guardian rings without a matching class, is basic level one stuff." Alex offered the gold band back to Digby. "Here, you can learn one of my spells from it."

He waved the enchanter's hand away. "Keep it. We're better off getting something new rather than doubling up on spells we already have access to."

"Thank you." Alex slipped the band onto his finger for safe keeping.

"Now all we need to do is get you a few levels to find out what you can get." Digby continued down the tunnel trying his best not to step on a rat as it scampered by.

"That and we need to gather a horde to help your friend." Alex hesitated for a second. "I think her name was Becky, right?"

"What? No. Her name is Rebecca." Digby stopped short realizing he hadn't actually introduced them. The boy must have picked up her name from their interaction. "I just call her

Becky to annoy her. And I wouldn't call her a friend. More of an accomplice really. She still has a betrayal to make up for before I let her cozy up to me again."

"Oh, from the way you both talked earlier, I thought you were more friendly." Alex leaned his head to one side. "You did seem to want to rescue her."

Digby let out a sigh. "She's just in a tight spot and I don't think she deserves to be locked in her home while she starves to death. Also, I suppose I do enjoy having her around. She's fun to argue with."

"That's... good." Alex started off in the other direction. "So should we head back up to the street to try to gather some zombies?"

Digby stopped walking, having accidentally kicked a mass of wet fur that had been in his path. He dropped his eyes down to find the corpse of a large rat laying against the wall, only to furrow his brow at the deceased creature.

"Maybe we don't have to leave these tunnels to gather zombies." Digby focused on the lifeless body.

Corpse: Rodent, minimum cost to animate: 2 MP.
Animate corpse? Yes/No

"What does it mean by minimum cost?" Digby ran the back of a claw along his chin, realizing the Seed hadn't worded a message like that before. Looking back at the description of his Animate Corpse spell, he recalled that the cost to use it was associated with the experience he would have gained if he had defeated the target while it had lived.

Considering that he lost two points of experience from what he was awarded for every level he gained, he had hoped that would mean that he would eventually bring the cost to animate a corpse down to zero. Apparently that wasn't the case. It was likely that a lone rat wouldn't award any experience, but there must have been a limit to how low the animation cost could go.

The Heretic Seed cleared things up as he considered the question.

A transfer of mana is required to animate any and all corpses. Your cost will decrease with each level gained but it cannot fall below 10% of a target's full experience value.

Sorry, no free handouts.

"That's fair, I guess." Digby accepted the cost of two points of mana. The rodent was economical enough to experiment with. There was always the chance that it might have a trait or something that could help.

"What are you doing?" Alex crept closer.

"Raising the dead, what does it look like?" Digby beckoned for his apprentice to take a closer look as the rat began to twitch. Speckles of gray ran through its matted fur.

"Oh, that is awesome." Alex crouched down beside him.

Digby read over the traits that the rat came with, finding call of the dead and bond of the dead, the same as Asher, but considering the rodent didn't have wings, it lacked the flight of the dead trait that his feathered friend had. Instead, a different one sat in its place.

SPEED OF THE DEAD
As a rodent zombie, the attributes required to maintain the ability to move quickly have been retained. +3 agility, + 2 strength.

Digby watched as the new zombie scurried over to his feet. Asher cawed and flapped her wings at the creature.

"Easy, girl." He patted her head. "I'm not going to replace you. You're special, alright?"

The albino raven settled down a few seconds later. Technically she wasn't really special when compared to other animated zombies, but Digby meant what he said. Sacrificing her was never going to be an option. He hadn't fed her and healed her just to throw her away when it suited him. Asher huddled closer to his neck as he stared down at his new minion. As far as what to do with it, he had no idea.

Looking over the creature's attributes, he found that its speed trait had given it three agility and two strength. Digby dropped four of his bond points into intelligence, and split the rest to further increase the rat's strength and agility to give it an edge. Four intelligence wasn't much, but it was good enough to hold the vermin to a simple command. With that, Digby pointed to the nearest living rat and spoke one word. "Kill."

The deceased rodent darted across the stone of the tunnel and plowed into its prey.

"Oh god." Alex recoiled as the pair let out a series of horrible squeaks.

"Did you think being a necromancer's apprentice was going to be all sunshine and rainbows?" Digby gave a slow but exaggerated shrug like the horrible display had been unavoidable. A moment later, the squeaking stopped.

Corpse: Rodent, minimum cost to animate: 2 MP.
Animate corpse? Yes/No

Digby raised his hand as he willed a second undead rat into existence. Once it was up and about, he simply set the pair onto another two rodents. The overabundance of vermin made the process quite fast. So much so that, in just a few minutes, he had ten loyal rodents animated and awaiting his next command.

"Are rat zombies going to help us somehow?" Alex looked down at the creatures while keeping his distance.

"Patience." Digby held up a claw to his apprentice before addressing his miniature horde. "Alright, listen up."

The group of ten gray rats all stood facing him, each with their heads raised to meet his gaze. A chorus of attentive squeaks followed.

"I have a new mission for you all. It's a little more complicated, but I believe it is within your skillset." Digby paced as he spoke making sure to keep his orders simple. Each undead rat followed him with their eyes. "First, I want you to attack and eat other rats. As your master, I am ordering you to follow the Path of the Leader. That means you need to eat hearts and minds. Make that your top priority. The first mutation you'll get is Compel Zombie. Once you have that, just do what comes naturally. Bite and kill every rodent you find and add them to your numbers. Keep growing your horde until I call for you." Once he was finished, he clapped his hands and sent the zombified vermin on their way.

"Will they be able to follow all that?" Alex watched the little horde scurry away.

"It sounds complicated, but really, it's only guiding what they would do if given no orders. Feeding and growing their numbers is what zombies do naturally. I just gave them a little more focus. Once they get their first mutation, they'll get a bit more intelligence too."

"And rats will be helpful against Skyline?"

"Think about it." Digby held out his claws in the direction his miniature horde had gone. "These tunnels are full of rats and by the time we have to make our move, I bet they can gather quite a few to back us up." He gave the enchanter a villainous grin. "Just imagine being attacked by a few hundred zombified rats all at once. I'd say that would make for quite the distraction, if you ask me."

Alex paused as if picturing it in his mind. "Okay, yeah, that's kinda disturbing."

"Indeed." Digby continued walking down the tunnel only to stop short again at the sound of splashing coming from the passage that branched to the right behind them. He immediately thrust out a hand to halt his apprentice.

Silence filled the tunnel as they both stood stock-still. The sound had been innocuous enough but something about it screamed for him to pay closer attention. Perhaps it was due to his heightened perception, as if the sensory information had connected to something in his mind. That was when voices followed.

"The necro has probably moved on by now, but he could still be down here," a masculine tone echoed down the tunnel.

"Is there any way to see where they entered the sewer from?" a second voice chimed in.

"Negative. The necro was carrying the unit under their arm as they escaped, giving us a view of his armpit the whole time. We didn't get a shot of the tunnels until he set the drone down. Even then, the operator was standing in the way of the monitor for most of the footage."

Digby's chest tightened. Only one organization used words like necro. Skyline knew he was underground. Worse, they were nearly on top of him. All they had to do was turn down the next passage. For an instant, he debated on holding his ground. At most it was a squad, but even then, he had no way of knowing if they had any guardians among them, or what level they might be. Without being able to prepare a location in advance, he wasn't sure he would be able to win. That only left one option.

They had to run.

CHAPTER THIRTY-SIX

Becca cut the connection to her broken drone, leaving Digby and Alex in the sewer to prepare for their insane plan to rescue her. She hoped whatever they needed to do to get ready would go smoothly and that they could avoid any of Skyline's personnel that might still be looking for them.

A part of her wanted to smile at the fact that a centuries-old dead man cared enough not to abandon her. Another part of her wanted to cry that she couldn't say the same about anyone else in her life.

With no friends and an employer that had written her off as an acceptable loss, she had been forgotten by everyone else. Becca lowered her head to rest on the cool surface of the laminated particle board that made up her control console's desk. It was all too much.

"Stop it." She sat back up and pinched her cheeks to stop her eyes from welling up.

With her feelings shoved back down where they belonged, she ran to the bedroom. Digby wasn't the only one that needed to get prepared. If everything went according to plan, she would be leaving the safety of her comfortable prison soon.

With the undead curse spreading, the world might not be recognizable to the one she'd left behind when she'd signed on with Skyline.

"Fuck." Becca's legs gave way halfway through her bedroom, dropping her to the floor against the side of her bed. The reality of what was happening finally set in. It had been so easy to talk about it all through the lens of a drone, but now, she was going to abandon everything she'd ever known.

"Maybe I can call Easton and beg for Skyline to take me back. Maybe I can—" Becca slapped a hand over her mouth before she threw up. She breathed through her fingers until the nausea passed. Then she shook her head.

"Stop it! You're not this weak."

Becca tightened her hands around the edge of the bed's comforter that hung down, balling the fabric up until her knuckles turned white.

"Now get up."

Her legs trembled but obeyed. After a minute, the shaking stopped and she continued her task. She made sure to run back to her console to tap a key on the keyboard to keep it from locking her out due to inactivity.

The system had been severed from Skyline's network connection the same as her drones, so they couldn't boot her remotely, but she was pretty sure her identification cuff wouldn't unlock the console anymore if it was to sit idle for too long. Setting an alarm to remind herself to keep tapping a key every four minutes, she continued with her preparations.

Becca didn't have a backpack, or anything suited for travel. Why would she? It wasn't like she'd ever gone anywhere before. She wasn't even sure how many of her things she would need to survive.

"First things first."

Becca tore off her sweatpants, changed into a new pair of Skyline issued underwear, and pulled on a pair of jeans. It had been months since she'd worn anything close to real pants, making her glad that they still fit. As it was, they were tighter than she remembered.

Obviously, there hadn't been much opportunity for exercise being cooped up in a high-rise apartment. Beyond a treadmill, hand weights, and some workout videos, she had only done the bare minimum to stay healthy. She stretched her legs, trying to get used to the feeling of denim against her skin again.

Once she was more used to the fit, she fished through the shirt drawer of her dresser for a lightweight Henley and pulled it on over her tank top. For a moment she hesitated before throwing her hoodie back on. The Skyline logo on the back made her want to drop the garment in the trash shoot. Unfortunately, she didn't have any other options. She just didn't own anything else.

"I'll have to loot something new as soon as possible." She nodded to herself before turning to the kitchen and ransacking her pantry.

Gathering the necessities, she could only find enough non-perishable food for a couple days. Skyline hadn't made a habit of delivering much more than that, and most of what they sent her needed to be refrigerated. If she shared with Alex, her supplies wouldn't go far. There would definitely be more looting in her future.

Next, she claimed whatever toiletries she could reasonably use while on the run. A toothbrush and toothpaste, some soap, deodorant, and hand sanitizer. Becca tossed her meager possessions on the bed and added a change of clothes. Once she had enough, she grabbed a trash bag from under the sink and dumped everything inside. It wasn't at all appropriate for travel through the airport let alone a trek through the zombie apocalypse, but it was the best she had.

"That's going to have to do." Becca cringed at her luggage, then turned back to her drone console.

Unlike her clothing and supplies, her work equipment was easy to deal with. A case beneath her desk already held everything she needed. Skyline had seen to it that she would be able to perform her job in any condition. A high-end laptop and a modified game system controller were all she required to stay operational in the event of a power outage.

Becca checked the contents of the emergency case and booted everything up to make sure she could connect. After being locked out of the drone pod earlier, connecting to her drones took some time to get her software figured out and the laptop set up for what she needed it to do.

After twenty minutes, she had her last remaining drone connected and her comms ready. It was doubtful that anyone would want to talk to her, but she wanted her communications system up just in case.

She closed the laptop and let out a sigh just as her main console's comm-line clicked on. Becca scrambled to place a post-it note over her web camera just as the light beside it lit up. She should have done it earlier. It was only for a second but the camera had definitely caught a glimpse of her emergency laptop on the desk.

"Going somewhere?" A video chat window opened on her monitor with a man she didn't recognize sitting in the frame. "You might want to pack more than a trash bag."

Becca froze, realizing that she'd left the bundle of clothes and supplies in her bedroom where the webcam couldn't see it. A sudden chill crept down her back. There must have been more cameras in her apartment, even in the bedroom. She tried not to think about the private time she'd spent in there that someone could have been watching. Her eyes widened when she realized that it also meant that all of her and Digby's plans had been compromised. Skyline must have seen her monitor over her shoulder.

"Who are you?" Becca pulled off the post-it note she'd stuck on her monitor and leveled her eyes at the camera. She wasn't about to let this asshole see her shaken.

"My name is Henry Rickford." He sat casually at a desk with a wall of opulent wood paneling behind him. A handsome face with a rugged but well-kept beard gave her a charismatic smile. The sleeves of his tailored dress shirt were rolled up in a 'ready to get work done' sort of way. It was as if the man was somehow the complete opposite of Digby.

"Am I supposed to know who you are?" She was done being polite.

"No, actually." He leaned back. "I've gone through quite the trouble to make sure that no one does. But I am, essentially, your boss's boss's boss."

"You run Skyline?"

"In a roundabout way, yes." He placed his hand on his desk. "And I'm contacting you to try to appeal to your humanity."

"How so?"

"You are in a unique position to do a great service to the world. All you would need to do is locate and give me the necromancer's position."

Becca suppressed the urge to raise an eyebrow. If this man was still looking for Digby, then whatever they had seen through her monitor hadn't been enough.

They hadn't found him yet.

There was still a chance.

"You think I'll just give Dig up so you can use him for whatever spell you have planned?" She narrowed her eyes.

"Yes." Rickford didn't even try to lie.

"And what would that spell do?" Becca wasn't going to pass up an opportunity to find out more.

"Save the world." He brought up a screen showing a world map with multiple markings in several countries. "These are new outbreaks of your friend's curse. If nothing is done, it will consume the world. But with his help, we can stop it."

Becca let out a mirthless laugh at his statement. "That's what I was trying to say before your men decided to attack him and abandon me."

"Yes, that was unfortunate. We were lacking in information at the time and didn't realize how much help he could be. I assure you; things have changed. The curse is out of control and we are running out of time to stop—"

"Bullshit." Becca slapped a hand on her console. "You expect me to believe that you're suddenly trying to stop the outbreak? I'm not an idiot. I know you've been transporting zombies from Seattle to the rest of the world. Skyline is the only organization that has had access to the city and there's no way this curse, or virus, or whatever, could have spread so fast without help. So sorry, but no, I don't buy it."

Rickford's charismatic smile fell into a severe frown.

"That's what I thought." Becca gave him a smug grin. "No deal."

"Wait!" The man leaned forward as she reached for the 'end call' button.

Becca stabbed her finger down to sever the connection.

"I'm done being used."

CHAPTER THIRTY-SEVEN

Down in the sewers, Digby raised a claw to his lips, telling Alex to keep quiet as the sound of footsteps came closer down the tunnel. They had to get back above ground as soon as possible. He got moving, trying his hardest to put in some distance while keeping the noise of his footsteps quiet. Alex did the same behind him as they both struggled to avoid the rats that hurried through their path.

Digby's mind ran in circles as he searched for a way out.

Could Rebecca have lied again?

Was she still informing on him, even now?

No, that didn't make any sense. If that were the case, then it meant that everything Manning said about her would have to have been a lie and, frankly, it seemed far-fetched that they would have thought far enough ahead to plan that sort of deception. Not to mention, he didn't want to believe it. Rebecca had certainly told her fair share of lies, but at a certain point, he needed to trust someone. No, he wanted to trust her.

Digby shook off his doubts as they came across a manhole cover with a ladder. Together they climbed up and forced the metal barrier out of the way. From there, they kept off the main streets and regrouped near the park where Digby had been ambushed earlier.

"They must have Rebecca under surveillance," Alex said as they ducked into the apothecary store that Digby had hidden in earlier.

"What?" He shot the boy a confused look.

"They said that someone was blocking a monitor in their footage. That sounds like they're talking about Rebecca. Who else would be standing in front of a monitor with a view of us? That must have been how they found us before, when we were in the footbridge between the hotels. They can see into her apartment somehow."

"And I covered her camera when I tucked her drone under my arm to carry it…" Digby's mouth fell open when he realized how lucky they'd been. "That's why they lost track of us when we entered the sewer."

"It sounded like they were watching the drone's feed over her shoulder or something." Alex leaned against one of the store's shelves.

"That means she isn't aware of it, then." Digby forced out a lungful of musty air, feeling relieved that she hadn't betrayed him again. He wasn't sure if he could take another blow like that. Then he tensed back up. "That also means that they probably heard our entire plan as well."

"Shit, you're right." Alex's eyes snapped back to him. "Which means we can't meet her where we planned."

"Indeed. Skyline is sure to be there waiting for us. We'll have to wait somewhere else for her and hope she figures it out." Digby slapped a few items off a shelf in frustration. "Maybe we can pick a different place that I've met up with her before."

"That's a long shot, but it…" Alex's voice trailed off as his eyes drifted to the side and up to stare past him.

Digby deflated as soon as he noticed. "There's something behind me, isn't there?"

Alex nodded awkwardly.

"Really getting sick of this." That was when a heavy hand dropped onto Digby's shoulder where Asher perched. The raven flapped herself out of the way as the unseen assailant shoved Digby to the side.

"Hey, what the——" He stumbled into one of the apothecary's shelves as a zombie walked past him to approach his apprentice. It must have wandered into the shop after he'd left it open earlier. Probably heard the noise of him knocking things around a moment ago and came to investigate in hope of finding prey.

"Oh crap." Alex stepped away and held up a fist as his gloved hand began to shimmer. Without hesitation, he cracked the zombie in the jaw, just as he had the illusionist after they'd escaped the convoy earlier. This time, however, the attack merely staggered his target. The enchanter leaped back a second later, shaking his hand as if it hurt. "Ow, it's like hitting a rock."

"Keep your distance, boy. I'll take care of this." Digby pushed himself back off the shelf he leaned on and cast Control. "No sense killing a perfectly good minion..." He slapped a hand to his forehead as the spell washed over the walking corpse without taking effect. "I really need to start analyzing things before casting spells."

The zombie stopped as soon as it shrugged off the spell, turning around to reveal its face. A band of what looked like bone wrapped its head, sitting just above its brow like a crown. Two angular horns grew from the formation on the corpse's head.

Zombie Brute: uncommon, hostile.

Digby's mind hit a wall, unsure how the creature could be a brute without being any larger than a normal zombie. That was when he remembered the second mutation within the brute's path. Bone Armor.

"Damn it." Digby rolled his eyes at his own luck as the corpse turned toward him, clearly prioritizing him as the greater threat.

The new brute reached out with a hand covered in plates of interlocking bone.

"Oh no you don't." Digby leaped away and opened his maw on the floor between them. Casting Blood Forge, he sent a black shard up at an angle to pierce the creature's chest. His jaw dropped as the formation shattered on contact, dealing no more damage than tearing the zombie's shirt. The bleached white of solid bone showed through the ripped fabric. "Of course its chest is armored too." Digby slapped his thigh in frustration and glanced at his mana.

MP: 124/148

That was when Alex shouted from behind the brute.

"I got 'im." The enchanter jumped onto the zombie's back, causing the walking corpse to stumble to the side, where it swung its passenger into a rack of medical supplies. The corpse might have been heavily armored, but with nothing but its Bone Armor mutation, it wasn't any stronger or more coordinated than a common zombie. Though, that didn't stop it from trying to bite the poor boy.

Alex moved his hand just in time, wrapping his arm tight around the bone brute's neck right below its chin to hold its jaw closed. He locked his legs around the thing's waist in the same instant, pulling the armored corpse off balance and knocking them both to the floor.

"What are you doing?" Digby shrieked at the chaotic display.

"I don't know. I don't know!" Alex's voice climbed to a panicked wine. "It just happened. What do I do?"

Digby immediately spun on his heel and ran. "I'll be back."

"What?" the enchanter shrieked.

"Trust me," Digby shouted back over his shoulder as he headed for the aisle where he'd shared a meal with his horde earlier. As long as no one had stumbled through since he'd been there last, there should still be an arsenal of firearms just lying there. He didn't like guns, and he was terrible with them—that was why he'd left them behind. His previous horde had no use for the weapons, but his apprentice, well, the boy needed something to defend himself with.

Skidding into the aisle, Digby found the guns right where he'd ditched them. He grabbed a rifle and a pistol and sprinted back to his apprentice, finding him somewhat safe, still wrestling with the bone brute on the floor.

"You look like you could use some help there." Digby held up both of the weapons he carried. "Would you like a pistol or a rifle?"

"What?" Alex stared up at him, looking confused.

"Which do you think you can use to take that thing out easier?"

"Neither, just shoot the thing," Alex shrieked.

Digby glanced back and forth between both firearms he offered. "I'm not exactly proficient in modern weapons and I'm likely to hit someone I don't intend to."

"Shit, fine." Alex repositioned himself to reach one hand out. "Pass me the pistol."

"Good choice." Digby crept toward the boy, being careful not to get too close to the zombie's flailing arms as he handed the weapon over. Taking the gun, the enchanter carefully lined it up with the bone brute's head and pulled the trigger. Digby winced in preparation for a loud bang.

Click.

"What?" they both said in unison as they looked at the gun.

"Crap, the safety was on." Alex dropped his head back.

"What's a safety?" Digby watched as his apprentice searched the weapon for a small lever. Once he flicked it to the side, he took aim at the creature's skull again before pulling the trigger. This time the weapon barked.

"Oh, come on." Alex groaned as smoke wafted from a wound on the bone brute's head, a chipped portion of skull showing beneath the damaged flesh.

"Its bone must be harder than other zombies'," Digby stated the obvious.

"Of course it is." Alex shoved the gun against the brute's head again and cast enchant weapon before pulling the trigger. Again, the weapon barked, but this time the zombie didn't fare so well, covering the aisle—as well as the enchanter laying on the floor—with the contents of its skull.

Digby cringed. "Gross…"

"Oh god." Alex kicked at the now motionless corpse. "It's all over me. Arg. It's in my mouth."

"Indeed. I'd spit that out if I were you," Digby added unhelpfully.

"Blah." The boy gagged a few times.

"Well, you did say you wanted to help." Digby shrugged as he read over a new message from the Heretic Seed.

1 zombie brute defeated, 218 experience awarded.

"Holy shit." Alex suddenly stopped gagging. "I just gained experience."

"How much?" Digby arched an eyebrow.

"Two-eighteen." Alex looked up at him, clearly unsure if the amount was a lot or not. His eyes darted back and forth, reading another line. "And I leveled up."

"Very good." Digby thought about the number of points awarded for a second. "The Seed seems to have given us both the same amount of experience without dividing the points between us." Digby did some quick math in his head. "Though it seems to have applied my level's values to the rewards."

"What?" Alex grabbed a package of disposable towels from a shelf to clean his face with.

"We lose two points of experience for every level we reach. If you gained two-eighteen, then that means the Seed is basing our rewards off my level rather than yours. Otherwise you would have gotten two-fifty, I think."

"Oh, okay." Alex pulled a bottle of water from a cabinet with a glass door and enchanted it before washing out his mouth. He raised the bottle again to take a sip but stopped short, clearly reading something on his HUD. "What should I do with my extra stat point?"

"I suggest you toss it into whichever attribute you find lacking and make the best of things."

"You sure? Maybe I should choose what I'm strongest in to maximize the impact." Alex's eye seemed to sparkle as he weighed his options.

"Not a bad idea, but from what I've figured out, the average of a human's physical attributes is somewhere around twenty." Digby gave him a sympathetic look. "And you're a bit low on some of those."

"Oh…" Alex frowned. "That sucks."

"Indeed." Digby nodded. "Just be glad you haven't died. Had to work my way back up from zero after that."

"I guess I should probably try to even myself out then." Alex dropped his additional point into strength since it was his lowest. Then his eyes lit up again. "Oh yeah." He immediately pulled the gold ring from his finger and closed his hand around it. The enchanter's face fell a second later.

"Still no spells available?" Digby tried to read his expression.

"No, I can get a new one. It's just not anything cool."

"Spill it, boy, what is it?" Digby clawed at the air as if trying to draw out an answer.

"Detect Enemy." Alex read off the description. "Enchant an object with the ability to detect those that mean you harm. An enchanted object will grow cold in the presence of hostile forces. Oh, and the object has to be made of iron." He frowned. "I don't have anything made of iron."

Digby laughed. "Plus, I'm pretty sure this whole city is hostile to you, so—"

"So it would just tell me what I already know." Alex finished his sentence. "Maybe I should wait to see if something else becomes available if I level up some more."

"Or maybe you don't and rank up that spell until it becomes something stronger." Digby held up a claw to make a point. "Sometimes that happens. The Seed does say we grow stronger by using our magic. The same should be true of even the most basic of spells."

"You have a point." Alex closed his eyes for a moment, just before the ring crumbled to dust in his hand. "I just hope it really does lead to something better."

"Fair enough." Digby could tell from the excited look in the boy's eyes that he wanted nothing more than to head out into the city and hunt for more levels. Unfortunately, there was too much risk in wandering around out in the open. Not to mention, firing a gun would draw too much attention. As it was, they would need to get moving soon in case someone heard the two shots Alex had already fired.

"Gather up whatever supplies you can. We need to keep moving." Digby beckoned for him to follow.

"Oh, sure." Alex's tone sounded down.

"Don't worry, we'll try to find something else for us to kill later. You'll be level three in no time." He gave his apprentice a smile.

Alex returned a hopeful nod and quickly gathered up a rifle and a holster for his pistol. Both were spattered with blood from back when Digby had eaten each item's previous owners. He didn't mention that particular detail, but a few pointed glances suggested that the boy had figured it out anyway.

By his own admission, the enchanter didn't know anything about modern weapons either, but he had watched numerous movies, which Digby thought sounded interesting. If the enchanter was to be believed, they were like plays, but projected onto a screen or displayed on a portable device. Apparently they could be watched whenever the viewer wanted. At first Digby balked at the idea, but Alex produced a small glowing rectangle from his pocket to prove it.

Ducking into another small shop a few blocks away, Alex showed him how many things he could do with the tiny machine. It was easily the most impressive thing he'd seen since waking up. If he didn't know better, he would have thought it was magic.

Asher was equally enthralled by the device as she perched on Digby's shoulder.

As much as he wanted to huddle into a corner with the device and explore it for hours, they didn't have that kind of time. Instead they rummaged through the shop for anything they could use. There wasn't much beyond some basic food items that Digby ignored, having no need for such things anymore.

Out front, there were a number of stations with hoses hanging on each. Examining a few pictures hanging on the wall of the shop that bore the image of various vehicles, Digby surmised that the hoses had something to do with the cars that now littered the street. He didn't have enough information to work out the details, though.

He didn't bother asking Alex, considering he was still having trouble comprehending the little glowing rectangle the enchanter had shown him; he didn't want to add more questions into the mix.

Checking behind the shop's counter, Digby found a corpse with a hole in its chest as if it had been shot. The fact that the body was still appetizing told him that the death had been recent. There was no sense wasting a free meal, so he opened his maw and went to work while Alex collected everything he could into a pack that he'd found back in the apothecary. As it seemed, the shop held something for everyone.

After making the best of their shopping trip, they snuck out into the street in search of zombies to add to their attack force. Strangely, there seemed to be few zombies roaming about, causing the process to take longer than expected. With the horde surrounding Rebecca's building growing exponentially, it seemed to be drawing in most of the dead from the area.

In the end, it took nearly an hour to find the twenty common zombies needed to fill Digby's ranks as they searched the side streets of Seattle. Though it was regrettable that there weren't enough edible corpses around to help his horde mutate.

I just hope my rodent minions have been able to gather at least a few hundred friends down in the sewers while we've been hard at work up here. Digby thought to himself just as a seemingly random experience message came in.

1 armored human defeated, 118 experience awarded.
-75% due to distance. Total experience gained 29.

Alex leaned on the side of a building and blinked his eyes. "What did we do?"

"I'm not sure." Digby read over the line again, understanding that whatever it was had happened far enough away to cause the Seed to subtract points. "Maybe my rats stumbled upon one of the men looking for us in the sewers and managed to take him down?"

Digby focused on his bond with the ten reanimated rodents to be sure. The taste of blood flooded his mouth as his mind lit up with a flurry of squeaks. It was as if all ten of his rats were shouting all at once, each repeating the same concept.

Feed.

Digby shut down the connection before their frenzied cries overwhelmed him.

"Are you okay?" Alex stepped closer as Asher hopped off of Digby's shoulder to the ground and cawed.

"Yes, I'm fine." He steadied himself. "The vermin are just louder in my head than I expected. And yes, it seems that they have come out victorious against one of Skyline's sellswords."

"What about the rest of the squad down there? Can rats

handle that many—" The enchanter's words were cut off by another message.

1 armored human defeated, 118 experience awarded.
-75% due to distance. Total experience gained 29.

"It seems so." Digby arched an eyebrow and scooped Asher off the ground.

"And that was a person, that ah… just died." Alex's face fell.

"I will remind you that they intend to execute you?" Digby gave him a pointed look.

"I know. It's just weird, and hard to really take in." The boy fell silent.

"Unfortunately, killing seems to be a requirement in this cursed world we've been handed." Digby held out his empty hands as if there was nothing that could be done about it as another twenty-nine points were awarded to them.

Alex winced a little.

"We should probably check on my vermin." Digby changed the subject and beckoned to his apprentice as he skulked off to find a manhole cover to access the sewers again. Three more experience messages came in before he found what he was looking for. "Help me with this."

Together they pried off the metal plate and stared down into the shadows. Alex pulled a portable light from his pack and shined it down while Digby focused on his bond of the dead just long enough to call the rodent horde back to him. A few minutes of silence passed before one of his animated rats leaders arrived below. Well over a hundred rodents followed behind it.

Then more came.

One after another, his rodent leaders appeared in the space below, each bringing a larger horde of their own. Both Digby and Alex fell silent as the last of his reanimated rats arrived, filling the space below with speckled gray forms writhing in a mass of fur and tails.

"Holy shit." Alex began to tremble.

There was no way to count them all.

Digby raised his head, catching a look of absolute horror in his apprentice's eyes. He gave the boy an awkward shrug. "I may have underestimated the number of vermin dwelling beneath the streets."

CHAPTER THIRTY-EIGHT

Becca's forehead began to sweat as she sat with her finger on the end call button after hanging up on Henry Rickford, a man that claimed to be in charge of Skyline, despite the fact that she'd never heard of him. Even worse, it didn't even matter that she'd hung up on him. He had basically told her that they were watching her even now through hidden cameras in her apartment.

She pulled her hand away from the end call button and looked around as her skin crawled. There was no way to find the cameras. Even if she found some, there was no way to know if she'd got them all. Becca glanced back to her monitor. It wasn't just her being watched. Skyline would be watching everything her drone did over her shoulder.

"That's what you think."

If Skyline wanted to spy on her, then that was fine, but she would use whatever resources she had to get in their way. With that in mind, Becca rushed to the sofa and tore off the cushions before grabbing the comforter from her bed. She couldn't help but laugh as she implemented what was probably the world's first blanket fort in the service of espionage. Propping the sofa cushions on either side of the enormous monitor, she threw the comforter over the top and ducked underneath.

Checking the time, she noted that only a half hour had passed since she'd left Digby and Alex in the sewer. That left another fifty minutes before she was supposed to meet back up, enough time to do some reconnaissance.

Becca shoved her headset back on and connected to her last drone. Once it was in the air, she activated its optical camouflage and made a lap of her building to find close to three thousand zombies surrounding her home. She frowned at the sight. The larger the crowd got, the more zombies seemed to flock toward it. Flying low, she drifted over the sea of corpses writhing beneath her. Out of morbid curiosity, she flicked her microphone on. She flicked it off less than a second later.

"That's enough of that."

It sounded like hell on earth. The souls of the damned, crying out in a discordant chorus of fear and hunger.

"I won't be sleeping anytime soon now, will I?"

She let a full body shudder have its way with her before making a wider search of the area around her building.

"As expected."

She tapped an annoyed finger on her console as she confirmed her suspicion that she was being used as bait. What was left of Skyline's convoy sat a few blocks away. They were out of sight of the horde, but their lead vehicle could still move out and plow its way through the crowd at a moment's notice.

If Digby showed himself, they would simply run him down. His idea of sneaking in to rescue her was looking worse and worse by the second. There wasn't much his meager horde could do against the convoy's lead vehicle. Not to mention Skyline was certain to know they were coming. If they had cameras in her apartment, then they probably had microphones as well.

They had heard everything.

Becca groaned to herself and took off for the location that she had arranged to meet Digby and Alex earlier. To her surprise, It was empty. She didn't expect Digby to be there so early, but she had been sure she'd find some sign of Skyline lying in wait. To be sure, she switched her camera to infrared.

"Shit."

Twenty-five heat sources were distributed throughout the surrounding buildings. Skyline was already in position for another ambush.

"Shit," she repeated.

It had been hard enough to get Digby to trust her again, the last thing she wanted was to unwittingly lead him into another trap. That was when she realized something else. The corner of her mouth tugged upward into a smile.

"If they——" She cupped a hand over her mouth as soon as she started speaking, realizing Skyline was still listening and she was talking out loud. One of the drawbacks of living alone was that it was sometimes hard to keep her inner monologue inside where it belonged. She kept her hand over her mouth as she organized her thoughts.

If they're waiting to ambush Dig and Alex, as well as keeping the convoy on my apartment, then who did they leave back at the field base?

There was no way to know how many men were watching her place, but there had to be at least twenty to man the vehicles and stand guard. Add that to the twenty-five waiting at their rendezvous point, and that only left around twenty or so at the museum of pop-culture. Becca suppressed a Digby-like cackle as a new idea formed in her head.

Pulling away from the compromised meeting place, she headed straight for the museum. Spying on Phoenix Company through the windows from a few hundred feet out, she confirmed her theory by getting a rough count of twenty-five men, including Captain Manning, occupying the field base.

Damn.

It would have been better if the captain hadn't been there, but he must have realized the base was under-guarded and remained behind to pick up the slack. Becca considered her options, eventually panning to the three kestrels parked next to the museum. The drone-like aircrafts were designed to be piloted remotely. Not only that, but they each had an onboard charging pod for a single drone that could serve as an access point.

All she would have to do was switch the unit stored on board with her own and use the connection to hijack the craft. With that, she could go ahead and rescue her damn self. She could fly the craft straight to her building, shoot out the window and hop aboard. It was too perfect not to try.

Well, almost too perfect.

There were a couple snags. Mostly because all of that would depend on if she could get into any of the kestrels to begin with. Zooming in, she found their hatches shut tight. Obviously, Phoenix Company wouldn't leave their aircrafts open in a zombie infested city. That would be asking for trouble. Becca glanced down at the useless bracelet on her wrist that used to unlock her console. The kestrels would require a similar cuff from a member of Phoenix Company to get inside.

She let out a sigh.

There was sure to be a merc inside the museum that had an ID cuff with the proper authorization, but getting it was a problem. They didn't have to kill Manning, but there would almost certainly be a fight. Even if Digby was able to cause some chaos to distract the over-sized captain, she would still need someone to snatch an ID cuff, unlock the kestrels for her, and manually switch out the onboard drone with hers. She wasn't sure Alex was up to that kind of task.

Then again, what choice did they have? Between their options, taking a risk was unavoidable, and stealing a kestrel was probably the best bad decision they could make. She shook her head at the insanity flowing from her mind. It seemed Digby had been rubbing off on her.

"Screw it!"

Becca minimized her drone interface and began looking for an access point for the museum's systems. If they were going to try something that risky, then she was going to do everything she could to level the playing field. If she could get into their security cameras, the intel would be invaluable. Unfortunately, she was not the hacker she thought she was without Skyline's software to lean on. The only thing she could brute force her way into was the museum's sound system.

Good enough. I'll play spooky sounds over the announcement speakers if I have to.

Becca clicked over to a music app in search of something that might cause some chaos. A twisted impulse to cue up *The Monster Mash* flashed through her head for a second, but as she scrolled through her options, she stopped on something that felt more appropriate.

Well, Dig did ask what punk rock was.

She searched for a track, remembering the leather jacket that the ill-mannered zombie had been wearing when she'd met him. Once she was satisfied with her choice, she went back to her drone's interface and pulled away from the museum. She still had to track the necromancer down and warn him that their rendezvous point had been compromised.

Keeping herself camouflaged, Becca staked out their meeting place in hope of cutting Digby off before he was able to reach it. Her forehead began to sweat as the clock ticked closer to the time they had arranged to meet with no sign of the dead man or his hapless apprentice.

Where the hell are they? Becca groaned from within her hastily-built blanket fort and abandoned her stake out. *Maybe Dig caught on to the ambush and moved to someplace else.*

Running through a list of places she knew he'd visited, she cross referenced them with places the zombie knew she had also been to and flew her drone to the closest one. Minutes later, she found the pair in the same alley she had run into Digby earlier. The one that he'd destroyed one of her drones in while having a temper tantrum. To her surprise, they were sitting next to a dumpster, alone.

Digby was feeding what looked like blood pellets to Asher, like a child caring for a guinea pig, and Alex was munching on a protein bar. A rifle leaned against the wall beside the enchanter showing that they had at least found him a weapon. Despite that, her eye twitched at the fact that there wasn't a single undead minion in sight.

What the hell has Dig been up to for the last couple hours? She groaned again as she disengaged her optical camouflage.

The enchanter took a bite of his snack, chewing faster as soon as he saw her drone. He winced and choked down a mouthful before speaking.

"Hey…" He started to wave but froze a second later clearly realizing that there could have been anyone piloting the drone. "You are Rebecca, right? Not one of them?"

"Yes, it's me." She dipped her camera forward to suggest a nod. "And just Becca is fine," she added since Digby had neglected to introduce them earlier.

"I see you figured out that we changed the meeting place." Digby stood up looking proud of himself.

"I did, and I assume that means you figured out that I'm being watched," Becca added, matching his tone hoping he hadn't assumed she'd betrayed him again.

"Indeed." The zombie shrugged as if the situation had been obvious to him. "We ran into a squad of your former comrades down below, and had to deal with them. After that, it wasn't hard to figure out that you had unwittingly spoiled our plans."

"Yeah, unfortunately that's accurate." She humored him. "But I have covered my monitor so no one can't see what we're doing. Also, I'm using a headset, so they shouldn't be able to hear anything either of you say. They can, however, hear what I say."

"That is less than ideal." Digby glowered at her drone.

"If you want to talk about things that are less than ideal, then tell me, what have you been doing this whole time?" She panned back and forth, searching the ally for the horde Digby had promised her.

"We've been up to plenty." He gave her a smug look.

"Yeah, we have," Alex chimed in excitedly, before unzipping

a backpack sitting beside his rifle to show her its contents. "We stopped by a store and picked up some food. I wasn't sure what you'd want so I tried to grab a variety."

"Thank you." Becca let a smile sneak back onto her face, glad that someone was thinking about her. "I packed some supplies at my place too, but Skyline doesn't keep me well stocked, so that will help." She peeked inside the backpack, finding it full of chips, protein bars, and instant noodles. "So when you say you stopped by a store, you meant a gas station?"

"Ah, yeah. It was better than nothing, and we were there anyway." He shrugged. "Lord Graves ate the clerk behind the counter."

"Did he now?" She shifted her camera back to the dead man who had returned to feeding his raven. "Dig, did you do a murder?"

"Nah, the poor bastard was already gone. Had a hole in him, he did. Figured he'd been shot. I think I ate the bullet, actually."

"Is that okay for you to eat?"

"Probably." He shrugged and tossed Asher a pellet.

"And I see you found some pet food while you were at it."

"Of course I did. Asher needs all the food she can get." He nuzzled the bird's beak. "Don't you?" Asher let out a happy caw and flapped her wings.

It would have been a cute scene except for the fact that they were both dead and eating human blood. Becca flicked her mic up, muting herself.

"This is my life now. Isn't it?" She flicked her mic back down and let her voice fall to an annoyed tone. "Well I'm glad you all found some food, but haven't you forgotten something?"

"Like what?" Digby tore his attention away from the raven.

"Like…" She trailed off, not wanting to let whoever was surveilling her hear any more. "Hang on."

Ducking out of her blanket fort, she left her monitor covered and headed to the kitchen with her headset still on. Short of options, she simply opened the fridge and pulled out whatever remained inside, shelves and all. With that, there was just enough room for her. Squeezing herself in, she tucked her legs close and pulled the door closed. "Try listening to me now, asshole."

"What was that, Becky?" Digby sounded indignant.

"I wasn't talking to you." She groaned. "But I just found a way to stop Skyline from hearing me for a few minutes. I can't stay like this but we can talk freely for now."

"Good. Where were we then, before you walked off?" The zombie's tone grew annoyed. "Oh yes, you were about to berate me for something I've supposedly forgotten."

"Oh yeah. What happened to the preparations you were supposed to be doing?" She slapped a hand against the wall of the fridge loud enough for her mic to pick it up. "I thought you were gathering a horde, and here I find you just sitting and having a snack next to a dumpster."

"Oh, pshaw." Digby dismissed her with a wave of his hand. "I have that taken care of. Not to mention I've put together a fun little surprise for Manning while I was at it. It's waiting just down the alley and around a corner."

"Thank god." She let out a breath that fogged in the cold of the refrigerator. "I was starting to think you weren't ready."

"You should know better than to doubt me by now. But more importantly, what are we going to do about the plan? With you being watched, the whole thing is pretty much shot to hell."

"I know, but I think I have a new idea." Becca made sure the door of her refrigerator of solitude was closed tight before explaining everything about hijacking a kestrel. When she was finished, Digby remained quiet for a long pause before breaking the silence.

"It's just as ridiculous as the previous plan. But it's better than no plan." The sound of him clapping his hands together met her ears.

"Good." Becca tried to adjust her leg to a more comfortable

position. "And what was that you said about having a surprise around the corner?"

Digby and Alex went quiet again before the zombie spoke up. "Should I show her?"

Becca assumed he was talking to Alex.

"Show me what?" She pushed her way out of the fridge and slipped back into her blanket just in time to see Alex zip up his backpack and sling it over his shoulder.

"Probably warn her first. I'll wait here," he added, pushing her curiosity to the limit.

"Thank you, boy." Digby placed Asher on his shoulder.

"And please stop calling me boy."

"Quiet, boy." Digby turned to Becca's drone and stood tall. "Despite your accusations, I'll have you know that I've been quite busy. Unfortunately, some of my new minions are a little different this time and my control is slightly limited over some of their numbers. Hence why I have them waiting around the corner. Couldn't let our new friends get too close to this tasty morsel." Digby jabbed Alex in the gut.

"Hey." The enchanter shrieked with a laugh inappropriate for the situation.

"Honestly, it's like trying to keep kittens away from a bucket of milk." Digby spun away and sauntered toward the gap between a pair of buildings further down the alley. "In the end, we opted to wait over here to avoid the hassle."

"Okay." Becca followed him to the mouth of the next alley-way, unsure of what he was getting at.

"Behold, my army." He stopped and gestured to a group of twenty zombies waiting in the darkened space next to a pile of garbage bags. They didn't look like much, all shambling around.

"Couldn't you have fed them or something?" Becca asked, making sure not to give any specifics to whoever was listening now that she was out of the fridge.

The dead man stepped closer to her camera and pointed

past the horde with a talon of hardened blood. "Look behind them."

Becca rolled her eyes before flicking them to the shadows at the back of the alley. "Okay, what am I supposed to be looking —" Her question ended, stuck in her throat like a bite of food that had activated her gag reflex as a countless number of tiny rodent-like eyes stared out at her. "Jesus fuck, Digby."

"I don't know what that means." He twirled around to take a bow, clearly proud of the horrors that he'd created.

"You're a monster," Becca whispered as her bladder threatened to evacuate itself without her consent.

He gave her a villainous grin.

"I know, right?"

CHAPTER THIRTY-NINE

Specialist Francis Easton packed up a few non-essential components of his communications station. Phoenix Company had just received recall orders. They hadn't seen hide nor hair of that necromancer or his apprentice for the last two hours, despite having two ambushes out there waiting for them. Manning seemed genuinely shocked that the necro hadn't at least made an attempt to rescue Rebecca. Now, they were out of time.

Easton fidgeted in his seat, an uncomfortable weight hanging on his shoulders. He'd lost hope that the captain would take the time to pick up Rebecca on their way out. With her helping an enemy, though, she'd signed her own death warrant. As for why she would turn on them, he had no idea. She didn't seem like the traitor to humanity that Manning made her out to be. He ignored a nagging suspicion that she knew something he didn't.

It wasn't the first time he'd turned a blind eye to Skyline's actions. They had raised him since he was thirteen and had trusted him with their secrets, after all. What else could he do? It was the same for half of his company, since most of them had been brought up through the same assistance program.

Still, the situation with Rebecca bothered him. There had to be a reason why she'd decided to bite the hand that fed her. He sighed and slouched in his seat. There wasn't a point in saying anything now. Manning wasn't the type of person to change his mind once it had been set.

The rest of Phoenix Company had started packing up the more important equipment. Anything basic, such as the majority of Easton's communication gear, would remain behind. They had to stay connected, which meant that he would have to stay on the line for as long as possible. Once everything that could be considered proprietary was stowed in the kestrels outside, they would head out and leave Seattle to its own devices.

Easton shuddered at the thought of abandoning the survivors that remained in the city's buildings. There was no way to know how many people were still out there. His thoughts were interrupted when a warning alarm went off at one of the other stations. He sat up straight and peered over his console at the sound.

"What's going on?" Manning stomped out of the Star Trek display that he'd been using as an office.

"We have a sentry turret malfunctioning," someone shouted.

Easton furrowed his brow and glanced out the front door's windows. The auto-turrets had worked well all night, taking down any zombies that got within twenty feet of the entrance.

"A second gun went down. Shit, we lost the third one. Could be a system error."

"Go fix them!" Manning sent out a squad.

Easton watched as they examined the sentry turrets positioned just outside the doors. After a quick once over, one of them poked their head back inside the museum.

"They've all rusted."

"Shit, get ready for a fight." Manning fell back to the center of the museum's entry hall as a low chuckle rumbled through his throat. "That idiot necro is actually going to make a run at us."

"Should I call the squads watching Crow's Nest and their rendezvous point back to base?" Easton stood up straight.

"Yes, there's no sense having them waiting out there if the target is going to throw himself at our feet, like an undead birthday present. I doubt I need the reinforcements to deal with him, but we have to evac anyway. They might as well pack it in and call it a night so we can head out once I kill this dumbass."

Easton followed orders and relayed Manning's instructions to the units in the field, then returned his attention to the doors, wondering what Rebecca's dead friend could do against twenty-five heavily armed men. According to the data that had been collected, his control over other zombies was limited.

His forehead started to sweat the moment his comm line clicked on and Rebecca's voice met his ears.

"Easton?" Her tone sounded serious.

He opened his mouth to respond but she cut him off.

"Don't answer. Just listen."

He froze, realizing that she was watching him. He sat down behind his station to hide.

"You helped me a little earlier, so I'm returning the favor. I know you have no reason to trust or listen to me, but Skyline is not intending on saving anyone in Seattle or the world for that matter. They have something planned. Something bad. They've been spreading zombies through the world as part of it. Now, you can go ahead and warn Manning or even stay and fight us. But with what we're sending your way, I suggest you run. If you make a break for it now, you might have a chance. Either way, the choice is yours."

Her line went dead.

Easton sat for a moment, unsure of what to do. She had to have been mistaken. It was true that Phoenix Company had loaded up a large number of specimens from the outbreak and shipped them back to base, but that was for research purposes.

Wasn't it? Skyline couldn't have had a hand in spreading the curse. His mind stumbled, having trouble thinking of another way the outbreaks could have started so far away without help.

Eventually, he stood and made the only choice he believed available to him.

He tattled.

A few friendly conversations with Rebecca weren't enough to cancel out years of training and obedience. Doubting his employers just wasn't an option, no matter how convincing the opposition was.

"Captain, I was just contacted by Crow's Nest."

"What?" Manning spun around to face him with a perplexed expression. "Why would she call you?"

"It was a warning, sir."

The giant of a man shook his head, letting out a laugh. "And what did her warning say?"

Easton shrugged before answering, "Run."

The moment the word left his mouth, the museum's speaker system clicked on. A quiet static filled the entry hall for a few seconds as the squad working on the auto-turrets suddenly stopped. They seemed to be looking at something beyond the building's stairs.

A dated guitar riff took over the sound system, along with a familiar beat. The volume rose, climbing until it was hard to hear anyone speak. Easton could feel the vibrations in his chest. In the space of a few notes, the squad outside opened fire. Easton scrambled forward to see what they were shooting at. From his angle he couldn't glimpse much. The beat of drums blended in time with muzzle flashes. Then came the vocals.

"Hey ho. Let's go."

Manning rushed forward to the doors, only to stop the moment he reached the glass. The squad outside stopped firing, many stumbling back to retreat. Manning acted fast, locking the main door before anyone could make it inside. He scrambled away an instant later, his face white as a ghost. "It's too late for them."

Panic surged through Easton's mind as one of the men outside slammed his body against the window. His face was contorted in fear as he shouted something. Their words were drowned out by the vocals of Joey Ramone belting out the lyrics of *Blitzkrieg Bop* over the loudspeaker. The man outside screamed again with everything he had.

"Raaaaaaaats!"

His cry bled through the doors a second before a wall of grayish-black fur slammed into the glass.

Easton stumbled back in terror, knocking over his equipment as thousands of tiny, dead forms writhed against the doors to engulf the squad outside. The mound of matted hair and milky eyes moved as one, tails whipping back and forth in a frenzy. Screams trailed off into a chorus of squeaking chaos. Blood sprayed against the glass only to smear into a layer of wet gore as the mass of tiny creatures piled against the entrance.

Everyone inside raised their weapons, taking aim at the windows.

"Hold your fire! You want to break the glass and let them in?" Manning snapped the sword from the sheath on his back. "Get the flamethrowers."

Easton reached for his sidearm, not having needed to fire it in over a year since being assigned as Phenix Company's communications specialist. The doors groaned under the pressure of ten thousand zombified rats. It was only a matter of time before they made it inside. The men around him trembled.

Rebecca's warning echoed through Easton's mind.

Run.

She had been right.

Manning made a break for the stairs to the second level, getting off the ground floor that would be taken first. The rest of the men followed suit with Easton dashing for the second floor near the hallway that led to the monorail station.

Punk rock poured from the speakers as he ran. He would never be able to listen to the song the same way again.

Hey Ho. Let's Go.

CHAPTER FORTY

6 armored humans defeated, 708 experience awarded.

Digby stalked toward Skyline's field base as his army of undead rats tore apart the mercenaries attempting to repair the mechanized guns that guarded the museum's entrance. Asher perched on his shoulder. With a simple Compel, the sea of frenzied rodents parted to let him through. He glanced at his HUD.

COVEN
Digby: MP: 104/128
Alex: MP: 114/114
Asher: MP: 30/30

MINIONS: 10 rodent leaders, 20 common zombies.

His mana had recovered a few points after taking out the base's turrets. They had gone down with just a few Decay spells. As for the swarm of rodents, well, they had worked better than expected. His ten animated rat leaders had gathered over ten thousand newborn zombies and formed a command structure to steer his army in the direction he wanted.

Their numbers weren't completely loyal but between his leaders and his Zombie Whisperer spell, he was able to keep the tiny creatures in line wherever his furry army got distracted. With everything in place, all he had to do was lead his forces to the museum of popular culture where Skyline thought they were safe, and let his undead army's hunger take care of the rest.

Digby walked in time with the catchy tune playing from the museum's external speakers. He had to admit, music had come a long way since he'd died.

I should have Rebecca show me more of what humanity has produced in my absence. These Ramone fellows are something special.

He shook off the distraction and focused on the entrance of the building. Digby frowned, finding his rodent army unable to breach the entryway. No matter, he'd expected that. He raised his hand, sending another Decay spell sweeping across one of the doors. The windows held for a second, then all at once, the glass shattered into thousands of sparkling fragments.

"Seek!" Digby compelled his forces forward with a wild cackle. "Seek and feed!"

The rats poured in through the opening, like water filling a basin. Screams erupted from inside.

3 armored humans defeated, 354 experience awarded.
1 level 14 Fighter defeated, 1368 experience awarded.

That Fighter didn't put up much of a fight.

Digby chuckled at the Heretic Seed's snarky comment, glad for once that it wasn't making fun of him. It had been a while since the Seed had even weighed in on any of his notifications. He was starting to think whatever demon was inside it had been ignoring him. A new message caught his eye before he had time to think about the Heretic Seed further.

You have reached level 17.
3,347 experience to next level.

He would have let out another bout of wild laughter but another notification reminded him to stay focused.

2 animated rodent leaders lost.
Maximum mana returned to 139.

Digby dropped his extra point into strength and raced up to the entrance behind his army. Fire poured from the broken door in his direction. Ducking back down the stairs, he raised his arm to shield his face. The leather of his coat's sleeve shrank and curled under the heat as the smell of burning rats filled his nasal cavity.

"Scatter," Digby shouted, telling the vermin to fall back.

Two men brandished strange weapons just inside the door. They looked like rifles, only thicker, with a hose connected to a tank worn on each man's back. Fire spurted from the weapons like a dragon's throat. Digby cursed. He didn't know weapons like that existed.

Flame Thrower: uncommon incendiary weapon.

Fire swept across a thousand rats, filling the air with count-less tiny howls from the unfortunate ones on top of the pile. Digby crouched low, hoping that no one had spotted him. He hesitated. There were no bullets fired in his direction. He assumed that meant he hadn't been noticed in the chaos yet despite his cackling.

1 animated rodent leader lost.
Maximum mana returned to 141.

Digby crept forward. There wasn't time to be hiding. The horde needed his help. Rats scampered away from the men in all directions, leaving a clearing of empty space on the floor around the two men and their strange weapons. Digby opened his maw near one of their feet and prepared to cast Blood Forge. He pictured the image of a crimson spike impaling his target.

Before he had a chance to cast the spell, another two mercenaries pushed forward to stand next to the men wielding flame throwers. Through his Blood Sense, Digby felt both moving mana through their bodies. He Analyzed them as fire began to coalesce into their hands.

Guardian: Level 8 Mage, hostile.
Guardian: Level 9 Mage, hostile.

Damn! He refocused on his open maw, changing the image in his head to align with a theory working its way through his necrotic gray matter. Whatever fuel flamethrowers were firing, it was probably carried from the tank on their backs through the hose connected to the weapon. Digby pictured the form he needed to forge, sending a serrated edge of crystalized blood up from his maw. The attack tore through the flame thrower's hose before shattering against the mercenary's body armor.

A pungent liquid sprayed from the hose, lighting up the entrance with a fiery mist. The tank detonated in a sudden burst of flame that engulfed both mages as well as the man carrying it. Fire spread through the room as they flailed on the ground.

1 armored human defeated, 116 experience awarded.
1 level 8 Guardian Mage defeated, 766 experience awarded.
1 level 9 Guardian Mage defeated, 866 experience awarded.

Digby checked his mana.

MP: 84/141

The rise in his attributes from his recent level up had almost increased his maximum mana capacity to the point where it made up for the amount he'd sacrificed to animate his rat leaders. Granted, it had only increased what he could hold without actually replenishing any, leaving him down over a third. Blood Forge was his best attack spell, but it was also hungry. If he was going to cast it again, he needed to get as much out of it as he had with that last one.

The remaining mercenary wielding a flamethrower had been knocked down by the explosion, but he wasn't dead. Digby sent in his rats to swarm the unfortunate man before he could get up and start firing again. He ignored the experience message that followed. It was just another armored human like most of the others.

Fire roared, blocking the path inside. Digby glanced back as a large truck that he and his apprentice had salvaged before the attack drove up to the area at the bottom of the stairs. Alex leaned out the window. Nodding to the boy, he told him to release the twenty zombies waiting in the vehicle's cargo compartment. Then he held his arms out to compel his rodent horde.

"Push."

His obedient rat leaders squealed, echoing his command through their army. The sea of tiny bodies responded by scampering toward him. Two thousand rats pushed forward around him. The sheer volume of the mass snuffed out the flames so he could enter the building unscathed. Once the path was clear, the rodents parted to let Digby through. The last of his army poured in the door behind him.

Asher flapped through last to land on his shoulder where she cawed menacingly at his foes. Rats raced around his legs, spreading into the room once again like a flood of greasy fur.

Manning stood halfway up the stairs, his face pale as the sea of rodents covered the floor and piled up at the bottom of the stairs. He gripped his sword tight. His men trembled around him.

"I have come for a reckoning." Digby raised a hand, extending his blood forged talons.

"The rats are a nice touch, but you're going to have to do better than that." Manning regained his composure and leveled his blade in Digby's direction as the Ramones playing over the speaker system faded to static.

"Well then." Digby cracked a smile. "Hey ho. Let's go."

The men on the stairs raised their weapons as he threw out both arms and dropped to one knee.

"Protect your king," he compelled his horde, calling a tidal wave of rats to cover his body in a layer of hair and flesh dozens of rodents deep as the mercenaries opened fire.

Beneath the writhing mass of vermin, Digby held his ground as the thud of bullets peppered his army. The sound of gunfire was drowned out by thousands of screeching rats. He clutched Asher to his chest to make sure she was safe. It was unlikely that any of the shots would get through, but he wasn't taking any chances with her.

"They actually think they have a chance, don't they?" he whispered to his pet.

That was when the horde of twenty zombies from outside pushed through the broken doors to join in on the chaos and pull the gunfire away from their master. Digby reached under his coat with his clawed hand and retrieved the skull of the gas station clerk he'd eaten earlier. Its cavity sloshed with blood.

Another Compel told the rats to carry him to the right, moving him within the mass until he was no longer in the line of fire. Crawling out from his blanket of safety, Digby snuck off out of sight, leaving his army with a Compel to scatter while Manning and his men were focused on the new wave of zombies that had entered a moment before.

Creeping across the museum floor, Digby made his way to a stairway on the far side of the room. From there, he watched as the rats dispersed into a thin layer that covered the floor. He smirked at the confused expressions that fell across the faces of Manning and his men as he appeared to have vanished into the mass of rodents.

That's right, you big jerk. Keep looking at where I was.

Digby crouched low and made his way up to the second floor, where he looped back to get behind the mercenaries still standing on the stairs with Manning. He left Asher behind to fly to the ceiling where she hid behind a strange vehicle hanging from a series of wires for decoration. She cawed from behind cover to draw their attention.

"Did he turn into rats?" one of the men asked from the top of the stairs. "Can he even do that?"

"Don't be an idiot, Easton. The necro just ran away," Manning spat back at the nervous man standing at the top of the stairs behind him. "Head to the monorail and get it ready to leave. We'll be right behind you as soon as we kill this asshole."

The man who had asked the question saluted and ran off down one of the hallways on the second floor. Digby ducked behind a display case as they rushed by, clearly unaware that he was already on the second floor with them.

"Alright, Graves, you made your point," Manning shouted into the entry hall below. "You're a necromancer, we get it. Now stop hiding and get out here. We might still be able to work something out."

Digby readied the skull he carried and crept up behind the group while their attention was still on the entryway, expecting him to pop up somewhere below. He Analyzed the remaining members of Skyline's forces. There were ten left, their captain being the only one that wasn't a normal human.

"You hear me, Graves!" Manning stood tall. "You can't just hide like a coward all night."

"I don't intend to." Digby commented as he reached the top of the stairs behind them. He cast Cremation like it was a period at the end of his sentence.

Green flames engulfed the skull as he threw it at the beast of a man's face. Manning raised his sword to block, a shimmer of blue light sweeping across his skin. The skull burst on impact, showering everyone on the stairs behind him with immolated blood. Manning remained unharmed, protected by some sort of barrier.

"Rend!" Digby shouted to his rats and remaining zombies below as he drew back his talons.

The mercenaries turned to take aim at him just before he slid his claws across the throat of a man unlucky enough to be within arm's reach. Digby grabbed his victim tight and pulled their body in front of himself to stop a barrage of bullets from below.

Manning rushed forward, thrusting his sword up the stairs. Digby kicked the dead body he held down at the Captain. Manning tried to pull back, but the corpse fell straight on to his sword, impaling itself down to the hilt. Another Cremation spell gave the holy knight something to worry about. The body burst into emerald flames, forcing Manning back to deal with the burning corpse.

His army of rats converged behind them, devouring the two men nearest the bottom of the stairs and working their way up. A series of messages streaked across Digby's HUD. He ignored them all.

Out of bullets, one of the men lunged forward with a knife. He grunted in victory as the blade buried itself in Digby's chest. His face went white when his hand kept going with little resistance. A shadow, leaking black fluid, surrounded the mercenary's wrist as he thrust his own arm into Digby's open maw waiting on the surface of his body armor. He snapped the gateway shut, consuming the unfortunate man's arm whole. A scream erupted from his victim just before being cut off as Digby buried his claws in his side.

Another few messages passed by as Skyline's remaining troops attempted to reload their weapons. Unfortunately for them, Digby's forge spell was faster. A pair of crimson spikes erupted from the corpse in Digby's arms, impaling whoever was in the way. The impact shoved others back into the sea of rats at the bottom of the stairs.

Pulling his sword from the flaming corpse of one of his own men, Manning whipped the weapon to the side, flinging burning remnants across the stairs with an awful squelch. Digby swiped a claw at his face while his blade was out of position. Manning dodged back, only to receive a kick to the chest as Digby sent him tumbling into the rodent horde below.

He cackled with wild abandon as the hungry rats converged on the meal. He couldn't believe it had been that easy. A moment passed. Then another. Digby arched an eyebrow waiting for a message telling him that a level-twenty-seven holy knight had been defeated.

It never came.

The mound of rats began to rise, their tiny bodies falling from a very much alive holy knight as Manning stood back up.

"Did you really think a bunch of rats was going to be enough?" A strange glow shimmered across the man's body forming a barrier that the pint-sized zombies had been unable to bite through.

Digby glanced at his mana.

MP: 24/141

It wasn't much. He opened his mouth to speak. Manning stood still as if waiting for whatever Digby had to say. He closed his mouth awkwardly a second later.

"What, no arrogant declaration this time?" Manning smirked.

"No..." Digby trailed off. Then, he spun on his heel and ran away.

It didn't matter if Manning was dead or not. All that mattered was that he'd created an opening for Alex and Rebecca to get what they needed and take one of the aircrafts outside.

I've done my part. The rest is up to you, boy.

"Get back here!" Manning shouted from behind him.

Digby glanced back over his shoulder as he sprinted through one of the museum's exhibits. "Not a chance in hell!"

CHAPTER FORTY-ONE

Becca hovered outside the Seattle Museum of Pop Culture, watching as Digby taunted Manning before running away. It didn't exactly make him look brave, but he had certainly held up his half of the plan. Actually, he had gone above and beyond. She could hardly believe how easily his horde had overwhelmed Skyline's personnel.

"I'm starting to see why Manning was so concerned about him."

Below, Alex huddled against the back of the truck after driving it up to the museum's steps and releasing twenty zombies from the back. The poor guy's mouth hung slack with shock. A lump rose in her throat, hoping that he really was up to the task that she needed him to do. Swallowing her doubt, she dropped down beside him.

"How is any of this real?" He spoke up as soon as she deactivated her camouflage.

"Tell me about it." Becca peeked around the truck to make sure the museum's entryway was clear of mercenaries.

"I just leveled up twice from what Lord Graves did in there.

Jesus, he just killed, like, twenty people." His expression was a mix of excitement and horror.

"Yeah, he does that." She looked at him a little closer. "Wait, you leveled up?"

"The Seed subtracted seventy-five percent because I wasn't in there with him, but even that was enough for two levels. God damn, it feels weird. My head has never been this clear before." He leaned forward, shutting his eyes tight. "I kind of wish it wasn't. It's like we've been pulled into a survival horror game. So many people have died, and I'm getting the rewards." He held his rifle tight to his chest.

"Hey, you with me!" Becca spun her camera to stare him in the face. He was spiraling. "We don't have time for a crisis of morality."

He opened his eyes and shook his head. "Sorry, yes. I said I would help, I'm ready."

Becca observed him for a moment. He was clearly out of his depth, but trying his best. It was actually impressive that he'd held himself together throughout the night after everything he'd been through.

"Good, and don't worry, you're not just some office worker. You're a goddamn heretic now, so let's go steal us an aircraft." She tried her best to cheer him on before adding, "Because the rest of Phoenix Company will be back here soon and we need to have a kestrel off the ground and pick up Dig by then." She darted off toward the building hoping he would follow.

"Right." Alex lived up to her expectation, ducking low as he climbed the front stairs. Rats scurried this way and that as he moved.

As soon as Becca got a good look through the front doors, she took in the scene. Most of the zombies from the truck had been gunned down, but a few still wandered the entryway. Alex seemed to relax as soon as he saw them, Becca did the same, blowing out a sigh of relief. She couldn't help but notice the absurdity of the fact that having a few of the monsters around made them both more comfortable.

"Give me a hand here." Becca floated through the broken doors and into the now unguarded entry hall of the museum. She passed over the floor, searching for a corpse that might have the ID cuff they needed. The kestrels were usually flown remotely but there were sure to be a couple pilots amongst the corpses in the field base. All she had to do was find one beneath the rodents that feasted on the bodies. "There's too many rats."

"I'm on it." Alex slipped through the doors behind her and pushed a few rodents aside to make room for his foot. They obliged for the most part, though, every now and then a few would squeal and snap at his ankle. It seemed Digby's control over the horde as a whole was limited. Alex shooed the rats away only to have them return with friends. The enchanter winced as one of the rodents chomped into his pant leg. He swatted at the deceased creature, smacking it off into a nearby mound of fur and tails and shouting at the rats. "Get away!"

Becca's mouth dropped open the second the words left his mouth as the hundred rats that surrounded him all reacted. Scurrying away from him, the cursed rodents left a circular patch of bare floor tiles around him.

"Oh wow." Even Alex's eyes widened.

"Shit, since when can you compel them?" Rebecca spun back to face him.

"Lord Graves cast something called Zombie Whisperer on me. Said it will help me keep the rats in line if they get bitey. I thought he was making it up earlier to make me feel better about doing this."

"I wouldn't put that past him, but I'm glad he wasn't lying." Becca went back to searching over the corpses in the room. "Why do you call Dig Lord Graves, by the way? You know he isn't a lord, right?"

"I kind of figured that. He doesn't act very lordly." Alex shrugged. "But calling him that seems to make him happy, and it doesn't hurt anyone. So why not?"

"You're a weird dude."

"I know." His eyes flicked to something that Becca couldn't

see. She assumed it was something in the Heretic Seed's HUD. A moment later he slipped a plastic bottle from a pouch. The liquid glowed for a few seconds as he held it. The enchanter threw back a mouthful as soon as the light faded. "Something tells me I'm going to be using that spell a lot."

"What?" Becca snapped her camera back to him.

"Sorry, Purify Water." Alex gestured to his ankle. "I got cursed when I got bit."

Becca nearly crashed into a wall in surprise. "And that spell just wipes it away?"

"Yeah."

"Holy shit, that could stop everything." Becca's mind raced. "If we could create more enchanters, clinics could be set up and this curse could be slowed, maybe even stopped." Her shock was immediately replaced by a wave of anger at her former employers, who had the money, personnel, and resources to do just that, yet chose to do nothing. Actually, it was worse, Skyline had purposefully spread the deadly ailment further.

"I wish I'd become a heretic sooner." Alex sighed, sounding sincere. "Lord Graves gave me these amazing abilities, but it's frustrating that I met him too late to really be useful."

"Yes, but that makes you more valuable. If Skyline's guardians are going to abandon the world, then you heretics are the only ones left with the power to help." Becca tightened her grip on her drone's controls and refocused on her search. "Getting you and Dig out of the city just became way more important."

"Ah, good?" Alex stood awkwardly as rats circled his feet.

"Yes, good. Now help me search this corpse." Becca had caught a glimpse of something on one of the bodies.

Alex visibly cringed as a layer of zombified rats stripped the flesh from the corpse of one of Skyline's men. If it hadn't been for his armor slowing the creatures down, there wouldn't be anything left. As it was, the guy had no face. The enchanter slapped a hand over his mouth as if he was going to throw up. "Oh no."

"Don't you dare hurl." Becca didn't wait for him.

"Sorry, I was hoping I'd gotten used to seeing stuff like this."

"Maybe you shouldn't have eaten so many protein bars before attacking a base full of mercenaries." Becca dropped down to the corpse, ignoring his unease.

"I couldn't help it, leveling up made me hungry." The enchanted downed another mouthful of water before regaining some color. "Oh thank god, that spell works on nausea too."

"Lucky you." She flicked on her drone's light and shined it down on the corpse. "Now Compel the rats to move along."

Alex did as he was told. At first the rats were reluctant to leave their bounty, but after a few tries a pair of rats came to his aid. Becca couldn't help but notice their fur was lighter than the rest as they raised up on their haunches to give their attention to Alex. They both squeaked at their zombified brethren. The rest of the rodents moved on to another corpse in response.

"Thanks." Alex gave the pair a somewhat comedic salute.

"Are those some of Dig's animated leaders?" Becca watched as the two gray rats disappeared back into the horde.

"Yeah, Lord Graves gave them a bunch of intelligence and ordered them to help me." With that, he turned back to the corpse and knelt down. "Okay, what am I looking for?"

"That." Becca shined her light at the dead man's wrist. "That's the cuff we need to open the kestrels."

"Okay, so I just take this bracelet to the planes outside?"

"Pretty much." Becca pulled away to give him space. "We should be good to go once we're inside. Just need to wait for Dig."

"Gotcha." Alex took another sip from his water bottle, probably to keep his nausea in check before reaching for the blood smeared cuff around the corpse's wrist.

"Don't bother trying to get it off." Becca stopped him. "It's locked around his wrist. Just take the whole arm."

"What?" Alex recoiled from her drone.

"You heard me, go for the shoulder. The rats did most of the work for you, so you should be able to pop it out."

"Oh god." Alex froze. "Looting a corpse is one thing, but ripping off its arm is another altogether. I'm gonna need a moment."

"We don't have a moment."

"Crap, okay." Alex immediately chugged half his purified water. Then he reached for the combat knife strapped to the dead mercenary's body armor.

After a fair amount of gagging and a little crying, the enchanter got the job done, popping the limb out of its socket. A full body shudder racked him, clearly horrified by what he'd done. Afterward, he wrenched the limb free.

"Well done, boy," Becca quoted Digby as she pulled away to head back outside.

Alex sighed. "Please, don't call me boy."

"No promises." She slipped back out through the building's broken doors.

"How are you able to look at this stuff without throwing up?" Alex kept pace behind her.

"I'm usually assigned to war zones. This is nothing compared to what the living do to each other," she responded matter of factly.

"Oh..." He didn't push the subject.

Leaving behind the few zombies that still roamed about, they made a break for the aircraft waiting to the side of the museum. Becca reached the kestrels first, turning back to keep watch as her partner caught up. The severed limb in Alex's hand bounced against his thigh as he ran.

Becca assumed that the life of an enchanter wasn't looking as bright to the awkward nerd as it had seemed earlier, but she had to admit that he'd held himself together better than she had expected. Becca spun and shined her light on an access panel near the kestrel's rear hatch to guide him. "Place the I.D. cuff against there."

Alex did as he was told, raising the grotesque key up to

where she aimed her light. A green square lit up above the panel and the rear of the kestrel began to lower like a ramp. Inside, crates sat between rows of seats that lined the walls. Each chair was fitted with a three-point harness. A narrow door led to a cockpit at the other end.

Becca flew straight for a box built into the wall, labeled 'drone pod.' "I need you to get this open."

"Got it." Alex searched for a latch and popped open the top. A drone similar to Becca's sat inside. The only difference was a pair of additional compartments mounted to its sides.

"Perfect, now switch that drone out for mine." Becca landed on one of the crates. "Once I'm in, I can hijack the system and start her up."

Alex disconnected a pair of wires from the back of the inactive drone and pulled it free from the pod. Picking up Becca's unit, he placed it in the box and plugged the cords into the same ports.

Becca's monitor went black immediately as her drone shut off its camera to link into the craft. She lost her audio connection as well, cutting her off from Alex until she could start up the craft.

Using the direct connection, she removed the kestrel from Skyline's network just as she had her drone units earlier. Next, she ran a check of the craft's systems, making sure to deactivate anything that might allow it to be tracked. She flicked on the cabin's internal microphone and camera, getting a close up of Alex's nose shoved into the lens.

"What do we do? What do we do?" The enchanter's voice was a mix between a whisper and a shriek.

"Bah, what's happening." Becca jumped in her seat, not sure what she'd missed while connecting to the kestrel's system.

"That convoy is coming." Alex threw a hand out toward the open ramp. "That huge tank thing is pulling up to the museum and Graves isn't back yet."

"Shit." Becca turned on all of the craft's external cameras, opening several windows on her monitor. Alex was right, the team that was sitting on her apartment building had just returned. They had made it back faster than she'd expected. The other team that had been ready to ambush their original meeting place wouldn't be far behind. She immediately tapped the command to close the kestrel's rear hatch.

Alex stepped back toward the cockpit door as the ramp began to rise up ever so slowly. "Come on, come on. Close, damn it."

More trucks pulled up to the front of the museum. The kestrel's ramp locked shut a second later. Becca watched the enchanter holding perfectly still in the cabin. Only the dim glow of a few blinking lights kept the darkness from filling the internal camera's view.

"Do you think they noticed us?" Alex crouched down behind one of the crates in the cabin.

"Only one way to be sure," she whispered through the overhead speaker.

"And what's that?" Alex kept his voice low as well.

"They'll either come knocking, or they won't." She tried to sound hopeful, but her voice wavered regardless.

Alex tightened his grip on his rifle.

They both held their breath.

CHAPTER FORTY-TWO

Digby sprinted through the costuming wing of the Seattle Museum of Popular Culture. His heart pounded like thunder in his ears.

Wait...

The unsettling fact that he was dead flooded back to remind him that his heart had a shard of the Heretic Seed nailed through it and couldn't possibly be pounding. This raised an important question, just what was that noise?

Oh yes... him.

The boots of Captain Manning assaulted the floor in a steady rhythm. Closer and closer, the beast of a man rushed forward.

Damn!

Any hope of escaping crumbled. Being dead, Digby could potentially run forever without getting tired, but that didn't change the fact that he wasn't fast enough. His physical attributes may have been a bit higher than what he'd had back before he'd died, but from what he could tell, they were still only average at best when compared to a normal human.

Manning was anything but normal.

Unable to do much else other than run through the costuming wing of the museum, Digby passed one outlandish costume from humanity's imagination after another. His mana sat at the corner of his vision, as if taunting him.

MP: 31/141

He'd gained a few points while on the run through the museum, but it wasn't enough.

Or was it?

Digby added up what he knew. Manning was powerful. A holy knight, whatever that was. At best guess, the man's starting class had been something close to a fighter, which meant that he had more strength than intelligence in the beginning. With twenty-seven levels of points thrown in there.

That would push him up around…

Digby immediately stopped thinking about it. The math wasn't friendly. At best, Manning's weakest stat would be intelligence, and even then, he would have a bit more than Digby. With that much, Manning could think faster and hit harder. The only advantage he could think of was simple desperation. He could become pretty dangerous when backed into a corner.

All thought crashed to a halt when he burst into a new exhibit. A sign hung over the entrance, reading 'Worlds of Myth and Magic.' Once inside, the walls of a castle surrounded him with imitation tapestries hanging on fake stone. For a moment, he thought he was having another immersive flashback of his past before he realized that his surroundings were real. It was like someone had attempted to recreate the castle where his life had ended, but had gotten lazy halfway through. Looking up, there was no ceiling, just modern lights shining down on the facade of medieval textures.

Cases of glass were set into the castle's walls to display objects or costumes from humanity's fantasies so that they could be viewed from both sides as people walked around the exhibit. Digby couldn't help but slow to a stop even as the footsteps behind him grew closer.

Snapping out of his haze, he spun back just in time to deflect a sword aimed at his neck. The blade slid against his arm, biting into his wrist and scraping against bone. The tip of the weapon veered up to split his ear in twain.

Manning grunted as he missed his mark. Then he followed up with a punch to Digby's gut.

The world blurred with the sound of breaking bone and glass as Digby flew through one of the display cases. He exploded out the other side of the fake stone wall in a cascade of glittering shards. He let out a ragged cough, choking on his liquefied organs as fluid worked its way into his lungs. It was just like before when he'd been hit by that fighter, confirming what he'd already assumed. The holy knight class had its roots in something simpler.

Digby cast a Necrotic Regeneration to pull himself back together, bringing his mana down to twenty-one. He started to get up, but found himself tangled in a dress that had been in the display he'd been thrown through. A meaty hand clasped the collar of his coat before he could get up.

"Don't even think about fighting back." Manning yanked him from the ground, only to throw him into another display case. Digby clutched the dress against his chest and head, using it to absorb the impact as glass shattered all around him.

This time, the other side of the case held, leaving him slumped against the wall of the display with a dress wrapped around his shoulder. A second costume fell in his lap.

Manning followed up with a boot to his face that knocked out a pair of teeth. The pane of glass behind him shattered, dropping him to the floor back on the side of the wall he'd started on.

Determined to get to his feet before Manning could stomp around the obstacle, Digby scurried backward and pulled himself up. Leaning on another case for support, he noticed the gleaming edge of a blade within one of the displays.

Ignoring the potential damage, he smashed his fist through the case and curled his fingers around the grip of what appeared to be a claymore. The blade was clearly dull and not meant for combat, but still, it was heavy. The plate mounted to the side of the display held few words. 'There can be only one.'

Sounds good to me. Digby took a wild swing the instant Manning came around the wall.

The knight didn't even use his sword to block. Instead, he simply held up an arm. Blue sparks flew from the impact, sending a ripple of light across his body. Digby's heart sank. The spell Manning had cast on himself back in the lobby that had rendered his rats ineffective was still active. He would have to overpower it or wait it out.

The barrier had to wear off at some point. *Right?*

Manning swiped at Digby's side, making it clear he wasn't going to give him time to find out. The attack put a gouge in the center of the stolen body armor that covered his chest before tearing through the lapel of his coat. The knight's blade continued downward until there was a three-foot slash in the garment on one side. The severed flap of leather dangled limp from his back, threatening to throw him off balance.

Digby jumped back, dragging the dull claymore along the ground. The phony blade actually had a dent from where it had struck Manning's arm.

Oh god, he's going to kill me. Digby's legs shook as he tried to regain a stance that passed for defensive.

Manning didn't stop. His boots stomped forward with his sword raised.

Digby attempted to retreat, but his back hit a wall. It was already over. Then, out of nowhere, the white feathers of a reanimated raven streaked through the room. Manning let out a confused shriek as Asher crashed into his head to claw and peck at his eyes.

The knight's barrier held, but the distraction gave Digby time to move. Darting to the side, he put in some distance. A sudden squawk echoed through the empty museum as Manning backhanded Asher in the side. The bird went silent, its body hurtling into one of the broken cases.

"No!" Digby snarled, before slamming his replica sword into the floor, blunting the tip. Out of desperation, he opened his maw and cast Blood Forge. Just one point of mana left.

Black fluid surged up the dull blade from a shadow on the floor, coating the imitation claymore with a hardened shell of razor-sharp blood. Without hesitation, Digby drew back the sword and leaped forward.

Manning thrust his weapon, pushing it through Digby's body armor. The tip pierced his chest before being stopped by the bulletproof plates on his back. It didn't matter; it was only a lung. The dead didn't need to breathe.

Digby swung with every point of strength he had, slamming his blood forged claymore into Manning's side. Motes of blue light burst from his barrier along with black fragments of crystalized blood from his sword. The impact shoved the burly man to the side, forcing him to pull his sword out of Digby's chest as he regained his balance.

"I'm not done!" Digby rasped, pushing air up from his undamaged lung.

He raised his claymore up and dropped it down like a blacksmith hitting an anvil. Both swords connected in a shower of blood fragments. Manning held firm, strong enough to hold back the attack without pause.

A fist slammed into Digby's chest, shoving him away and pulverizing several ribs. He struck back with a thrust to Manning's stomach. Shards of hardened blood snapped off the blade to expose its blunt tip. The knight's barrier shimmered with a flicker, like it might be reaching its limit.

Spurred on by the momentary progress, Digby followed up with another strike. His enemy raised an arm to block as he let out an unhinged cackle. The claymore bit into Manning's wrist, the blood forged edge of his blade cracking down the length of the weapon on impact. Fragments of black blood fell from the sword one after another, shattering on the floor.

Manning held firm, the claymore's blade only drawing a trickle of crimson from a tiny scratch on his wrist.

Digby's victorious laughter was cut off as a ball of white light began to form in the palm of Manning's hand. The knight thrust the glowing orb into his own chest, sending a wave of energy across his body. Without hesitation, Manning simply shoved his sword through Digby's chest until the hilt slammed into his sternum.

The giant of a man didn't stop.

Instead, he pushed on to bury the blade of his weapon into the fake stone of the museum's fantasy exhibit. Digby's back hit the wall; his body pinned in place as a terrifying numbness began spreading from the wound, slowly purging the curse from his body. His imitation claymore clattered to the floor.

"I can't believe I thought you were dangerous." Manning lowered his head down to look Digby in the eyes.

"Who says I'm not?" Digby argued, having no options left but to annoy the man as the horrible feeling in his chest grew stronger.

"The sword pinning you to the wall says otherwise." Manning twisted the blade in his chest. "Let's see if you have the will to hold off my spell."

If Digby had the mana to cast another Regeneration to stop the spreading numbness, he would have. Unfortunately, his one point of MP wasn't going to cut it. That was when something strange happened. The spell chasing the curse from his corpse stopped spreading.

At the same time, his heart seemed to grow ice cold, the feeling radiating out to force sensation back into his chest. Digby furrowed his brow, unsure what had saved him. His will value was nothing to thumb his nose at, and he wasn't sure if it was enough to fight off whatever purging spell the knight had used. That was when the reason became obvious.

The shard.

That must have been it! The fragment of the Heretic Seed was pushing back. Realizing this, Digby cracked a smile. "'Fraid my curse is a tad stronger than your magic."

"Fine, we'll do it the hard way." Manning shoved harder on his sword, cracking one of the few ribs Digby had that wasn't already broken.

"Alright, alright!" He squealed like a prey animal in the claws of a predator, completely dropping his smug expression from a moment before. "What if you and I... make a deal here?"

"Like what?" The knight asked as if he didn't see his captive as a threat anymore.

"We work together, like you offered me earlier." Digby did what he could to stall.

"That sounds like you." Manning chuckled. "You just change your mind and beg as soon as you know you've lost."

"True." Digby wheezed, deliberately making his words harder to hear. "But I wasn't suggesting that I join you."

"Then what?" Manning arched an eyebrow and leaned in closer.

"I was suggesting that you join me." Without warning, Digby jerked his head forward and snapped his claws around the back of Manning's head. He tasted blood as he sank his teeth into his enemy's nose.

"Fuck!" Manning recoiled in horror while trickles of crimson flowed from his face.

"Welcome to the horde!" Digby snarled. "I killed your enchanter, so good luck removing that curse. Maybe that will teach you to get too close to a desperate zombie." His snarl faded to a wicked laugh.

Manning swore a few more times as he touched his nose. The damage wasn't bad, but it didn't really have to be. It was the curse that mattered.

"Do you really think I don't have access to another enchanter?" The knight wiped at his blood and calmed down. "I'm not an idiot. I have one waiting at our evac point, where they're safe, for this exact reason."

"Really? That's awfully smart of you." Digby smiled, showing his enemy a mouthful of bloody teeth. "But will you make it there in time? You never know, maybe the curse works fast this time."

"Whatever." Manning wiped his face again with the back of his hand then reached out to grab Digby by the hair. "The rest of my men will be back here any second to evacuate, and I'm sure I have what it takes to hold out for the thirty minutes it takes to pack up and ride a monorail."

"Well then." Digby made sure to speak in his most irritating tone. "I guess you may as well pull me down from here and take me back to your lords, then. We can find out your fate on the way."

"Sorry, but you're not coming." Manning gave a nonchalant shrug.

"What's that now?" Digby narrowed his eyes.

"No point in taking you with me after I've crushed your skull." The knight lowered his hands to the sides of Digby's head.

"Huh?" His face fell.

"My lords can find another zombie to help with their spell." Manning tightened his thumbs on Digby's forehead. "You aren't worth the trouble."

"Wait, wait—" Digby's words were cut off by an intense pressure.

Without another word, Manning squeezed harder, as if trying to prove the difference between their strength. The sound of fracturing bone splintered into Digby's ears. He flailed in desperation, only succeeding in scraping the man's body armor.

Manning growled in his face like a brute, his voice climbing into a scream of effort.

Digby squirmed, his body thrashing to defend himself. "I'll

kill you." He snarled his words through a blurry haze, his eye sockets cracking as his forehead buckled inward.

Manning's primal roar was the last thing he heard before his skull collapsed.

Then, there was nothing.

CHAPTER FORTY-THREE

The sound of water sloshing from side to side filled Digby's ears as the gentle sway of the ocean rocked him awake. Sunshine warmed his skin. His eyes snapped open to a cloudless blue sky, the sides of a small boat surrounding him.

What the...? Digby sat up.

Sea water pooled around his legs as his mind struggled to wrap itself around where he was. He recognized the boat immediately, but couldn't work out how he'd gotten there.

It was the same craft he had died in. The boat that he'd drifted to the frozen north and hibernated in for eight hundred years. Somehow, he was back where he'd started.

Hope flooded his chest.

It had all been a dream. Everything.

The future, Skyline, the curse; even Rebecca, Alex, and Asher. He wasn't sure if he should cheer or cry. Then he caught a glimpse of his clawed hand.

"Wait a second..." He lunged to the side of the boat and peered into the water. The waves broke against the bow, occasionally showing his deathly visage in their reflection. "That's unfortunate."

Digby slumped back into the boat to lay down. The last thing he remembered was his head being crushed by that over-muscled knight, Manning. He stared up at the sky. It didn't feel like he was in hell, and after the life he'd lead, it was probably unreasonable to think he'd gone to heaven.

"Oh well, purgatory is good enough." Digby rested his head back to relax for the rest of eternity.

"You're not in purgatory."

"Gah!" Digby leaped up at the sudden sound of a voice in his empty boat. "Who the hell—" His words got stuck in his throat as he raised up to find a version of himself sitting at the other end of the boat, looking very much alive.

"Close your mouth, you look like the village idiot." The copy of Digby leaned forward on his knees with his fingers interlocked in front of his face. A pair of crimson eyes stared down at him. "And before you ask, you're not dead either."

Digby closed his mouth, partly because he was just about to ask if he was dead, but also because he probably did look like the village idiot. Silence fell over the boat as they both stared at each other. The sound of gentle waves filled the void between them until Digby finally spoke.

"Why am I—"

"Here?" Human Digby finished his sentence as if he'd already known what he was about to ask.

"Yes."

"Because this is where I was born." The doppelgänger shrugged. "This is where we became one."

"I'm sorry, I don't follow."

"That's to be expected. Try to keep up, would you?" Human Digby's tone was rather arrogant.

"Now I know why no one liked me back home." Digby rubbed at what was left of the bridge of his nose, annoyed that his copy still had one. "Was I always this irritating?"

"Yes, you were. But despite appearances, I am not you. At least, not entirely."

"Then who are you?"

"Who do you think?" The doppelgänger threw both hands out to his sides as if the answer should have been obvious.

Digby couldn't argue that there was something familiar about the human's way of speaking. Well, something besides reminding him of himself. He'd definitely been spoken to in the same manner before. That was when it hit him.

"You're the demon." His eyes widened. "The one within the Heretic Seed that has been making snarky comments all night."

"Close, but no, I'm not a demon, and I don't live inside the Heretic Seed." The human doppelgänger locked eyes with Digby. "I am the Heretic Seed."

"What?"

"And, in a roundabout way, so are you."

"I say again, what?" Digby splashed water at the thing for speaking nonsense.

"It's not that hard to understand." The Heretic Seed folded its arms. "When the original monolith was shattered by you and that half-wit Henwick, a shard was lodged in your heart."

"I remember." Digby glanced down, placing a hand to his chest.

"As luck would have it, that shard was able to remain active."

"How?" Digby leaned forward.

"By connecting to you." The Heretic Seed gestured to Digby with its human hand. "Or, more accurately, it absorbed you."

"What?" Digby's tone fell flat.

"All living things contain their own system of essence circulating in their body. The outer layer of which is where mana comes from." The Heretic Seed placed both hands on its chest. "But within the center of that system there is a spark. Something special that's unique to everyone."

"Like a soul?" Digby raised an eyebrow.

"Yes, something like that. It holds everything that makes you, you, and it leaves your body when you die." The Heretic Seed's representation nodded in a self-satisfied manner. "When you expired, your spark was no longer needed by your body. And as it happened, that spark was just enough energy to stabilize the shard's unique mana flow. So, the Heretic Seed simply gobbled you up, and here we are."

"What do you mean you gobbled up my spark?" Digby narrowed his eyes. "Are you saying you ate my soul?"

"Yes, that sounds about right."

"What?" Digby leaped up, rocking the boat as he stood and stabbed a finger in the smug thing's direction. "You ate me?"

"Oh relax, it worked out." The Heretic Seed folded its arms and turned up its nose. "If it wasn't for that, you would be nothing but a mindless zombie like the rest."

"How so?" Digby froze mid-point.

"Your skull has been crushed, leaving your brain nothing but a smear on a wall. Where do you think your consciousness is really stored?"

Digby dropped his accusatory finger to his side. "It's in the shard, isn't it?"

"It's in the shard," the Seed repeated. "It's simple, really. When the fragment absorbed your spark, it merged the Heretic Seed's functions with you. The result is a saved instance of yourself at the time of your death." The thing gestured to itself. "Hence, this representation of the Heretic Seed's system."

"So that's why the messages are so snarky."

"Yes, you are a bit of an ass, and therefore the Seed reflects that."

"Great." Digby rolled his eyes. "I'm basically just talking to myself then."

"Exactly. But this version of you is capable of updating and reactivating your brain. That's why you retained your consciousness when you resurrected as a zombie. The Heretic Seed's mana system is still tangled up with your body's. And that's why you aren't dead now. The Heretic Seed is constantly recording everything you do, think, and say, so it can repopulate your brain as soon as it's functional again."

"Wait." Digby furrowed his brow. "Are you saying I can't be destroyed?"

"Ah…" The Seed hesitated. "As long as the shard remains intact inside your body to maintain our tangled mana system, and your head is still at least partially attached to your body, then yes, you're a bit immortal. Or, at least, you can always be brought back."

"Well, what the hell are you waiting for? I have things to do and people to eat. Send me back already."

The Heretic Seed sighed. "You would have to regenerate the top of your head first."

Digby froze. "What?"

"This imaginary space exists within the shard as a holding ground for your mind while your body is regenerated. But you still have to cast a spell to do that."

Digby glanced at his HUD, realizing he could still see it. "I can still use—"

"You can still use magic while in here." The Seed rubbed at the bridge of its nose. "You can cast Necrotic Regeneration at any time. You'll be reactivated as soon as you do."

"Why didn't you say so?" Digby splashed a foot in the water that sloshed around the boat.

"Because you kept asking questions."

"Oh…" Digby looked over his HUD.

COVEN
Digby: MP: 155/155
Alex: MP: 114/114
Asher: MP: 30/30

"Asher is alive." Hope flooded back into his chest. "Or, at least, she's still undead. And that's alive enough for me." The last time he'd seen the raven, she had been backhanded into a broken display by Manning.

"Don't forget about Alex," the Heretic Seed added.

"Oh, yes. The boy is fine too." Digby grinned for a moment before frowning. "The last of my rats have been exterminated, though."

"Tragic."

"Hold up." Digby found the messages that he'd ignored during the intensity of the last fight. "What have we here?"

GUIDED MUTATION

Requirements for the brute's mutation, Bone Armor, have been met.

Accept? Yes/No

Digby's mouth dropped open as he realized that when he'd eaten a mercenary's hand back in the museum, he had pushed his bone resources up to meet the requirements of one of his mutations under the Path of the Brute.

"That would give you one mutation from each of the four paths," the Heretic Seed chimed in. "I suggest you accept it."

"But…" Digby hesitated, looking down at his clawed hand and remembering the bone growths on the brute he and Alex had fought back in the apothecary shop earlier. "I've changed so much already. How much of a monster will I need to become?" He looked his doppelgänger in the eyes. "I can hardly remember what it was like to be human anymore."

"Do you even want to be human?"

"I don't know." Digby scratched at the back of his neck. "I guess I assumed there might be a way to regain my life after all of this was sorted and I wasn't being chased by mercenaries. But is that even possible?"

"Who knows?" The Heretic Seed shrugged.

"Shouldn't you?" Digby gave the copy a sideways look.

"Maybe if we had more than just a shard of the Heretic Seed available, I would know more. But as it stands, I have no idea where this magic came from or the details of how it works. Perhaps if you were able to find another fragment, you might be able to learn more. Becoming human again might even be possible."

"So a treasure hunt?" Digby nodded. "No sense holding back then. My humanity will have to be put on hold." He focused on the Bone Armor mutation and accepted the costs.

GUIDED MUTATION
New mutation path available. By claiming at least one mutation from each of your current paths, you have unlocked the advanced path, Ravager.

AVAILABLE MUTATIONS:
SHEEP'S CLOTHING
Description: Mimic a human appearance to lull your prey into a false sense of security.
Resource Requirements: 10 flesh.

TEMPORARY MASS
Description: Consume void resources to weave a structure of muscle and bone around your body to enhance strength and defense until it is either released or its structural integrity has been compromised enough to disrupt functionality.
Resource Requirements: 25 flesh, 10 bone.
Attribute Effects: +11 strength, +9 defense.
Limitations: All effects are temporary. Once claimed, each use requires 2 flesh and 1 bone.

HELL'S MAW
Description: Increase the maximum size of your void gateway at will.
Resource Requirements: 30 viscera.
Attribute Effects: +3 perception, +6 will.
Limitations: Once claimed, each use requires the expenditure of 1 MP for every 5 inches of diameter beyond your maw's default width.

DISSECTION
Description: When consuming prey, you may gain a
deeper understanding of how bodies are formed. This will
allow you to spot and exploit a target's weaknesses
instinctively.
Resource Requirements: 10 mind, 5 heart.
Attribute Effects: +3 intelligence, +6 perception.

"Wow." Digby reread the list, imagining how dangerous he
would be if he was to claim each of them. Then he looked back
at the requirements, realizing how steep most of them were. He
would have to eat dozens of people to reach them all, and it was
unlikely he would stumble across that many fresh bodies
without having to kill them himself.

"Better get hunting," the Heretic Seed commented from the
other side of the boat.

"Quiet, you." Digby swatted at the thing's words, not appreciating the suggestion.

He glanced back at his HUD, ready to cast the Necrotic
Regeneration that would bring him back to the world beyond
the little boat he sat in. That was when he realized his mana
had reached its maximum.

"How long have I been here for? My mana is full."

"A few minutes." The Heretic Seed steepled its hands. "You
absorb mana faster while unconscious. Same as meditation."

"I tried meditating earlier when I first woke up and wasn't
good at it." Digby made a point not to look at the Seed.
"Haven't really had a moment to try again since."

"Well, you should, because you can't sleep without someone
crushing your skull, and I don't think that holy knight is going
to be willing to help out when you need to absorb mana faster."

"Fine, I'll think about it." Digby rolled his eyes and cast
Regeneration. "I'd like to say it has been a pleasure. But
honestly, you're a pompous ass and you don't have the answers
to most of my questions." Digby waved to the Heretic Seed.
"So... bye."

The ocean around him began to blur together with the sky until white light filled his vision. The sound of the surf and the smell of salt lingered as it all faded away.

CHAPTER FORTY-FOUR

Digby opened his freshly regenerated eyes to darkness.

"That's not right."

All he could see was a message hanging in a field of black telling him his Necrotic Regeneration had increased its rank to C, and that its duration had increased from ten seconds to twenty. It was good news since he usually had to cast it a few times to reach full functionality. However, that wasn't really helpful at the moment.

The problem was that he couldn't see anything.

For a moment he was afraid that his head hadn't regenerated properly, like when his finger refused to grow back after being severed. An image of himself without a face flashed through his mind. What if pieces of his skull had been lost after being crushed by Manning? He couldn't find a replacement for that like he'd done with his finger, could he?

That was when he raised his hand, feeling some resistance as if a layer of black material was covering his body.

"Oh good, I'm not blind." Digby relaxed. "I'm just in some sort of sack."

He thought about that for a second.

"Wait, that's not good either." He clawed at his prison, finding a zipper near his head. With a shrug, he pulled it down.

The happy cawing of Asher greeted him as he sat up from within a black bag the size of his body. A label reading 'Biohazard' ran down one side. Beyond that, he was still inside the myth and magic exhibit of the museum of popular culture. A bloody dent in the wall told him he hadn't moved far from where he'd been killed. He winced at the bits of hair and chunks of his gray matter that were pressed into the damaged surface.

"Oh well, at least that knight isn't around." He knocked on his head with one hand. "And everything is back where it belongs." Then he knocked on his head again, noting an odd sound.

A new plate of bone had grown around his forehead like a headband, disappearing into his hairline on the sides and wrapping around his skull. Feeling around, he found a pair of formations protruding from the front. They stuck out and angled up like horns, just like the bone brute he'd fought with Alex.

Glancing down, he found that his left hand now had a few small plates lining his knuckles. His right hand, that bore his claws, had changed even more. Interlocking sections of bone now covered his hand and wrist all the way to his fingertips where his claws stuck out. He flexed each digit, finding that everything moved with ease, like his hand had always been armored. He smiled down at his appendage. It reminded him of a knight's gauntlet.

Digby shimmied his legs out of the body bag he sat in, and removed the damaged Skyline body armor he still wore. It didn't seem to fit anymore for some reason. Once the gear was off, he found more bone, forming a natural chest protector made from several overlapping plates. A similar formation was attached to his back.

"That ought to keep the Heretic Seed safe for now." He rubbed at the plate that covered his impaled heart, feeling confident it was enough to protect the obsidian shard.

Running a hand down his leg, he felt more plates of bone through his pants running down his thighs and shins. He stretched out to test his movement. Everything seemed to work. His new armor was light and comfortable.

Checking his reflection in one of the unbroken display cases, he was shocked to find that the bleached white bone of his new armor actually looked good. The horned headpiece was a nice touch, suggesting some sort of demonic crown.

"What's this now?" Digby couldn't help but notice the word King written in the title of a description board mounted on the wall to one side. He took a step back from the display case he'd been using as a mirror and examined its contents. His inner thief began to stir.

A coat of exquisite, brown leather hung behind the glass. Digby couldn't help but admire its unique design. With an asymmetrical lapel that wrapped around into an exaggerated collar, he'd never seen a garment like it. It even had a pauldron attached to one shoulder. A photo of a slender man with a wild hair style was framed below it. The man's pants didn't leave much to the imagination. The coat though, was something special. Out of curiosity, Digby Analyzed the item. His mouth dropped open the instant he did.

Coat of the Goblin King: unique, legendary.
MASS ENCHANTMENT: Due to belief and admiration shared by a large quantity of people, this item has gained a power of its own.
PASSIVE TRAITS:
MAGIC DANCE
Wearer's maximum mana is increased by 50.
PUPPETEER
Increases the wearer's influence when commanding targets with less intelligence.

Don't you dare think about stealing things now.

Digby ignored the Seed and raised a hand to smash the glass, hesitating for a second.

Isn't this how I got into all of this?

He couldn't help but remember that it was his desire to steal things that had placed him in Lord Axton's castle with Henwick all those years ago. Not to mention, the rest of Skyline's forces must have returned by now. Why else would he have been placed in that body bag? Manning must have ordered his men to pull him off the wall and wrap him up so they could bring his corpse with them when they left. In fact, the sellswords could return to pick him up at any moment. It certainly wasn't the right time to be making any loud noises.

All of this weighed on Digby's mind.

Then he shrugged and smashed the glass anyway.

The coat was simply too good to leave behind. Making a point not to waste any time, he grabbed the garment, along with the vest and frilly shirt beneath it. Digby tossed them on, buttoned the vest, and fastened the Goblin King's coat with a buckle at his waist. The collar curled around his neck, standing tall with a wicked curve while a tail of leather hung from his back like a cape.

Maximum mana has increased to 206.

"Fits like a glove." Digby nodded to himself just before catching the sound of boots in the distance. "Damn, they heard the glass." He beckoned to Asher. "I need you to find Alex; he should be in one of the airships outside by now. I'll call to you as soon as I can so you can lead him back to me and help me escape."

Asher cawed in understanding, then flew off toward the exit furthest from the approaching noise. Once the raven was gone, Digby spun to greet Skyline's mercenaries head-on. He made sure to make his appearance as intimidating as possible, holding his claws out to his side.

Then he realized there was a better, more cowardly, option.

Scrambling back to the floor, he shimmied his way back into the body bag he'd escaped from. He tucked his new coat underneath him and zipped himself. Then, he held as still as possible.

Seconds later, broken glass crunched beneath boots as footsteps entered the room.

"Are you sure you heard something?" a man asked.

"Yes, it sounded like a window being smashed," another responded.

"Well, no one's here now, and that necro is right where we left him."

"Watch out for rats. I don't want to lose anyone else." Manning's voice entered the room. "This whole night has been a shit show. After all the trouble this asshole caused, I can't wait until Seattle is a smoking crater in the ground."

"Should we load the necromancer's body into one of the kestrels out front?"

"No," Manning answered. "The crafts outside are crawling with more of those god damned rats."

Digby suppressed a chuckle at Manning's frustration. It was nice to hear the holy knight shaking.

"Take the necro to the monorail. We'll use the kestrels parked at the evac site at the other end. I have to head there anyway to deal with my fucking cursed status. Shit, we've lost so many men that we don't even need the aircraft out front any more. Christ, this operation got messy."

"What about that enchanter kid that was working with the necro?"

"Forget him, he'll burn along with Crow's Nest and the rest of Seattle. If they manage to get one of our aircraft off the ground, we'll just swing back and shoot it down."

I don't like the sound of that.

Digby wasn't sure what the man had meant about Seattle burning, but someone needed to make sure Manning wasn't able to go after Alex and Rebecca's airship. His thoughts were interrupted when the bag he was hiding in was suddenly lifted off the ground. From the motion, he assumed he was being carried by two men.

He glanced at his mana.

MP: 156/206

It wasn't bad, but he'd rather have more. He could wait until they brought him to wherever they were going; by then he would have absorbed enough MP to reach the new maximum that his new coat provided. Then again, if he waited that long, they might bring him somewhere with more enemies.

Then again, more foes could also mean more minions. Digby decided to stay put.

A minute later, the men carrying him placed his body bag down on a solid surface. Manning left them with instructions to guard Digby's corpse. Once the captain was gone, he sat still and watched his mana. As much as he hated to give the Heretic Seed's arrogant imitation of himself the satisfaction of being right, he closed his eyes and relaxed.

Meditation it is, then.

It was as good a time as any to try something new.

Becca went over a last-minute check of her recently hijacked kestrel's systems and prepared to fire up its rotors. The troops that had returned from watching her apartment had made their way inside minutes ago, without investigating the aircraft parked outside. The rats remained a problem, but without Digby actively commanding them, the rodents mostly remained content to mill about the entrance with many surrounding the kestrels.

She slapped a frustrated hand against her console.

The plan had been for Digby to meet them back outside so they could take off together and rescue her. At this point, she already had everything she needed to make her escape. The only thing missing was an eight-hundred-year-old zombie that didn't seem to know how to follow his own plan.

There was nothing really stopping her from leaving him behind and rescuing herself, but after everything they'd been through, that didn't feel right. Plus, Digby was their primary combatant, and they were going to need him in the days or weeks to come.

According to Alex, Digby was still listed on his HUD, but that didn't mean he was safe. Becca let out a sigh, realizing that all she could do was wait. That was when Alex spoke up.

"What was that?" He jerked his head to the side as if listening to something.

"What was what?"

"I thought I heard something." He looked into the camera mounted inside the kestrel's rear compartment. Again the enchanter stood too close to the lens, magnifying his nose until it was all Becca could see in the tiny window nested at the corner of her monitor. "It sounded like something tapping on the roof."

Becca switched to the kestrel's external cameras, finding an albino raven pecking at the kestrel.

"It's Asher." Becca opened the ramp to let the bird in.

The deceased raven flapped up to Alex's feet as soon as she was inside and cawed in a manner that could only be described as urgent. She flew back outside a second later, only to land a few feet away and squawk in their direction.

"I think she wants us to follow her." Alex crouched down to watch her.

Just as Asher cawed again, the monorail parked at the

museum left the station. The feathered zombie took flight after it, making her point clear. Digby was on board.

"Damn it, Dig. You are not making this easy." Becca's hands ran across her keyboard to fire up the kestrel's rotors.

The monitor came alive with a dozen different readouts.

A reticle appeared at the center of her screen. The words 'Weapon Systems Armed' flashed across Becca's HUD as she curled her hands around the controls.

"Better strap in, Alex, we're going hunting."

CHAPTER FORTY-FIVE

Digby held back the urge to murder the two men guarding him. Now that Manning had left them alone, all they seemed to do was complain, entirely ruining his efforts at meditation.

"Why the shit are we guarding a corpse? It's not like it's going anywhere."

"It's what the captain wants, and I'm not telling a guardian no. Don't want to end up with my head crushed in like this guy." One of the men kicked at Digby's bag with a foot.

Again, Digby held back the urge to murder. Instead, he opened his maw near his hand and forged a new set of blood talons, earning him a rank up message for the spell.

RANK INCREASE
Blood Forge has advanced from rank D to C. Objects forged will have greater strength and flexibility.
It's about damn time.

Digby couldn't help but agree with the Heretic Seed's comment. Blood Forge was arguably his most versatile spell, yet it had taken much longer to improve than his others. The only exception was Regeneration, which had only ranked up a few minutes before. Honestly, it was like some half-wit was deciding these things with a die roll.

The two mercenaries' conversation went on for a couple more minutes while Digby continued his attempts at meditation to replenish his mana. In the end, he wasn't successful with the constant distraction beside him, but he was still able to absorb most of what he needed due to the time he spent waiting. It was nearly full when the surface his body bag rested on lurched forward.

"Gah!" Digby slapped a hand over his mouth, realizing he'd shrieked out loud when the unexpected movement caught him off guard. He held as still as the grave with the hope that neither of the guns for hire guarding him had noticed.

"Did that corpse just say, 'Gah?'"

"Yeah, it did."

Digby recognized the sound of both men changing position to aim their rifles at him. The motion of his surroundings continued as, again, someone kicked at him with their boot.

He checked his mana.

MP: 206/206

Finally! Digby thrust his talons up in the direction of the nearest voice, shredding through the body bag and burying his claws in the side of one of the guards. The other tried to adjust their aim, but Digby was too fast, opening his maw on the wall and casting Blood Forge. A jagged blade of black fluid flew from the side to tear through his enemy's throat. He was getting better at aiming his attacks.

2 armored humans defeated, 232 experience awarded.

Digby ducked back down, dropping the body he'd run through with his claws to check his sides for more enemies. There were none. The room he was in was long, with seats and windows lining the walls. Outside, buildings passed by. The whole place was moving.

"What the?" Digby glanced to the rear of the compartment, catching the museum's oddly shaped building disappearing into the distance. He'd assumed that the monorail the sellswords were talking about was some sort of vehicle, but he hadn't known what to expect. Now that he was onboard, it was rather impressive.

Digby shook his head. Now wasn't the time to be amazed by modern inventions. He still had a train full of armed mercenaries to deal with.

Creeping toward the door at the front of the car, he peeked through the small window, finding the next compartment full of Skyline's men. He ducked back down the instant he saw them. There had to be at least fifteen and he didn't have a rat army to back him up anymore.

"But that doesn't mean I'm alone." Digby turned back to the dead bodies behind him and checked the cost to animate one.

Corpse: Human, 66 MP required to animate.
Animate corpse? Yes/No

Even with the additional mana provided by his new coat, he wasn't willing to sacrifice the amount needed to animate both bodies. He settled for just one before shoving whatever he could of the other into his maw to fill his void's resources.

Without wasting time, he put all his new minion's attribute points into intelligence, bringing the value to eight. He didn't need it screwing things up by misunderstanding a simple command. Once it was on its feet, he shoved a rifle into both of its hands and tossed the straps over its shoulders, so it didn't have to carry the weight on its arms. Then he tightened the straps on its helmet.

"Okay, here's what I need you to do." Digby positioned the zombie in front of him. "We're going to enter that compartment and you're going to pull the triggers of those weapons. Don't worry about aiming, you just leave that to me."

The zombie nodded.

"Perfect." Digby clapped his hands and pushed his minion forward.

It took him a moment to figure out how to open the door, but a second later it slid to the side and Digby stepped into the next car with his minion in front of him. One of his enemies spoke up right away.

"What are you...?" His voice trailed off before he finished the question. "Oh shit, he's dead!"

Digby pressed himself up against his zombie's back and reached around to steady the rifles. His minion opened fire without hesitation, filling the car with death. Digby did his best to keep the weapons pointing in the right direction while firing blind. Panicked shouts erupted from the other side of the compartment until both guns ran dry.

Peaking over his minion's shoulder, Digby hoped the volume of bullets had been able to strike the weak points on each of his enemies' armor. No such luck. An experience message confirmed it. Six men still stood in varying stages of readiness.

"Damn!"

A second message made him feel a little better.

You have reached level 18.
2,963 experience to next level.

Digby dropped his extra point into agility and ducked back behind his minion as the mercenaries returned fire. It was the only attribute that made sense. He would never be stronger than Manning, so mobility seemed like his best bet, even if it was only a little. Either way, there wasn't time to think about it.

Bullets filled the air, hitting his minion's body armor with dozens of solid thuds. Digby struggled to hold the corpse up under the barrage. The windows around him shattered and sparks flew from a hundred impacts.

Several bullets tore through the abdomen of his unfortunate minion, two of which lodged themselves in Digby's gut. Two more were stopped by the Bone Armor on his leg. Only one bullet hit home, drilling through his left hand and shattering two of the knuckles. A pair of his fingers hung limp. He cast a Necrotic Regeneration just as the last of the mercenaries' weapons ran out of ammunition.

Digby made his move, shoving his now inanimate minion's corpse down and leaping forward. One of the men raised a pistol level with his head. Digby blocked with his right hand, taking the bullet with the bone gauntlet that covered his wrist. His armor cracked and chipped but held firm as he thrust his claws up through his enemy's chin. With a gurgling scream, the sellsword fired off two more wild shots that struck one of his comrades in the jaw.

Digby yanked his claws free just as a bullet tore through his side from behind. He ignored it and cast Decay on the window across the monorail car to shatter it. The distraction caused two of his enemies to look back. While they were distracted, Digby grabbed ahold of a handrail for leverage and threw his legs out, connecting with both of the vulnerable targets to kick them through the opening. They fell into a horde of zombies below as Digby dropped to the floor. As he stood back up, a bullet slammed into the back of his head. The band of bone that wrapped his skull took the impact. His vision blurred nonetheless, causing him to stagger forward. On reflex, Digby cast Cremation on the corpse of his inanimate minion, hoping to catch an enemy in the blaze.

A second bullet ripped through his lower back to tell him he'd missed.

Even worse, the bullet had hit something important in his spine, causing his legs to collapse out from under him. Digby didn't know how much time had passed but it must have been less than twenty seconds since he'd last cast Regeneration, as it started to repair the damage before he hit the floor. Glancing back, he caught his enemy out of the corner of his eye. One of

Skyline's sellswords stood just to the side of the burning corpse of Digby's unfortunate minion.

The mercenary fired again, putting a bullet in the seat next to Digby's head. He scurried backward to retreat while regaining the function in his legs and focusing on the floor near his attacker. The sellsword adjusted his aim as a shadow formed around his foot. With a yelp, the foe slipped into Digby's open maw.

His gun barked as he fell.

A shout from behind drew Digby's attention as the stray bullet struck the last of Skyline's men in the throat. Snapping his maw shut, he took his attacker's leg off at the knee. The wretch toppled over, face first, into the burning remains of Digby's minion. The mercenary flailed and rolled for several seconds, but in the end, the fire claimed his life.

Standing back up in the monorail compartment, surrounded by lifeless bodies, Digby couldn't resist a good cackle. His victory was interrupted by the stomping of boots coming from the next car. There was only one man with feet big enough to make that much noise.

Manning.

Digby cast a Decay the instant he caught Phoenix Company's leader through the window of the door at the end of the compartment. Rust spread out from the sliding track at the top, causing the door to get stuck halfway. Manning probably had the strength to force the mechanism open, but instead he chose a show of force.

Digby sensed mana flowing through his foe just before Manning's fist exploded through the monorail's door. Metal tore and bent as the brute of a man shoved his massive body through the opening. Four more men slipped through behind him to stand at the holy knight's sides.

Digby stood to meet them, the wind blowing through the compartment as the tail of the Goblin King's coat billowed behind him. His shadow stretched across the car in the light of the Cremation flames.

The sound of the monorail racing forward filled the silence before either of them spoke.

"I crushed your skull. How the fuck are you here?" Manning reached back and ripped his sword from the mechanized sheath on his back, nearly slashing one of his own men that stood too close in the confined space of the monorail's compartment. "You're a damn cockroach."

"I've been called worse." Digby flicked his talons out to his side with a flourish.

Without another word, Manning charged. His sword tore through the air. Digby ducked back, then to the side as the blade slashed up to the ceiling. Sparks flew from the roof as the weapon's edge scraped against metal.

Two of the men behind the knight fired, one hitting Digby in the leg while the other shredded a seat cushion behind him, sending bits of stuffing into the air. Manning blew the fluff out of his face as Digby shielded his eyes with his left hand and reached out with his right to strike.

Manning reacted, swiping down to meet Digby's gauntlet. Steel hit bone, cracking plates of armor as the blade bit into the necrotic flesh of his palm.

"Fool!" Digby closed his armored fingers around the blade and cast Decay, increasing the damage to the weapon by physically touching it. Rust spread down the sword from his hand like a curse. He slapped his left hand against the flat of the blade in the same second, snapping it in two. He hopped back and claimed the severed weapon's tip as his own. The dagger-sized blade no longer had a handle, but he could always regenerate a damaged hand later.

Manning's face contorted with anger as the men behind him began to push forward. Before they were able to raise their weapons, the holy knight turned on the closest one to shove the mercenary into the monorail seats.

"Get the fuck back to the front cars, you're in my goddamn way."

The four men froze, clearly afraid of the giant of a man.

With a stomp of his foot, he sent them all running from the compartment.

"I think I might keep this." Digby drew the knight's attention back to him as he swiped the broken piece of sword like he was testing the improvised weapon's balance. Not that he really knew how to tell. He was just trying to irritate his enemy after seeing how reckless Manning's anger had made him.

"Go ahead." The knight held out his hand, letting light gather in his palm like he had earlier.

Digby froze, remembering what that spell had done to him before. Manning gave a ferocious grin as he slammed the orb of light into his chest. A threatening aura filled the air as the holy knight's body glowed.

"This spell is called strength of the faithful, and it isn't available to your Heretic Seed. It's particularly good against undead." The glow around his body faded as the edge of his broken sword gleamed.

"How do you even know? It's not like you've faced my kind before tonight," Digby spat back.

"True, but I'm not the first guardian to face a necro, and we leave detailed reports."

"Good to know." Digby's mind raced with possibilities, wondering if whoever had started Skyline might have run across the witch that had created him all those centuries ago.

"Not that it will do you any good." Manning cast a second spell, sending a blue shimmer sweeping across his body. "This one is a barrier against physical attacks, and you don't have anything that can get around it." He laughed. "That's the thing about necromancers. They depend too much on minions to do their fighting for them. Death magic can only get you so far by yourself."

"I make do with what I have." Digby glanced to one of the bodies that littered the compartment, running through his options. Blood Forge was his most economical.

"Nice try." Manning stepped back before he could cast the spell and send a shard of blood for him. "And by all means, go ahead and try to animate one of them, I'll cut them down before they can even get up."

Digby frowned. Manning was right. Animating a zombie would seal his fate. It would cost too much mana and would be too easily destroyed. His body tensed. He had no idea of what to do next. Manning charged forward, clearly having no intention of giving him time to think. Lacking options, Digby flipped his makeshift dagger in his hand and plunged it down.

Manning didn't even notice.

The blade hit his neck with a hard ping as it scraped across the barrier surrounding his body. Without the need to defend, the knight simply swiped low with what remained of his broken sword. Digby didn't even feel the attack. Instead, he just wobbled as his left shin split in two, his foot no longer attached to his body. Before he fell, Manning slammed a fist into his stomach. The force of a mana infused punch ripped him from the ground and hurled him back across the monorail car.

Glass shattered and metal buckled as Digby slammed into the door at the back. He slumped to the floor, shaking his head until his vision refocused. Even his HUD was hard to see. Without waiting to find out what part of him was broken and what wasn't, he cast a Regeneration. Tissue knitted itself over the stump of his leg. The severed portion lying somewhere near Manning.

The hulking figure of Skyline's holy knight lumbered toward him, the fire on the floor twisting his features into something inhuman and bestial. Sweat ran down his face. The curse was taking its toll. Unfortunately, Digby was pretty sure he wouldn't survive long enough for his enemy to turn so he could take control of him.

Digby felt around for something to hold off the monster of a man coming for him. His hopes soared when the fingers of his left hand curled around the grip of a pistol. It must have been dropped by one of the sellswords earlier.

Without hesitation, he raised the gun and fired. The weapon kicked as a bullet shredded one of the monorails seats. He fired again, striking Manning in the arm. Blue sparks flew from his barrier but nothing more. Digby continued to pull the trigger, missing half his shots while the rest were stopped by the holy knight's magic.

Only after several hits did the barrier flicker enough to let a bullet through. It punched into the body armor covering Manning's chest with a hard thump, leaving the scrap of lead flattened on the surface. The Captain took a step back with a sudden cough, but that was all the attack accomplished. Nothing could hurt him.

Digby's pistol clicked as a part on top of it locked back. With no more use for the empty weapon, he threw it from where he sat on the floor. The useless hunk of metal bounced off the man's leg.

"You're not a very good shot, are you?" Manning let out a gravelly laugh.

"I don't like guns." Digby shrugged as he ran out of options. He glanced at his HUD.

MP: 72/213

It was something, but with the spells he had available, there just wasn't a way to win. Digby looked over his coven's status, finding Asher and Alex listed below his name just as they had been.

At least they're alive.

With a little luck, Rebecca could still be saved and Manning might not be able to pursue them before removing his curse. It was a meager comfort, but it was all Digby had. If he was honest, he had already made it far further than he ever thought possible. Still, he smiled knowing that his allies might survive.

I hope they can get along without me.

He pictured Alex feeding Asher a bit of brain in his absence. Her happy caws met his ears.

That was when he realized the sound wasn't in his imagination. He actually could hear Asher cawing somewhere in his mind. Digby reached out with his thoughts to call to his pet. The connection was distant and quiet, but he was certain it was there. He glanced out the broken window to his right, catching a white speck flying between the buildings.

His eyes widened.

The last time he had seen Asher, she had been on her way to find Alex. She'd either gotten lost and returned to him, or...

Rebecca will be right behind her with a fully armed airship.

Digby snapped his vision back to Manning as he stomped closer.

I have to buy time.

He reached up to grab a nearby handrail and hoisted his body off the floor. Hopping on his remaining foot, he found the broken half of Manning's sword lodged in one of the monorail's seats. Digby claimed the blade again and placed it between his teeth.

"What do you intend to do with that?" Manning's voice sounded labored.

"It's better than nothing." Digby spoke through gritted teeth, still holding the makeshift dagger and attempting to stall. "You're not looking so good, maybe you should have a lie down before you become one of my minions."

"You're not looking great either." Manning kicked Digby's severed foot into the Cremation flames still burning in the center of the car.

"That was uncalled for." Digby narrowed his eyes as his unfortunate extremity burned.

"Then do something about it." Manning held out both arms, inviting him to try as another blue shimmer swept over his body to reapply his defense spell.

Digby steadied himself as if accepting the challenge. There was only one choice. To place his faith in his allies. They had either found him and were getting in position to attack or they had left him behind.

He raised his hand and opened his maw.

Manning stepped backward as a flood of necrotic blood

erupted from a shadow on the wall. He would have been successful too, if Digby had been attempting to forge another spike, but no, that wasn't his goal at all. The torrent split into crystalline shapes with multiple jagged points. Black shards reached for the knight, shattering on contact against his barrier, unable to penetrate his defenses.

"Is that all you have?" Manning didn't even try to dodge as the forged shapes broke off against his skin, only to be replaced by more surging from the shadow.

"Yes, and it's all I need." Digby forced the contents of his void out, the blood carrying bits of flesh and fragments of bone with it. He even reached for the blood cooling in the bodies of Skyline's men lying scattered on the floor.

Manning attempted to push through as the entire night's worth of devoured humans solidified around his legs and waist. His face dropped as his error became clear. Digby wasn't attacking. No, he was just holding his target still.

Digby spat out the blade in his teeth, then focused on his own leg. With so little in the way of resources left in his void, he cast Blood Forge on the viscous fluid crawling through his own dead veins. A thick form burst from the stump of his left leg. Bridging the gap between his severed limb and the floor, it crystallized into a wide peg that could carry his weight. With his severed foot more or less replaced, he limped his way to the window and screamed in the direction he'd last seen Asher.

"I know you're out there, Rebecca!" He gripped the sides of the monorail's window and leaned out, so the wind whipped through his faded hair. "Give him everything you've got!" He finished by thrusting a finger in the direction of the immobilized holy knight.

Manning hacked at the solid blood surrounding his legs, chipping away at his prison little by little with his broken sword.

"Now who's the idiot?" Digby cackled and used the last of his mana on a Cremation spell that set the man's gory restraints aflame. Turning back to the window, he called again, "There! I lit up your target for you."

Manning shouted a long string of curse words, most of which Digby hadn't heard before.

"Now, Becky!" he snarled. "Now!"

"She's not coming!" Manning slapped at the fire surrounding him, his skin cracking and bubbling to demonstrate the incredible amount of punishment he was capable of withstanding. "That traitor abandoned you just like she did us."

Digby's shoulders sank as nothing happened.

"Face it, you put your trust in the wrong people." Manning cracked away the blood surrounding one of his feet as the monorail passed between two buildings. "Why would they even want to take a monster like you with them?"

Digby rested his hands on the ridge of the broken window and deflated as the excitement that had swelled in his chest a moment before drained. Again, Manning wasn't wrong. People hadn't liked him even when he was alive. Why would they risk their lives for him now?

That was when the monorail passed by one of Seattle's taller buildings.

A building large enough to hide an aircraft.

Rebecca's stolen kestrel emerged from behind just as two panels near the front of the craft opened. Digby's heart soared when a pair of the largest guns he'd seen since waking up slid into place. A ring of multiple barrels spun as he turned back to his enemy to gloat.

"I may be a monster, but I'm a monster with friends."

Manning stopped hacking at the blood that imprisoned him and lowered his hands to his sides to speak one word. "Fuck."

The walls of the monorail tore apart like paper as the kestrel opened fire. Manning's barrier winked out in seconds. Raising a hand, he shielded his head as white-hot metal ripped through the air around him. Impacts rocked his body, thumping into his armor and skin. For a moment, it looked like he might even be able to take it.

Then, pieces of him began to break away.

A finger, an ear, a kneecap. Fragments spattered against the wall as the hail of destruction shredded everything in its path. Manning's defense could only hold him together for so long before his entire body came apart at the seams. He let out a final enraged roar just before his lower jaw exploded.

"Easy now, Becky." Digby held out a hand to tell her to hold up. "That's enough!"

The barrage came to an abrupt stop as both guns ceased firing. Once it was safe, Asher flew through the devastation that remained where Manning had stood. There was barely anything left of the seats and walls, let alone the holy knight. The albino raven landed on Digby's shoulder to nestle against the collar of the Goblin King's coat. A joyful smile spread across his face as the kestrel outside rotated and lowered its ramp.

Digby limped over to where Manning had been and picked up a scrap to toss to his loyal zombie companion. Asher caught it out of the air and scarfed it down.

"That's a good girl. I'm going to make sure you have all the prey you can eat." Digby placed a hand over his stomach, feeling his void gnawing at him. He had lost most of his resources on that last forge spell.

"I should probably take a little something for the road as well. Else I might start looking at Alex as a snack." He opened his maw to kick in whatever pieces of the holy knight were lying about.

"What's this?" Digby crouched down to pick up a glove. Fishing around inside it, he pulled out part of a meaty hand, complete with a golden band around its middle finger. He plucked the ring off and bit off a mouthful. Digby pocketed the item. "I'll have to see what sort of spell I can get from this once we're someplace a little more secure."

Digby turned toward the front of the monorail compartment, catching several of Skyline's sellswords through the broken door where Manning had told them to wait. They looked ready to fight but lacked the confidence to make the first move. Digby locked eyes with the closest and took a sudden step forward.

They all flinched.

"I thought so." He turned away and stepped up to the opening that had been torn through the wall as Rebecca lined up the kestrel's ramp. It was a shame to leave the bodies behind, but with the next compartment filled with more of Skyline's men, he didn't want to press his luck. Instead, he scratched at Asher's chin and stepped toward the kestrel's ramp.

"Come along, girl, we still have a princess in a tower to rescue."

CHAPTER FORTY-SIX

Becca tapped her console's sticks to the side to rotate the stolen kestrel. She did her best to line the aircraft's loading ramp up with the damaged monorail, but the vehicle proved much more difficult to maneuver than a drone. Despite the controls being similar, it had been a while since she'd flown one.

"You're going to have to help Dig up." She glanced to the window at the edge of her monitor that showed the inside of the kestrel's passenger compartment.

Alex gave her a thumbs up and inched his way down the ramp to lend Digby a hand. Fortunately, the zombie had been getting stronger all night and now seemed to possess the physical prowess of a normal human in their prime.

"Many thanks." Digby clawed his way up before standing on the aircraft's open ramp with Asher held close under one arm to keep the raven from being sucked into the rotors.

Wind blew through the compartment, causing the necromancer's coat to trail off to the side behind him while an asymmetrical collar wrapped around his neck. The image stuck in Becca's head, drawing her back to her childhood. A memory of watching movies with her mother back before her parents sold her off to Skyline.

"Dig, what the hell are you wearing?" She arched an eyebrow at her monitor.

"I did a little looting back at the museum." The zombie tugged on his collar to straighten it as the kestrel's ramp closed behind him.

"That is freaking awesome." Alex stepped closer to study the garment.

Becca shook her head at the pair and pulled away from the monorail. Taking one last look with her exterior camera, she caught a glimpse of Easton at the front of the tram, manning the controls. For a second, he seemed to be looking at her.

Half of her was glad he'd survived, while the other was afraid he'd hunt her down. In the end, she just hoped he would reach the evac point and get the hell out of the city. A group of Skyline's men stood with him, the last remaining members of Phoenix Company.

Muting herself for a moment, she glanced back to Digby having trouble comprehending that he had actually won. "You crazy, dead man." She couldn't help but grin as she added a quiet, "Lord Graves."

The zombie plopped himself down on one of the seats that lined the kestrel's interior and lounged back like a wealthy lord out of a fairy tale. He bounced one leg on the other, drawing her eye to the odd formation attached to his left shin.

Becca unmuted herself.

"Jesus, Dig. Are you missing a foot?"

"Don't worry about it." Digby knocked on what looked like a peg-leg made from crystalized blood. "I handled it."

She rolled her eyes and looked away from the interior view to focus on flying. They were nearly free and clear; it wouldn't do for her to crash into a building now. It wasn't long before she banked onto her apartment's street. Her heart raced the moment she began her approach. The horde that had gathered around her home had grown.

There must have been ten thousand. Even with Digby on their side, there was no way to control that many of the dead at once. Becca swallowed hard and slowed to a stop near the building's third floor, then she tapped the controls to bring the kestrel up to her apartment near the top. She peeked over her monitor as the aircraft came into view outside her window.

Her hands began to shake as the reality of what she was about to do slithered through her mind. The moment had seemed so far away when she'd packed her things earlier. She let out a final terrified whimper, before stamping the fear down and reaching for her emergency gear.

Bringing the aircraft to a stop, she set it to standby and disconnected from her console to reconnect with her laptop. The screen was small. So small it felt claustrophobic. The kestrel's HUD overlay loaded around the perimeter, tightening her view even further. She tapped a few commands and brought up the craft's weapon systems. A reticle appeared at the center of her screen.

Becca's eyes widened, remembering that the guns were aimed into her apartment. She hopped up from her chair and raced to the bedroom where she was furthest from the window. She could still hear the rotors outside. Taking a few more steps away from the door she ducked down behind the bed. It wouldn't do much for her if a stray round ricocheted in her direction, but it kept her from hyperventilating.

That was when she remembered that she forgot to pack something important.

Becca took a deep breath before reaching under the bed. It took a few seconds of feeling around before she found what she was looking for. A shoebox that she hadn't thought of in over a year slid out from under the bed.

She hesitated before opening it.

A few dozen envelopes filled the box, each with a red approval stamp from Skyline's security screening. They were the letters that her parents had sent back when she'd entered her employer's training program. They used to come every week.

Then every other week. Then the letters just stopped. After that, Becca had thrown them under the bed and vowed never to open them again.

Her heart ached to look at the box, let alone read any other letters, but still, she couldn't leave them. Becca glanced at her trash bag of supplies, then back to the letters. There wasn't room for the whole box. She grabbed a random envelope from the middle and stuffed it into the pocket of her jeans.

"Sometime this century." Digby interrupted her reminiscence, shoving his face into the kestrel's interior camera. A magnified image of his empty nasal cavity filled the window nested at the corner of her laptop's screen. "Is the window too thick to Decay?"

"It's rated to stop small arms fire, so you're not going to get through it like that." Becca minimized the interior view so she didn't have to look at him, and grabbed the modified game controller to adjust the kestrel's targeting reticle. She took aim at her workstation in the other room. It seemed fitting to destroy the equipment that she'd been shackled to for years. All that was left was to fire. She placed her finger on the right trigger of her controller.

Hesitating for a second, she whispered one word, "Goodbye."

Then, she destroyed her home.

Through the claustrophobic view of a laptop, the window shattered as a hail of bullets punched through the thick window and shredded her drone console. Sparks flew as computer towers fragmented and her wrap-around monitor was reduced to flickering scrap.

Becca pressed her hands over her ears to drown out the noise. She'd heard gunfire across dozens of war zones, but never this close. Never in person. It only lasted a few seconds, but it was enough to carve the sound into her memory.

Removing her finger from the controller's trigger, she flinched as the kestrel's guns stopped spinning. Becca picked her laptop up off the floor and stepped to the door. Devastation greeted her the instant she entered the living room.

Nothing was left of her drone console but shattered plastic and particleboard. A cold breeze caressed her cheek, highlighting that the window that had separated her from the world was no longer there. Beyond it, the kestrel floated, its rotors blowing a few stray post-it notes around the room. The aircraft looked so much more real than it had moments before.

Becca set her laptop down on the back of the sofa and raised her controller to rotate the aircraft's rear to face the window. She hit the open command to bring down the ramp.

"Your coach awaits, my dear." Digby bowed as he came into view, clearly trying to act as regal as possible, like he wanted to make a good first impression. He held the bow, waiting for her to greet him back. "It's nice to finally meet you."

She let an awkward silence go by.

"Hey Becca." Alex waved from his place beside his zombie lord.

She waved back unsure what else to say.

"Come on, then." Digby raised back up, sounding less formal as he gave her a good look at his face. It took everything Becca had not to gasp.

He was a monster.

Of course she already knew he was dead, having seen him through a monitor all night, but now, seeing him in person, there was so much more detail. He even had a scrap of what she assumed was Captain Manning stuck between his teeth.

"Quit staring. It's not like this is the first time you've seen a zombie." He looked away. Asher flapped her wings and cawed to interrupt the awkward moment.

"Easy there." Digby patted the raven's side. "We'll be on our way in no time."

Becca relaxed. He may have eaten dozens of people that night, but he was still just Digby, the dead man that thought there were demons in his blood. The same man that had risked everything to get her drone to the kestrel so she could rescue herself. The same man that had stood up to an army of mercenaries, and said no when they'd offered him the same comfortable prison that she had said yes to years ago.

Alex grabbed a handle at the side of the kestrel's door and held a hand out to her. The enchanter had lost his job and had his world turned upside down but still managed to come through when it mattered most. Both he and Digby had been cast aside by society, centuries apart from each other.

Becca raised her head and smiled. They were misfits the same as her. She snatched up the trash bag that contained everything she owned in the world and tossed it to Alex. Next, she passed him her laptop. Then finally, she approached the ramp herself.

The sound of a thousand mouths moaning drifted up as she reached one foot out over the gap. The chorus below was audible, even over the sound of the kestrel's rotors.

"Don't look down." Alex snapped her mind back to the ramp as she took his hand.

"There we go." Digby dropped himself back into one of the seats. "Now, can we leave?"

"Yeah, yeah, keep your pants on." Becca pushed aside her worries and sauntered through the passenger compartment to grab her laptop.

"Why would I take my pants off?" Digby furrowed his brow.

"It's an expression." Becca sat down in the cockpit to get a feel for the controls. Her face fell when she realized they were more complicated than she expected. After ten seconds of touching things she didn't recognize, Becca opted to drop her laptop on the console and continue using its controller. It had worked so far, so why change things?

Testing the sensitivity a little, she closed the ramp and pushed the aircraft away from her apartment. It was unnerving to be riding in the same vehicle she was controlling by remote, like she'd been shrunk down and placed inside a drone. Eventually, her nerves faded, and she pulled the craft up above the buildings. It was a straight shot out of the city from there, she just hoped the kestrel's stealth capabilities would keep it off the military's radars.

That was, if there was even a military left still.

They were nearly halfway out of Seattle when a screen on the craft's console lit up with an incoming call. She didn't get the option to deny it.

"Ms. Alverez."

Becca froze at the sound of her last name coming from the lips of Henry Rickford, the man who had contacted her earlier. The man who controlled all of Skyline. He didn't wait for her to say anything.

"My offer still stands. Lock the cockpit door behind you, and deliver that necromancer to me. You have my word that no one will harm a hair on your head."

There wasn't anything he could say that would make her believe him.

"Sure, and maybe Dig will magically regrow a nose. No thanks." She reached out to hit the end call button only to jump halfway out of her seat when Digby burst into the cockpit.

"Wait!"

Becca turned to the zombie, her blood running cold the instant she saw his face. She didn't know a corpse could turn white with fear.

Digby let out an astonished whisper, "How?"

"Graves, is that you?" The man on the other end of that call squinted.

Digby's eyes narrowed into a hateful glare.

"Hello, Henwick."

CHAPTER FORTY-SEVEN

Digby tightened his grip on the side of the cockpit door until his claws scraped the metal.

How?

The word sat at the front of his mind.

How is Henwick alive?

How could the same man that had rallied a tavern full of idiots to attack a lord's castle centuries ago be talking to him at the other end of a screen. The last time he'd seen the charismatic hunter, Digby was helping to smash the Heretic Seed's monolith. He had assumed Henwick had died when the...

Digby's eyes widened.

...when the Heretic Seed exploded.

No. Digby leaned closer to the screen, his mind working out the only possibility. *It couldn't be.*

Henwick let out a relaxed sigh. "Graves, you look terrible. But I'm glad you survived. I thought you'd been killed all those years ago. I had no idea you had been connected to the Heretic Seed." The man glanced to the side. "How did that happen, by the way?"

"I stole a ring from the castle's study before you coerced me into helping you destroy the monolith." Digby would have lied, but he didn't want Henwick to know about the shard embedded in his heart. By telling the truth, he offered a plausible answer that wouldn't raise any additional suspicion. He slapped his hand on the console. "Who cares how I got magic? How are you——"

"Alive?" Henwick finished his question for him. "It was when the obelisk exploded." He raised a hand to show a scar peeking out from the rolled cuff of a white shirt. "A piece of that infernal thing got lodged in my arm right before I fell from that platform. I survived the fall, but apparently having a shard embedded in my arm was enough to link me into the Seed's system. After the castle burned down, I used its power to hunt down the witch that brought that curse to our village. I've been alive ever since."

"And you gave that power to Skyline?" Digby narrowed his eyes.

"No." Henwick dropped his arm back down. "It took me centuries to find a way to remove the fragment from my wrist. After that, I assembled a team to study and recreate the Seed's system into the Guardian Core that my men use now."

"About your men," Digby let a growl rise in his throat, "Skyline has been trying to destroy me all night."

"And I apologize for that. I had their orders changed to capture as soon as it was reported to me that a zombie named Digby was responsible for all this."

"Don't act like it was some sort of favor because you knew me lifetimes ago. You didn't like me when I was alive, so I doubt you have some sort of interest in my wellbeing now."

"You just need him for your spell," Rebecca chimed in from her place in the seat beside him. "You went through the trouble of spreading zombies throughout the world. Now you need a way to keep them in line."

"That is the crux of it, isn't it?" Henwick's face grew serious. "This curse is unique, and we've never had anyone come even close to cultivating a pure mana balance before now. Between the two, we have an opportunity."

"And you want to control the outcome, is that it?" Rebecca's voice rose.

"Quiet, woman." Henwick's demeanor turned in a heartbeat, dropping his charismatic tone. "I'm not speaking to you, and there is such a thing as being too smart for your own good."

"So you admit it?" Digby spat his words.

"Yes." Henwick glared at Rebecca before returning his attention to him. "Like I said. This curse is an opportunity that I have been unable to create. Now that it's begun, it needs to be refined and controlled. With the right spell and the right mana balance, we can modify the curse into something stronger while making it more manageable."

"So that's it, then? You just want to be the one with all the power." Digby was tempted to disconnect the call right then, but he didn't know what button to press.

"Why?" Rebecca asked, before adding, "And don't tell me to be quiet again, you asshole."

"Is it so wrong to want control over humanity in order to keep people safe?" Henwick glared at her with disdain.

"Keep people safe?" Rebecca scoffed. "You're going to kill billions."

Henwick gave her a smug smile. "Saving humanity, doesn't mean all of humanity."

"You just want to save the people that will follow you, and let the rest die? That it?" Digby stomped his improvised peg-leg on the floor of the cabin.

"Of course. If I can unify the world under one rule, it will be better for everyone in the long run."

"And what qualifies you to sit at the top?" Rebecca flicked her eyes between him and the kestrel's front window.

"I have pulled the strings of this world for centuries and it has turned out well enough."

"That's what you think," Alex chimed in from the passenger compartment.

Henwick ignored him. "All I'm doing is eliminating the obstacles that consume my time and resources." He raised both hands. "Just look at how long it has taken me to get a nuclear strike in the works."

"What?" Rebecca's mouth fell open.

"Shit." Alex's jaw followed suit.

"Whatever." Digby brushed off the man's comments, having no idea what a nuclear strike was. "I'll never help you. I didn't like you back home, and I don't like you now. For all I care, you can go—"

"Dig!" Rebecca pointed at a blinking light on the kestrel's controls.

"Yes, very nice. But I'm trying to insult our enemy. Can it wait until—"

"No, Digby." Rebecca's tone grew dire. "We have bigger problems. A missile just launched off the coast."

"What's a missile?" He looked to Alex who continued to hang his mouth open.

"I wish I could have convinced you to give yourself up." Henwick turned away from the camera. "But it seems you're just as short sighted as you were when you were alive. It's not like you're the only one I can use. You were just the most convenient. I'm sorry to have wasted my time." He reached toward something off screen. "Goodbye, Graves."

The picture went blank.

"Shit shit shit." Rebecca strapped herself into her seat as she pushed on the little sticks on the device in her hand.

"What's happening?" Digby nearly fell backward as the kestrel accelerated.

"That guy fired a nuke at us." Alex belted himself into the seat beside Rebecca in the pilot's compartment.

"Not at us, but close enough." Sweat formed on Rebecca's forehead. "They're going to wipe Seattle off the map."

"What does cartography have to do with anything?" Digby regained his balance.

"It's a bomb, Dig!" Rebecca reached back and grabbed the sleeve of his new coat. "It's a really big bomb. One that can destroy the whole city."

"Oh." His eyes bulged. "Well, what are you waiting for? Fly faster."

"What do you think I'm doing?" Rebecca hunched over as if leaning forward would help the craft move. "This is as fast as we can go, and I don't think we can make it. The blast is going to tear us apart!"

Digby froze, having trouble comprehending how he had come so close to escaping yet still fail in the end.

"I was so close." He shook his head. "No. I am not about to let Henwick get me killed again." Shoving his hand into his pocket, he pulled out the two rings he carried. The shiny black obsidian band of the Heretic Seed sat in his palm next to the gold ring he'd plucked from Manning's cold, dead hand.

"I need a barrier." Digby grabbed the gold band, hoping he could learn a spell from it. He prayed the barrier spell Manning had been using wasn't exclusive to a holy knight as he closed his fingers around the ring.

Compatible spells detected, Kinetic Impact and Barrier.
You better hope this works.

Digby didn't bother looking into kinetic impact, assuming it was what Manning and the fighter earlier had knocked him around with. It was strong, but not what he needed.

BARRIER
Create a layer of mana around yourself or a target to absorb an incoming attack.

That's it! Digby willed the Heretic Seed to extract the spell prompting the gold band to crumble in his hand.

Barrier extracted.

Digby took one step toward the back of the kestrel, then stopped. He'd almost forgotten something important.

"Rebecca!" He shoved his arm through the door at the front to drop his last heretic ring in her lap. It fell to the seat cushion and slid under her leg. "If things look bad, and you can't keep this craft in the air, put that on. It might give you the power you need to survive."

Leaving her to fish the obsidian band out from under her rear, he gave Alex a nod and headed toward the back of the passenger compartment. Asher flew up to his shoulder.

"No." Digby pulled the raven from her perch and placed her under one of the seats behind a crate. "You need to stay safe. I don't know if this will even work, but I need to do it alone." He gave the bird one last pat and returned to the kestrel's ramp.

Digby slapped the open button, letting in a gust of wind and noise.

"What the hell are you doing?" Rebecca shouted over her shoulder from the cockpit.

"I'm giving us a chance." Digby checked his mana.

MP: 213/213

In the distance he saw a light trailed by a plume of smoke. It was heading for the city's center. He grabbed the handle at the side of the ramp and leaned forward. Gusts of wind whipped through his hair as he focused on the kestrel and tried to cast Barrier.

Barrier cancelled due to incompatible mana composition. Minimum 10% mana required of each heat, vapor, soil, fluid, and life.

"Damn it! Of course it requires everything but death essence to cast." He tried again.

WARNING: Continued attempts to cast improperly balanced spells may yield unpredictable results.

I hope you know what you're doing.

Digby ignored the Heretic Seed and repeatedly tried to cast the spell as a sudden burst of light lit up the world. For an instant there was no sound, then it hit all at once. A surge of information burned through his mind as the light threatened to blind him. Collapsing to the ramp, it took everything Digby had not to fall from the craft.

Barrier has evolved into Absorb.

ABSORB
Description: Absorb the energy of an incoming attack. Absorbed energy may be stored and applied to a future spell to amplify its damage.
Rank: D
Cost: 30
Duration: 10 seconds (+50% due to mana purity, total 15 seconds.)
Range: 10ft (+50% due to mana purity, total 15ft.)

Digby didn't even try to focus the spell on anything specific; the incoming blast was simply too big. Instead, he knelt on the ramp and raised both hands as the spell activated. The buildings of Seattle burst into nothing as the kestrel hurled through the sky. The craft was at the edge of the city when the blast wave hit. Alex and Rebecca screamed from the cockpit behind him.

Digby held his ground, his hands outstretched as a green vortex formed before him. A strange energy hit him, flowing into the spell. Digby nearly fell over. It was like attempting to drink an ocean of dirty water. There was so much power. All of it trying to rip the world apart.

Digby's eyes went first. The image of the city's destruction burned away into a field of darkness. Next went his ears as the deafening sound burst the sensitive tissues in his head. Heat licked across his face like a day spent too long in the summer sun.

He cast Absorb again, making sure the spell didn't run out before they were clear of the devastation. Layering on a Necrotic Regeneration, his eardrums reformed to take in the noise of buzzers and alarms from the kestrel. The world faded back into view to show him a blurry image of his hands. Bones protruded from the tips of his fingers on his left hand, the skin having melted away. He cast another Regeneration to make sure he didn't fall apart.

"I can't hold it together!" Rebecca's voice shouted from somewhere behind him. She sounded so far away. "We're going down!"

"Graves!" Alex's voice came next. "Get belted in."

Digby collapsed to the floor, unsure of what was happening. Wind continued to whip through the compartment. It vanished with a sudden mechanical clack, like the kestrel's ramp closing. He rolled to one side feeling a feathered form nearby.

"Asher?" Digby pulled the bird close to his chest as it let out a weak caw. "It's alright, I have you."

The kestrel rumbled and shook like it might break apart at any moment. From the cockpit, a continuous sound rang out, reminding him of the fire alarms he'd set off back when he'd first awakened in the future. It didn't sound good.

Everything was a blur, leaving him with no idea of how much time had passed. He cast another Regeneration, struggling to get his head to focus as a line of text ran across his blurred vision.

WARNING: Void resources low.

"No!" Digby's jaw tightened as he realized what that meant.

His conscious mind began to fade into the background as he made a frantic attempt to keep his instincts under control. Then it all went away, leaving him alone with all that was left.

Hunger.

CHAPTER FORTY-EIGHT

Becca woke up with her head hanging forward. The straps of the kestrel's pilot seat bit into her waist and shoulders. Dirt trickled in through the broken windshield in front of her. She tried to move, setting off a throbbing ache in her skull as nausea swam through her stomach.

Somehow, she had survived the crash.

A white circle floating at the edge of her vision drew her eye. It darted out and expanded the instant she focused on it.

Name: Rebecca Alvarez
Race: Human
Heretic Class: Mage

She skimmed a list of attributes, stopping at a line at the bottom.

Ailments: Poisoned

Becca coughed, spattering blood across the kestrel's controls. The radiation from the blast must have taken its toll. There was no way to know how high a dose she'd been hit with. She might last a few days or a few hours. There was no point worrying about it now.

She looked down at her hand, noticing a string of runes trailing around her middle finger. The crash had been a blur, but she must have put on the ring that Digby had dropped in her lap.

Alex stirred in the seat beside her, letting out a labored grunt of pain. Becca slapped her seatbelt release, falling forward across the console. The kestrel must have crashed and skidded to a stop with its nose buried in the dirt at an angle. Once she got her feet under her, she turned to examine the injured enchanter, finding Alex hunched over with a deep gash on his face and one arm bending in the wrong direction.

"Hang in there." She hesitated to unbuckle his seatbelt for fear that there might be more damage.

"What class are…?" Alex's words trailed off with a wet gurgle.

"Huh?" Becca paused before realizing what he meant. "Oh, I'm a mage."

"Can you heal?" He struggled to hold his head up.

"I…" She would have slapped herself in the forehead if she hadn't been on the verge of throwing up. "Sorry, I forgot about magic for a second. I'm not used to it."

It took her a few seconds of poking around in her HUD before she found her spells. All she had was something called Icicle and another named Regeneration.

"How do I—"

"Just focus on me and think about what you want to cast."

Within seconds, she felt something moving within her. Something that had always been there, but she'd never noticed before.

Her mana.

Suddenly, Alex lurched back, gasping as if in extreme pain. His arm snapped back into place with a loud crack as the gash on his head began to knit itself back together.

"Holy shit…" Becca couldn't believe her eyes. "I did that?"

"Yeah. Thanks." Alex's breathing stabilized as he unbuckled his seatbelt and dropped forward. He keeled over clutching his mouth a second later. "Oh god, I'm poisoned."

"I think it's radiation." Becca stepped away; afraid he might throw up on her. "Don't you dare hurl. If you do, I will."

Alex took a few deep breaths and pulled a plastic bottle from a pouch on his armor. It glowed in his hand for a moment before he handed it to her.

"Drink this, it should help."

Becca took the bottle and unscrewed the cap. It was colder than she would have expected, considering it hadn't been refrigerated. Tipping it back, she felt the water's effect immediately. It tasted clean and fresh.

Then, just like that, she felt better.

"Oh, thank God." The poisoned status vanished from her HUD as well. "Here, get some in you too." Alex swallowed a mouthful and put the bottle away. Seconds later, he looked ten times better, like he'd just woken up from a full night's rest.

"We might have a chance here, after all." She regretted her words the instant they even left her mouth, jumping back as a clawed hand snapped around the edge of the cockpit door behind her. It was followed by a wicked howl. Becca froze as a new notification scrolled across her vision.

Heretic Zombie: Level 18 Necromancer, rare, ravenous.

"Dig, stop!" She slapped a hand down on the console beside her. "It's us."

The zombie's claws tightened against the doorframe hard enough to dent the metal. Alex pulled out his bottle of purified water and unscrewed the cap, ready to fling its contents at the threat. Becca wasn't sure if that would be enough to stop him.

The claws continued to scratch at the door but held back without coming closer.

"That's weird." Becca let out a breath she didn't realize she'd been holding. "Why isn't he tearing us apart?"

Alex answered her with a shrug before leaning to the side and peeking into the passenger compartment. He let out a quiet laugh a second later.

"What?" Becca stepped forward to look, feeling a smile slide across her face as soon as she saw the ridiculous corpse.

Digby reached out for her and snapped his teeth as a sticky froth formed at the corner of his mouth. Swiping with his claws, they streaked past her, unable to make contact as a three-point harness held him firmly in place in one of the kestrel's passenger seats.

"You crazy, dead man." She shook her head at the snarling monster. "He actually had the forethought to belt himself in to protect us."

Alex put away his water bottle and slipped past his ravenous lord. He jumped all the way to the other side of the craft when Asher cawed at him from under one of the seats.

Becca couldn't help but laugh before turning around to peer over the mountain of dirt blocking most of the kestrel's front window. The aircraft was nose deep in an open field. She pushed up on her toes to see more just as a hoof stepped into the dirt a few feet away. Becca flinched but kept watching.

A raspy neigh sounded as a familiar deceased horse trotted past the crashed aircraft.

"Looks like we aren't the only ones who escaped the city."

Becca leaned on the pilot seat as the sun rose on the horizon behind the silhouette of the undead horse. Orange and pink clouds filled the sky, bringing in the dawn after a night that seemed like it would never end. The horse let out a carefree yet horrifying whinny before galloping off into the light.

Alex stepped back into the cockpit to stare out at the sunrise beside her. "What happens now?"

"I have no idea." Becca shrugged. "But things are going to be different."

They both remained silent for a moment before Digby let out a ravenous growl.

Alex shook his head at his lord. "We better get him something to eat."

Becca let out an inappropriate laugh.

"...Or someone."

EPILOGUE

Clint Howland rushed through the hall of one of Skyline's high security facilities. There was so much going on. The strongest members of Phoenix Company had been annihilated, leaving himself and a monorail car full of his comrades as the only survivors of the operation in Seattle.

He had seen the face of evil that night.

A corpse, with the mind of a man.

That monster had looked right at him back on the monorail a few hours before. He'd nearly lost control of his bladder. If that necromancer had decided to attack, he was sure he wouldn't have made it back alive. If he had known that sort of creature existed, he never would have accepted his transfer to Phoenix Company, even considering the power that came with his assignment.

He glanced at the Guardian Core's status screen.

Clint Howland, Guardian Level 2, Mage.

He still couldn't believe he was alive. The captain had been level twenty-seven, and that necro and his accomplices had still beaten him. A chill traveled down his spine at the thought of it. There had to be a way to get out of his contract. He wasn't cut out for any of the shit that had gone down in Seattle.

Unfortunately, getting out wasn't an option, not since his parents had signed him over to Skyline years ago. Now, he had no choice but to report for debriefing. The unusual part was that he had been sent to a different building than Easton and the others. He'd never been inside any of the high security areas of the base before. He didn't even know anyone with clearance.

Wasting no time, he jogged into a small waiting room at the end of the hall. A young woman wearing a dated dress like something out of the fifties sat behind a desk with her hair done up.

"Mr. Howland?" She didn't look up to greet him.

"Present." Clint tried his best to stand tall.

"Mr. Rickford will see you now." She gestured to an elevator door positioned on the far wall.

"Thank you." Clint made his way across the waiting room, unsure if he should mention that he had no idea who Rickford was. He opted to stay quiet and do as he was told.

The elevator door opened as soon as he approached with no need for a call button. Even stranger was the fact that the door was made of gold and bore a strange emblem. It looked like a cross but with two diagonal branches coming off each side to form an x at its center instead of a horizontal one. Stepping inside, the walls were covered with extravagant wood paneling that surrounded a triptych of oil paintings.

It was all a bizarre display of wealth that didn't fit with the decor of a private military base. Clint glanced over the paintings, finding scenes of angels looking down upon a mass of filthy people. He looked away, feeling uncomfortable with the judgmental expressions on the angel's faces.

The elevator climbed for nearly a minute, causing Clint to wonder if the building he had entered was actually that tall. Finally, the doors slid open to an empty cement room. The difference between the spaces was jarring. Peeking out, Clint swallowed with an audible gulp before stepping forward. Something felt off, but he couldn't put his finger on it.

"Oh good, you're here." A man in a white shirt and black suit pants pushed through a steel door. He was well dressed but retained a rugged appearance. "Clint, right?"

"Yeah, I mean, yes sir." He stood at attention.

"No need for that." The man held out his hand.

"Understood, Mr. Rickford." Clint nodded.

"And call me Henwick. Rickford is just a name I use down there."

"Understood," Clint repeated.

"I'm sure you're wondering why I've brought you here." Henwick turned and pushed back through the metal door he'd entered from as if expecting Clint to follow.

"Yes."

The hall beyond was dark and musty, making the well-dressed man seem more out of place.

"I've asked you here to help me with a problem." Henwick approached a door locked with a keypad. He typed in a code and pushed through, leading Clint into a room with a pit at its center. There was no railing around the side for safety.

"Of course. I'm here for whatever Skyline needs." Clint stopped near the edge of the pit, trying to hide how nervous and confused he was.

"Excellent." Henwick spun around. "That's just what I like to hear. Everyone should strive to do their duty, no matter what the cost."

"I'm sorry, what?" Clint stepped forward.

"Never mind." Henwick placed his hands on the wrinkled collar of Clint's uniform. Then, he pushed.

"Wait, wa—" Clint slammed into the floor of the pit nearly fifteen feet down. He coughed as the air escaped his lungs. "What's going on?"

"Try not to fight, Mr. Howland." Henwick stared down over the edge. "It will only make things harder."

Clint scurried back against the wall, his heart racing as a

door opened at the other side of the pit. A dark passage lay beyond.

"Sir! Please," he called up, giving in to the fear that had been gnawing at him since he'd boarded the elevator. "I don't know what——" His words froze in his throat as a familiar moan came from the open passage.

"No. Not again. I survived Seattle. I can't..." He trailed off as a lifeless form staggered into the light. The sight of it sent terror screaming down his spine.

It looked... Ravenous.

ABOUT D. PETRIE

D. Petrie discovered a love of stories and nerd culture at an early age. From there, life was all about comics, video games, and books. It's not surprising that all that would lead to writing. He currently lives north of Boston with the love of his life and their two adopted cats. He streams on twitch every Thursday night.

Connect with D. Petrie:
TavernToldTales.com
Patreon.com/DavidPetrie
Facebook.com/WordsByDavidPetrie
Facebook.com/groups/TavernToldTales
Twitter.com/TavernToldTales

ABOUT MOUNTAINDALE PRESS

Dakota and Danielle Krout, a husband and wife team, strive to create as well as publish excellent fantasy and science fiction novels. Self-publishing *The Divine Dungeon: Dungeon Born* in 2016 transformed their careers from Dakota's military and programming background and Danielle's Ph.D. in pharmacology to President and CEO, respectively, of a small press. Their goal is to share their success with other authors and provide captivating fiction to readers with the purpose of solidifying Mountaindale Press as the place 'Where Fantasy Transforms Reality.'

Connect with Mountaindale Press:
MountaindalePress.com
Facebook.com/MountaindalePress
Twitter.com/_Mountaindale
Instagram.com/MountaindalePress

MOUNTAINDALE PRESS TITLES

GameLit and LitRPG

The Completionist Chronicles,
Cooking with Disaster,
The Divine Dungeon,
Full Murderhobo, and
Year of the Sword by Dakota Krout

A Touch of Power by Jay Boyce

Red Mage and
Farming Livia by Xander Boyce

Ether Collapse and
Ether Flows by Ryan DeBruyn

Unbound by Nicoli Gonnella

Threads of Fate by Michael Head

Lion's Lineage by Rohan Hublikar and Dakota Krout

Wolfman Warlock by James Hunter and Dakota Krout

Axe Druid,
Mephisto's Magic Online, and
High Table Hijinks by Christopher Johns

Dragon Core Chronicles by Lars Machmüller

Pixel Dust and
Necrotic Apocalypse by D. Petrie

Viceroy's Pride and
Tower of Somnus by Cale Plamann

Henchman by Carl Stubblefield

Artorian's Archives by Dennis Vanderkerken and Dakota Krout

APPENDIX

ATRIBUTES AND THEIR EFFECTS:

CONSTITUTION: Attribute related to maintaining a healthy body. Allocating points improves the body's ability to fight off disease and lowers the chance of infection and food borne illness. Greatly affects endurance.

AGILITY: Attribute related to mobility. Allocating points will improve overall control of body movements. Greatly affects speed and balance.

STRENGTH: Attribute related to physical prowess. Allocating points increases muscle destiny to yield more power. Greatly affects the damage of melee attacks.

DEFENSE: An attribute related to physical durability. Allocating points improves skin and bone density. Greatly reduces the damage you take. Defense can be supplemented by wearing protective clothing or armor.

DEXTERITY: Attribute related to skill in performing tasks, especially with hands. Allocating points will increase control of precise movement. Greatly affects control of melee attacks and ranged weaponry.

INTELLIGENCE: Attribute related to comprehending information and understanding. Improves processing speed and memory. Greatly affects mana efficiency. (+4 per attribute point.)

PERCEPTION: Attribute related to the awareness of the world around you. Allocating points improves the collection and processing of sensory information and moderately affects mana efficiency. (+2 per attribute point.)

WILL: Attribute related to controlling your mind and body. Allocating points will increase your dominance over your own existence. Greatly affects resistance to spells that directly affect your physical or mental self. (+1 per attribute point.)

NOTEWORTY ITEMS

THE HERETIC SEED
An unrestricted pillar of power. Once connected, this system grants access to, and manages the usage of, the mana that exists within the human body and the world around them.

HERETIC RINGS
A ring that synchronizes the wearer with the Heretic Seed to assign a starting class.

THE GUARDIAN CORE
A well-regulated pillar of power. Once connected, this system grants temporary access to, and manages the usage of, the mana that exists within the human body and the world around them.

NOTEWORTY CONCEPTS

AMBIENT MANA
The energy present with a person's surroundings. This energy can be absorbed and use to alter the world in a way that could be described as magic.

MANA SYSTEM
All creatures possess a mana system. This system consists of layers of energy that protect the core of what that creature is. The outer layers of this system may be used to cast spells and will re[plenish as more mana is absorbed. Some factors, such as becoming a Heretic will greatly increase the strength of this system to provide much higher quantities of usable mana.

MANA BALANCE (EXTERNAL)
Mana is made up of different types of essence. These are as follows, HEAT, FLUID, SOIL, VAPOR, LIFE, DEATH. Often, one type of essence may be more plentiful than others. A location's mana balance can be altered by various environmental factors and recent events.

MANA BALANCE (INTERNAL)
Through persistence and discipline, a Heretic may cultivate their mana system to contain a unique balance of essence. This requires favoring spells that coincide with the desired balance while neglecting other's that don't. This may affect the potency of spells that coincide with the dominant mana type within a Heretic's system.

MASS ENCHANTMENTS
Due to belief and admiration shared by a large quantity of people and item or place may develop a power of power of its own.

HERETIC & GUARDIAN CLASSES

MAGE
Starting class for a heretic or guardian whose highest attribute is intelligence. Excels at magic.

POSSIBLE STARTING SPELLS:

ICICLE
Gather moisture from the air around you to form an icicle. Once formed, icicles will hover in place for 3 seconds, during which they may be claimed as a melee weapons or launched in the direction of a target. Accuracy is dependent on caster's focus.

TERRA BURST
Call forth a circle of stone shards from the earth to injure any target unfortunate enough to be standing in the vicinity.
Choose one spell to be extracted.

FIREBALL
Will a ball of fire to gather in your hand to form a throwable sphere that ruptures on contact.

REGENERATION
Heal wounds for yourself or others. If rendered unconscious, this spell will cast automatically until all damage is repaired or until MP runs out.

DICSCOVERED SPELLS:

NECROTIC REGENERATION
Repair damage to necrotic flesh and bone to restore function and structural integrity.

CREMATION

Ignite a target's necrotic tissue. Resulting fire will spread to other flammable substances.

CONTROL ZOMBIE

Temporarily subjugate the dead into your service regardless of target's will values. Zombies under your control gain +2 intelligence and are unable to refuse any command. May control up to 5 common zombies at any time.

ZOMBIE WHISPERER

Give yourself or others the ability to sooth the nature of any non-human zombie to gain its trust. Once cast, a non-human zombie will obey basic commands.

BLOOD FORGE

Description: Forge a simple object or objects of your choosing out of any available blood source.

ENCHANTER

Starting class for a heretic or guardian whose highest attribute is will. Excels at supporting others.

POSSIBLE STARTING SPELLS:

ENCHANT WEAPON

Infuse a weapon or projectile with mana. An infused weapon will deal increased damage as well as disrupt the mana flow of another caster. Potential damage will increase with rank. Enchanting a single projectile will have a greater effect.

PURIFY WATER

Imbue any liquid with cleansing power. Purified liquids will become safe for human consumption and will

remove most ailments. At higher ranks, purified liquids
may also gain a mild regenerative effect.
Choose one spell to be extracted.

DISCOVERED SPELLS:

DETECT ENEMY:
Infuse any common iron object with the ability to sense
and person of creature that is currently hostile
toward you.

FIGHTER
Starting class for a heretic or guardian whose highest attribute is
will. Excels at physical combat.

POSSIBLE STARTING SPELLS:

BARRIER
Create a layer of mana around yourself or a target to
absorb an incoming attack.

KINETIC IMPACT
Generate a field of mana around your fist to amplify the
kinetic energy of an attack.

SPECIALIZED CLASSES

NECROMANCER
A specialized class unlocked buy achieving a high balance of
death essence withing a Heretic's mana system as well as discover
spells within the mage class that make use of death essence.

STARTING SPELLS:

ANIMATE CORPSE

Raise a zombie from the dead by implanting a portion of your mana into a corpse. Once raised, a minion will remain loyal until destroyed. Mutation path of an animated zombie will be controlled by the caster, allowing them to evolve their follower into a minion that will fit their needs.

DECAY
Accelerate the damage done by the ravages of time on a variety of materials. Metal will rust, glass will crack, flesh will rot, and plants will die. Effect may be enhanced through physical contact. Decay may be focused on a specific object as well as aimed at a general area for a wider effect.

DISCOVERABLE SPELLS:

ABSORB
Description: Absorb the energy of an incoming attack. Absorbed energy may be stored and applied to a future spell to amplify its damage.

BURIAL
Description: Displace an area of earth to dig a grave beneath a target. The resulting grave will fill back in after five seconds.

HOLY KNIGHT (GURADIAN ONLY)
A specialized class that specialized in physical combat and defense. This class has the ability to draw strength from a Guardian's faith.

PASSIVE HERETIC ABILITIES

ANALYZE

Reveal hidden information about an object or target, such as rarity and hostility toward you.

MANA ABSORPTION
Ambient mana will be absorbed whenever MANA POINTS are below maximum MP values. Rate of absorption may vary depending on ambient mana concentration and essence composition. Absorption may be increased through meditation and rest.
WARNING: Mana absorption will be delayed whenever spells are cast.

SKILL LINK
Discover new spells by demonstrating repeated and proficient use of non-heretic skills or talents.

TIMELESS
Due to the higher than normal concentration of mana within a heretic's body, the natural aging process has been halted, allowing for more time to reach the full potential of your class. It is still possible to expire from external damage.

ZOMBIE RACIAL TRAITS (HUMAN)

BLOOD SENSE
Allows a zombie to sense blood in their surroundings to aid in the tracking of prey. Potency of this trait increases with perception.

GUIDED MUTATION
Due to an unusually high intelligence for an undead creature, you are capable of mutating at will rather than mutating when required resources are consumed. This allows you to choose mutations from multiple paths instead of following just one.

MUTATION

Alter your form or attributes by consuming resources of the living or recently deceased. Required resources are broken down into 6 types: Flesh, Bone, Sinew, Viscera, Mind, and Heart. Mutation path is determined by what resources a zombie consumes.

RAVNOUS

A ravenous zombie will be unable to perform any action other than the direct pursuit of food until satiated. This may result in self-destructive behavior. While active, all physical limitations will be ignored. Ignoring physical limitations for prolonged periods of time may result in catastrophic damage.

RESIST

A remnant from a zombie's human life, this common trait grants +5 points to will. Normally exclusive to conscious beings, this trait allows a zombie to resist basic spells that directly target their body or mind until their will is overpowered.

VOID

A bottomless, weightless, dimensional space that exists within the core of a zombie's mana system. This space can be accessed through its carrier's stomach and will expand to fit whatever contents are consumed.

ZOMBIE MINION TRAITS (AVIAN)

FLIGHT OF THE DEAD

As an avian zombie, the attributes required to maintain the ability to fly have been restored.

BOND OF THE DEAD

As a zombie animated directly by a necromancer, this creature will gain one attribute point for every 2 levels of their master. These points may be allocated at any time. 7 attribute points remaining.

CALL OF THE DEAD

As a zombie animated directly by a necromancer, this minion and its master will be capable of sensing each other's presence through their bond. In addition, the necromancer will be capable of summoning this minion to their location over great distances.

ZOMBIE MINION TRAITS (RODENT)

SPEED OF THE DEAD

As a rodent zombie, the attributes required to maintain the ability to move quickly have been retained. +3 agility, + 2 strength.

BOND OF THE DEAD

As a zombie animated directly by a necromancer, this creature will gain one attribute point for every 2 levels of their master. These points may be allocated at any time. 7 attribute points remaining.

CALL OF THE DEAD

As a zombie animated directly by a necromancer, this minion and its master will be capable of sensing each other's presence through their bond. In addition, the necromancer will be capable of summoning this minion to their location over great distances.

MUTATION PATHS AND MUTATIONS

PATH OF THE LURKER

Move in silence and strike with precision.

SILENT MOVEMENT

Description: Removes excess weight and improves balance.

Resource Requirements: 2 sinew, 1 bone
Attribute Effects: +6 agility, +2 dexterity, -1 strength, +1 will

BONE CLAWS

Description: Craft claws from consumed bone on one hand.
Description: .25 sinew, .25 bone
Attribute Effects: +4 dexterity, +1 defense, +1 strength

PATH OF THE BRUTE

Hit hard and stand your ground.

INCREASE MASS

Description: Dramatically increase muscle mass.
Resource Requirements: 15 flesh, 3 bone
Attribute Effects: +30 strength, +20 defense, -10 intelligence, -7 agility, -7 dexterity, +1 will

BONE ARMOR

Description: Craft armor plating from consumed bone.
Resource Requirements: 5 bone
Attribute Effects: +5 defense, +1 will

PATH OF THE GLUTTON

Trap and swallow your prey whole.

MAW

Description: Open a gateway directly to the dimensional space of your void to devour prey faster.
Resource Requirements: 10 viscera, 1 bone
Attribute Effects: +2 perception, +1 will

JAWBONE

Description: Craft a trap from consumed bone within the opening of your maw that can bite and pull prey in.

Resource Requirements: 2 bone, 1 sinew
Attribute Effects: +2 perception, +1 will

PATH OF THE LEADER
Control the horde and conquer the living.

COMPEL ZOMBIE
Description: Temporally coerce one or more common zombies to obey your intent. Limited by target's intelligence.
Resource Requirements: 5 mind, 5 heart
Attribute Effects: +2 intelligence, +2 perception, +1 will

RECALL MEMORY
Description: Access a portion of your living memories.
Resource Requirements: 30 mind, 40 heart
Attribute Effects: +5 intelligence, +5 perception, +1 will
Units of requirement values are equal to the quantity of resources contained by the average human body.

PATH OF THE RAVAGER
Leave nothing alive.

SHEEP'S CLOTHING
Description: Mimic a human appearance to lull your prey into a false sense of security.
Resource Requirements: 10 flesh.

TEMPORARY MASS
Description: Consume void resources to weave a structure of muscle and bone around your body to enhance strength and defense until it is either released or its structural integrity has been compromised enough to disrupt functionality.
Resource Requirements: 25 flesh, 10 bone.
Attribute Effects: +11 strength, +9 defense.

Limitations: All effects are temporary. Once claimed, each use requires 2 flesh and 1 bone.

HELL'S MAW

Description: Increase the maximum size of your void gateway at will.
Resource Requirements: 30 viscera.
Attribute Effects: +3 perception, +6 will.
Limitations: Once claimed, each use requires the expenditure of 1 MP for every 5 inches of diameter beyond your maw's default width.

DISSECTION

Description: When consuming prey, you may gain a deeper understanding of how bodies are formed. This will allow you to spot and exploit a target's weaknesses instinctively.
Resource Requirements: 10 mind, 5 heart.
Attribute Effects: +3 intelligence, +6 perception.

Made in the USA
Columbia, SC
25 July 2024

861e91cb-083a-463c-baf1-60600443e5eaR04